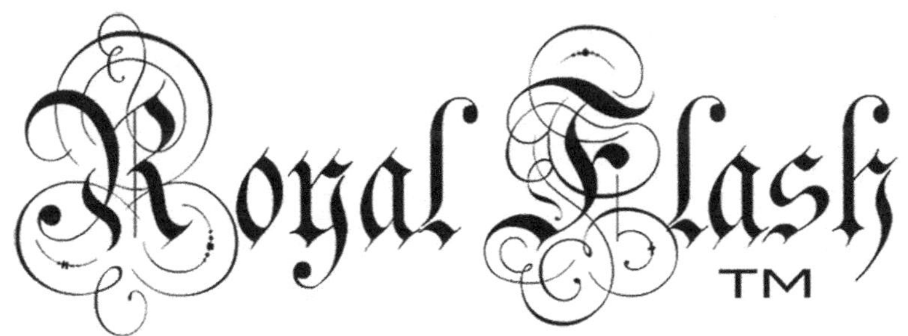


Presents

# "Tattoo Flash Coloring Book"

All Artwork and

*Cort Bengtson*

Published by Cort's Royal Ink Tattoo Company
Book Design and Layout by Cort Bengtson

 ISBN-13: 978-1-948187-13-8

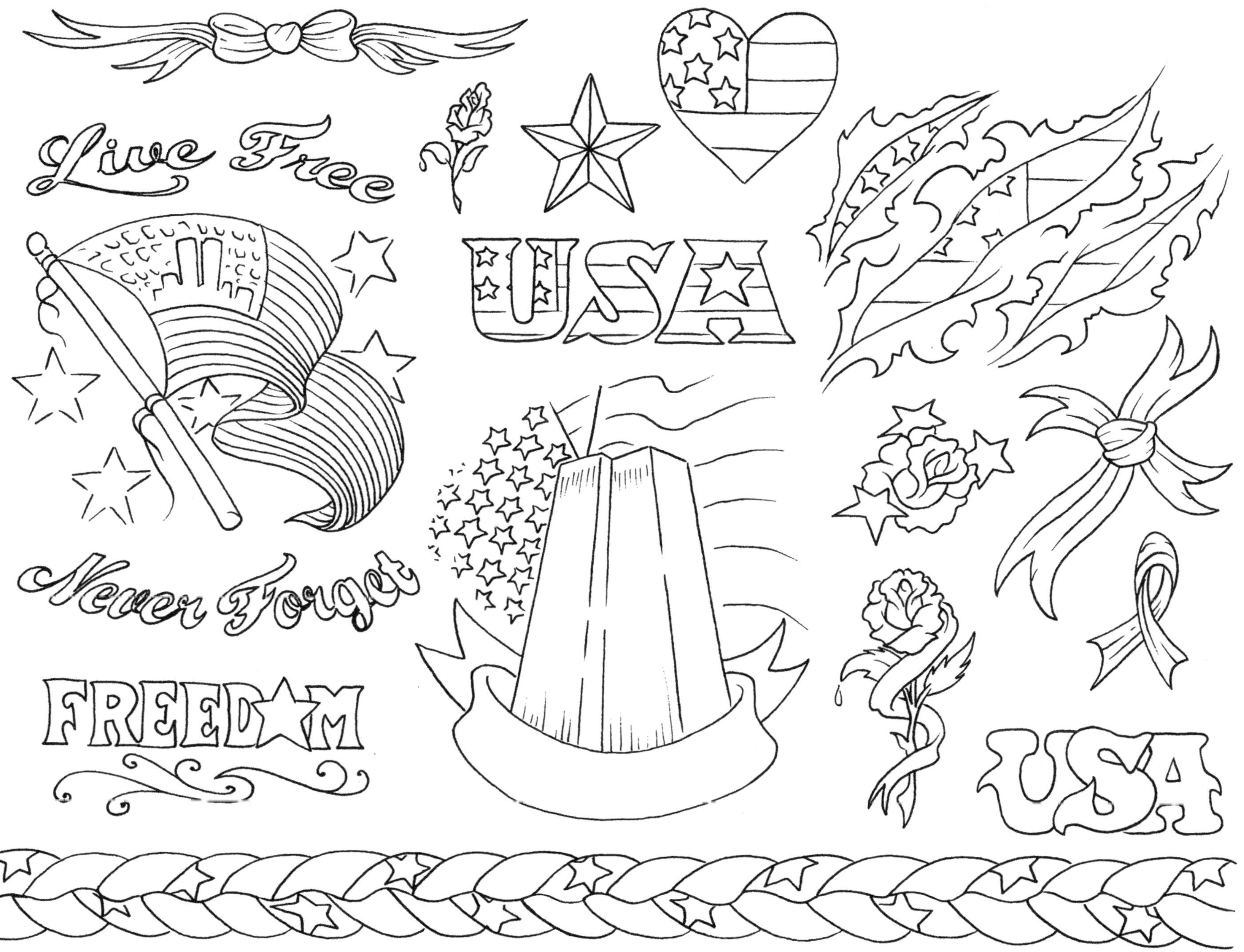

Live Free
USA
Never Forget
FREEDOM
USA

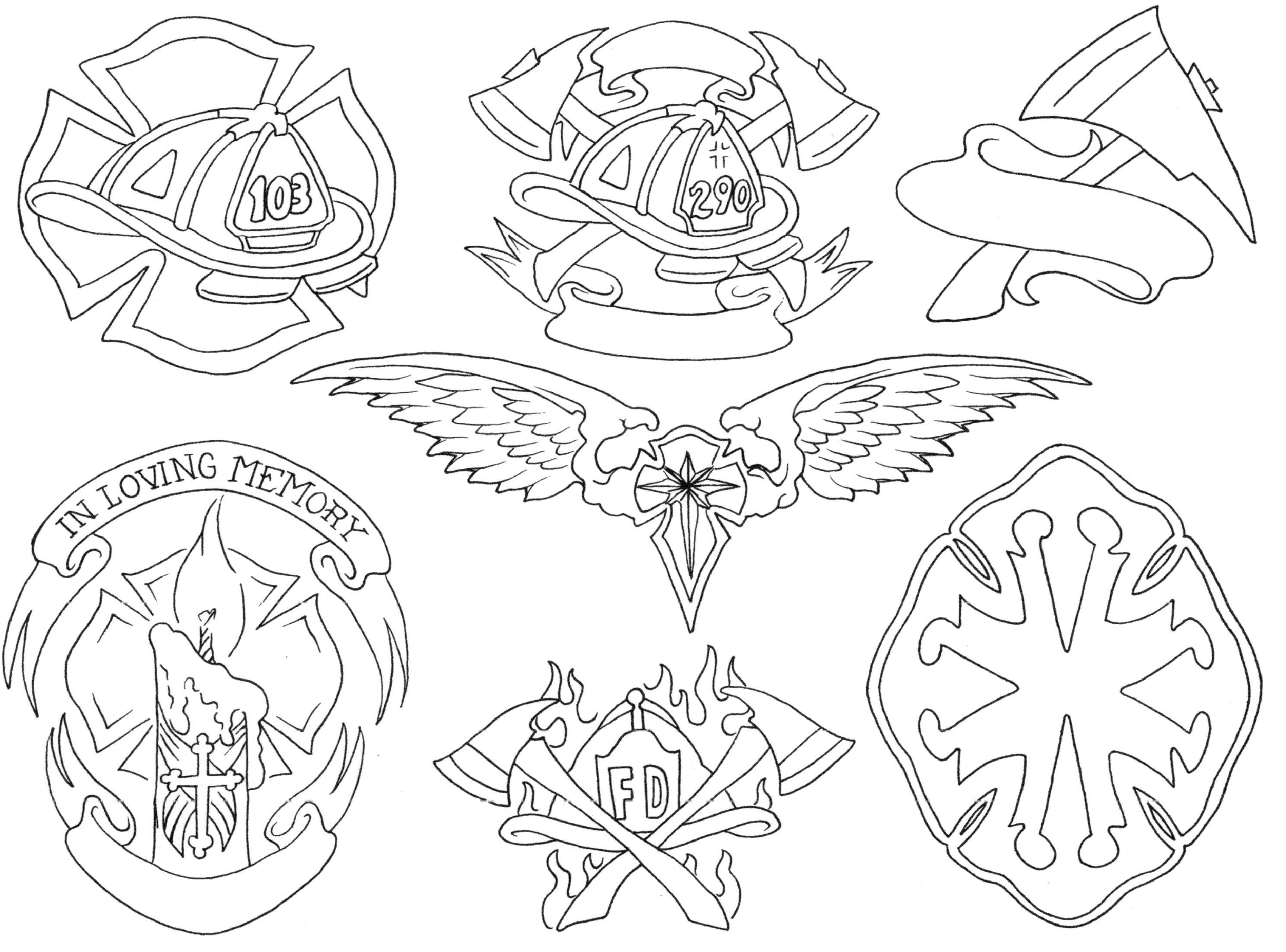

103
290
IN LOVING MEMORY
FD

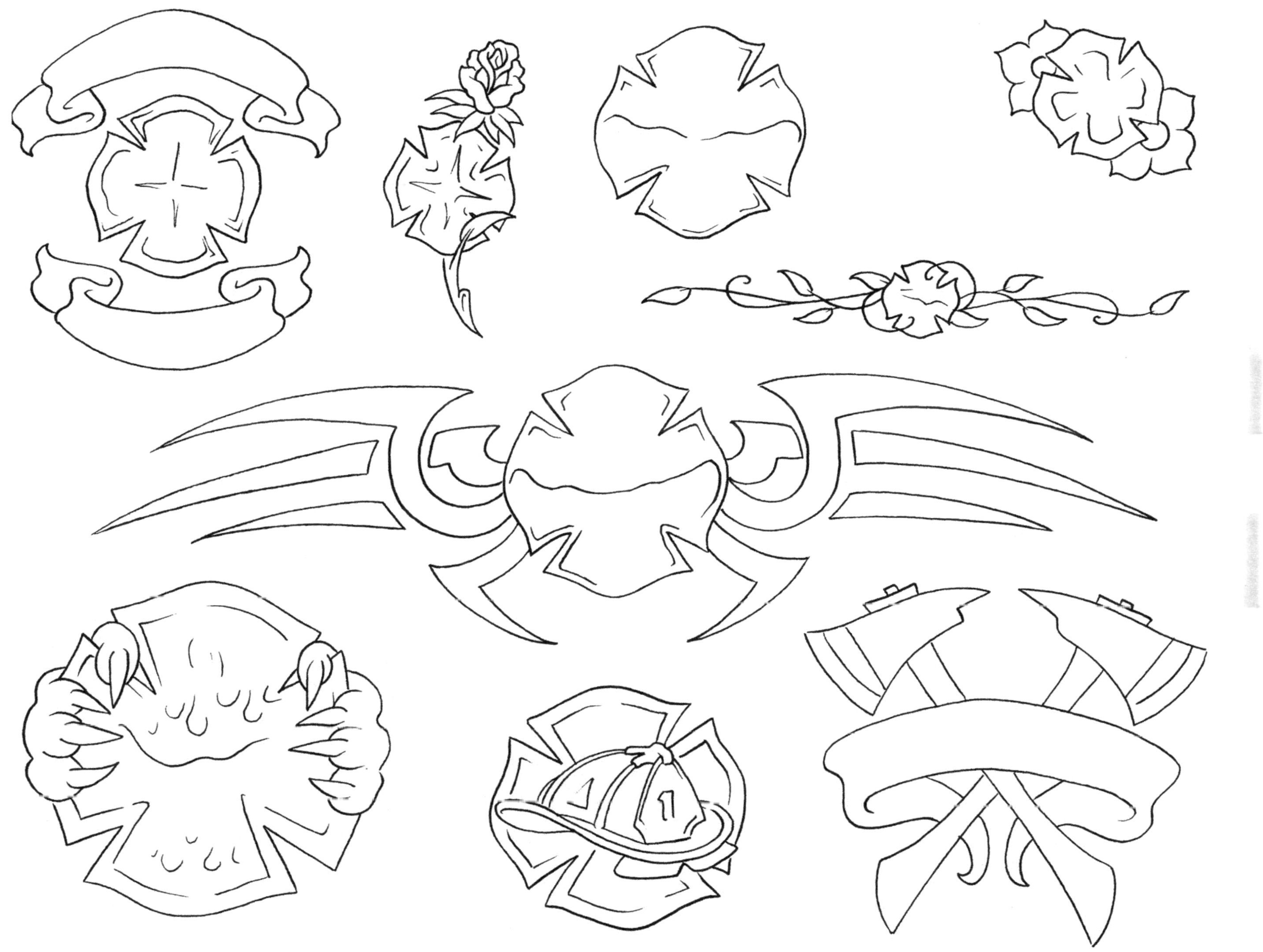

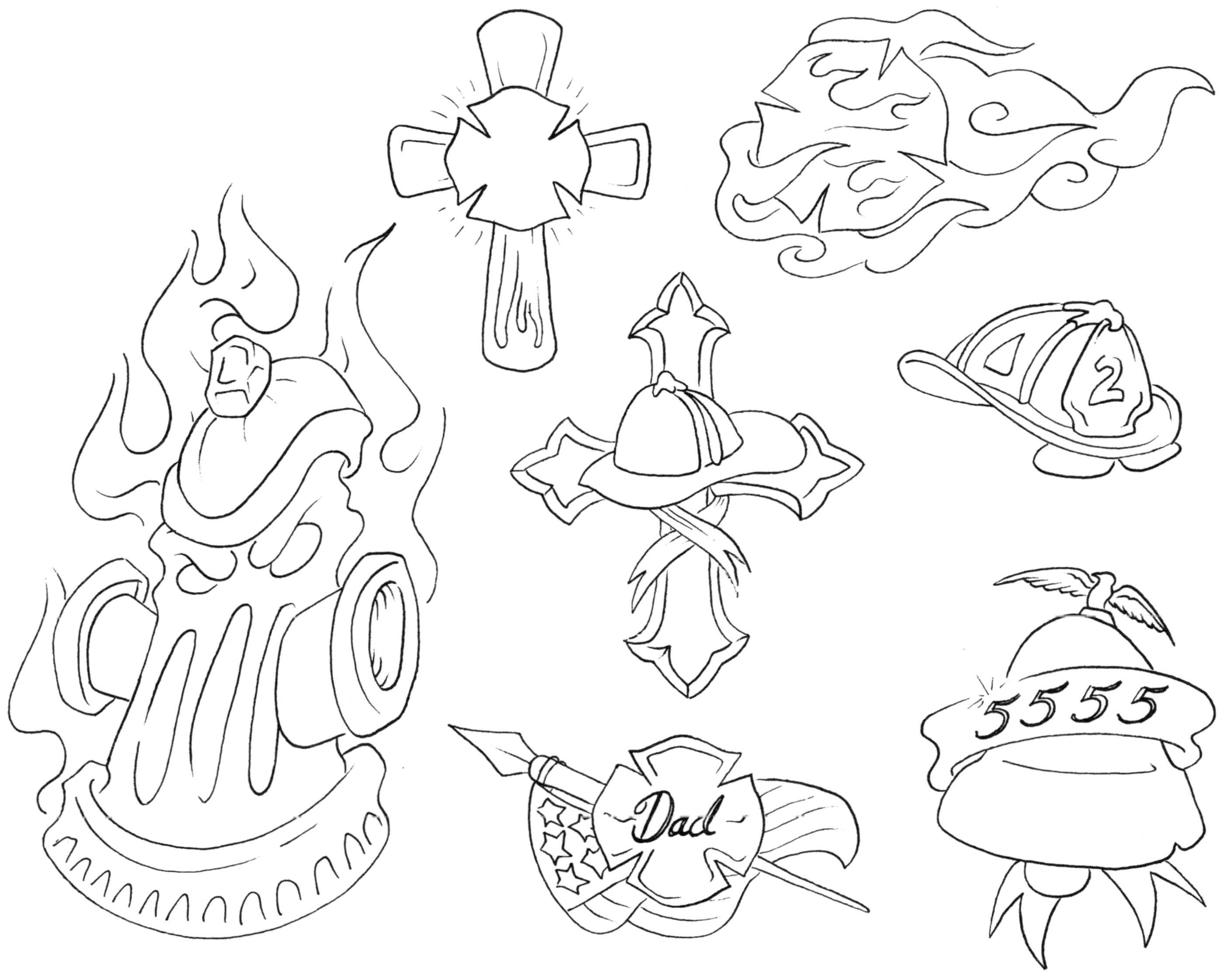

2
Dad
5555

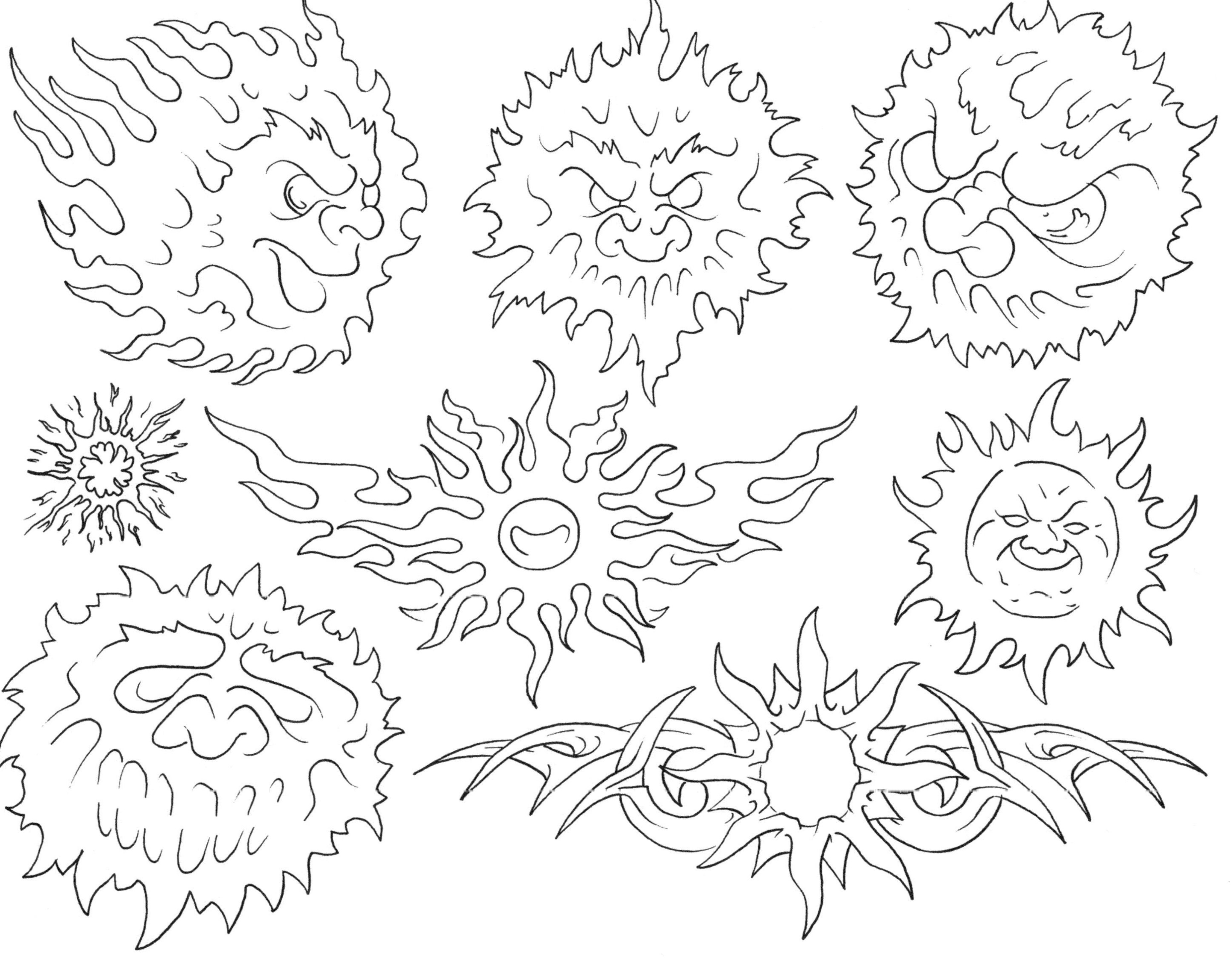

J.C.

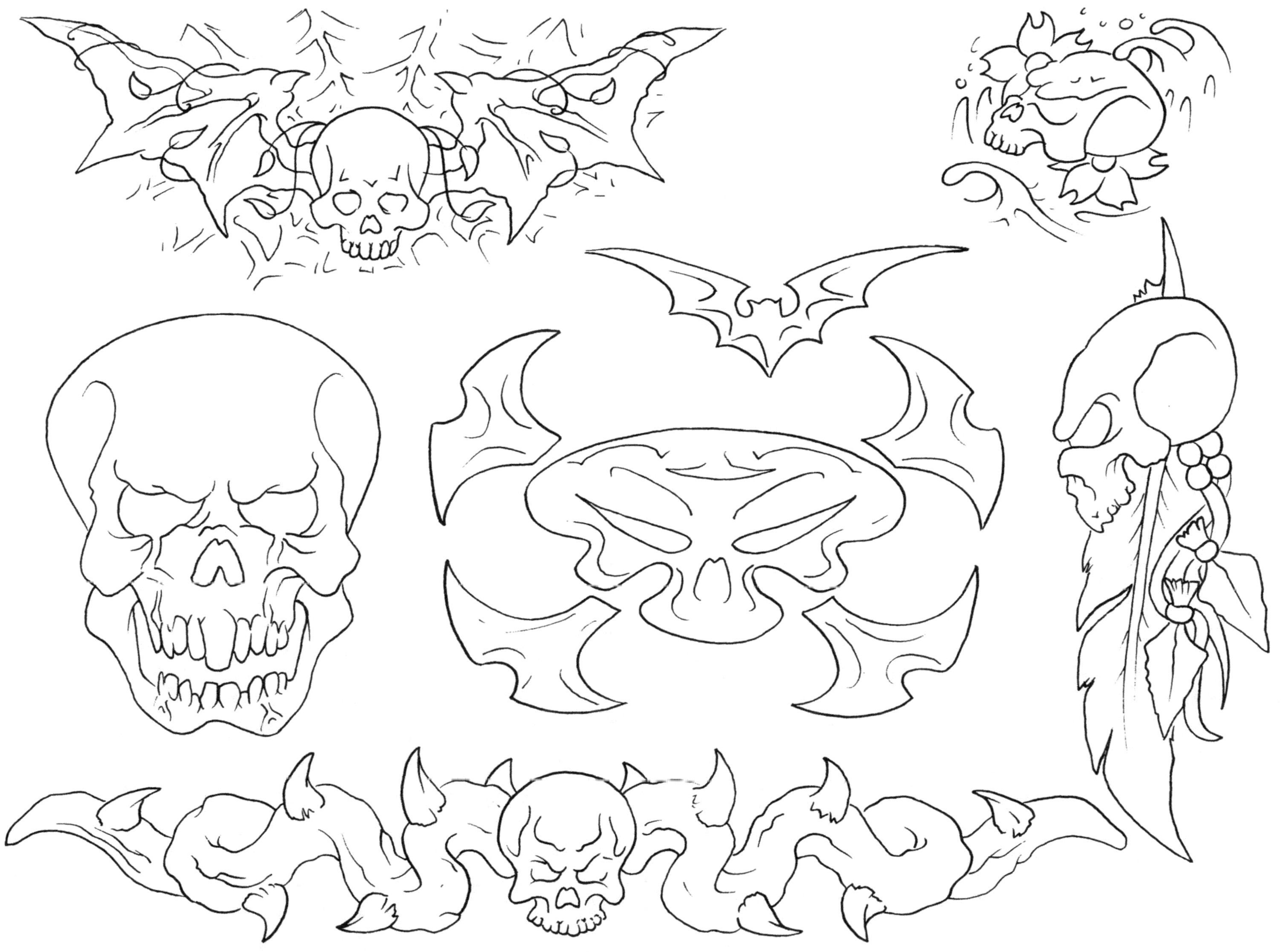

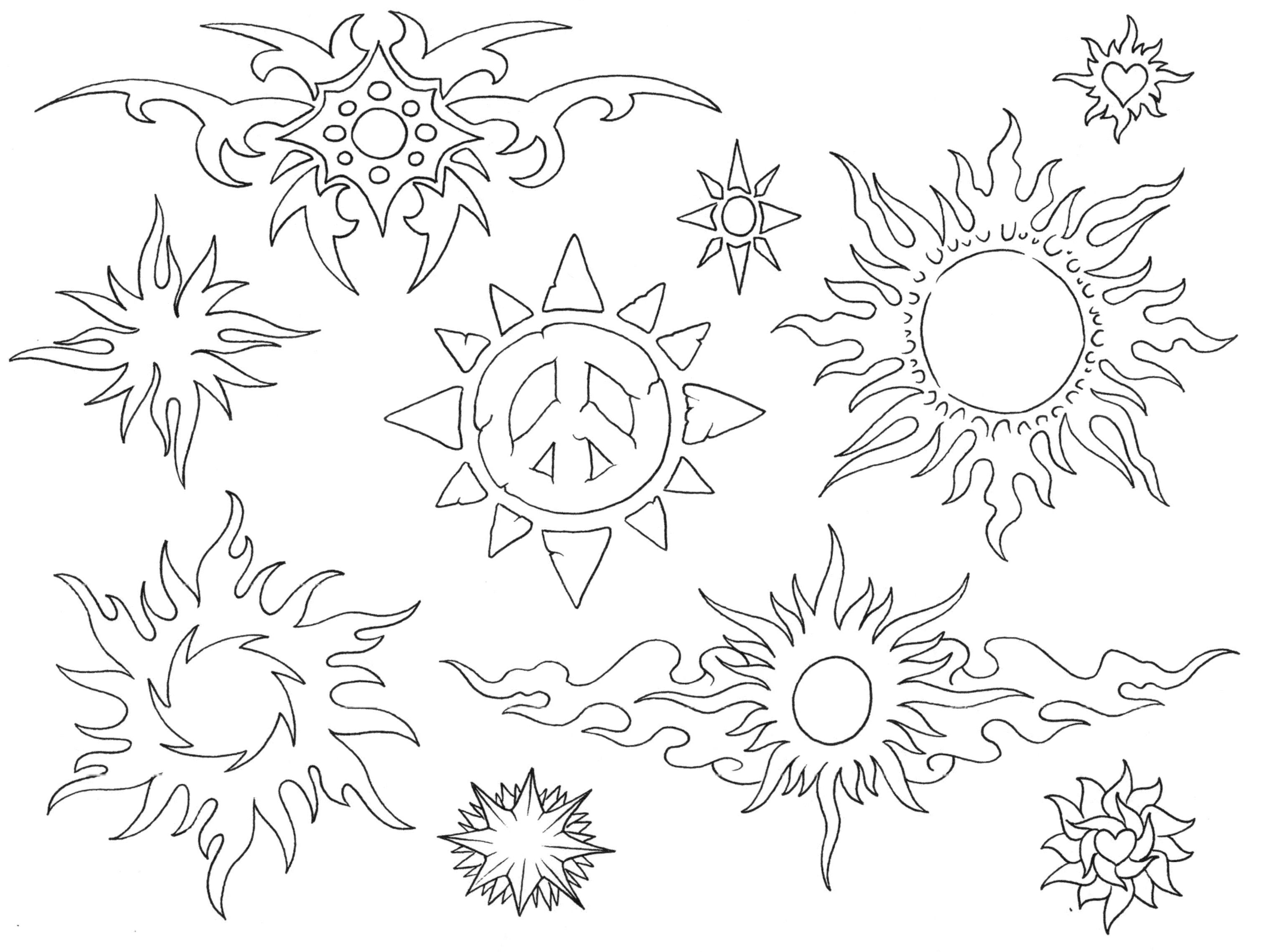

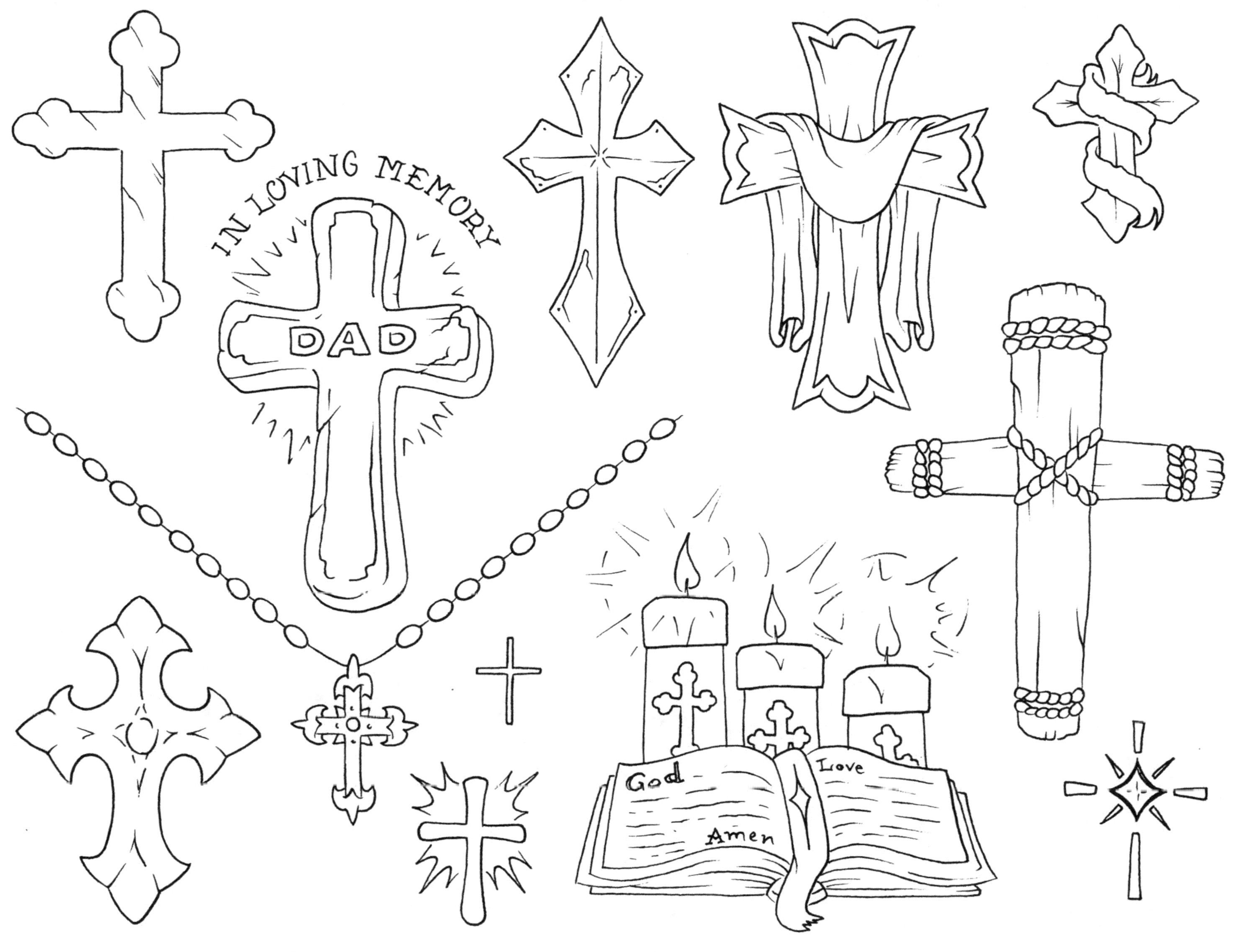
IN LOVING MEMORY
DAD
God
Love
Amen

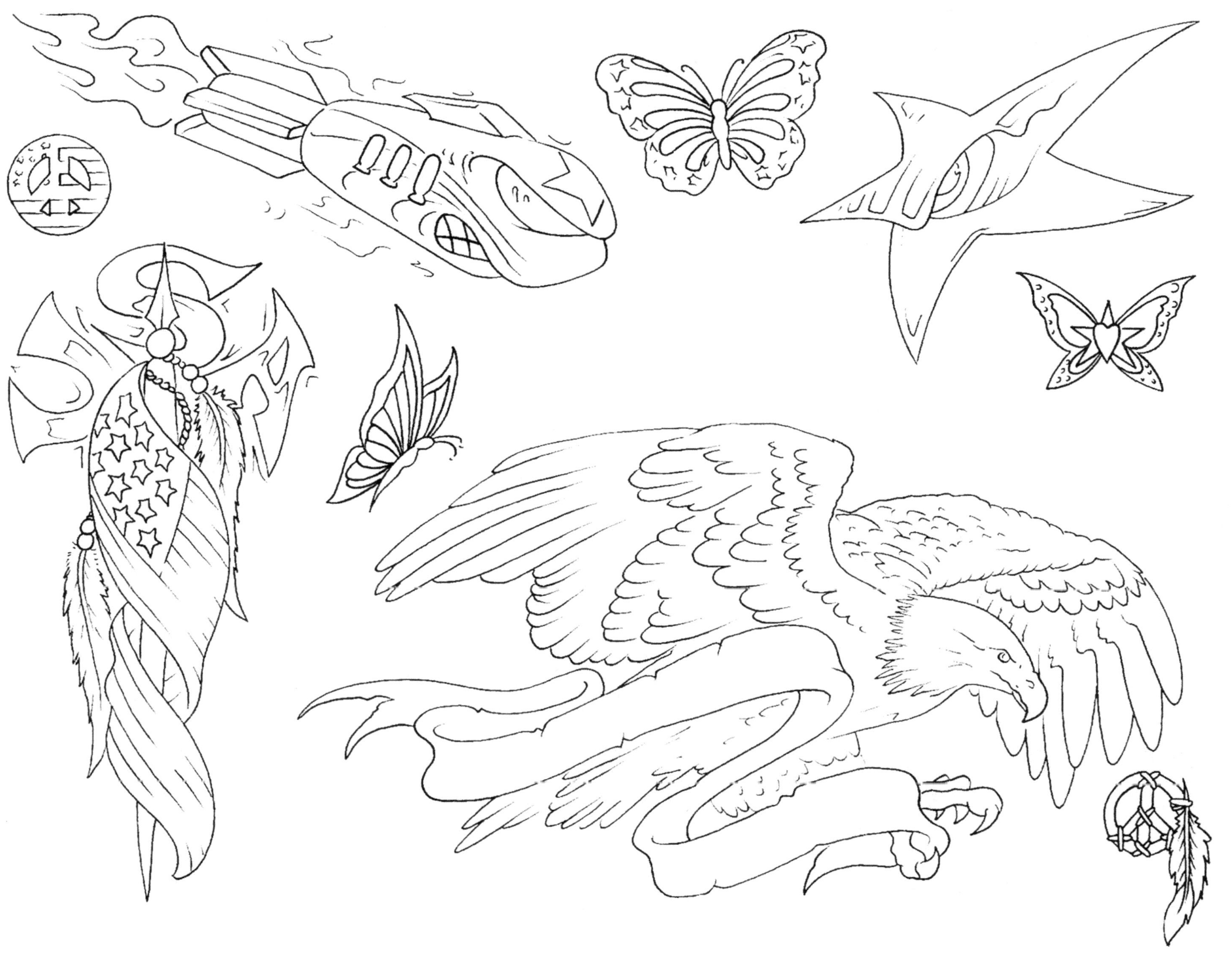

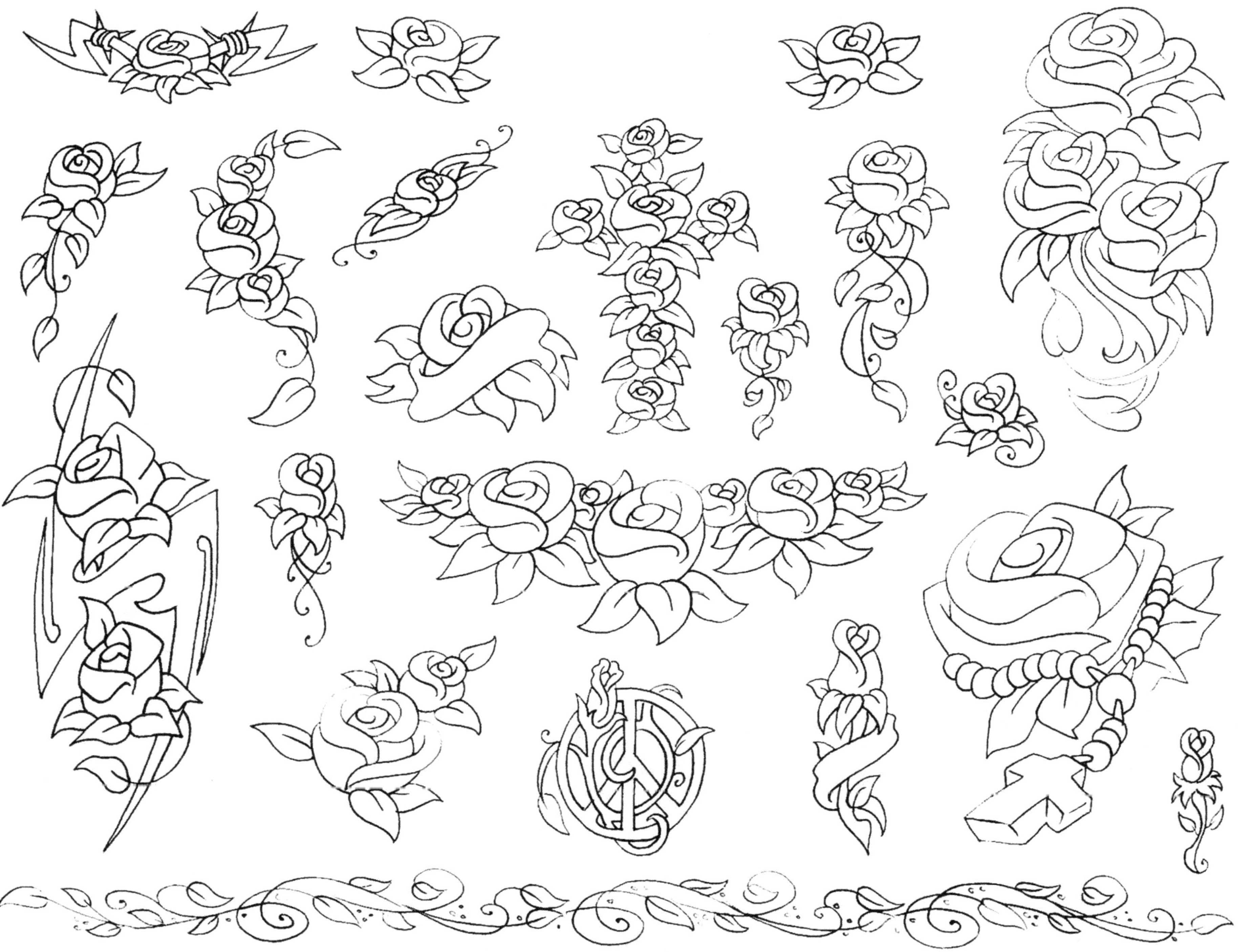

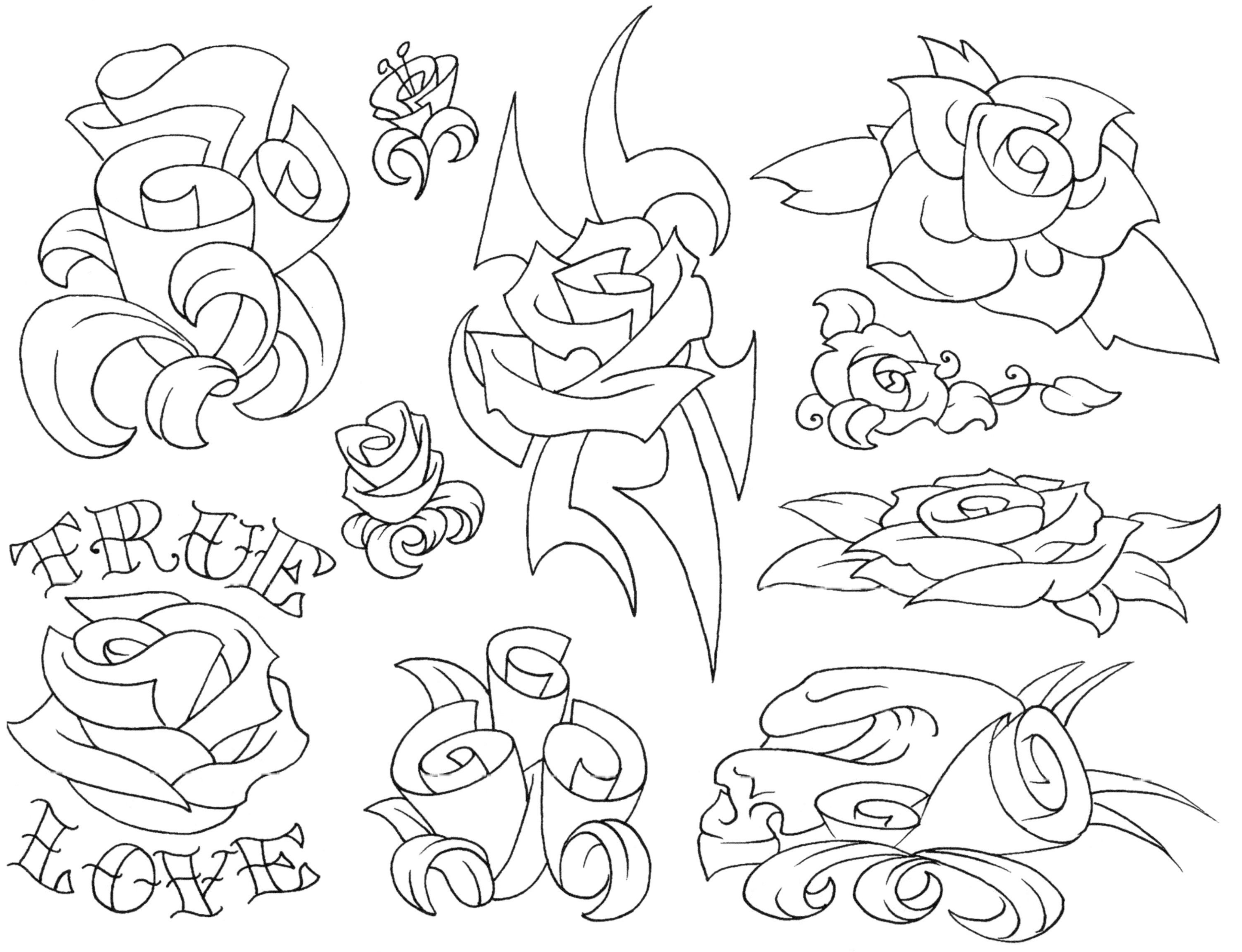
TRUE
LOVE

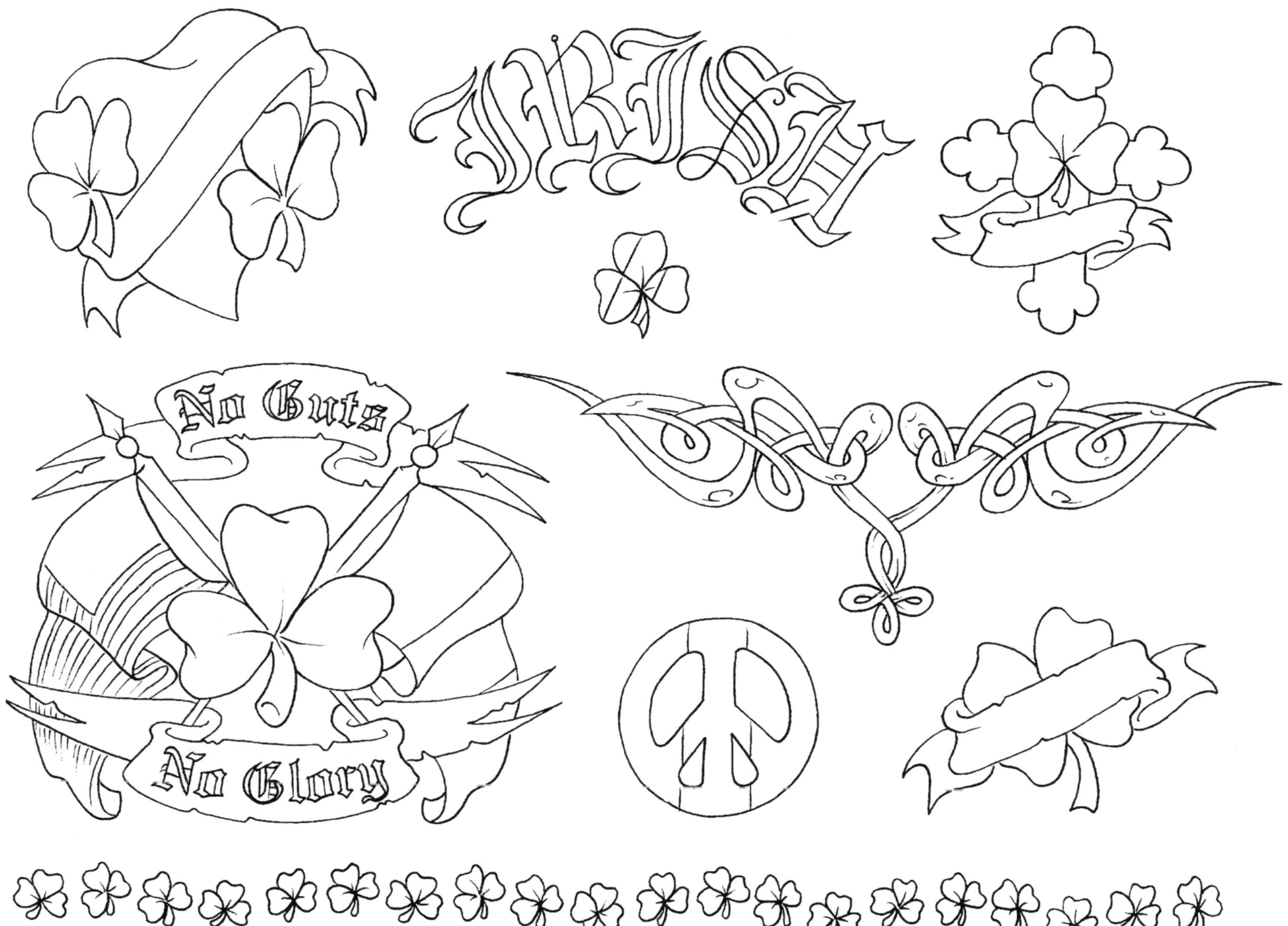
Irish
No Guts
No Glory

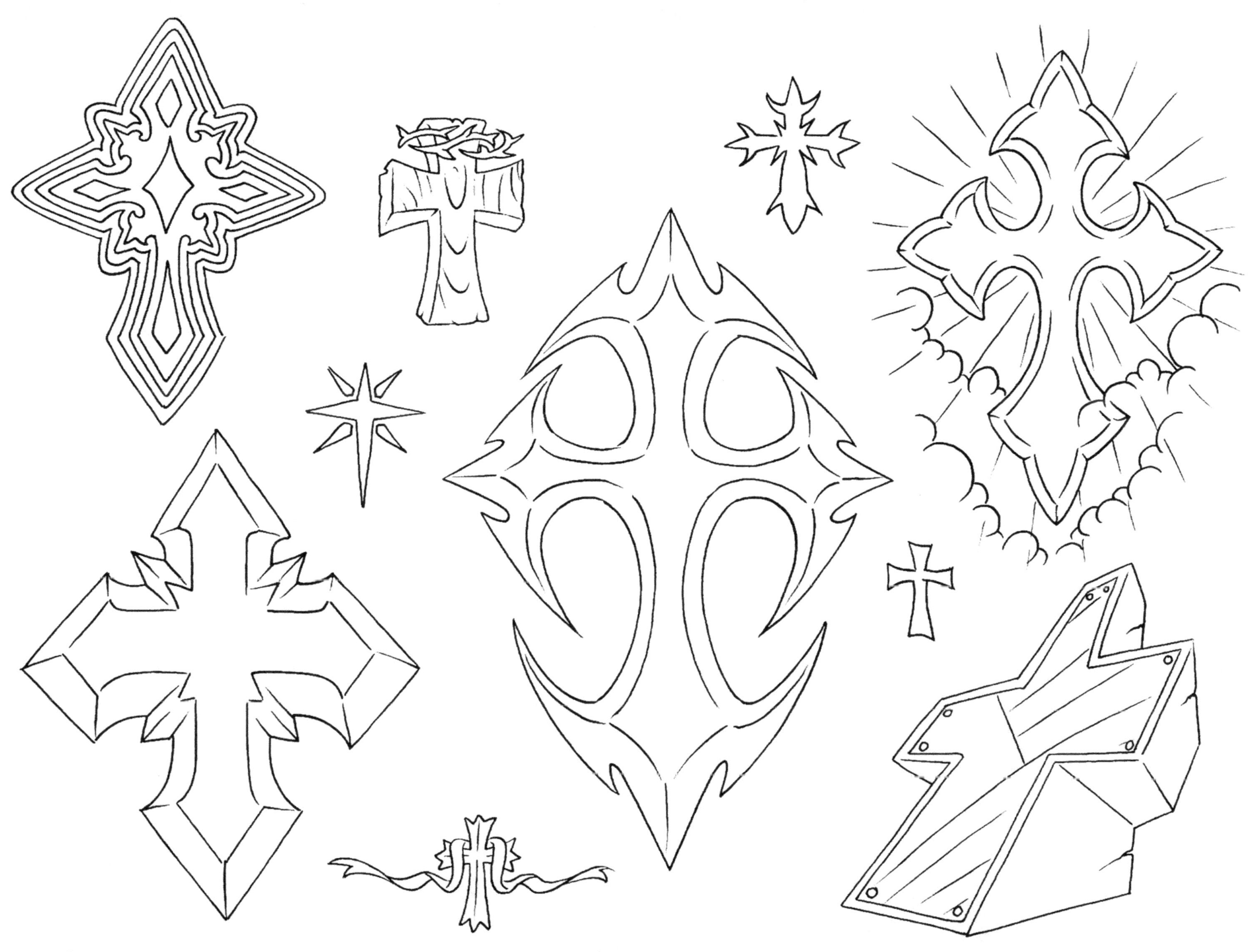

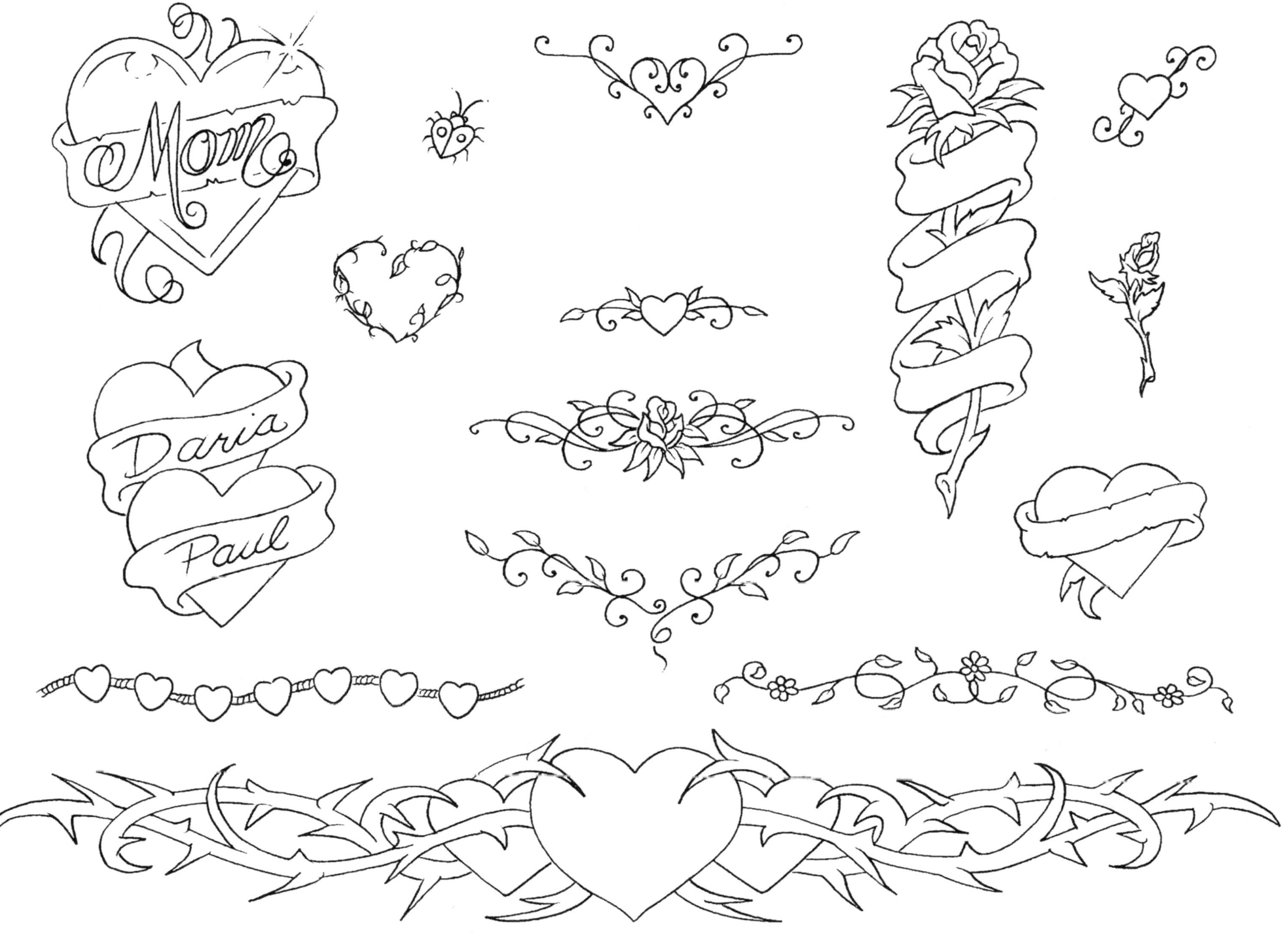
Mom
Daria
Paul

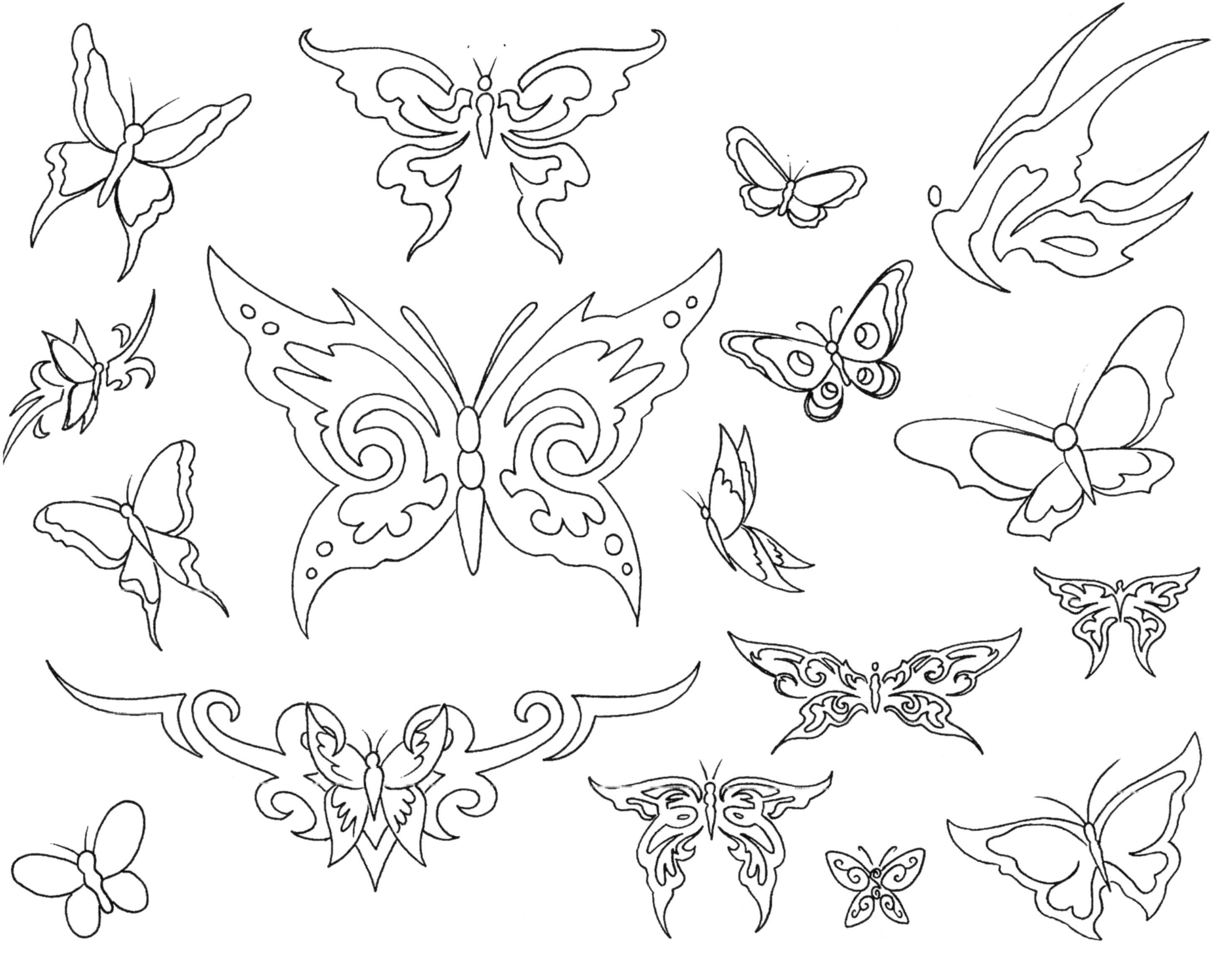

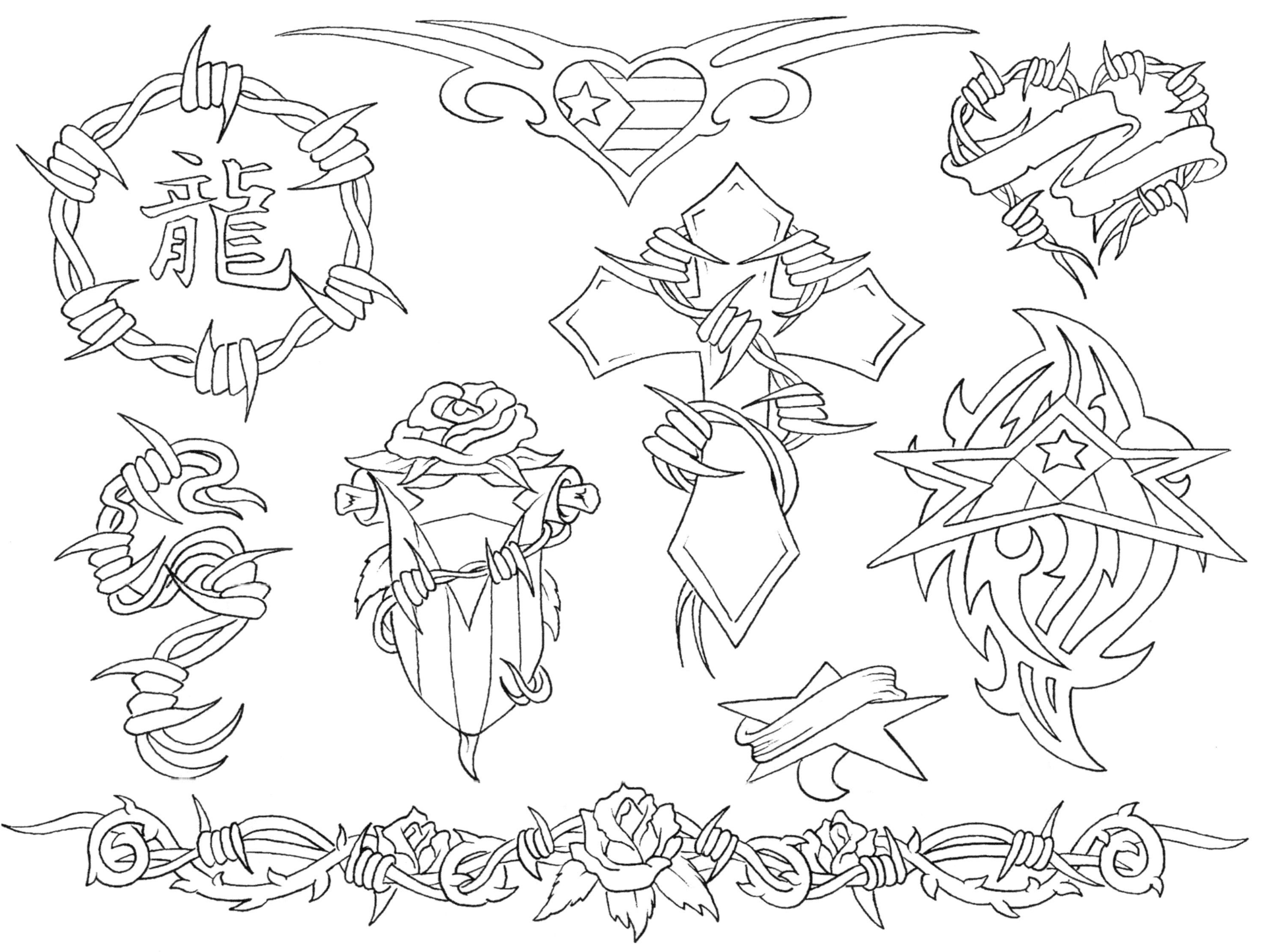
龍

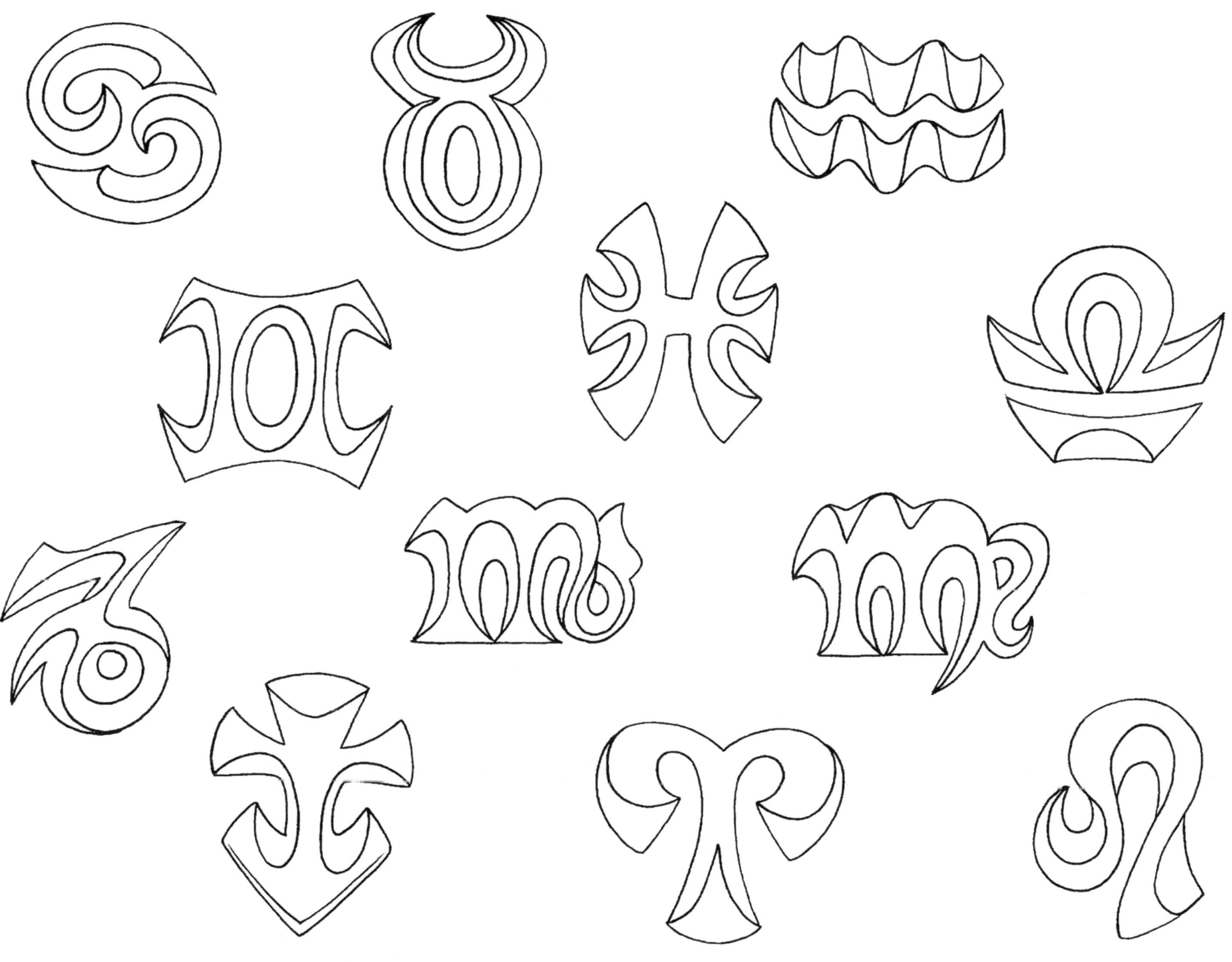

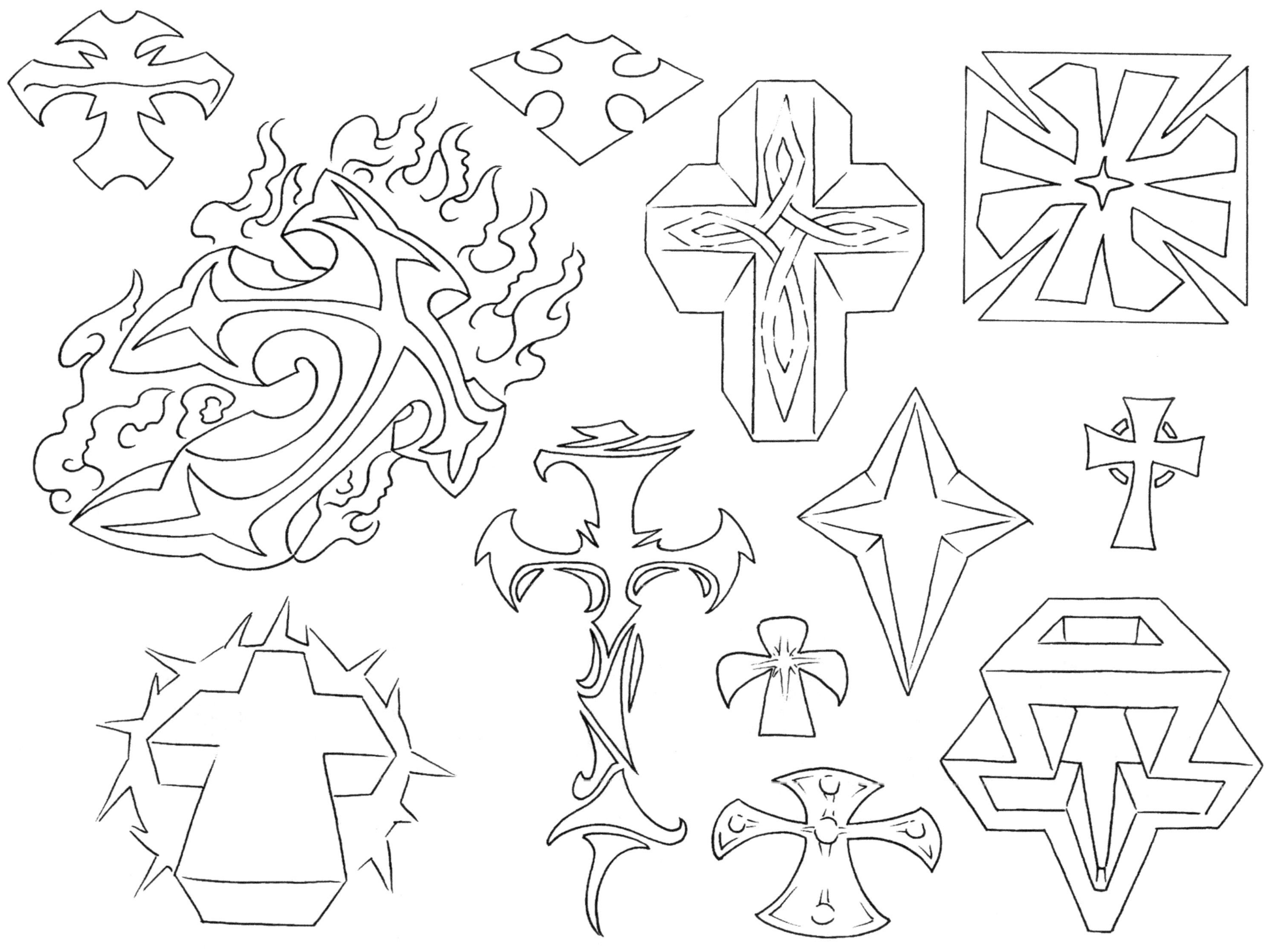

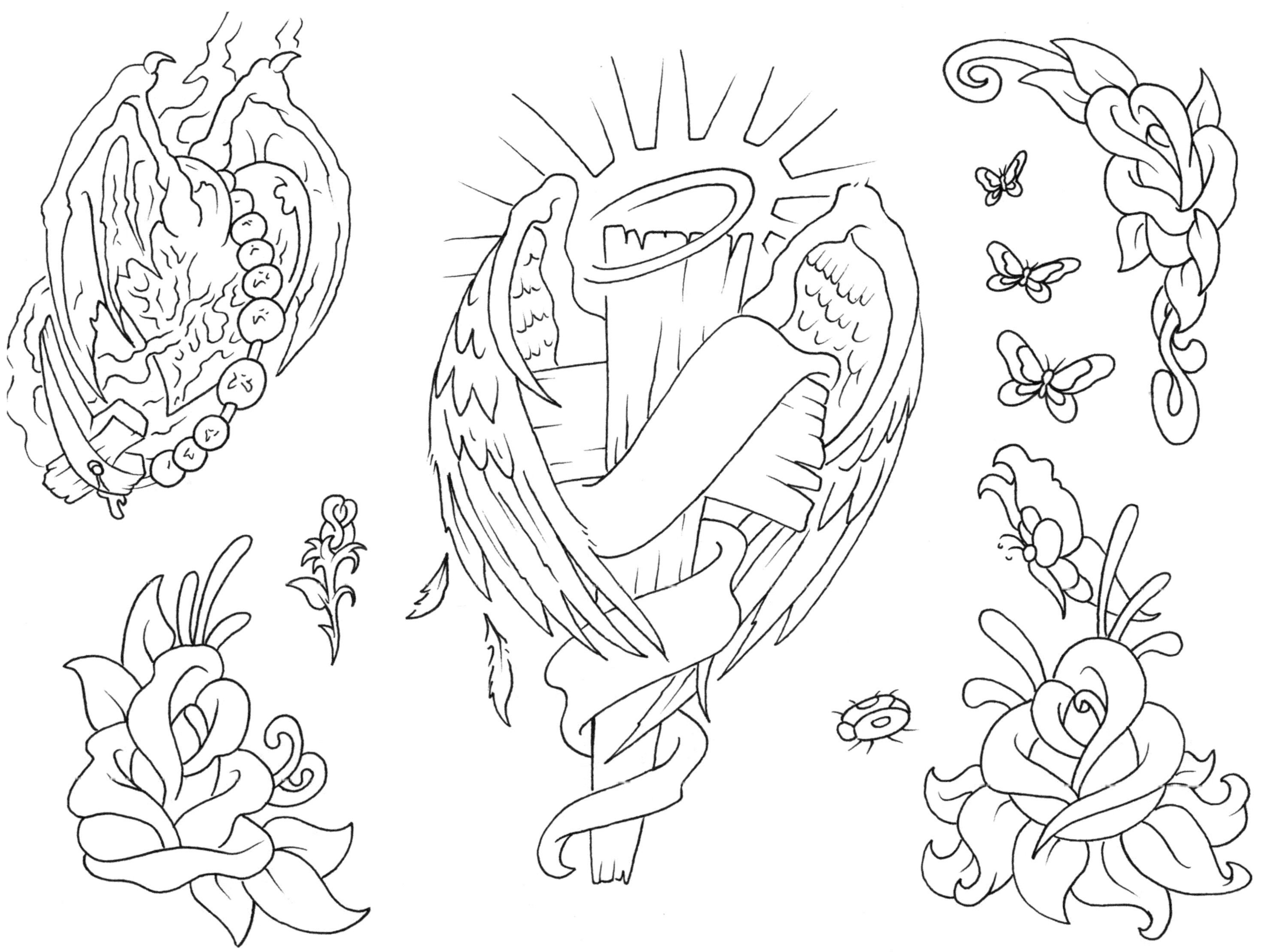

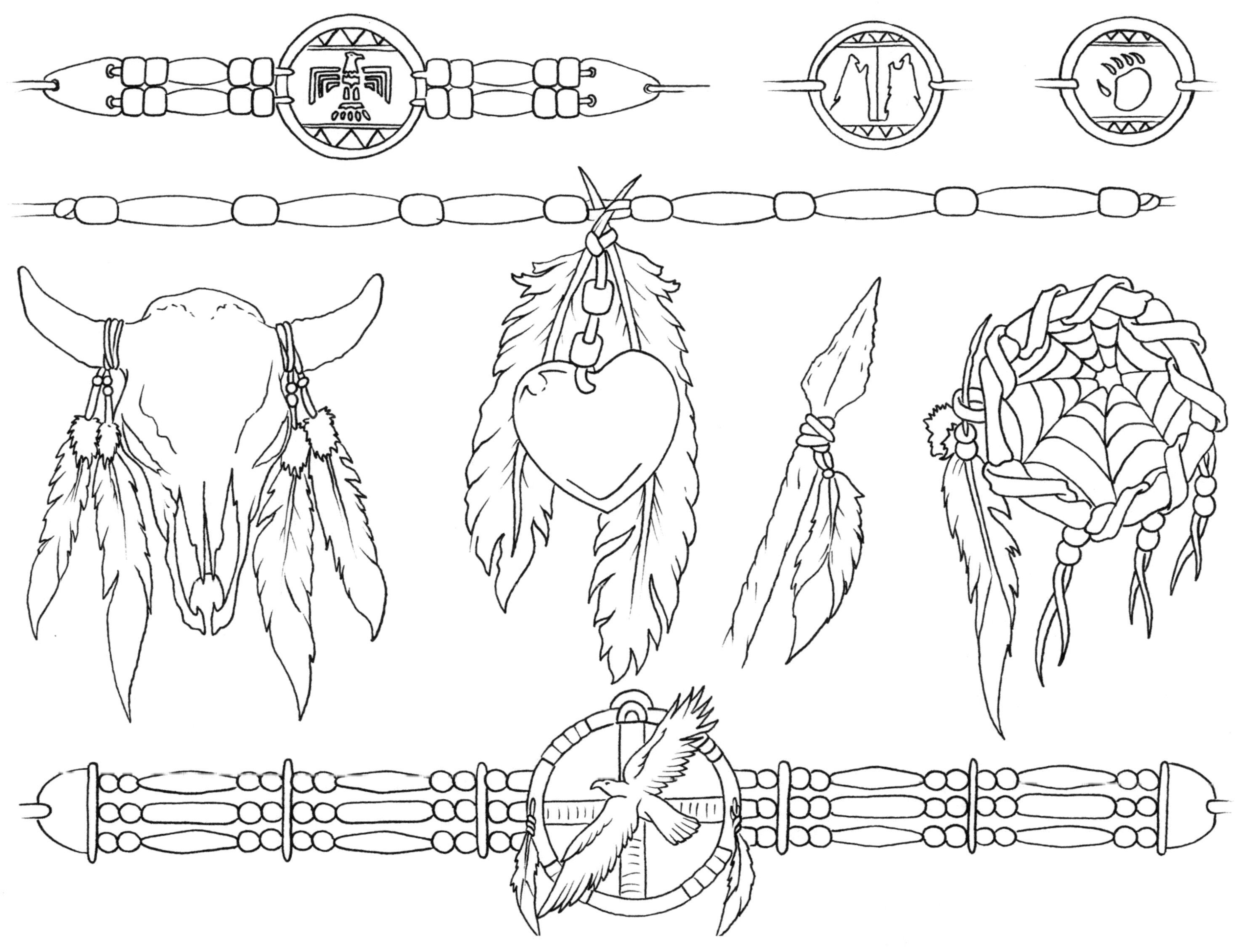

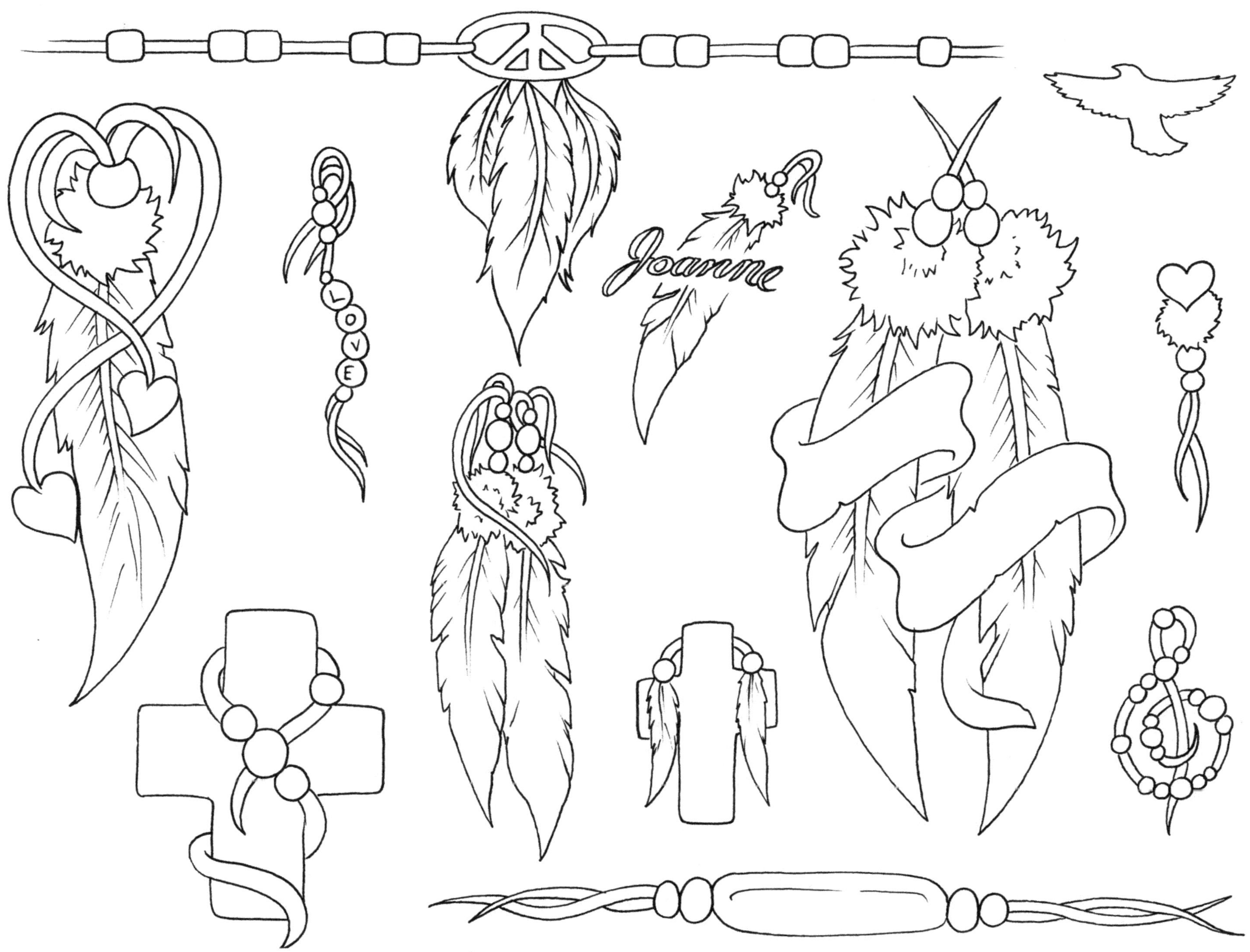
LOVE
Joanne

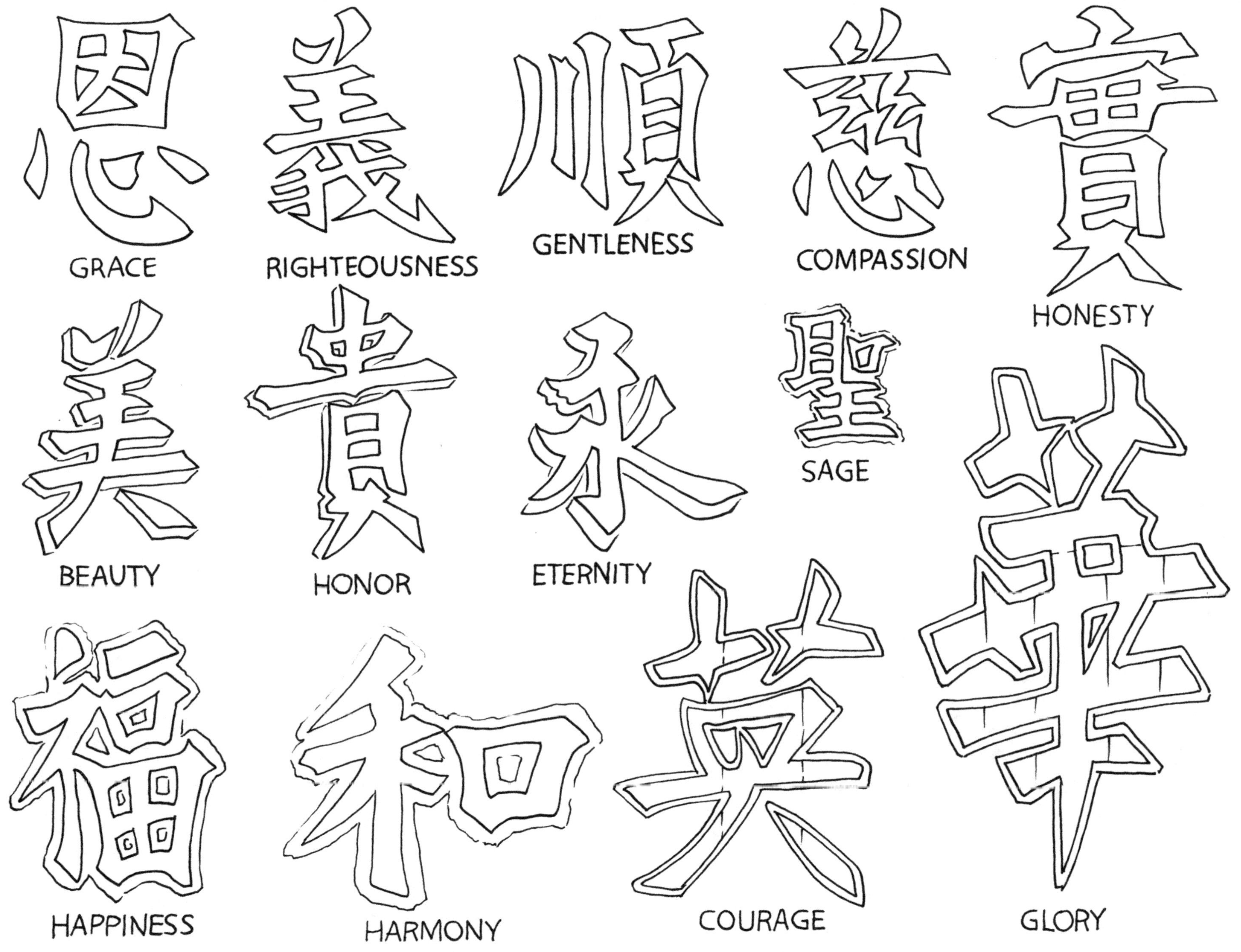
恩
GRACE
義
RIGHTEOUSNESS
順
GENTLENESS
慈
COMPASSION
實
HONESTY
美
BEAUTY
貴
HONOR
永
ETERNITY
聖
SAGE
福
HAPPINESS
和
HARMONY
英
COURAGE
華
GLORY

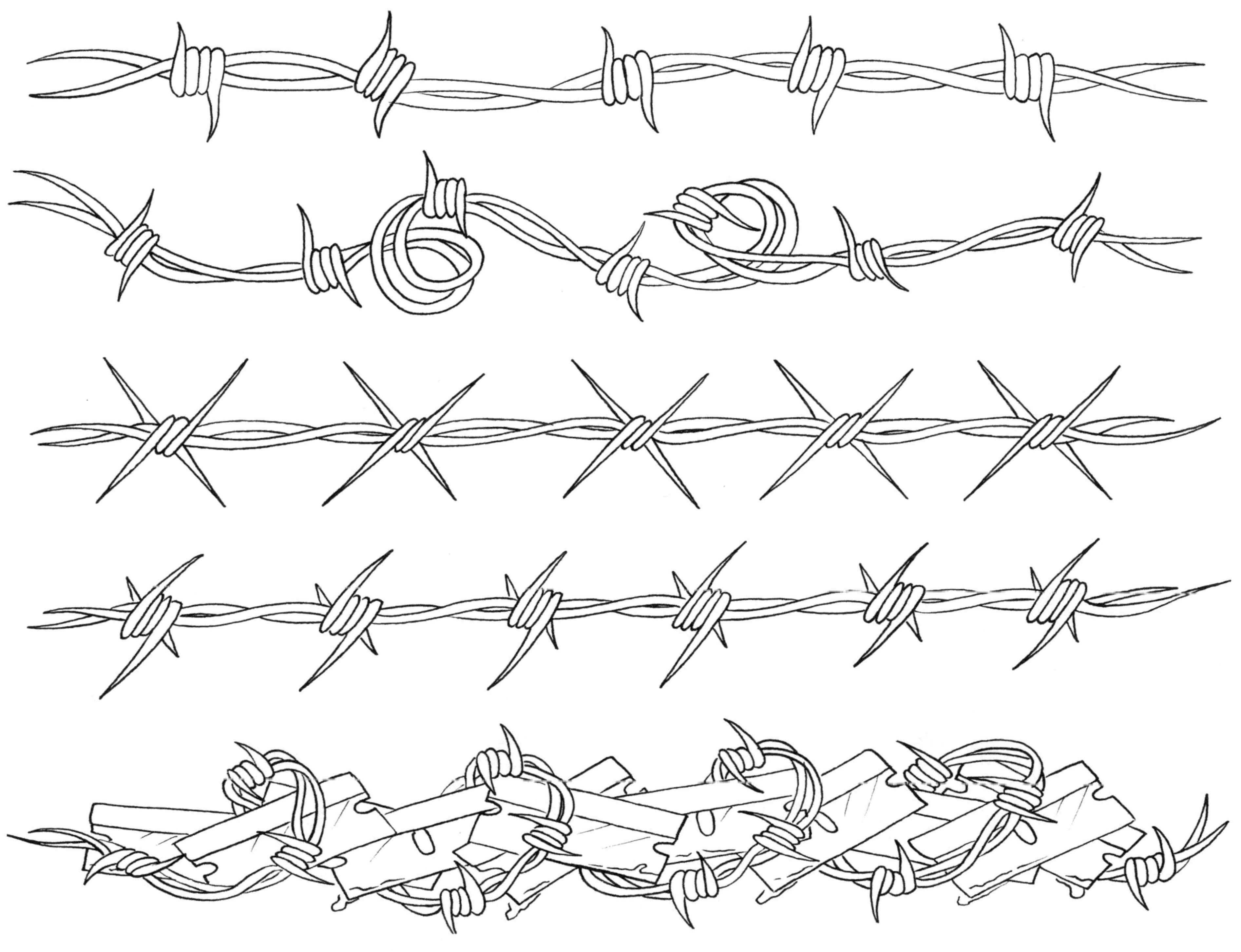

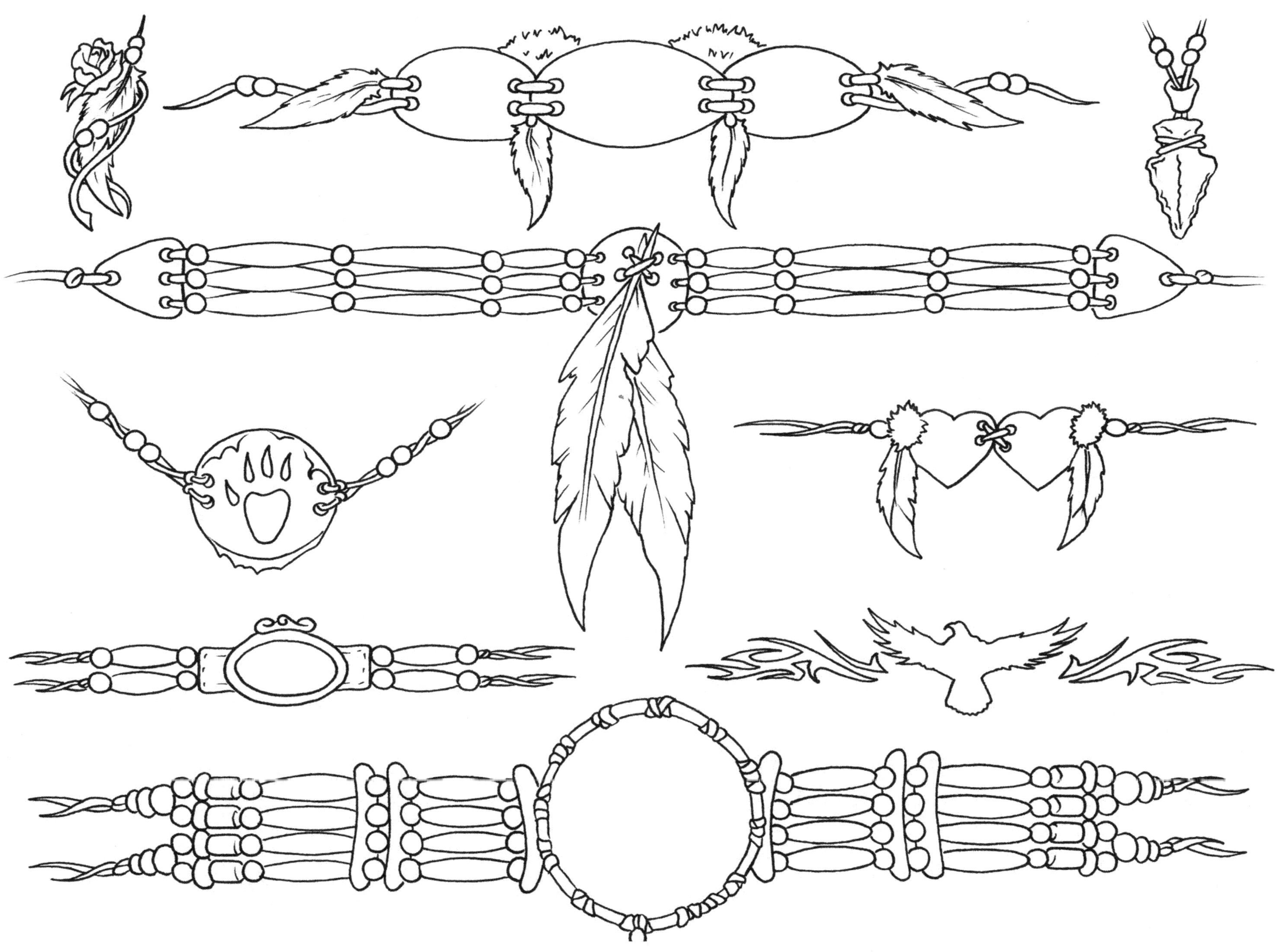

Alexis

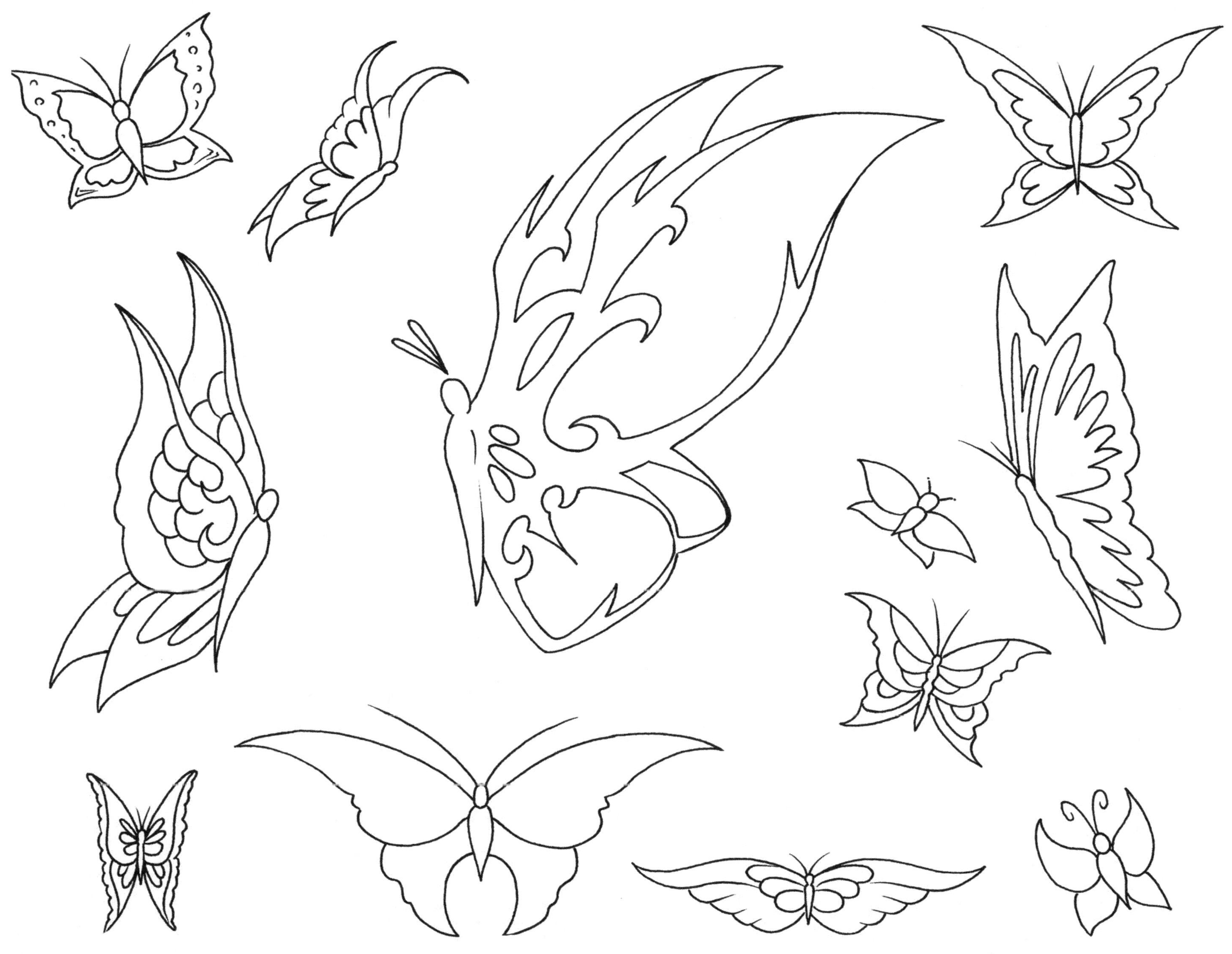

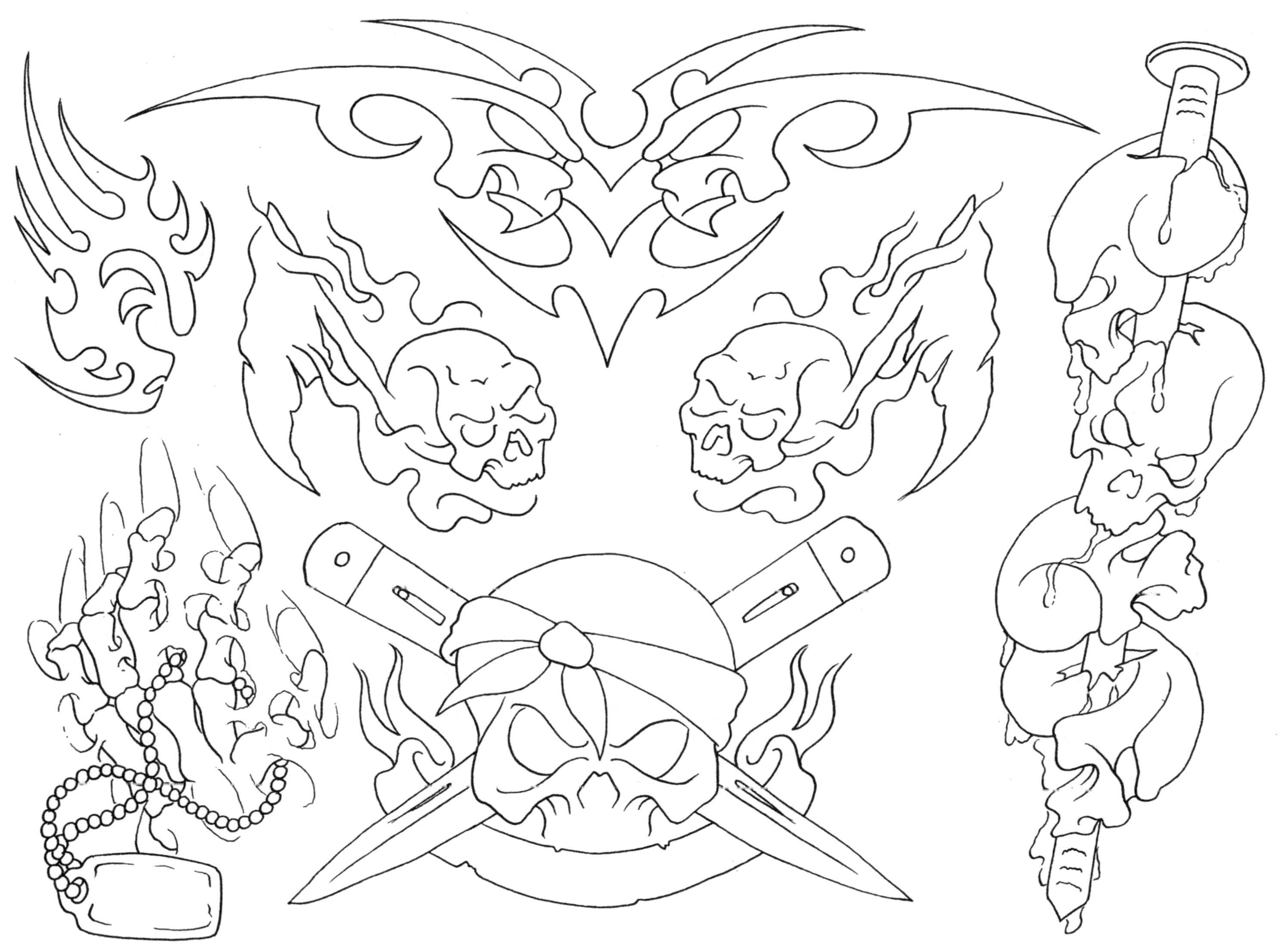

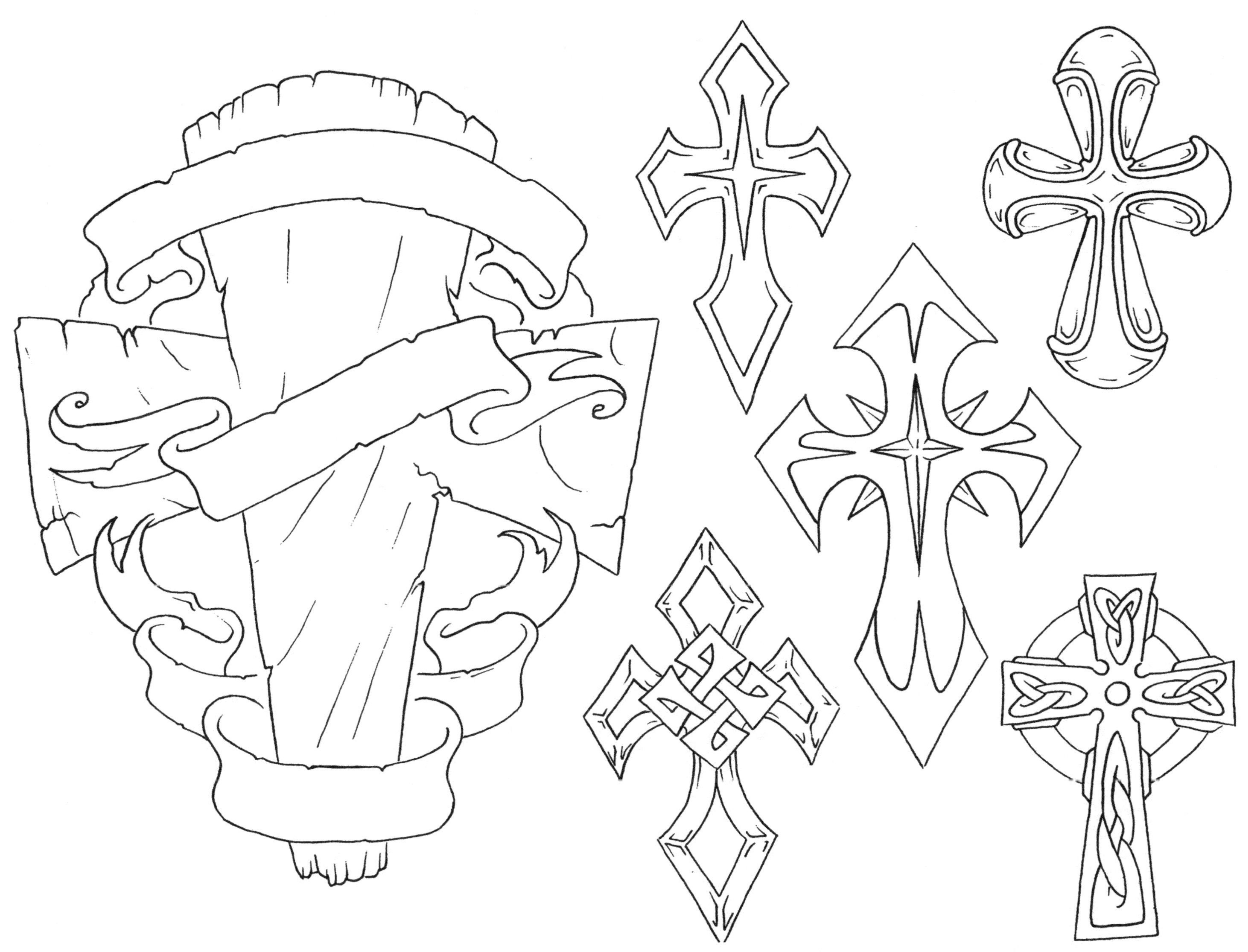

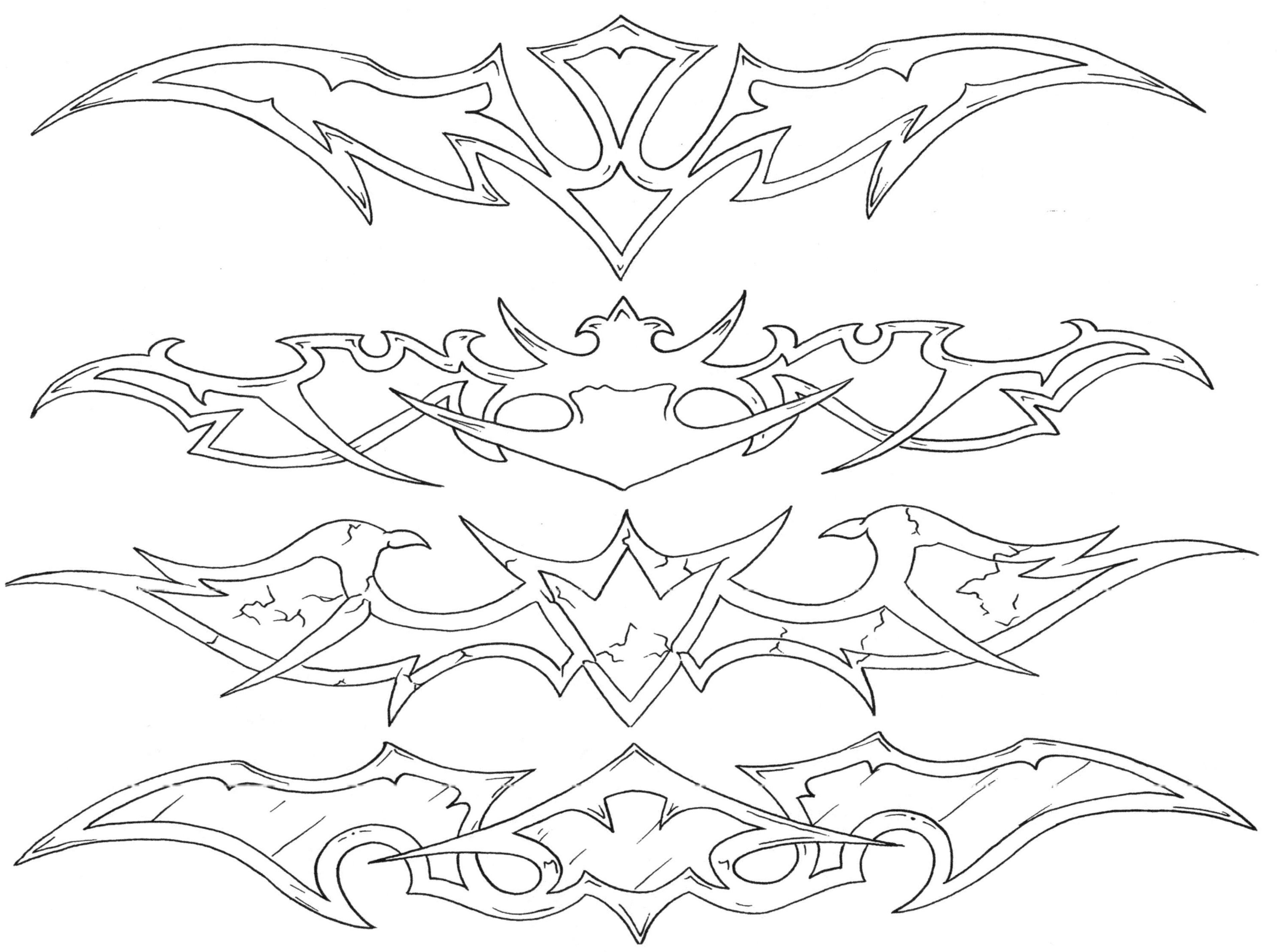

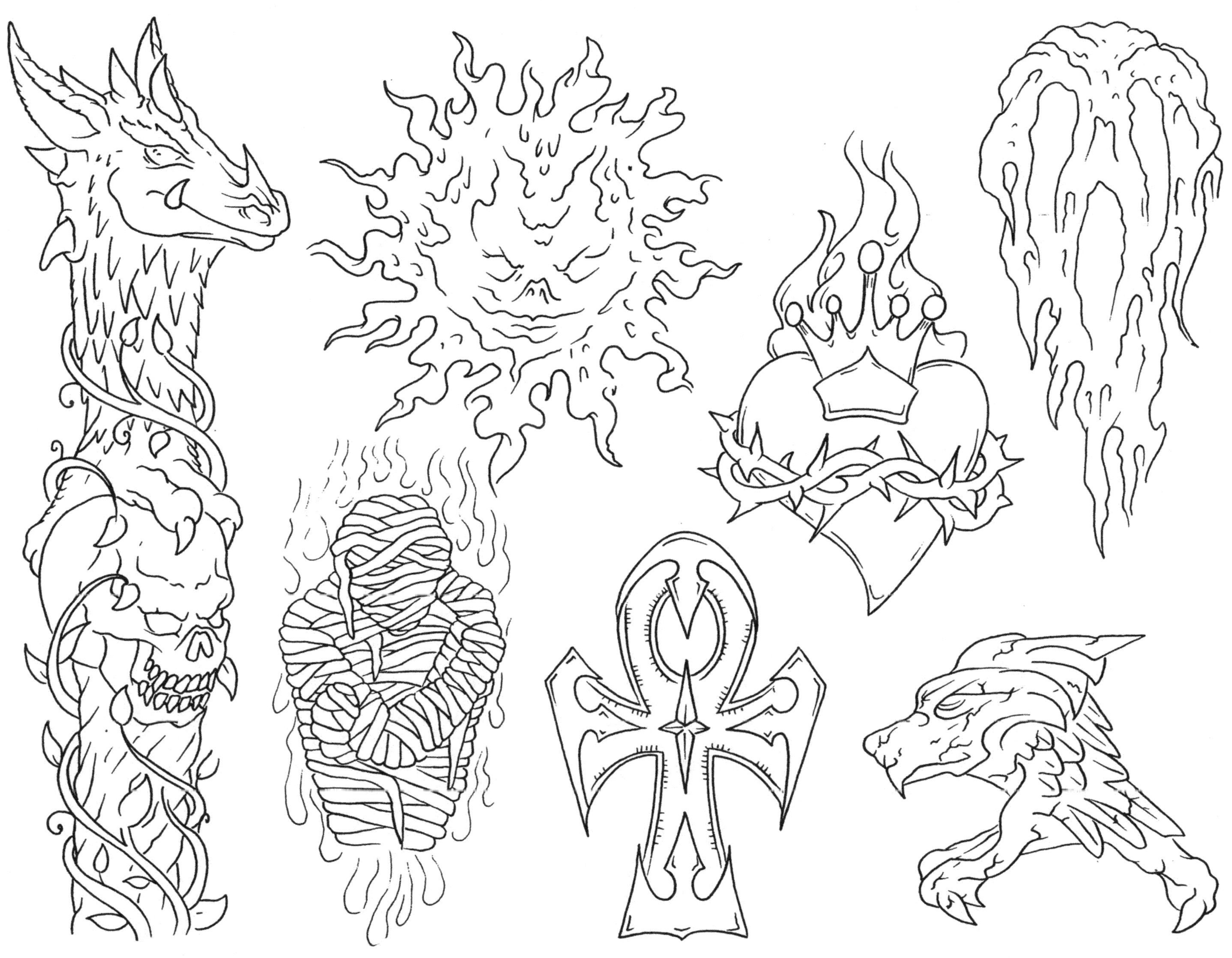

King
Queen
Lucky
JOKER

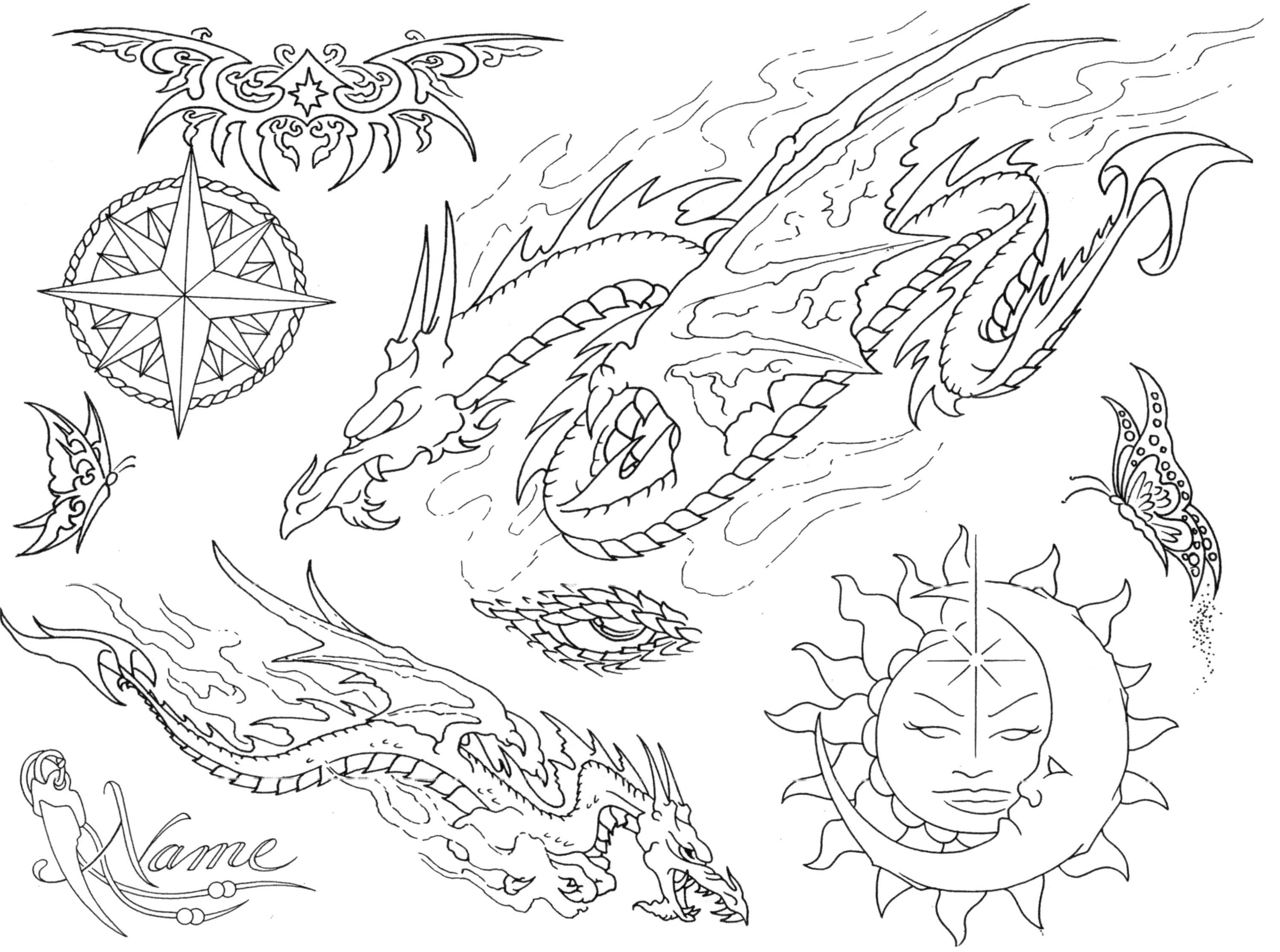
Name

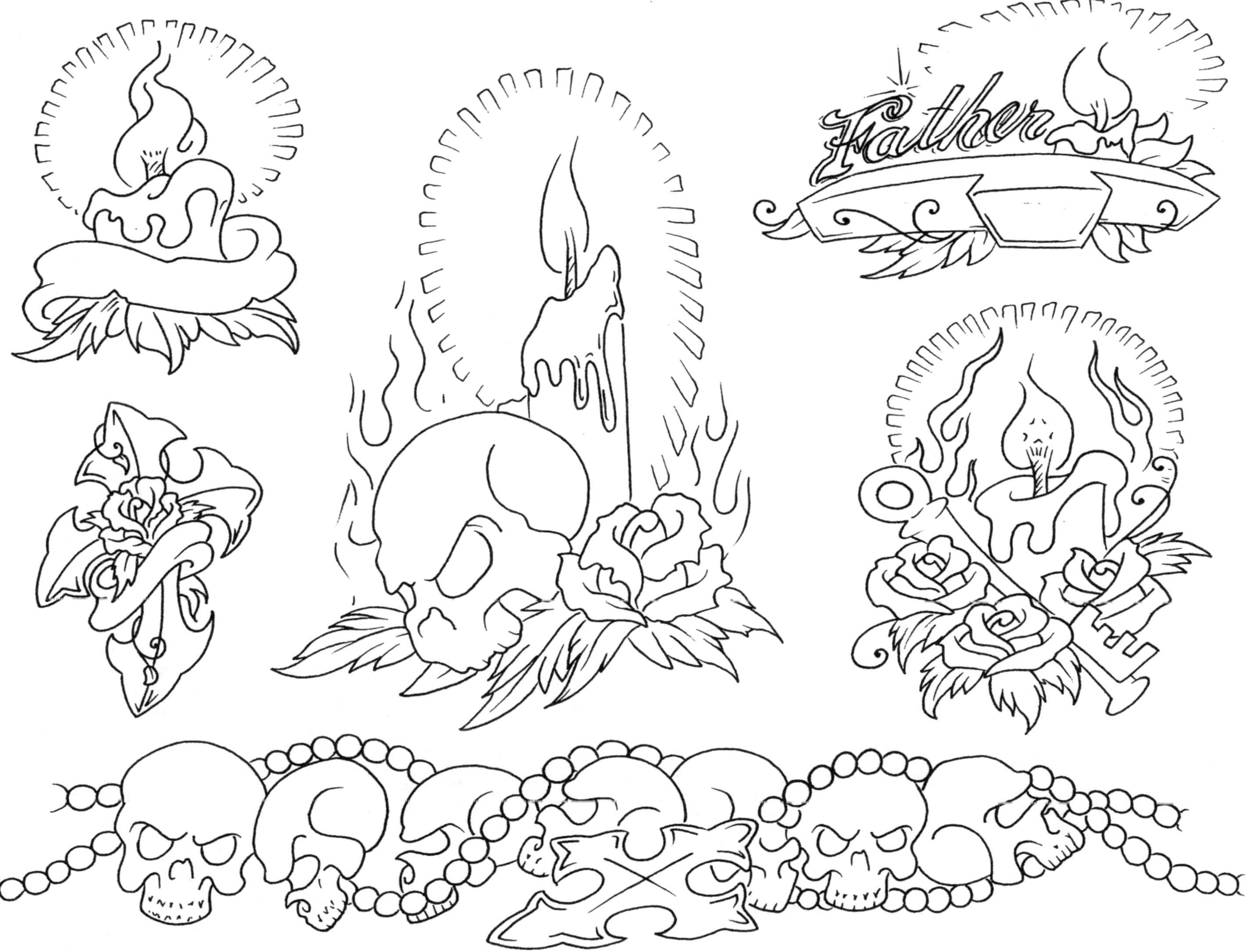
Father

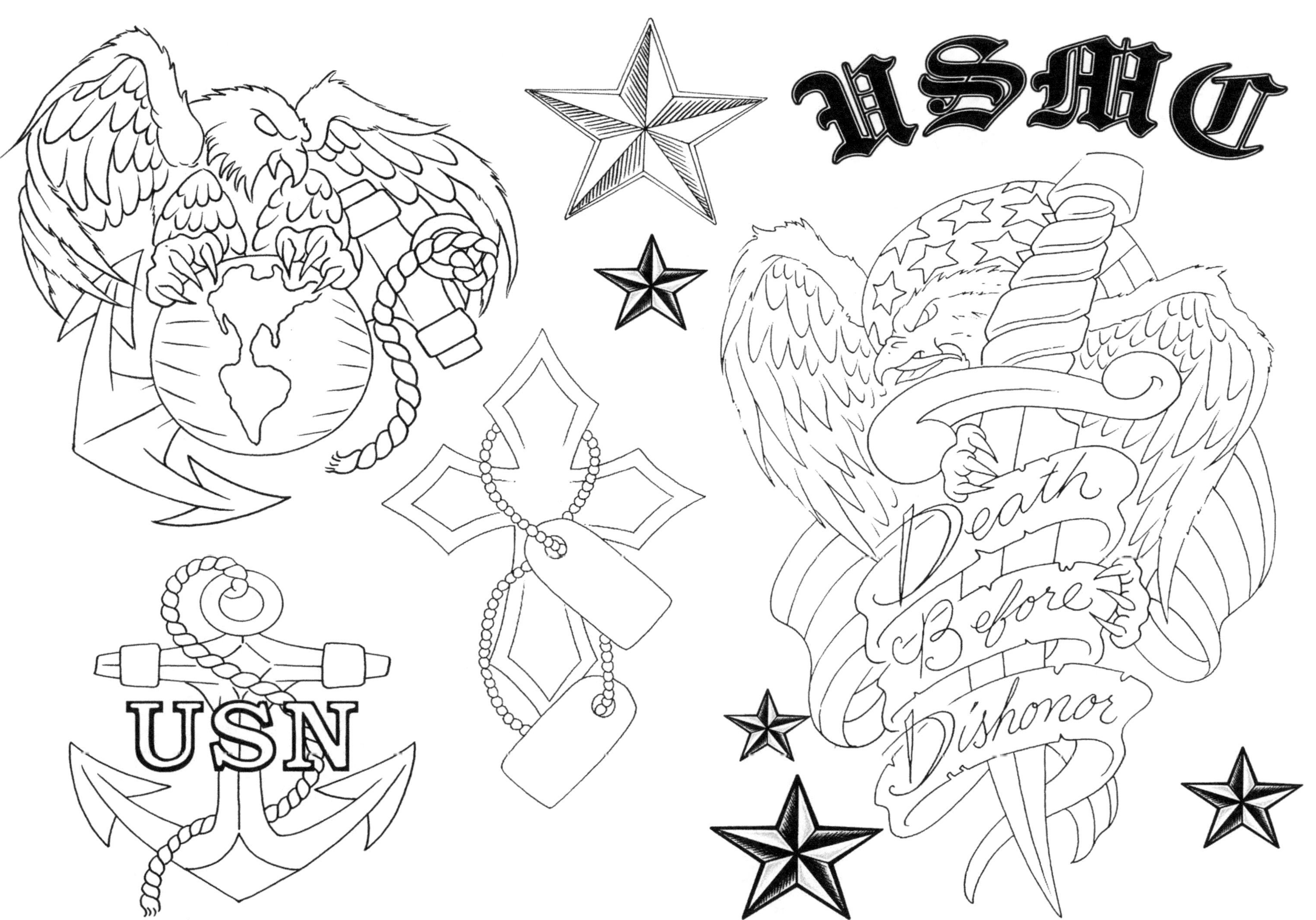
USMC
Death Before Dishonor
USN

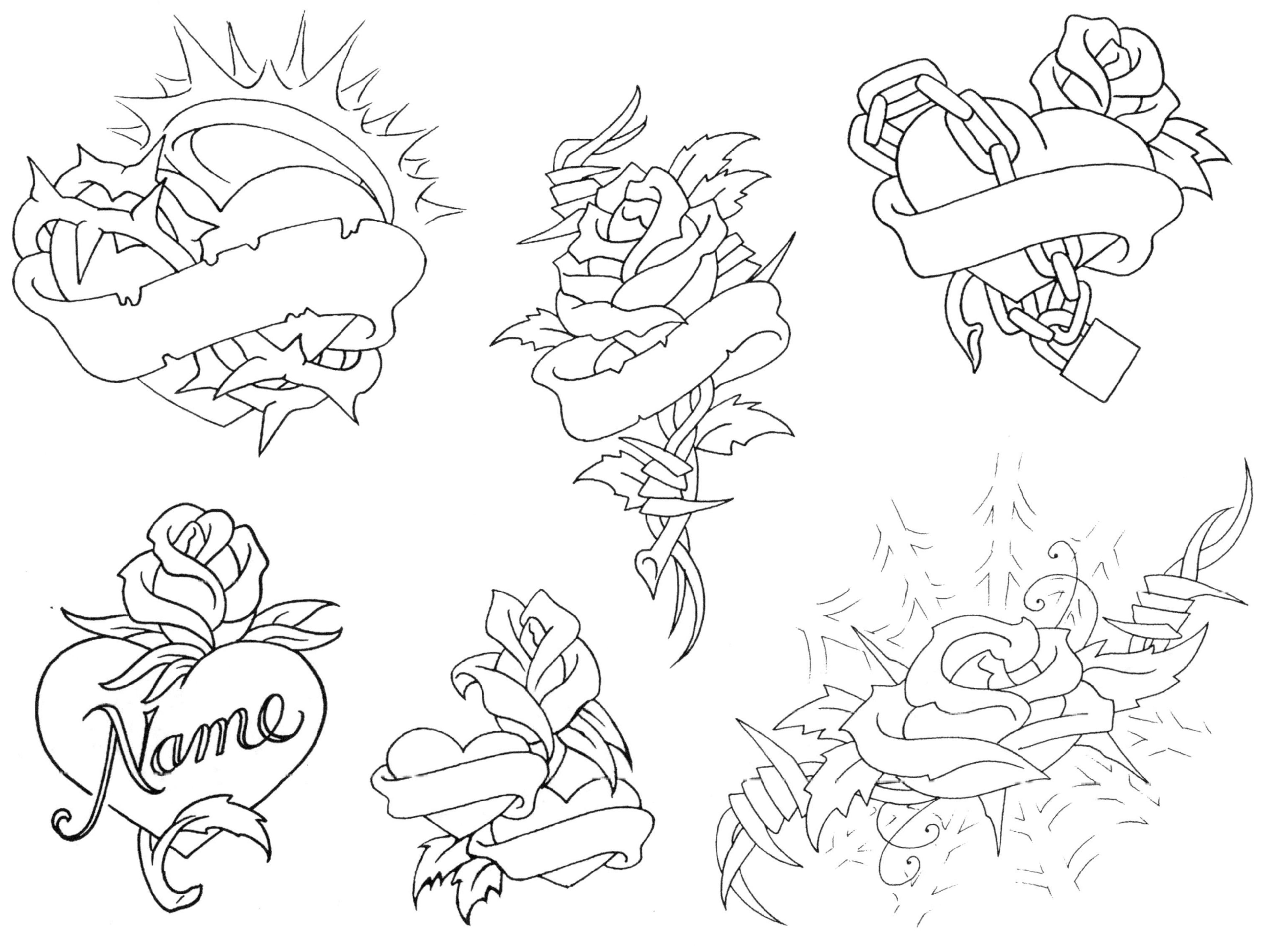
Name

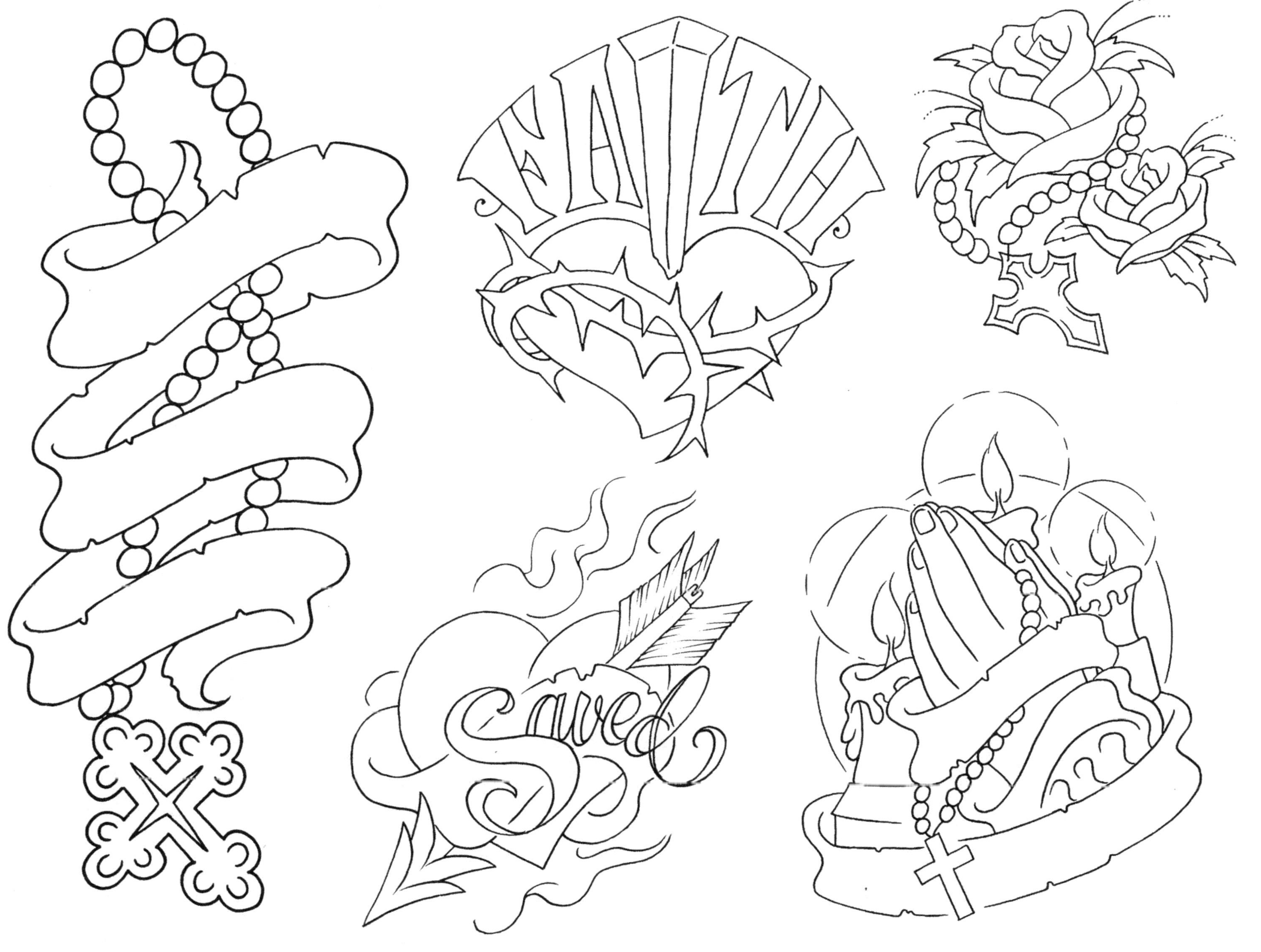
FAITH
Saved

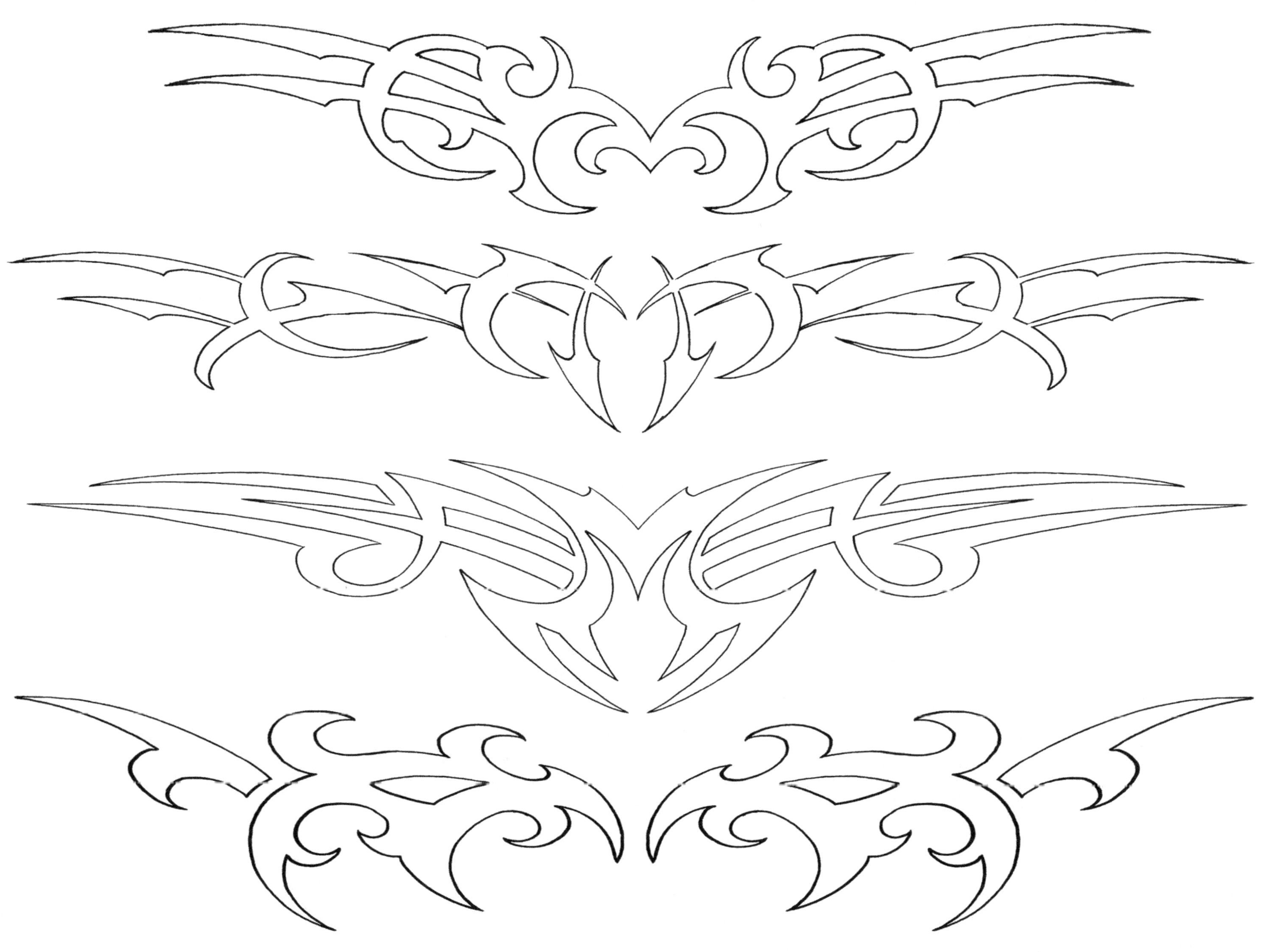

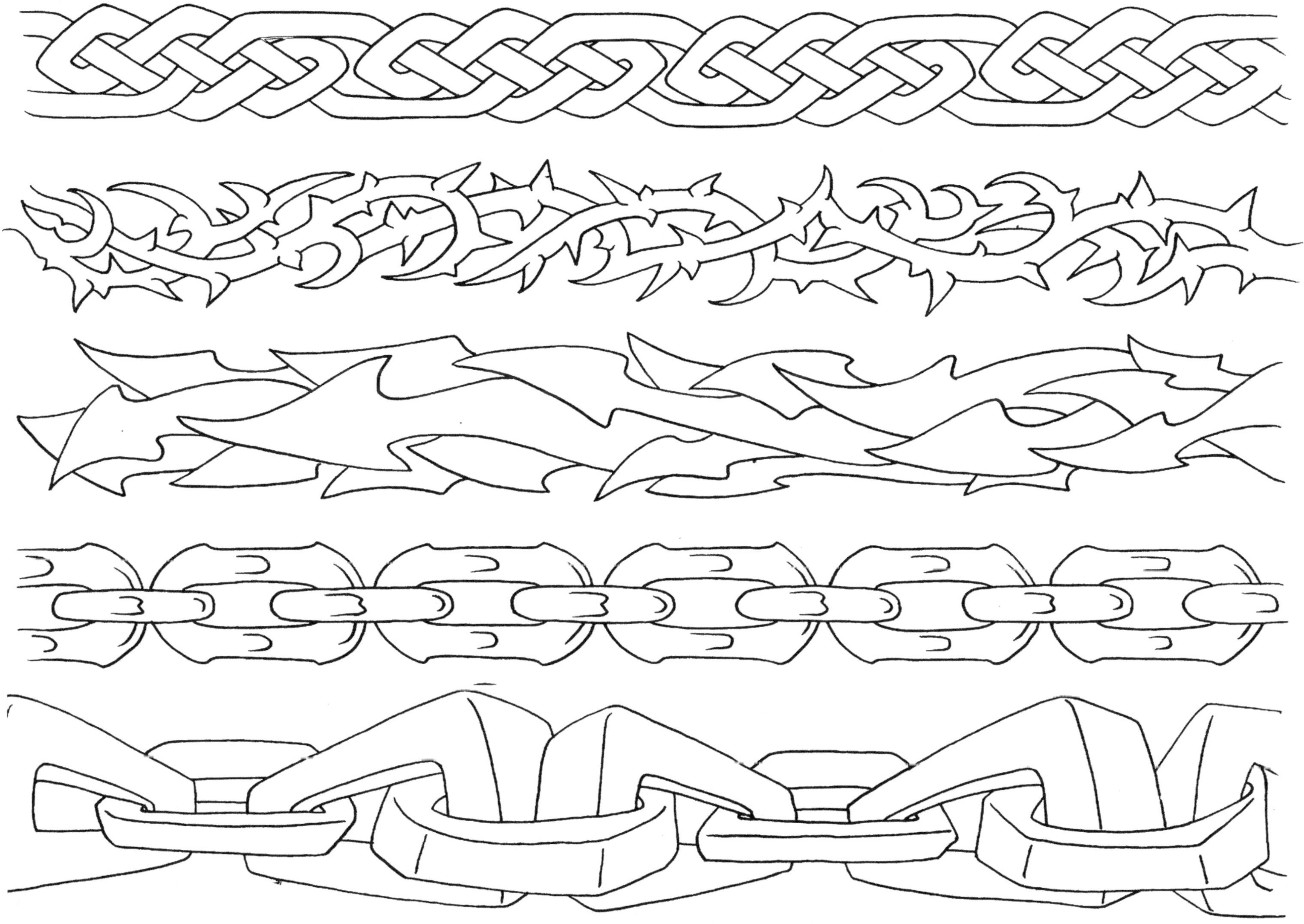

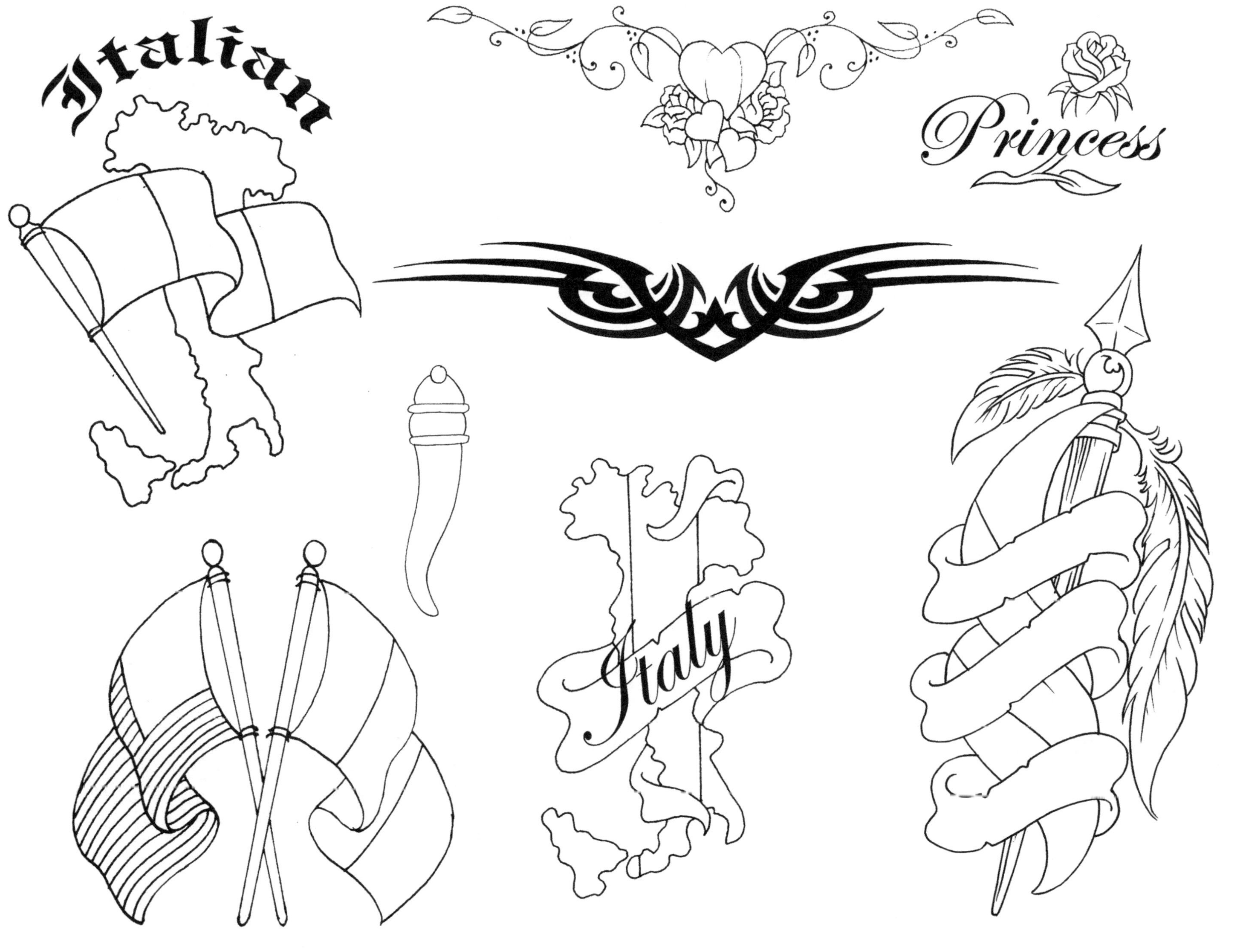

Italian
Princess
Italy

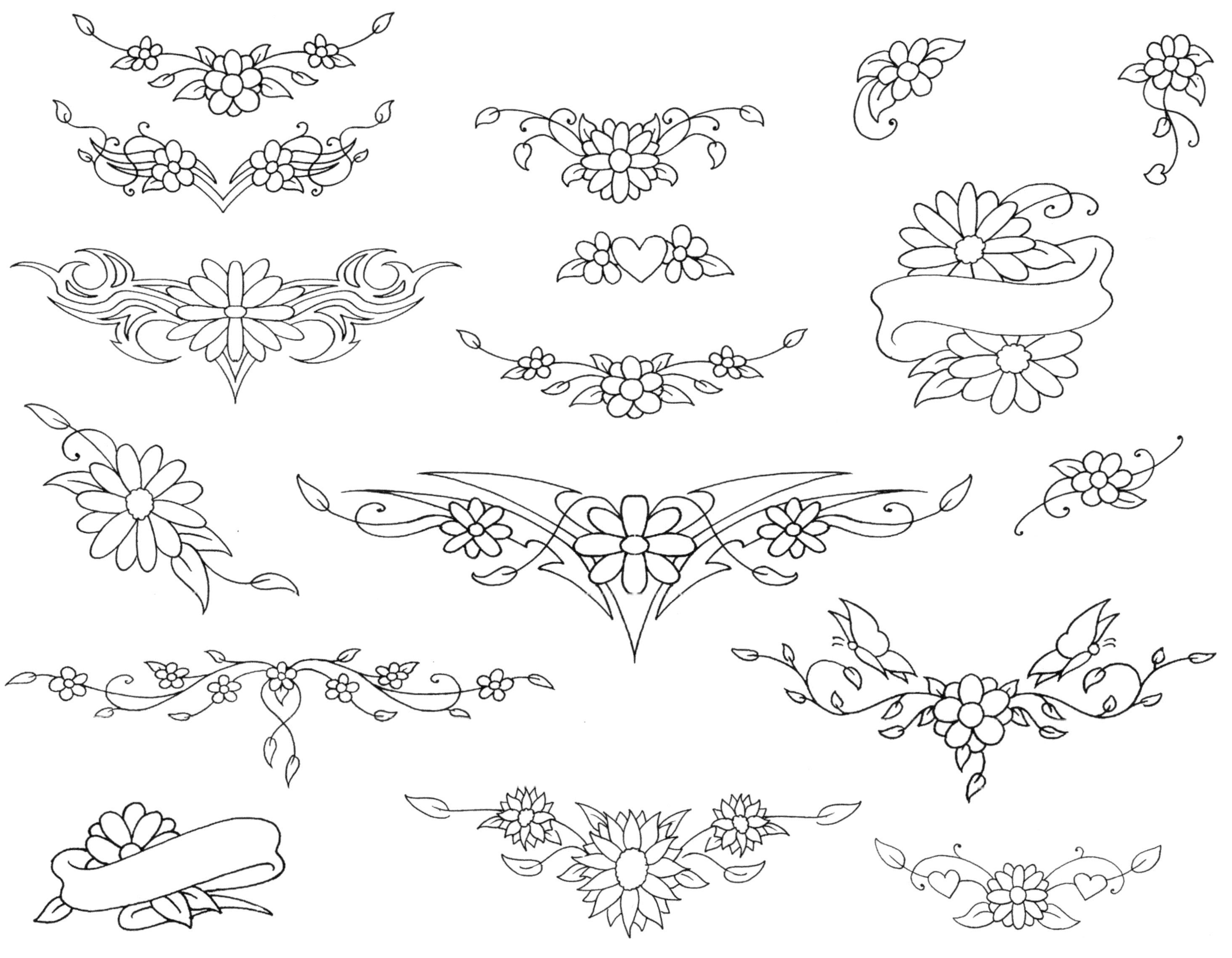

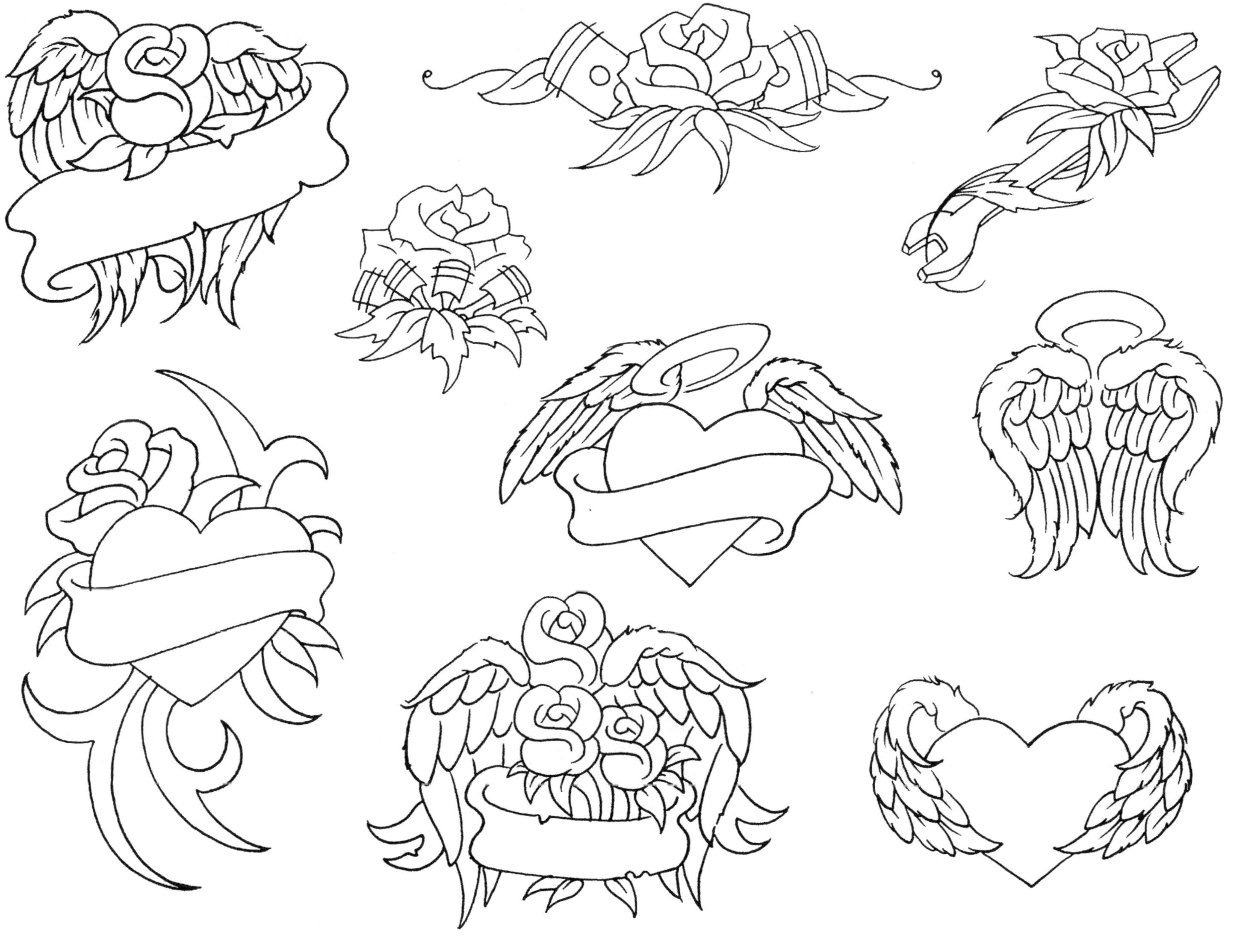

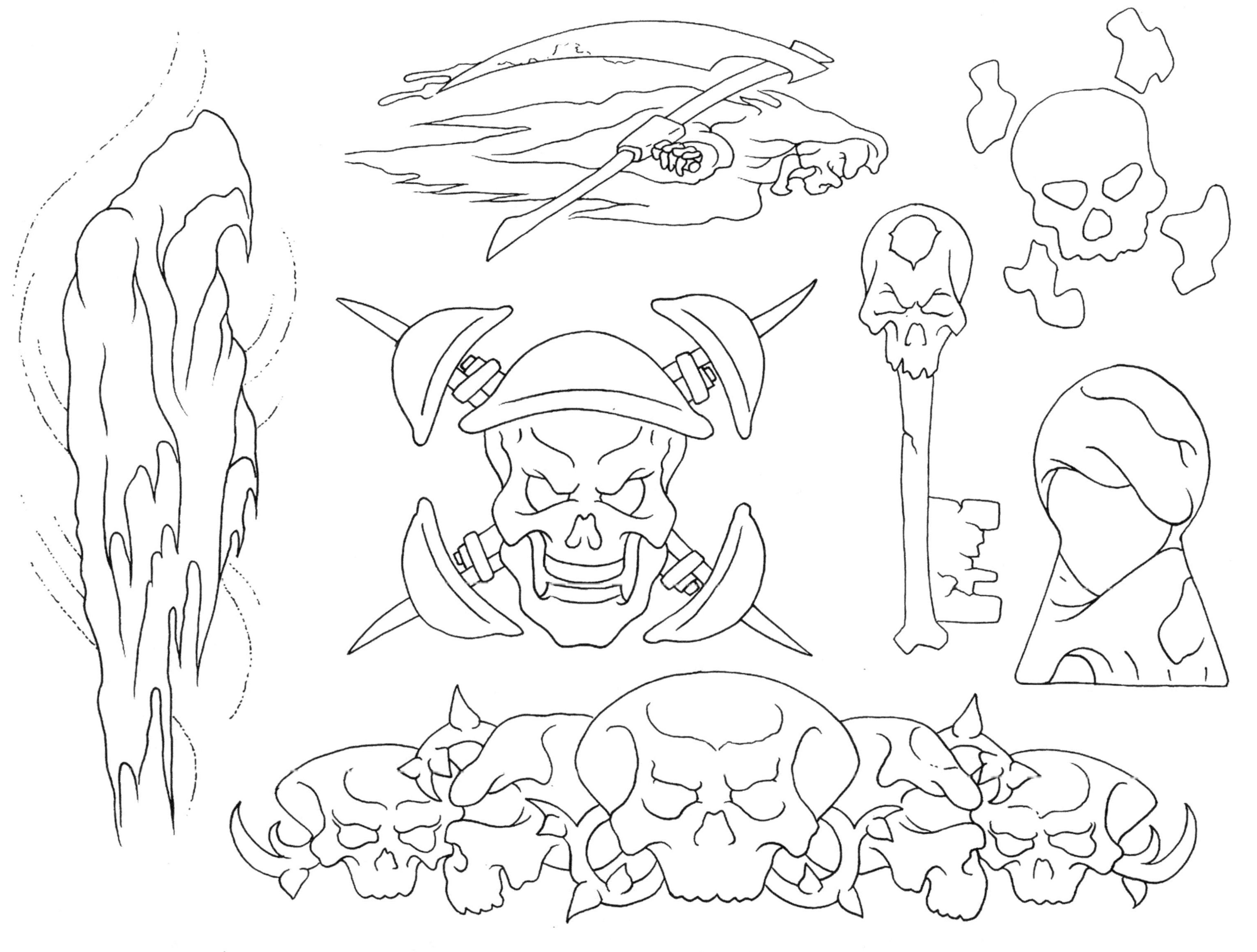

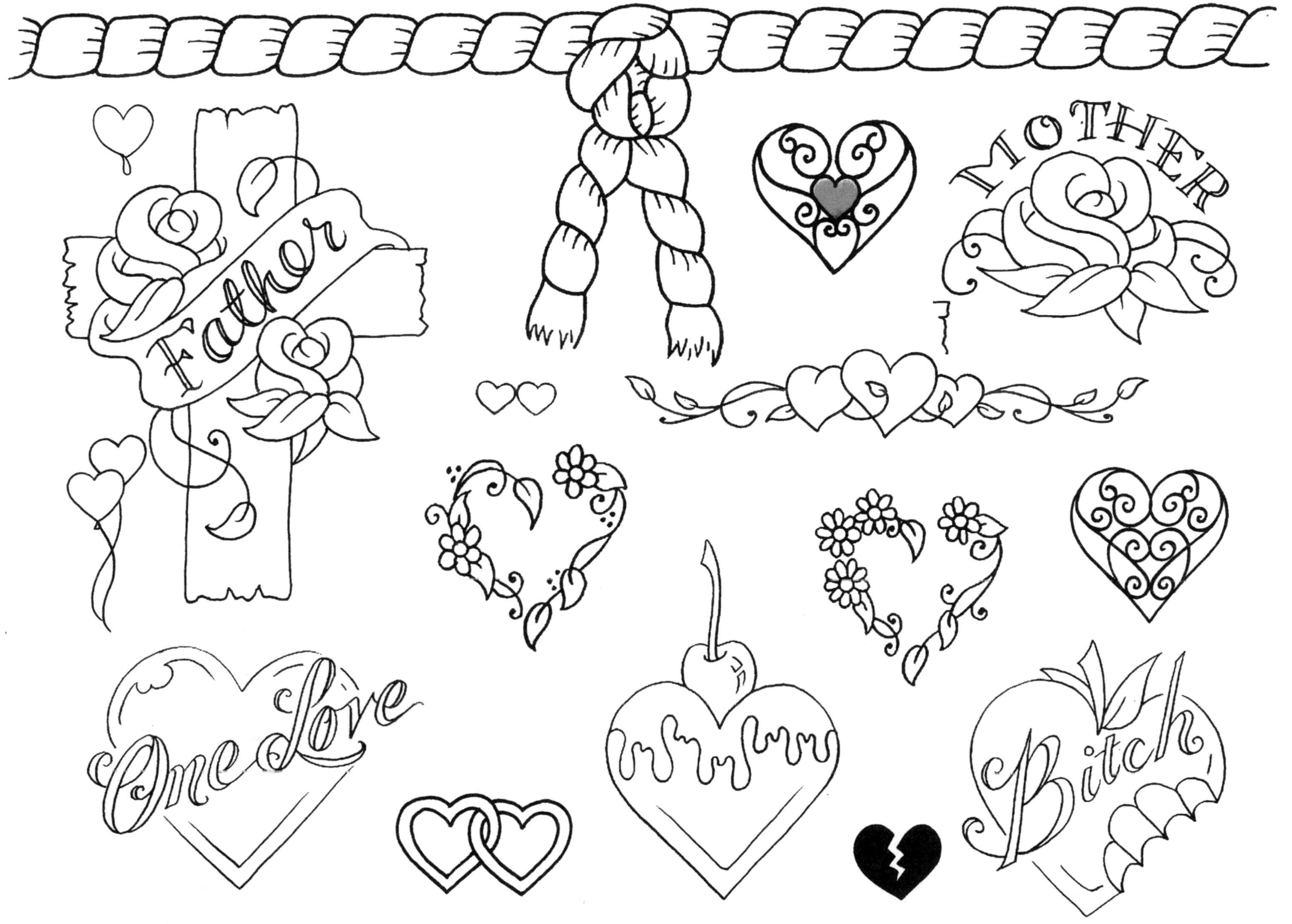

Father
MOTHER
One Love
Bitch

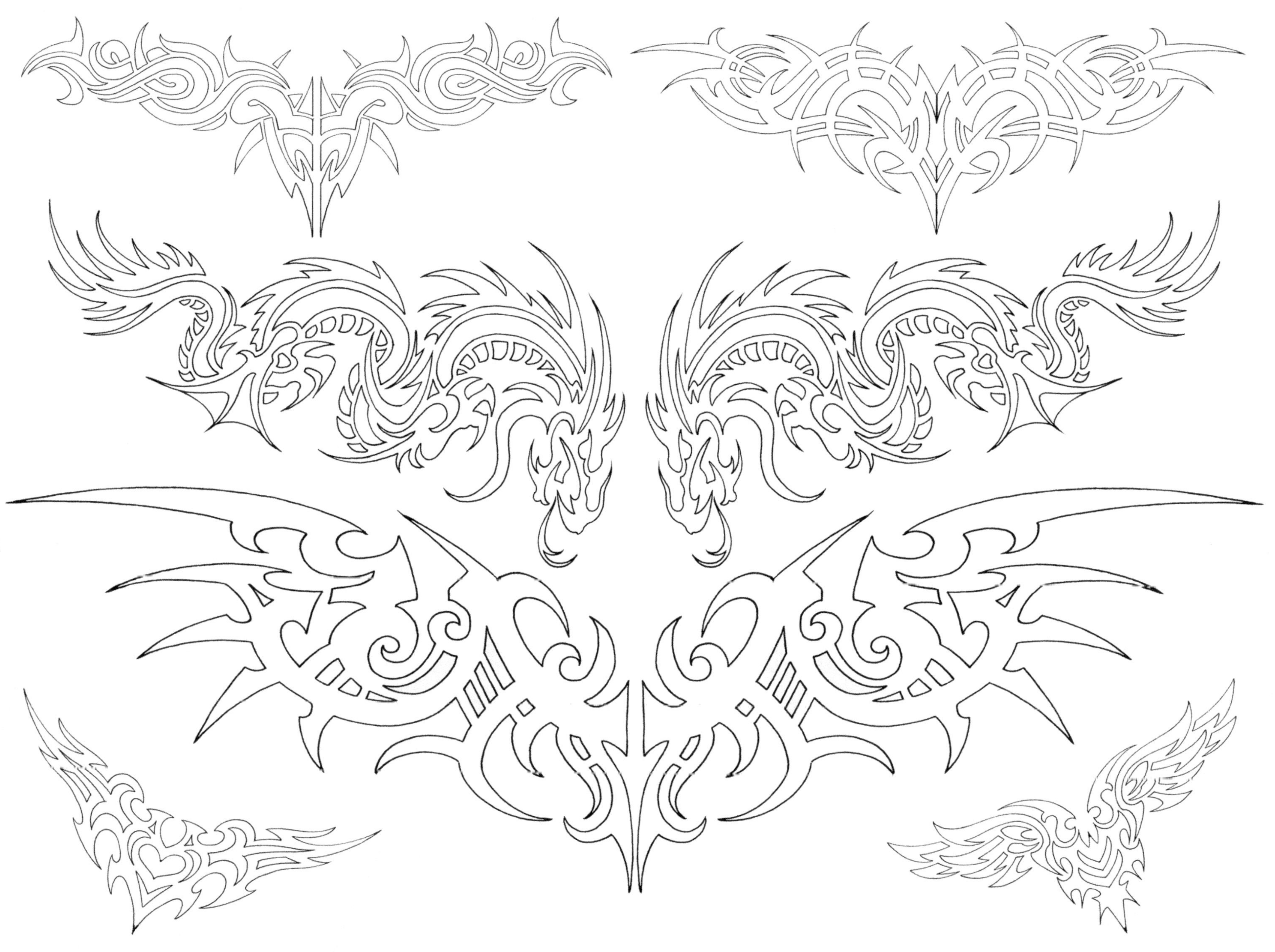

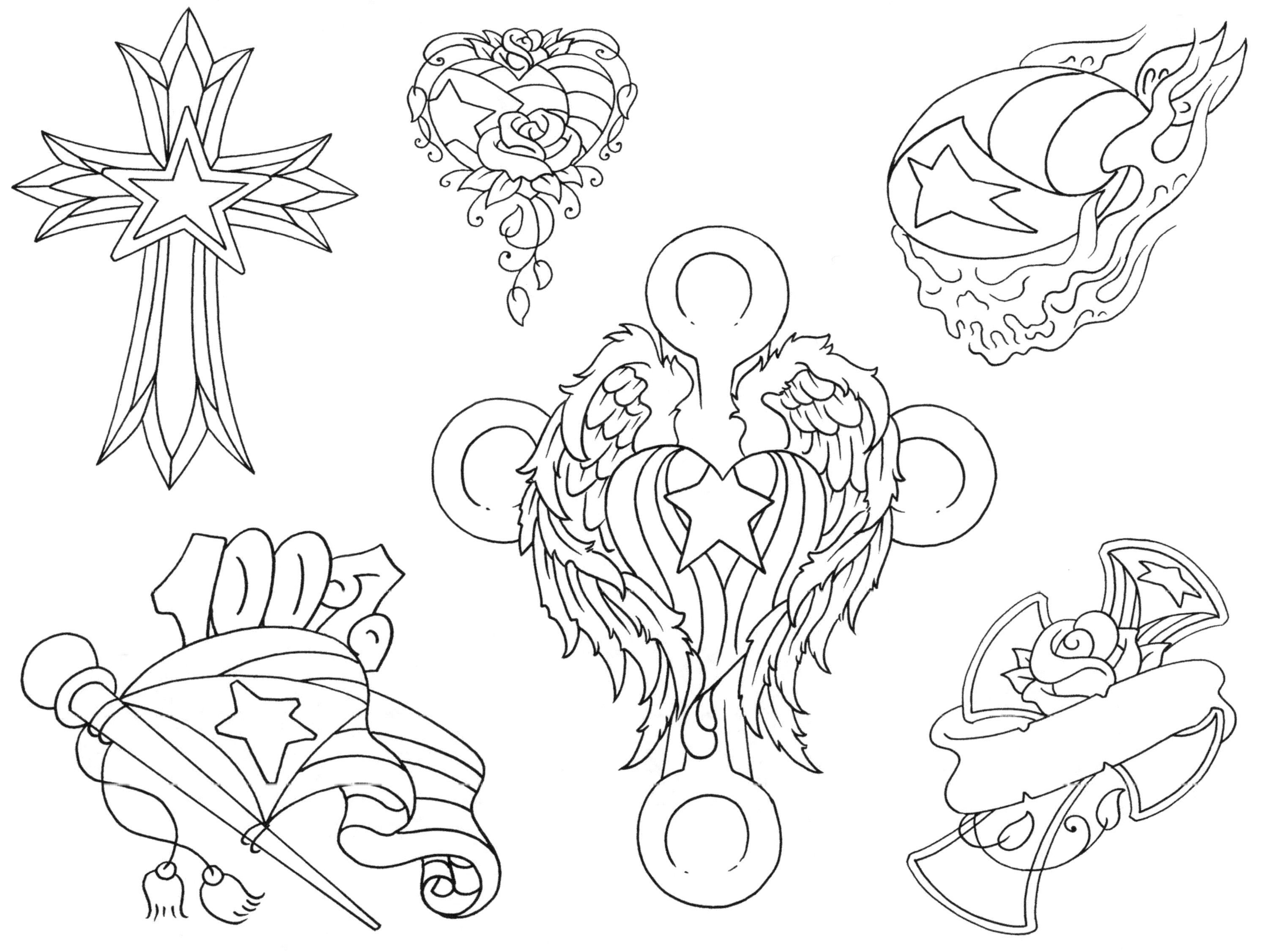

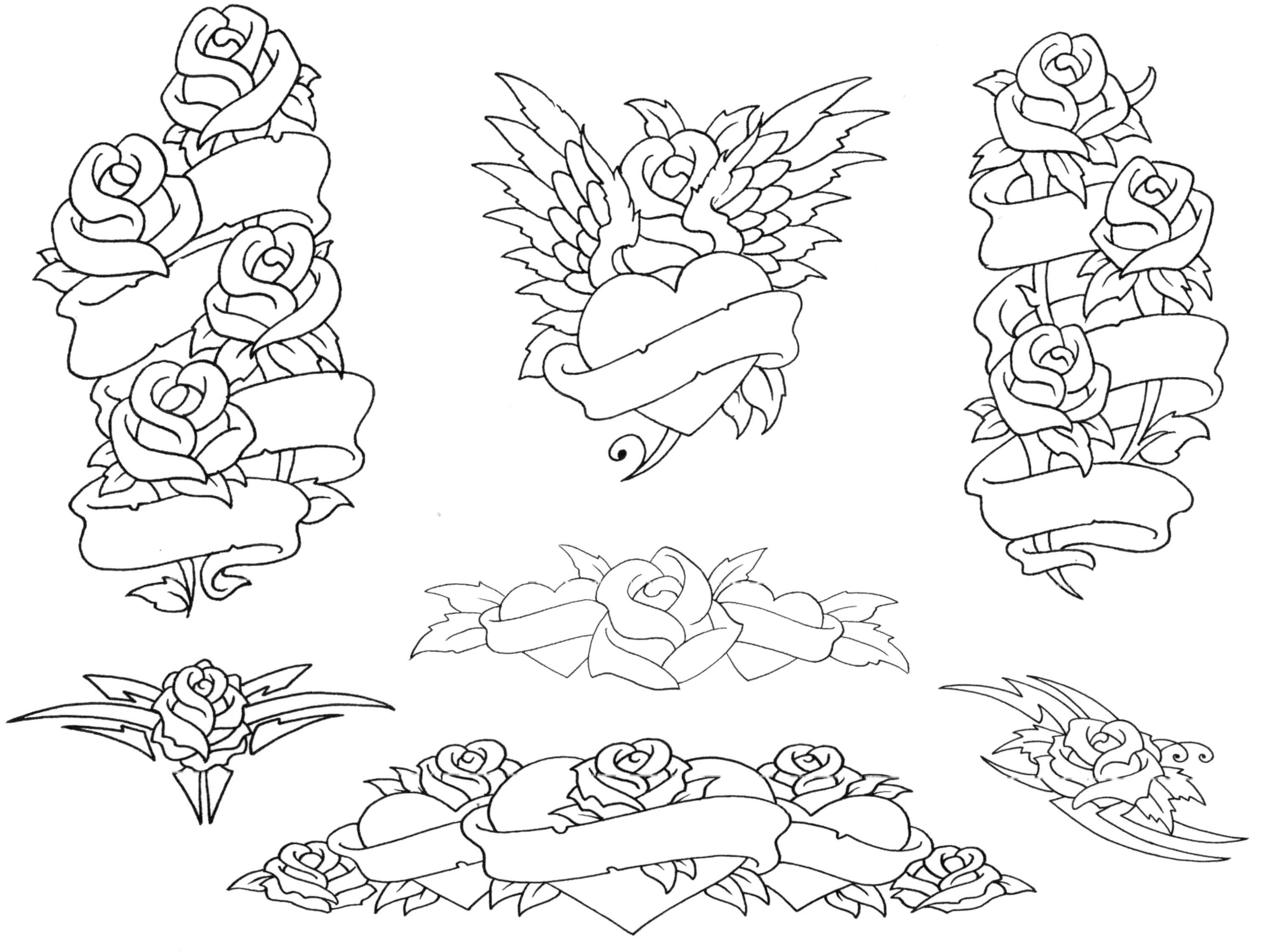

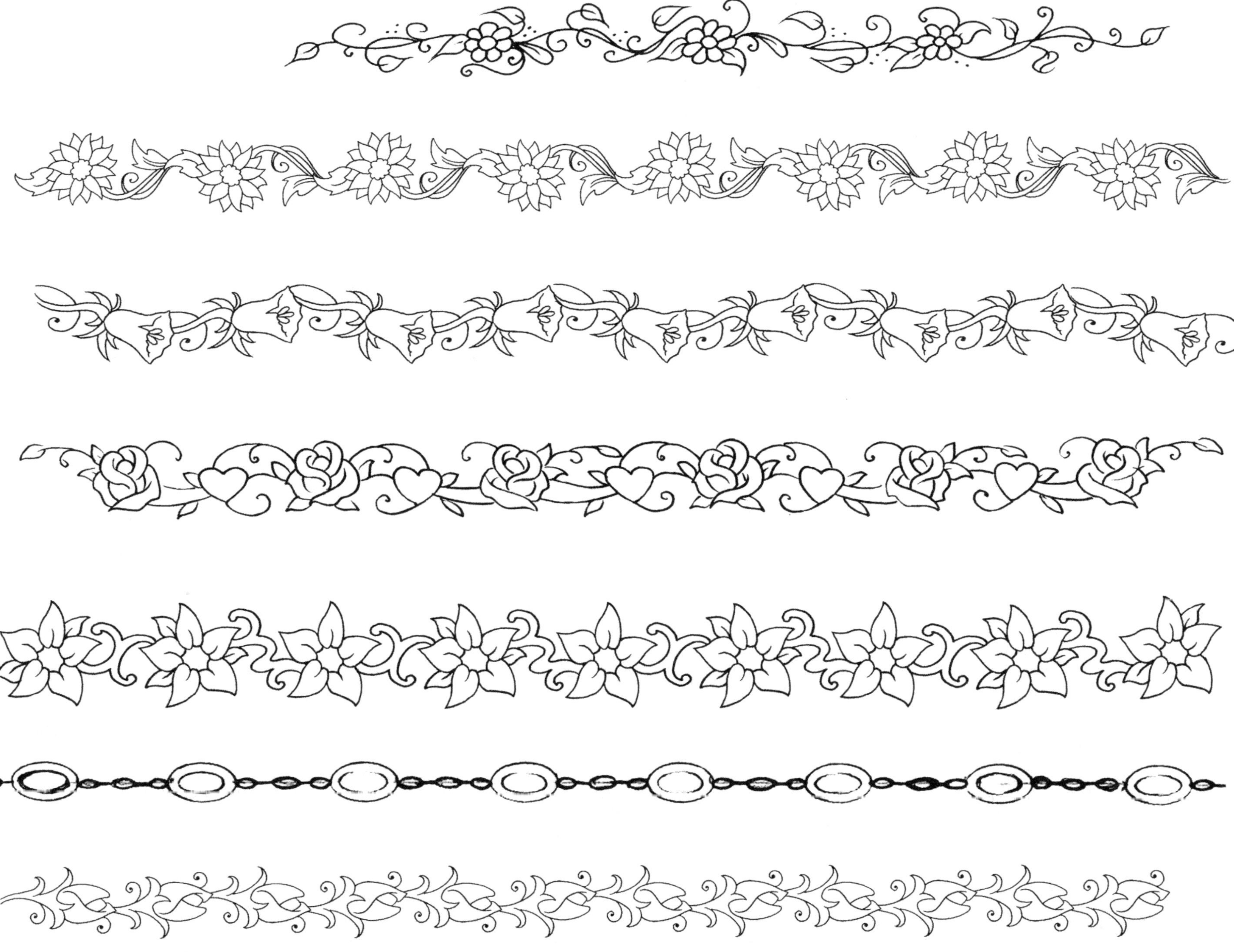

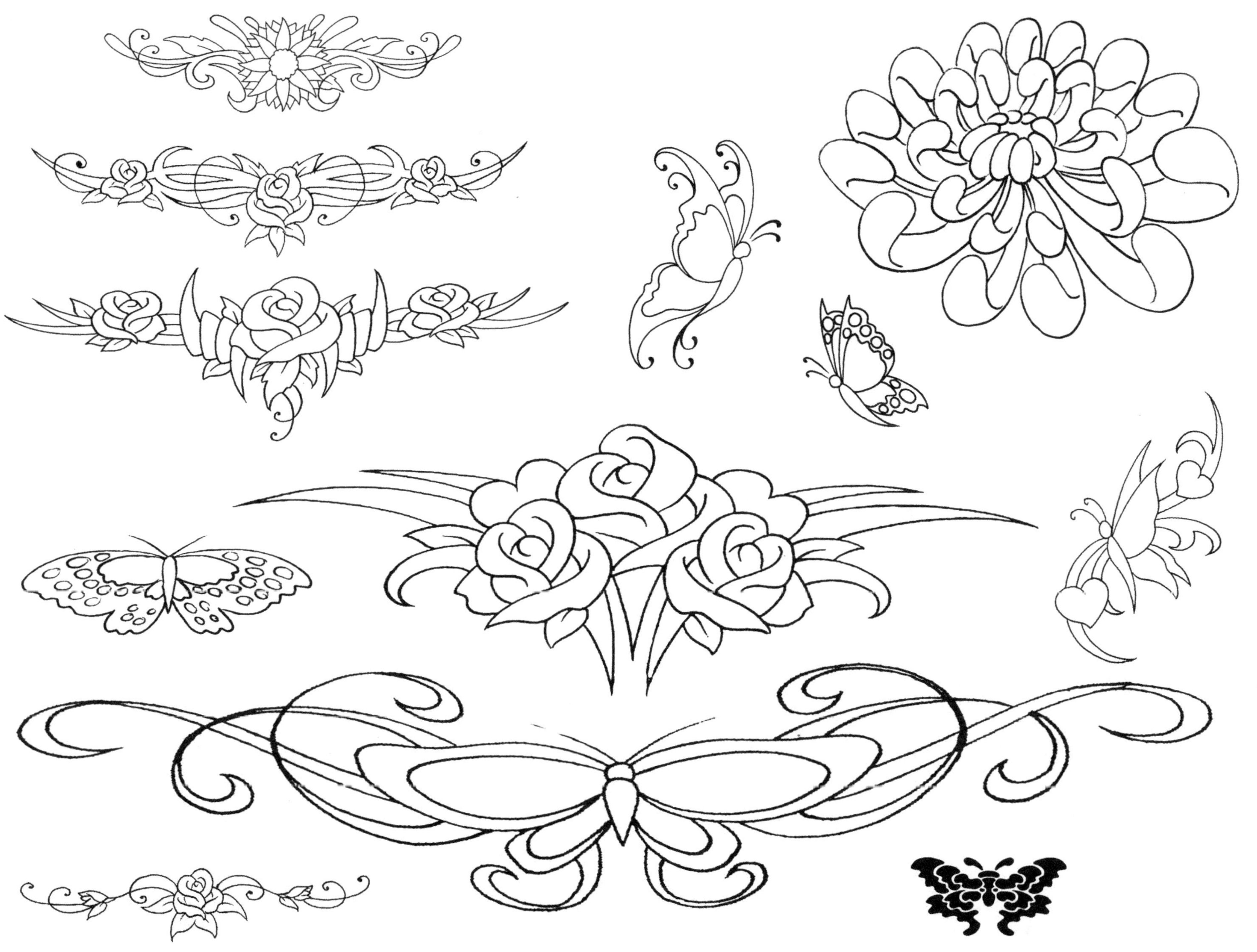

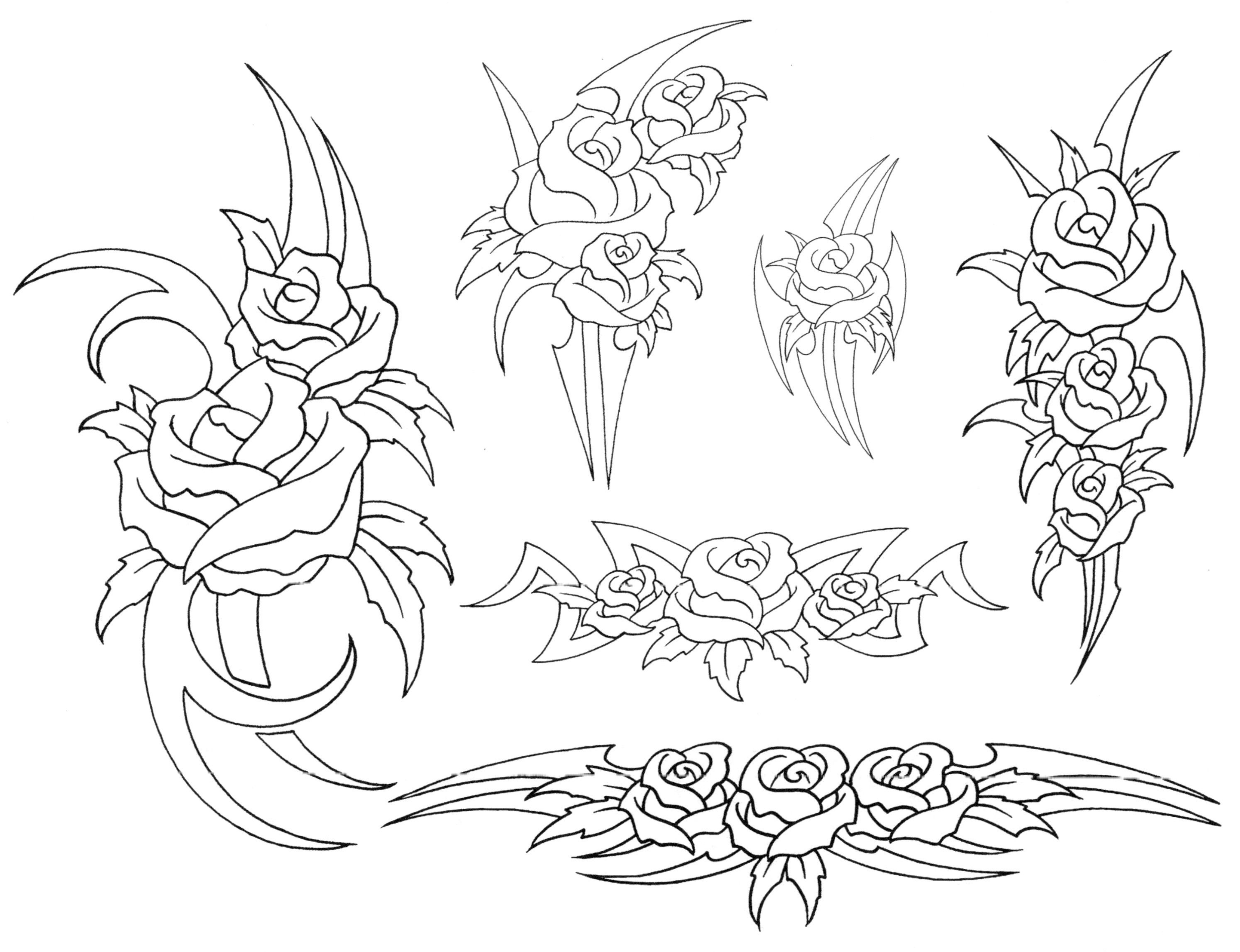

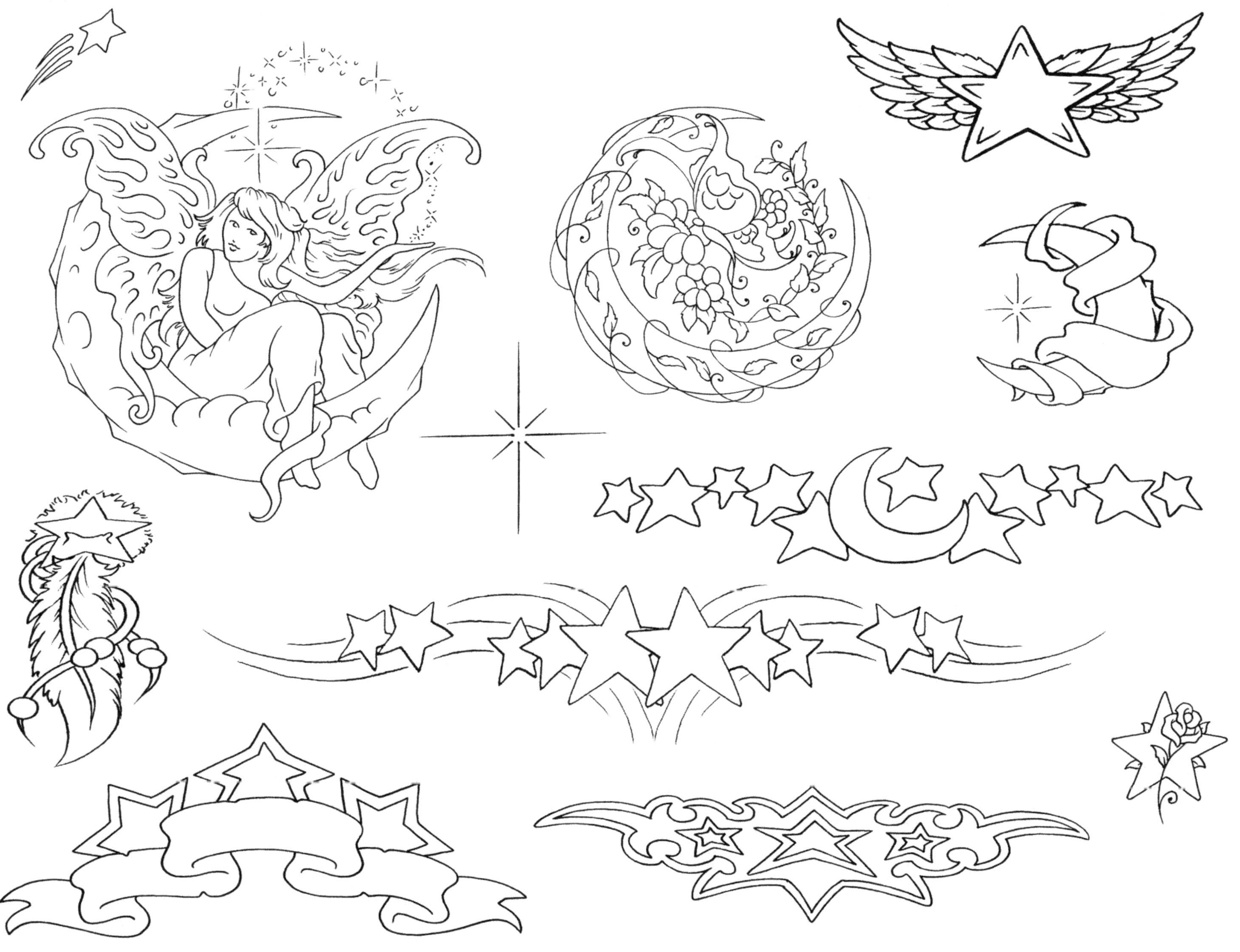

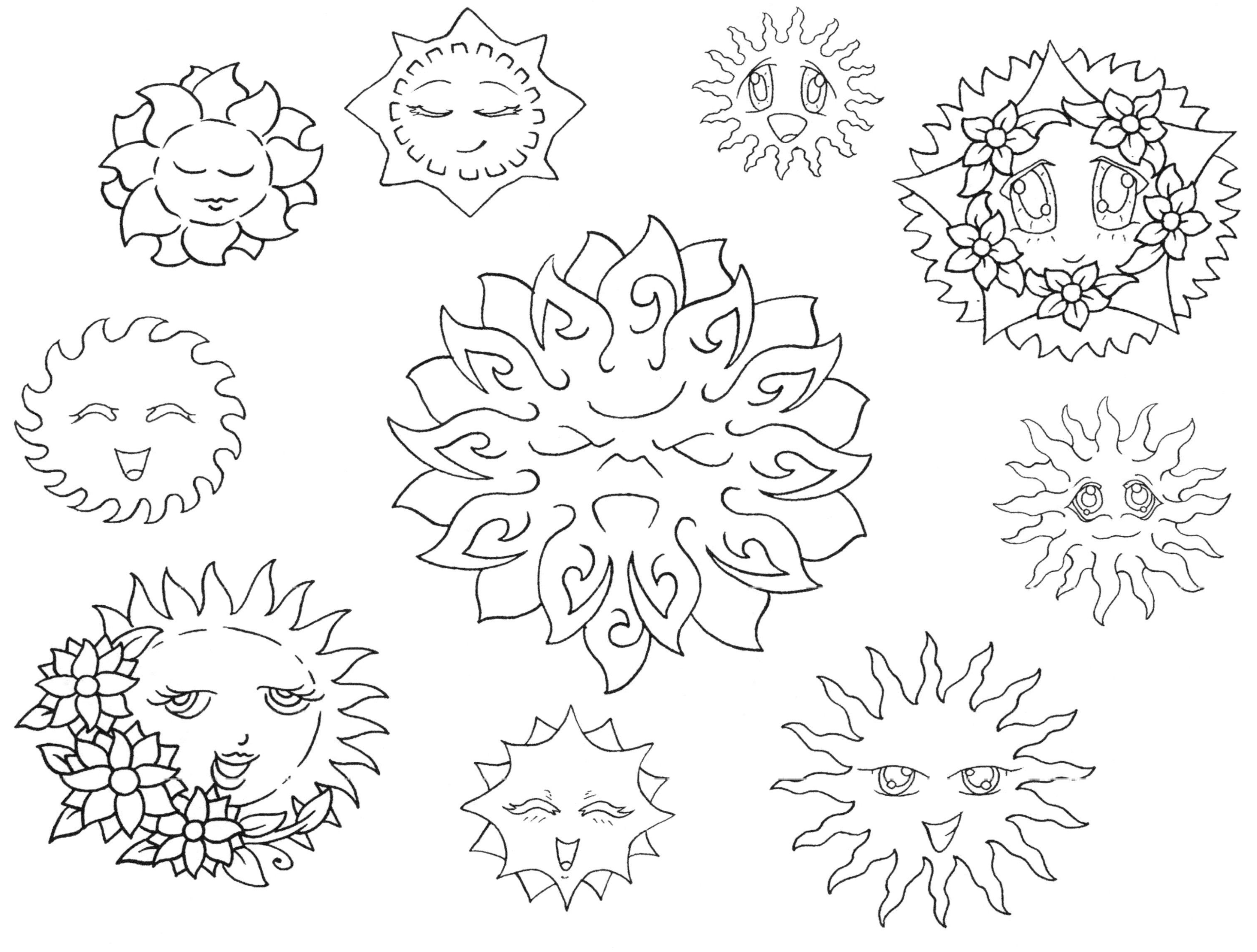

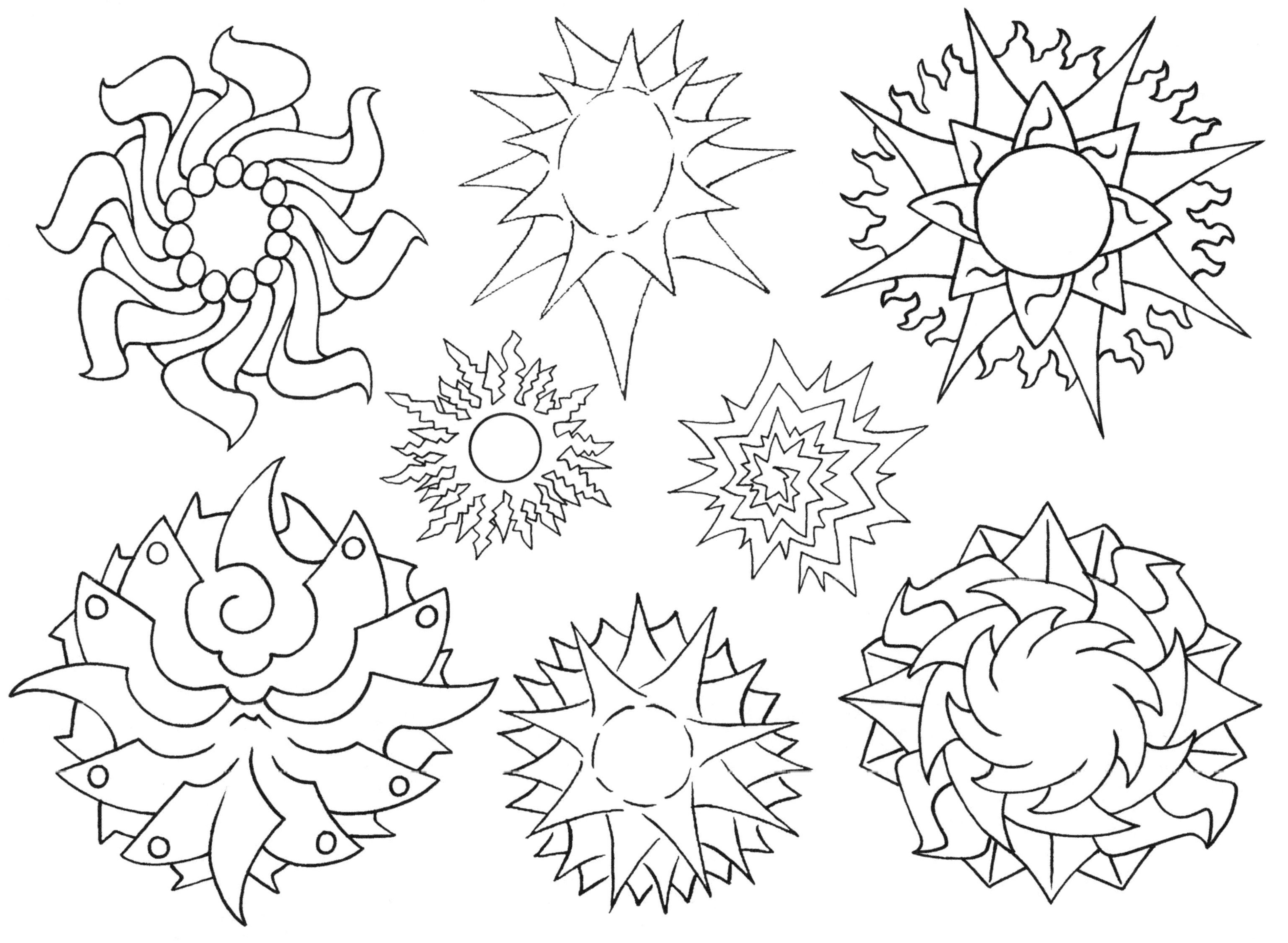

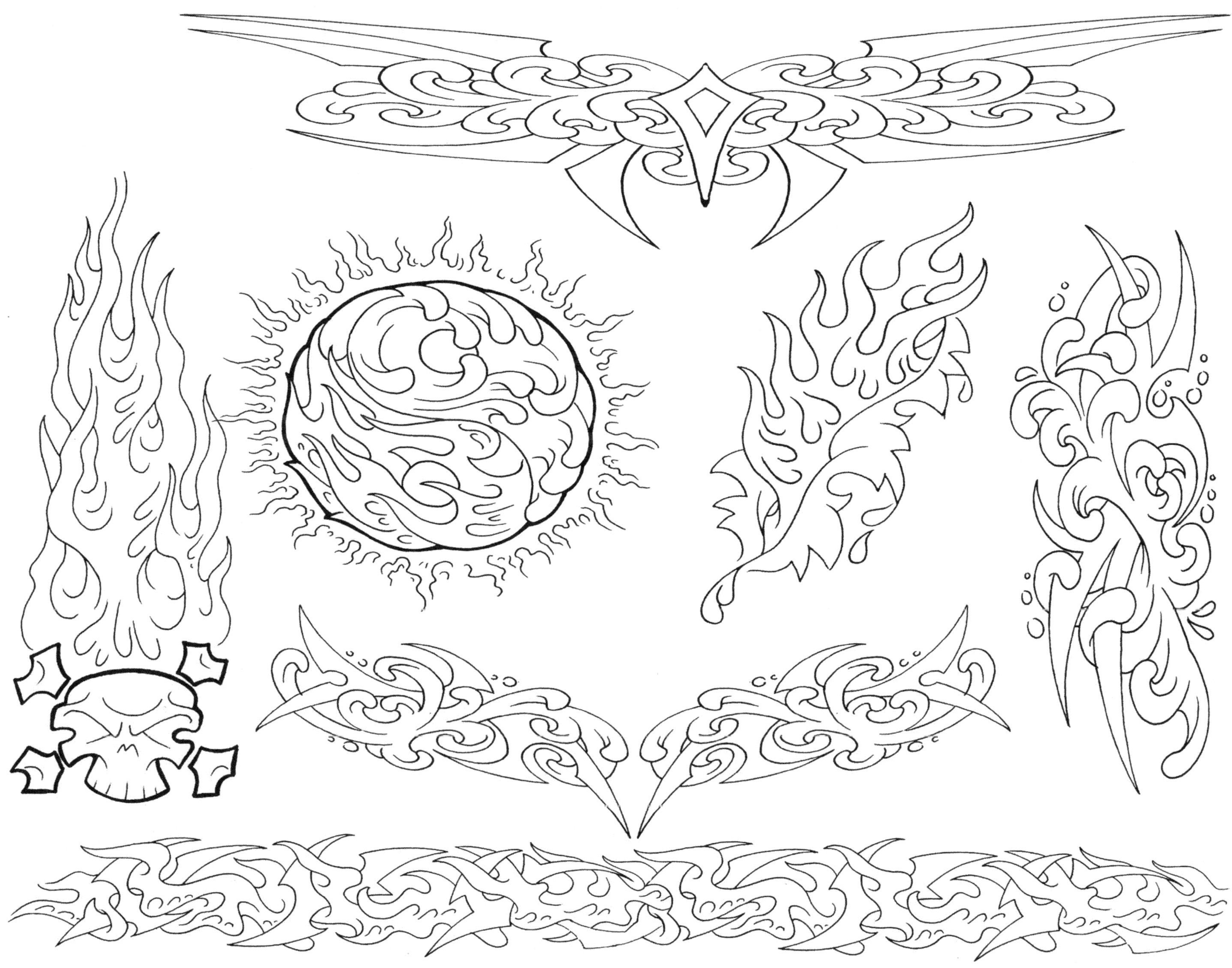

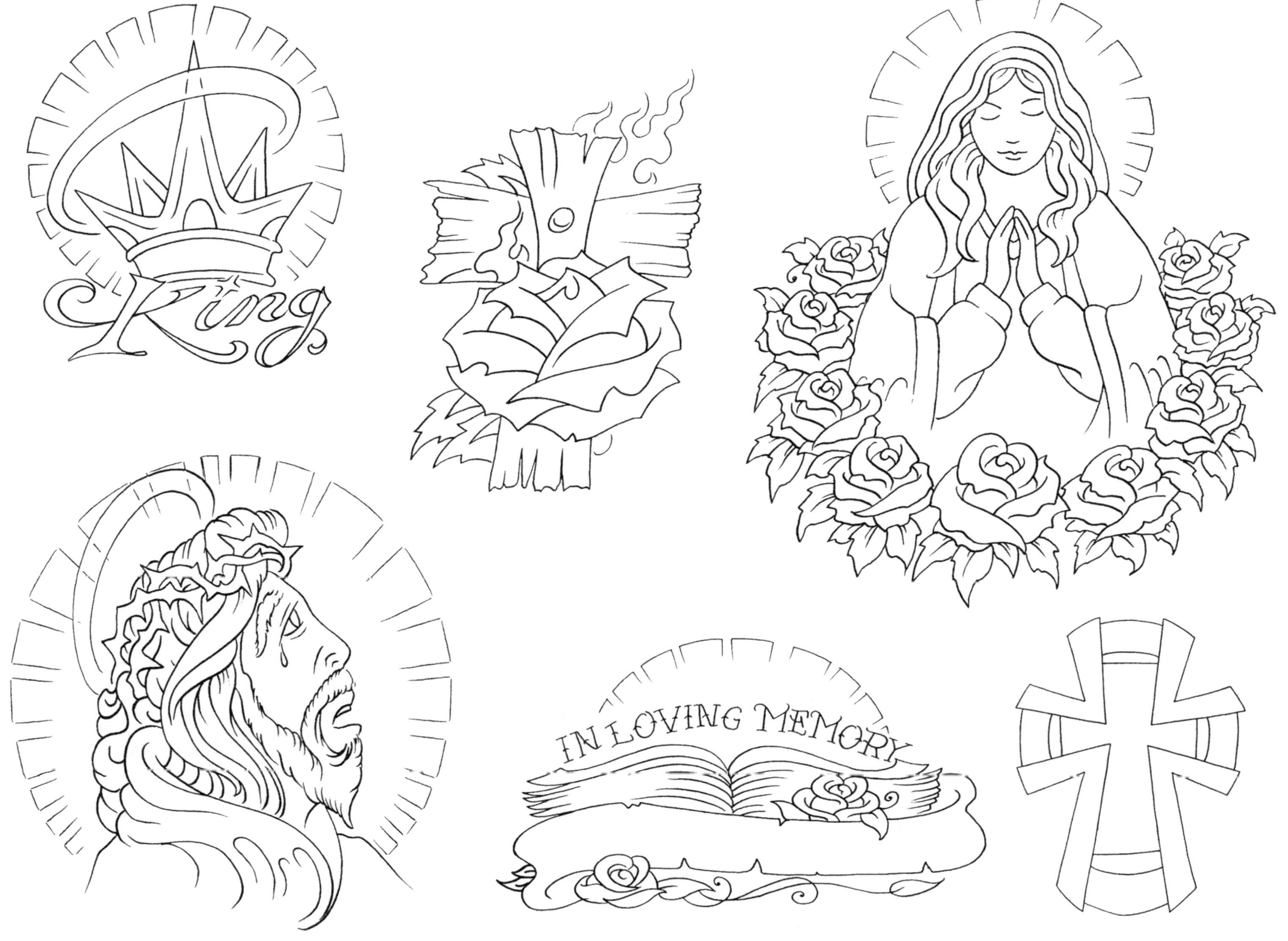
King
IN LOVING MEMORY

Saint
Sinner

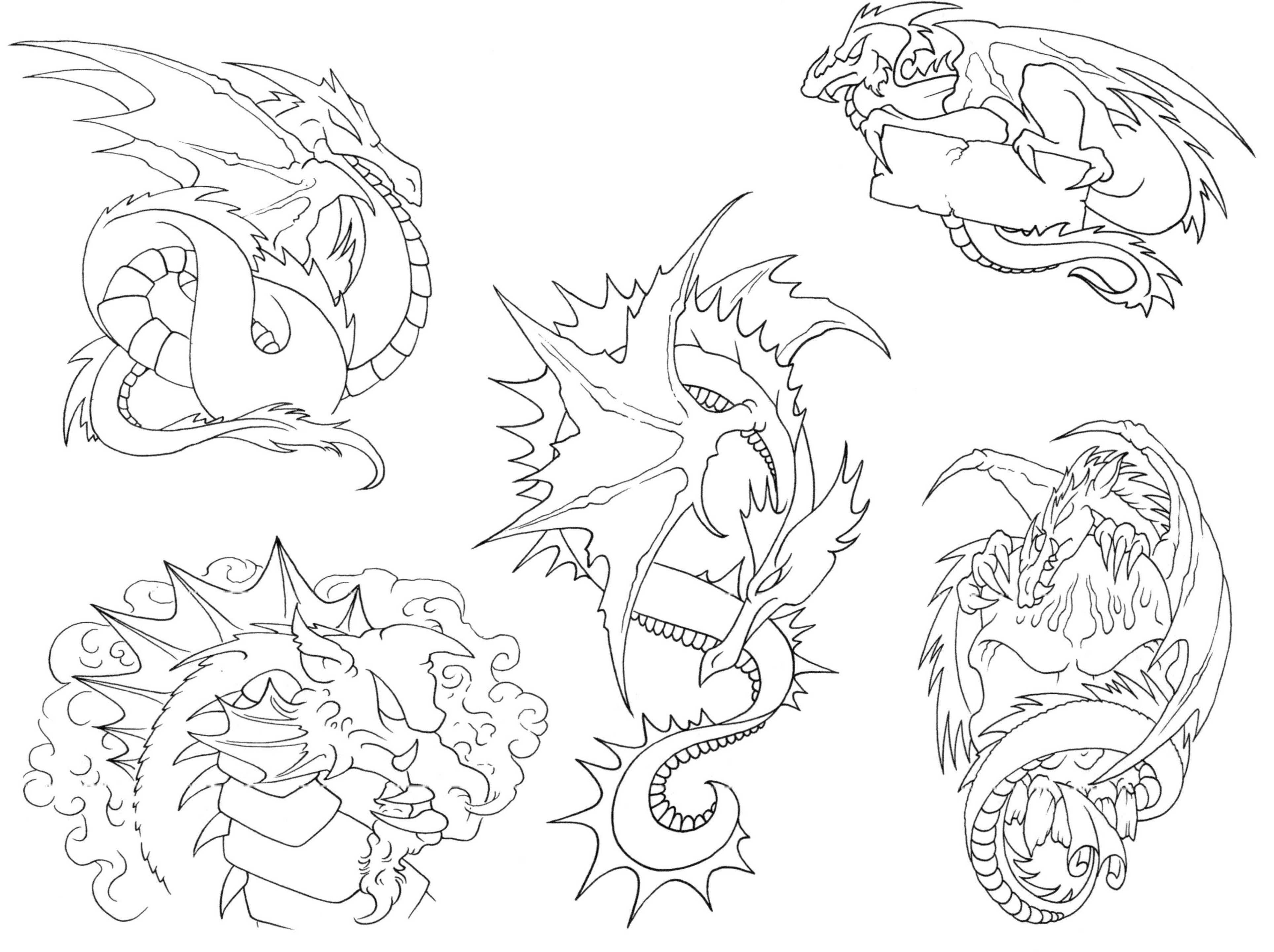

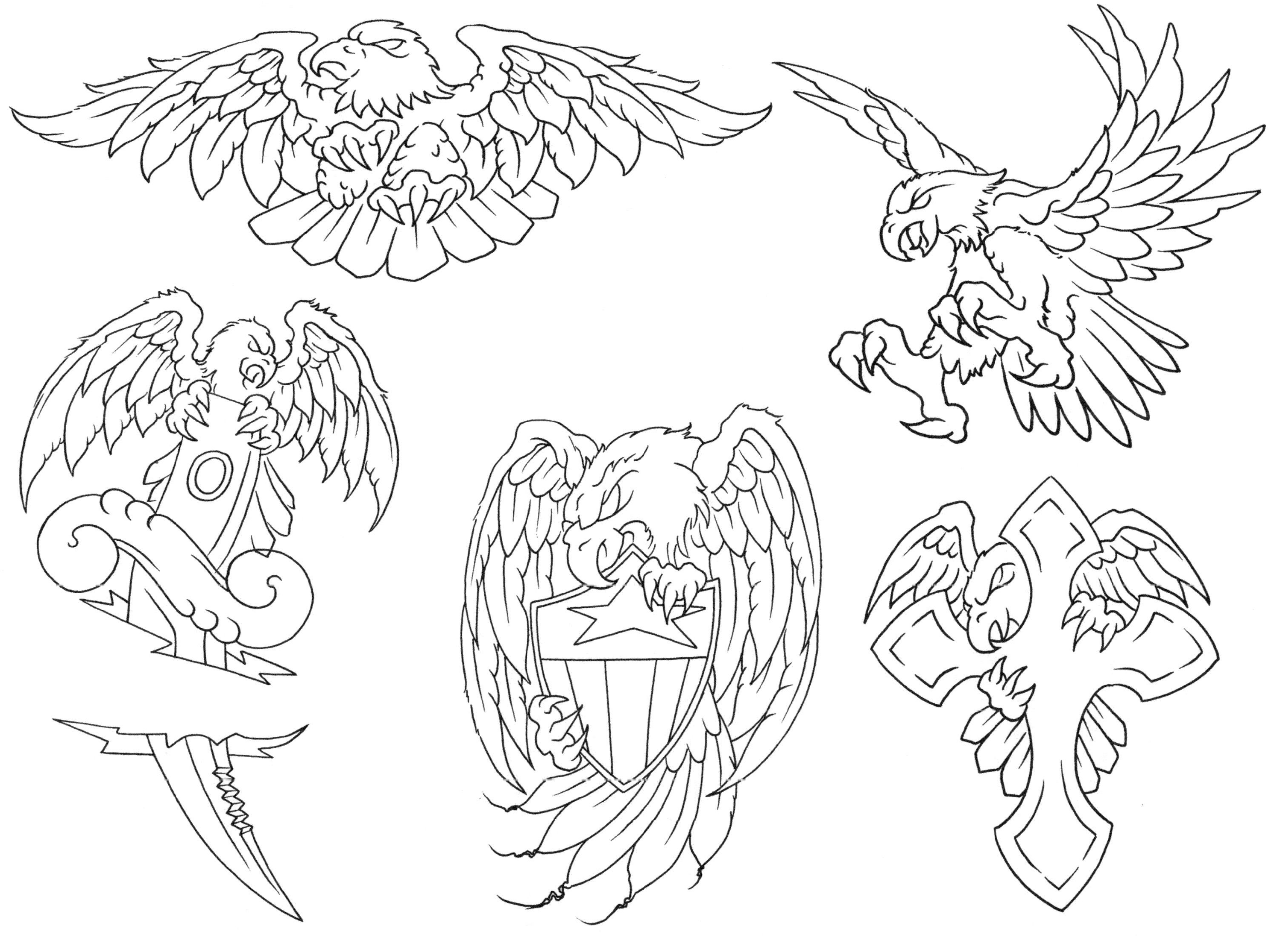

R10.5

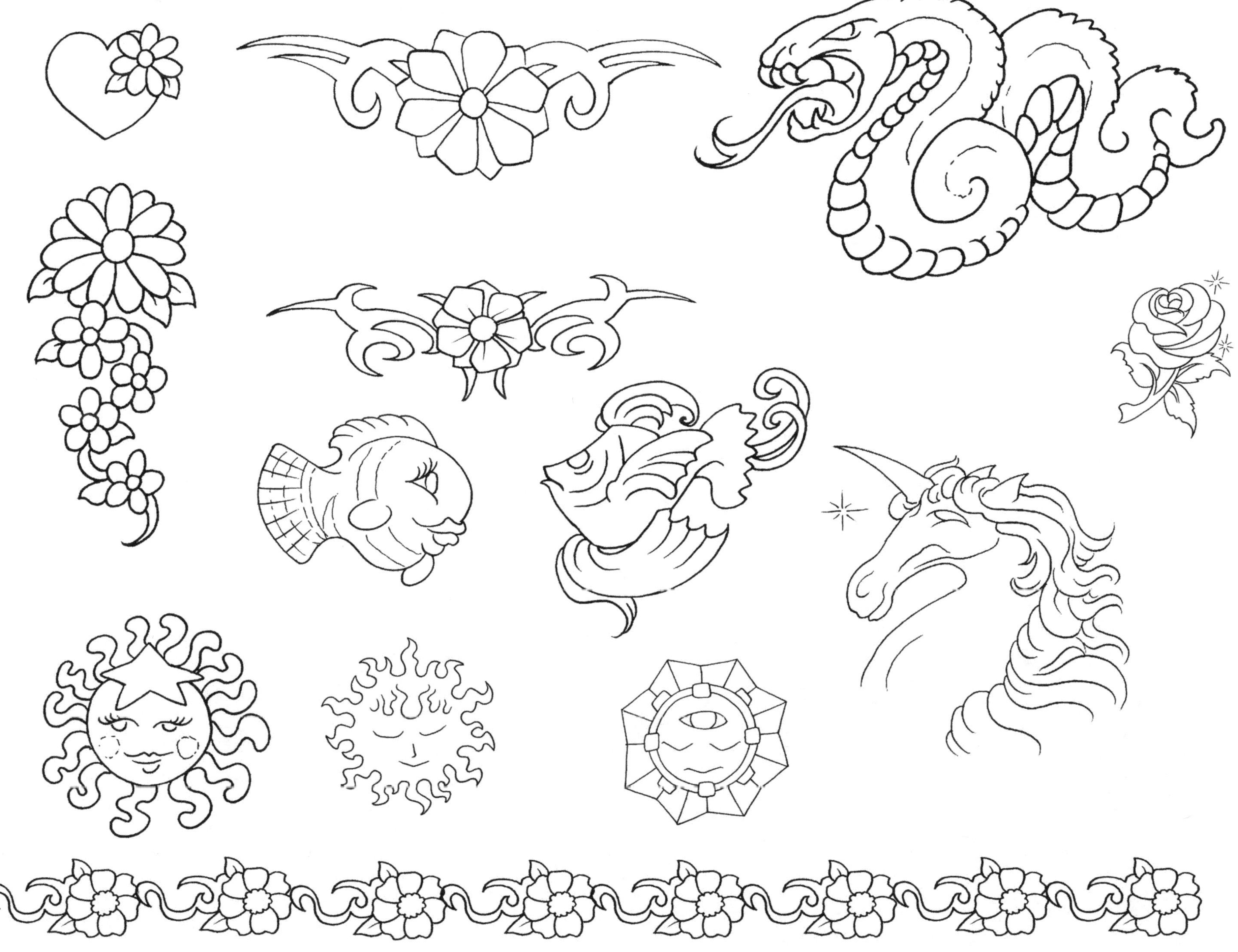

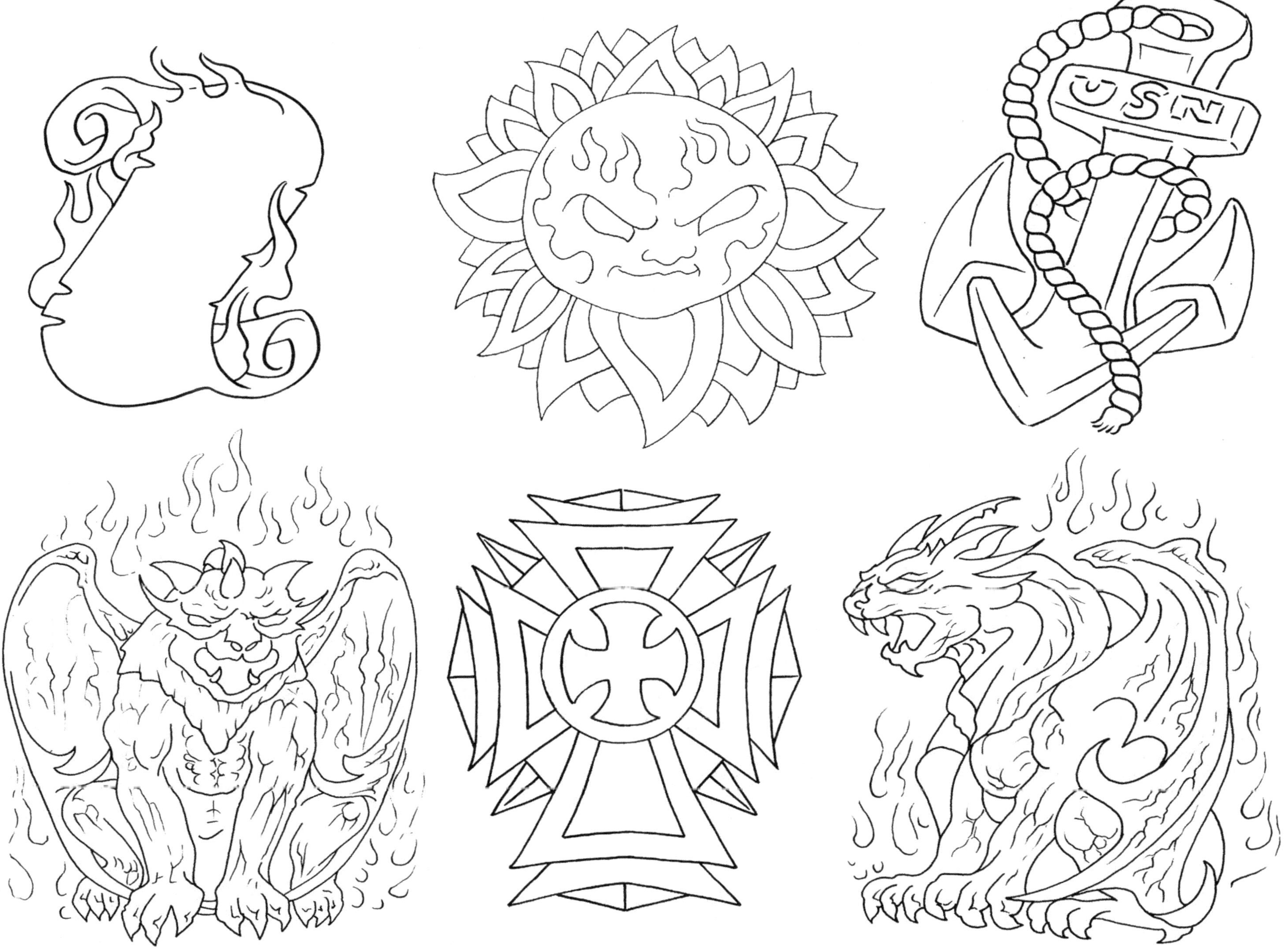
USN

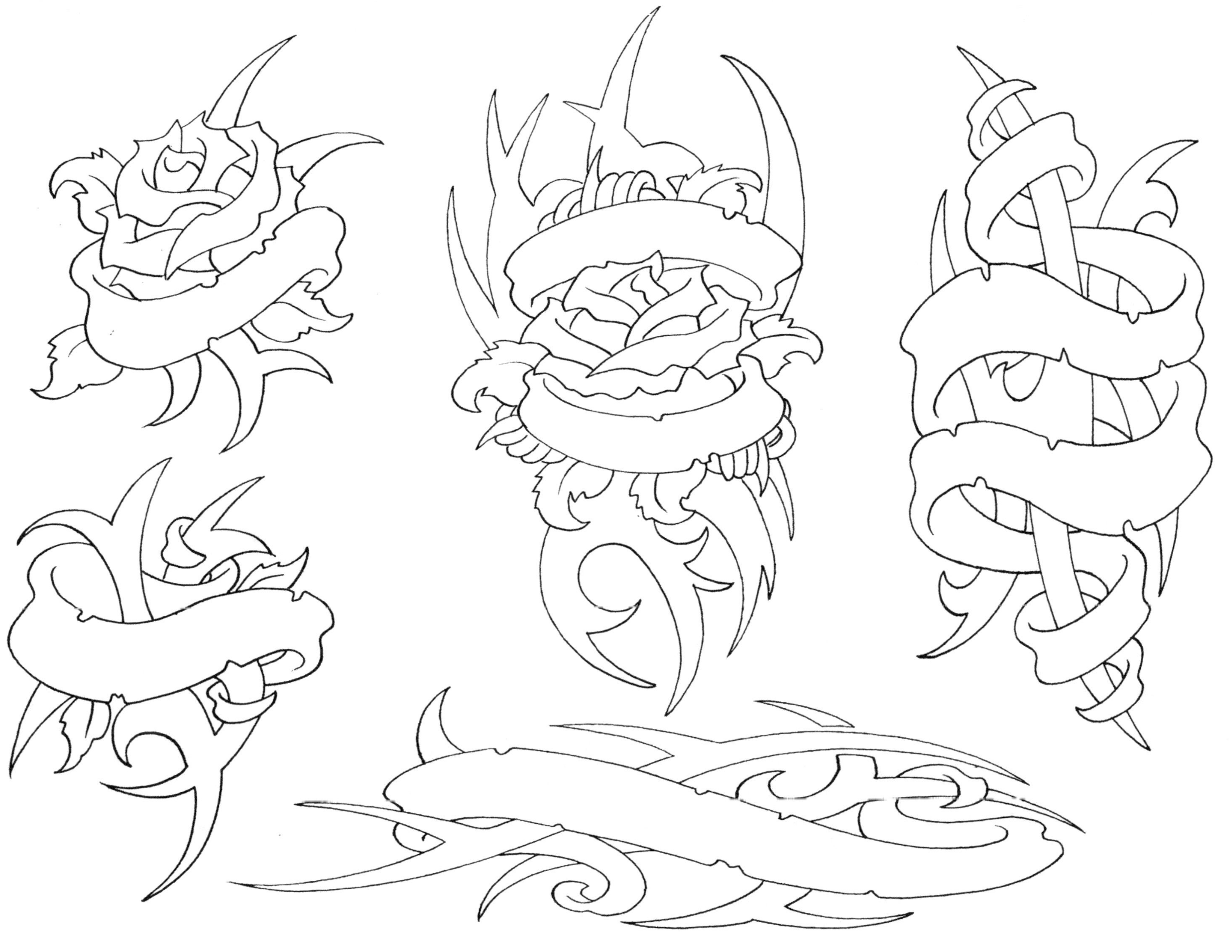

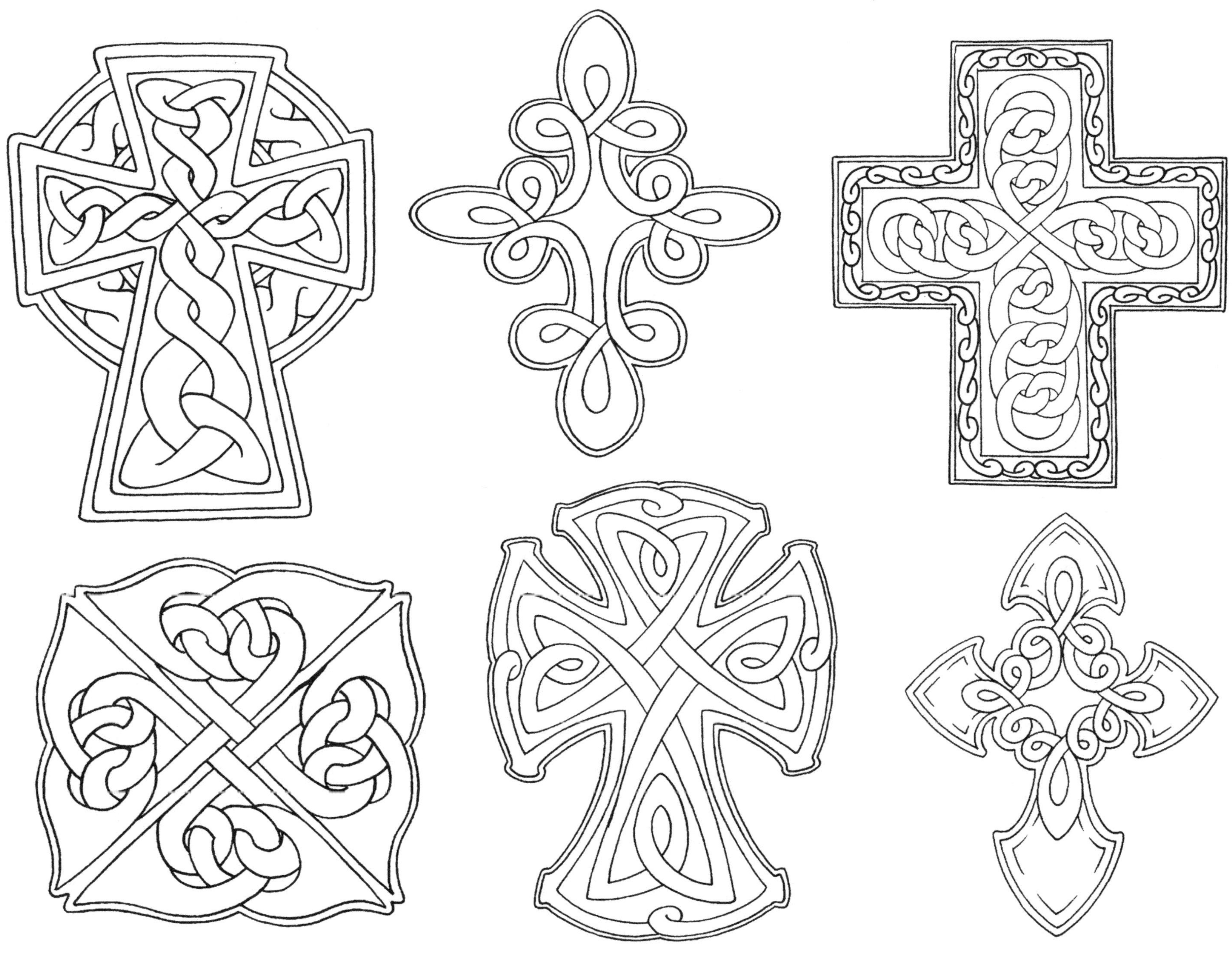

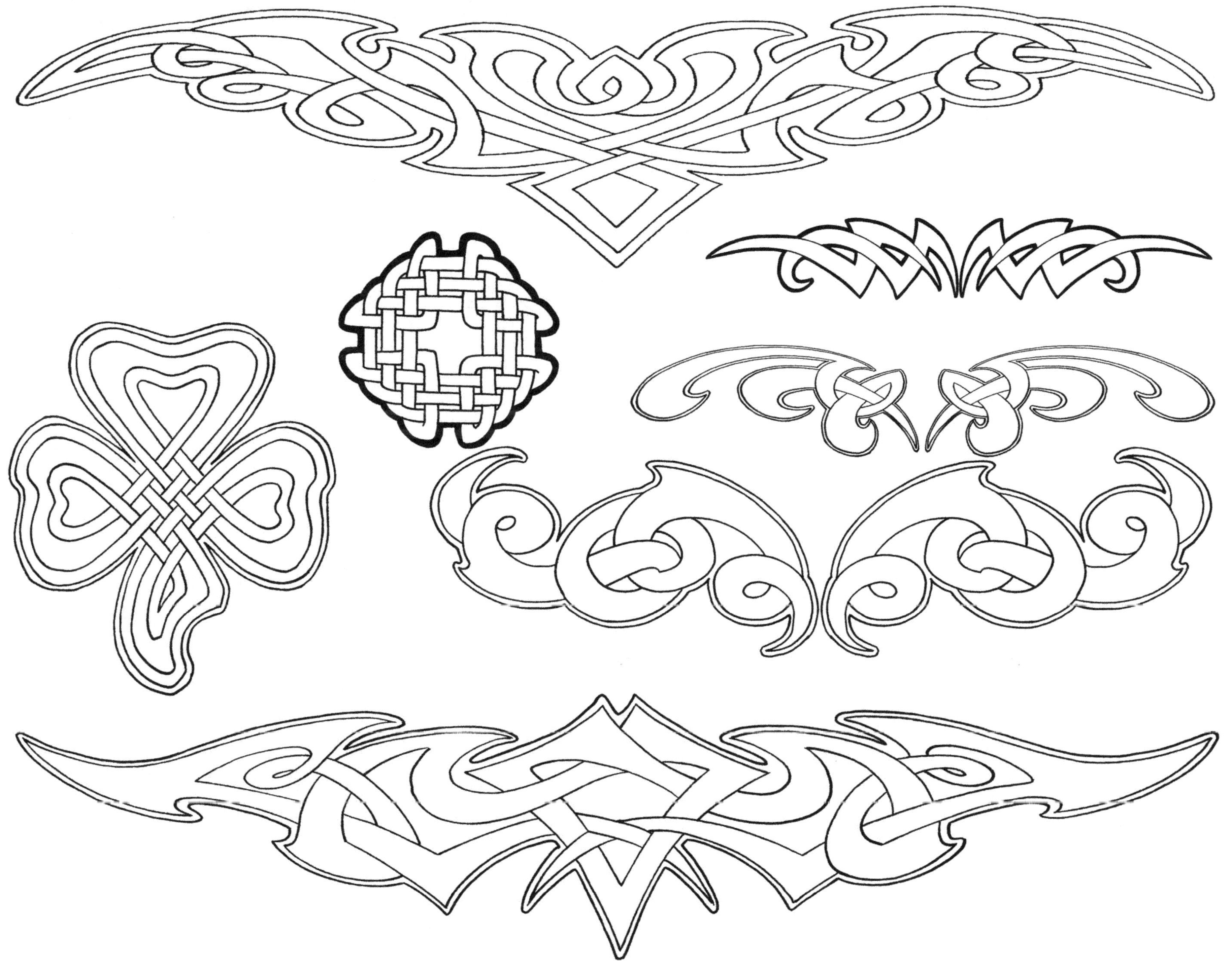

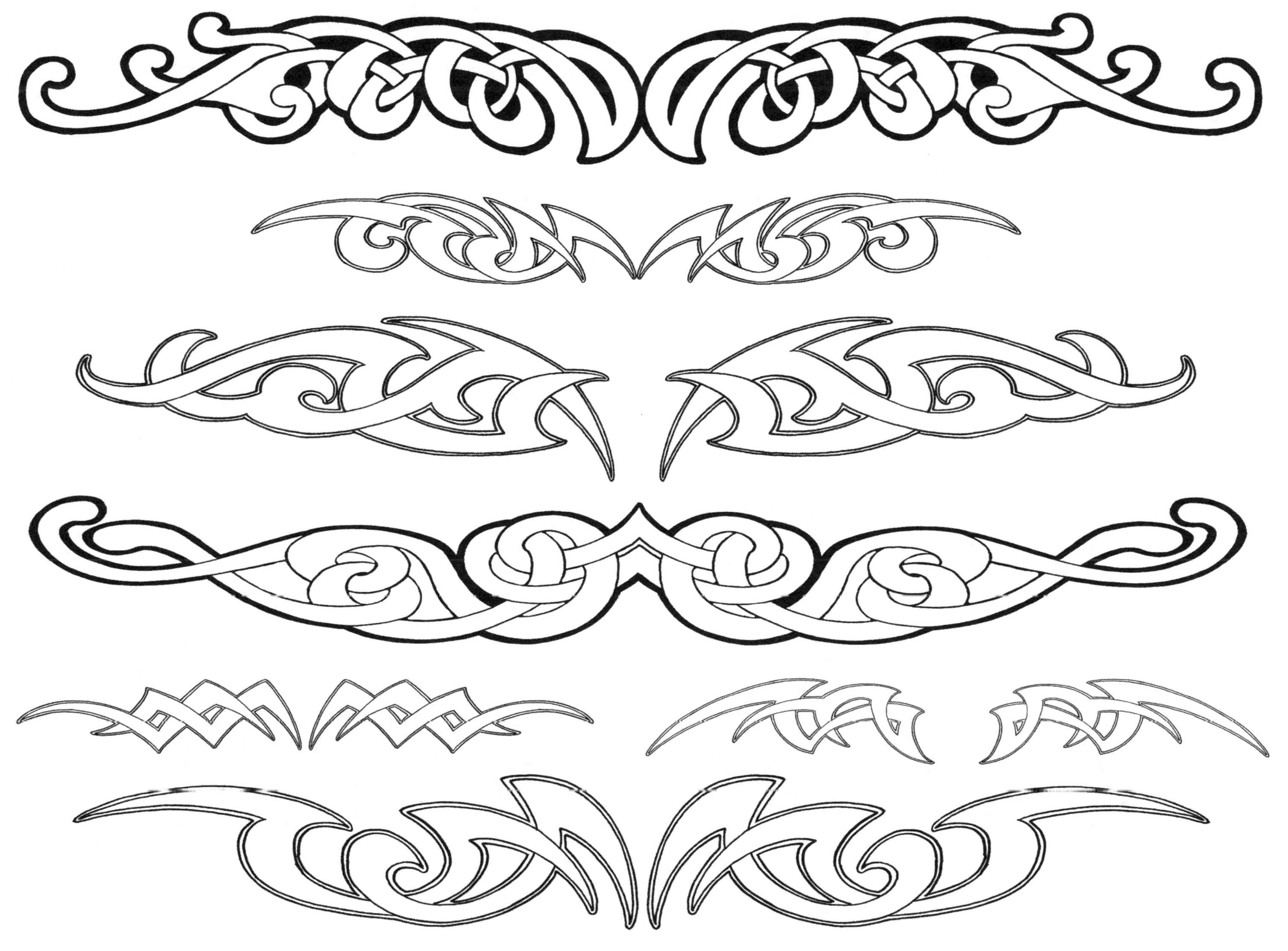

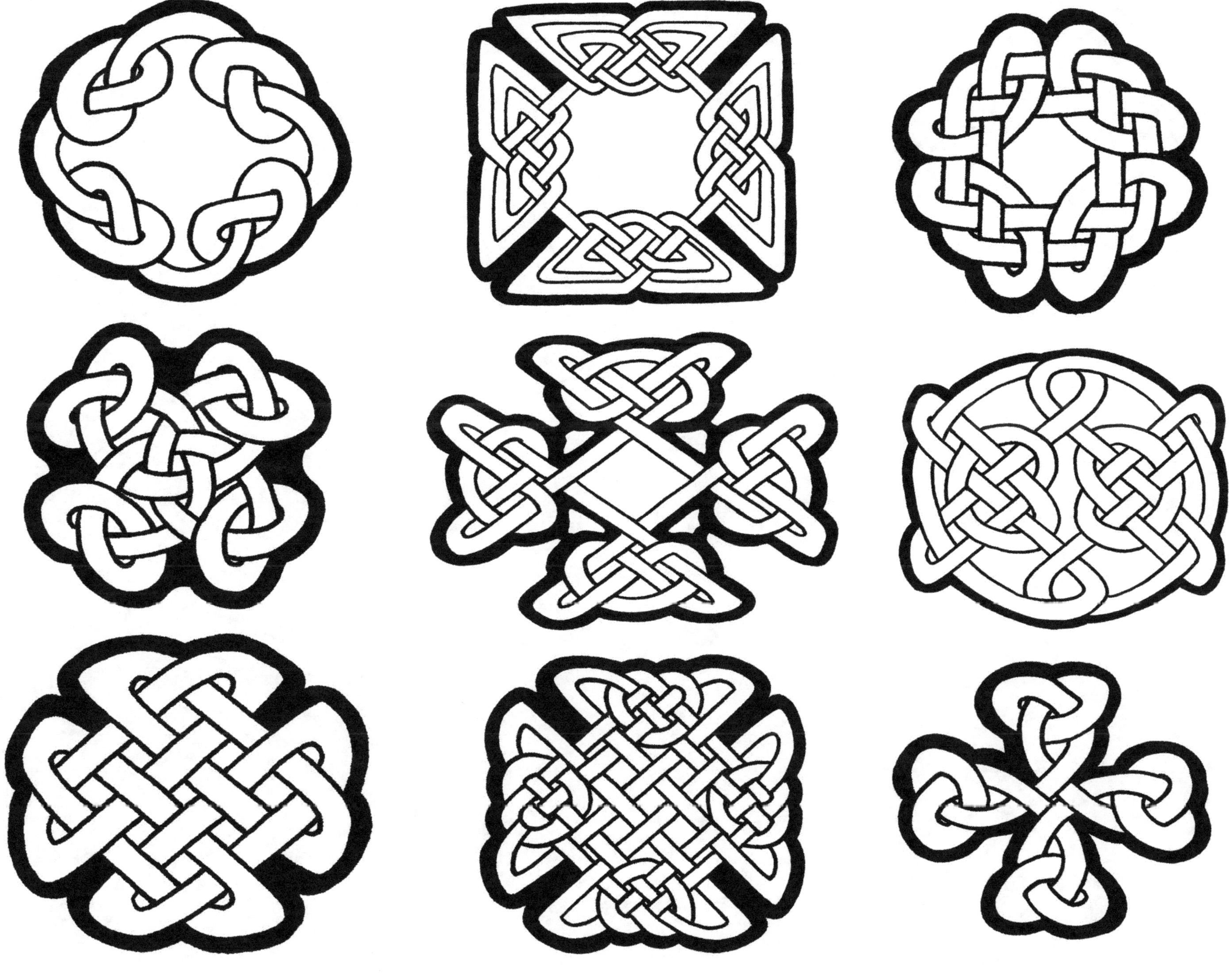

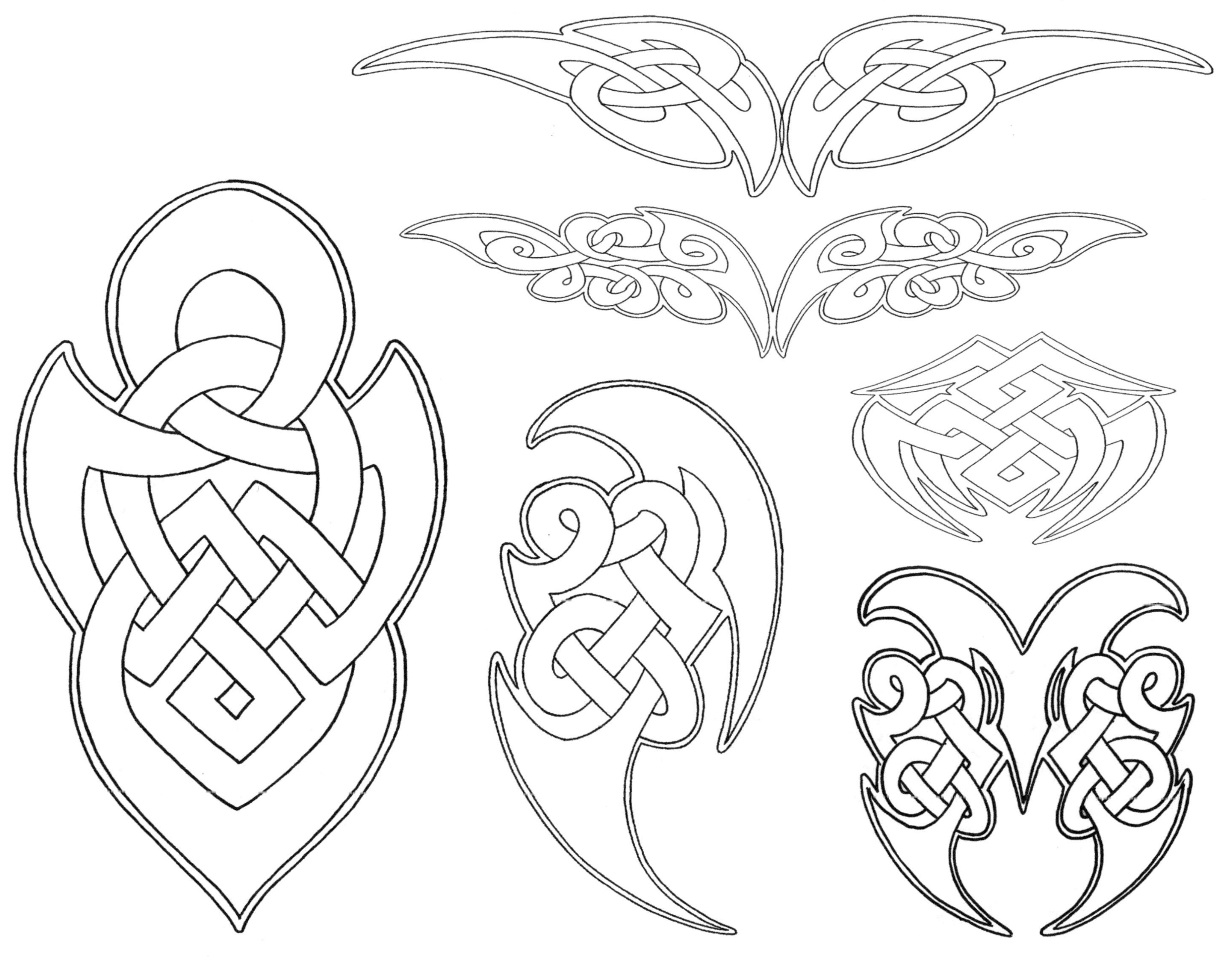

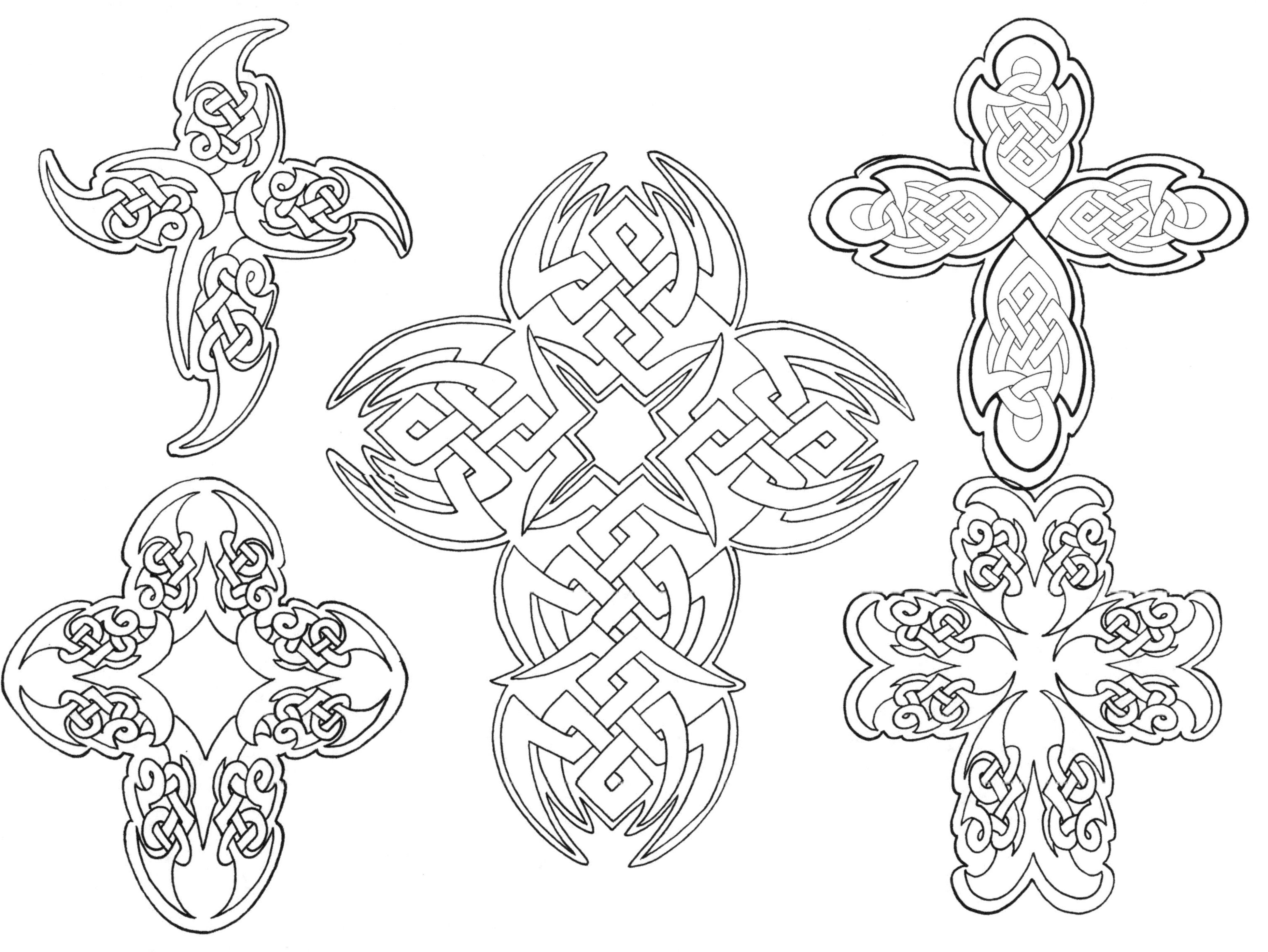

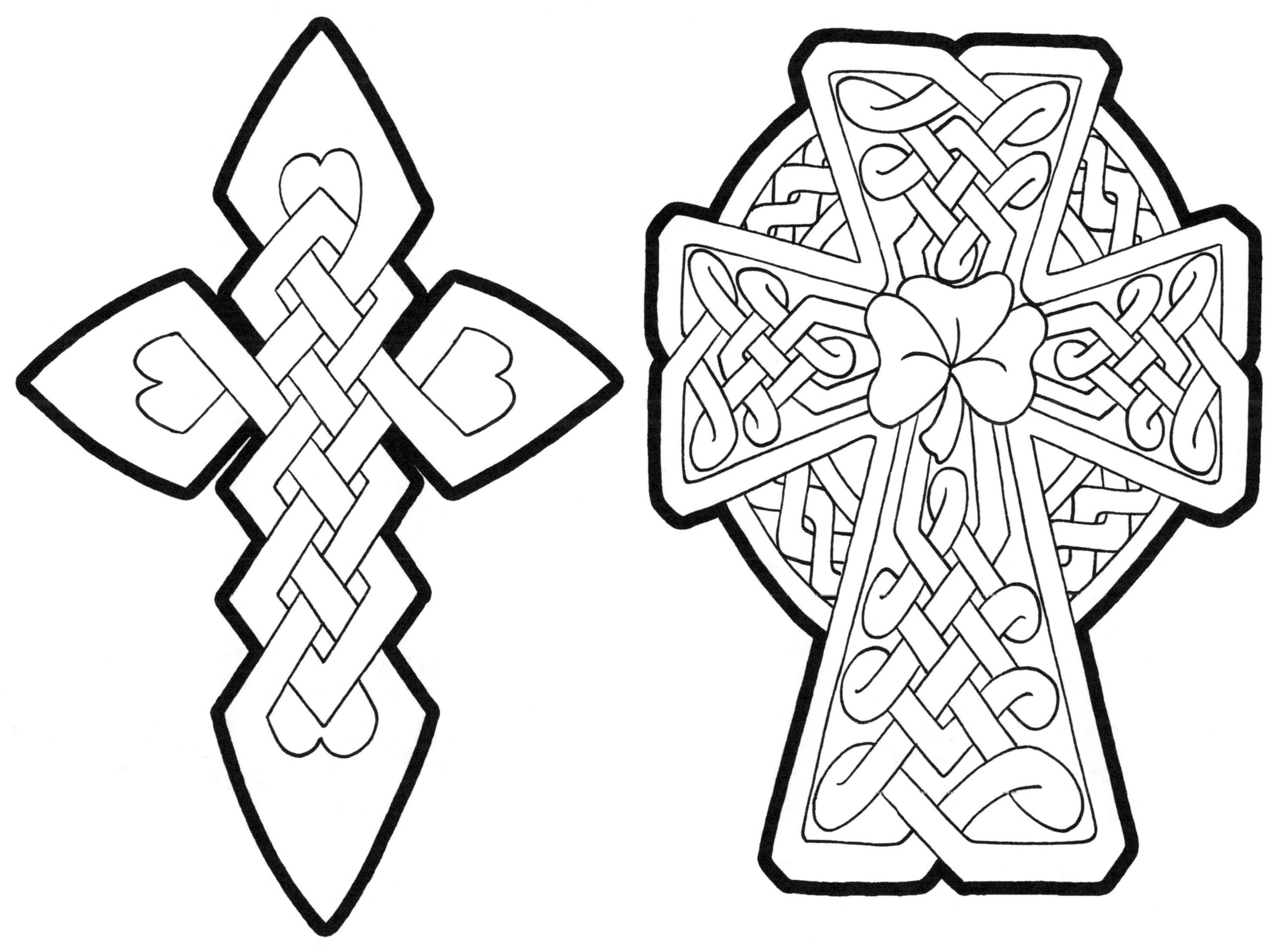

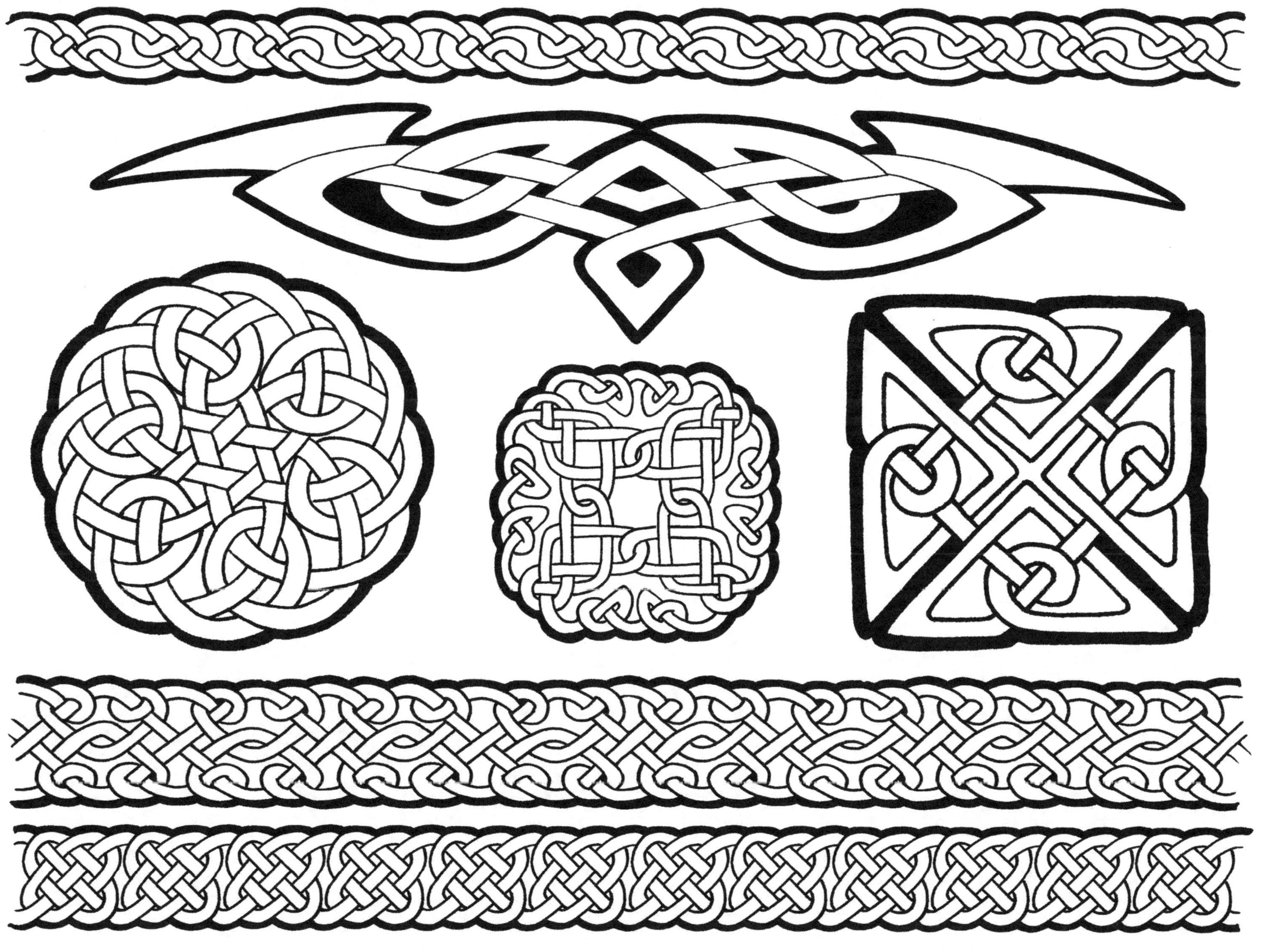

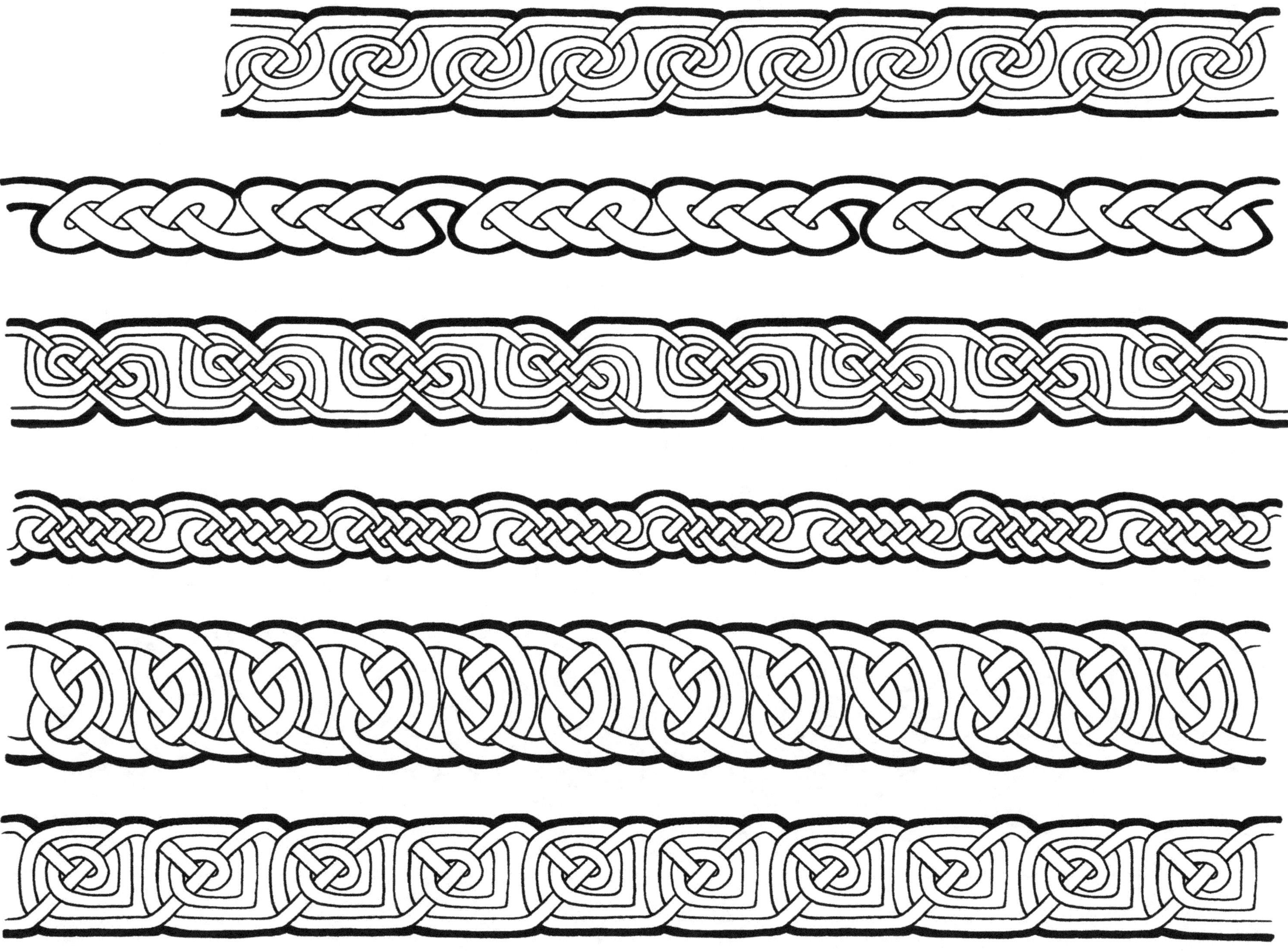

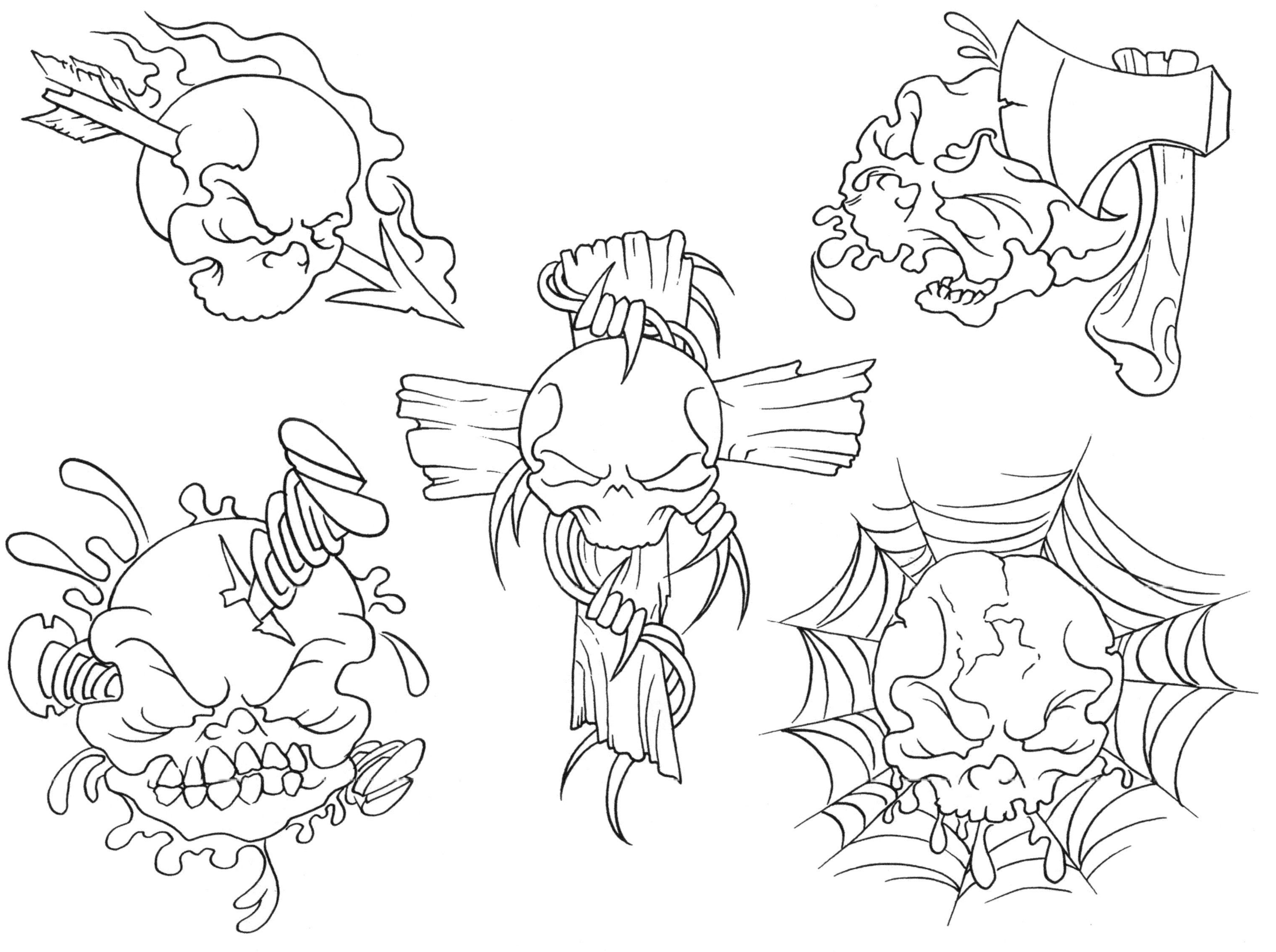

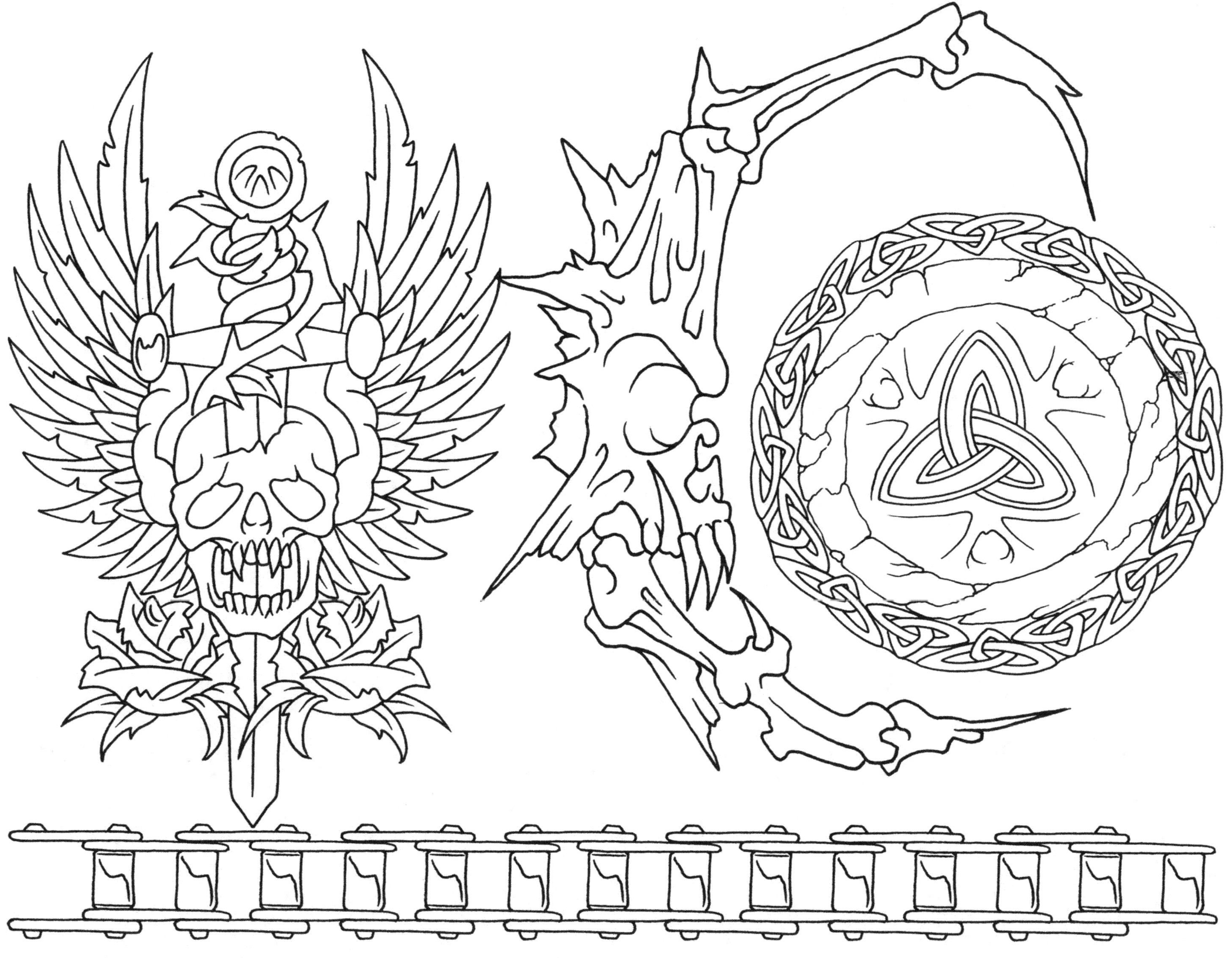

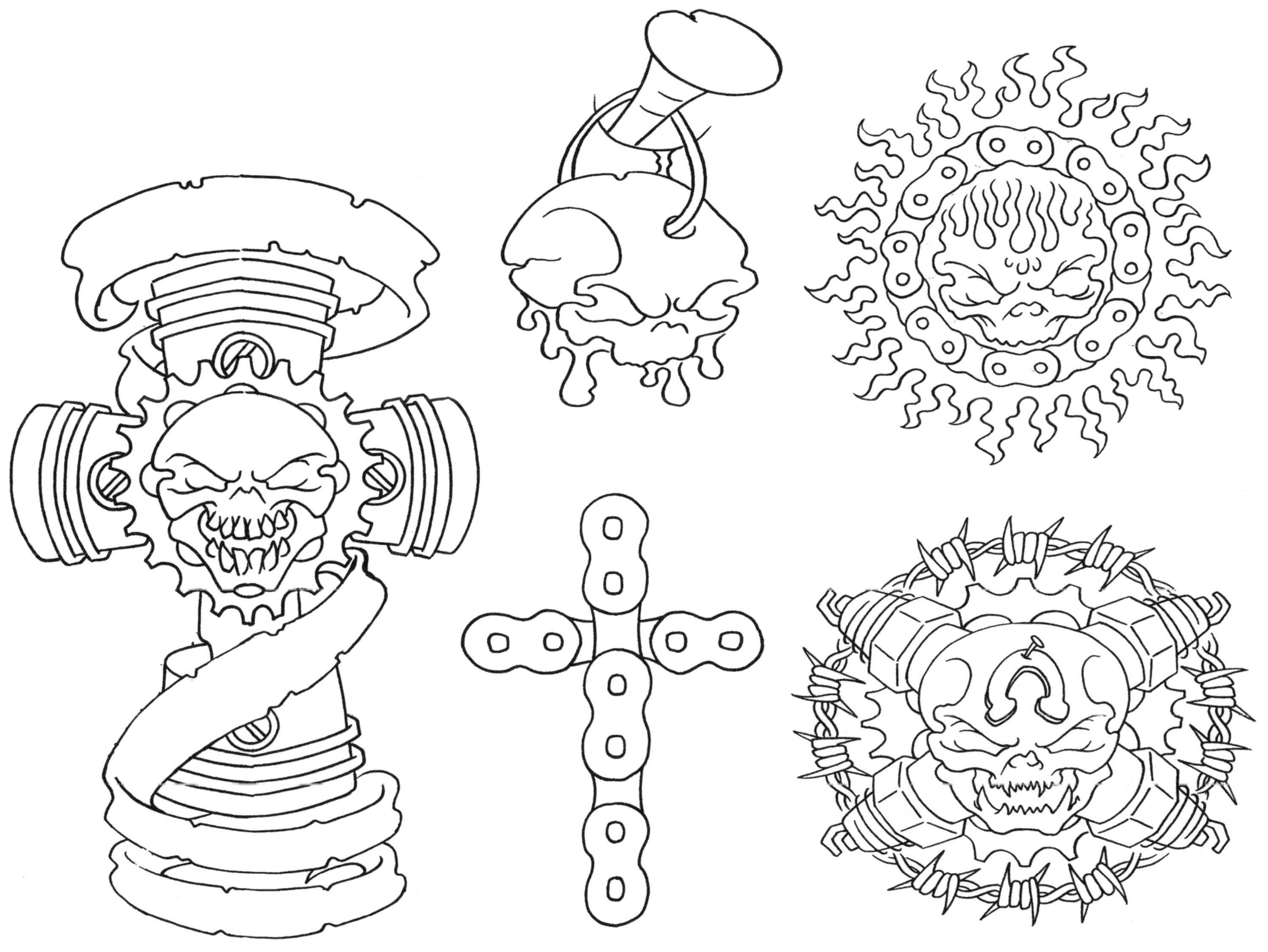

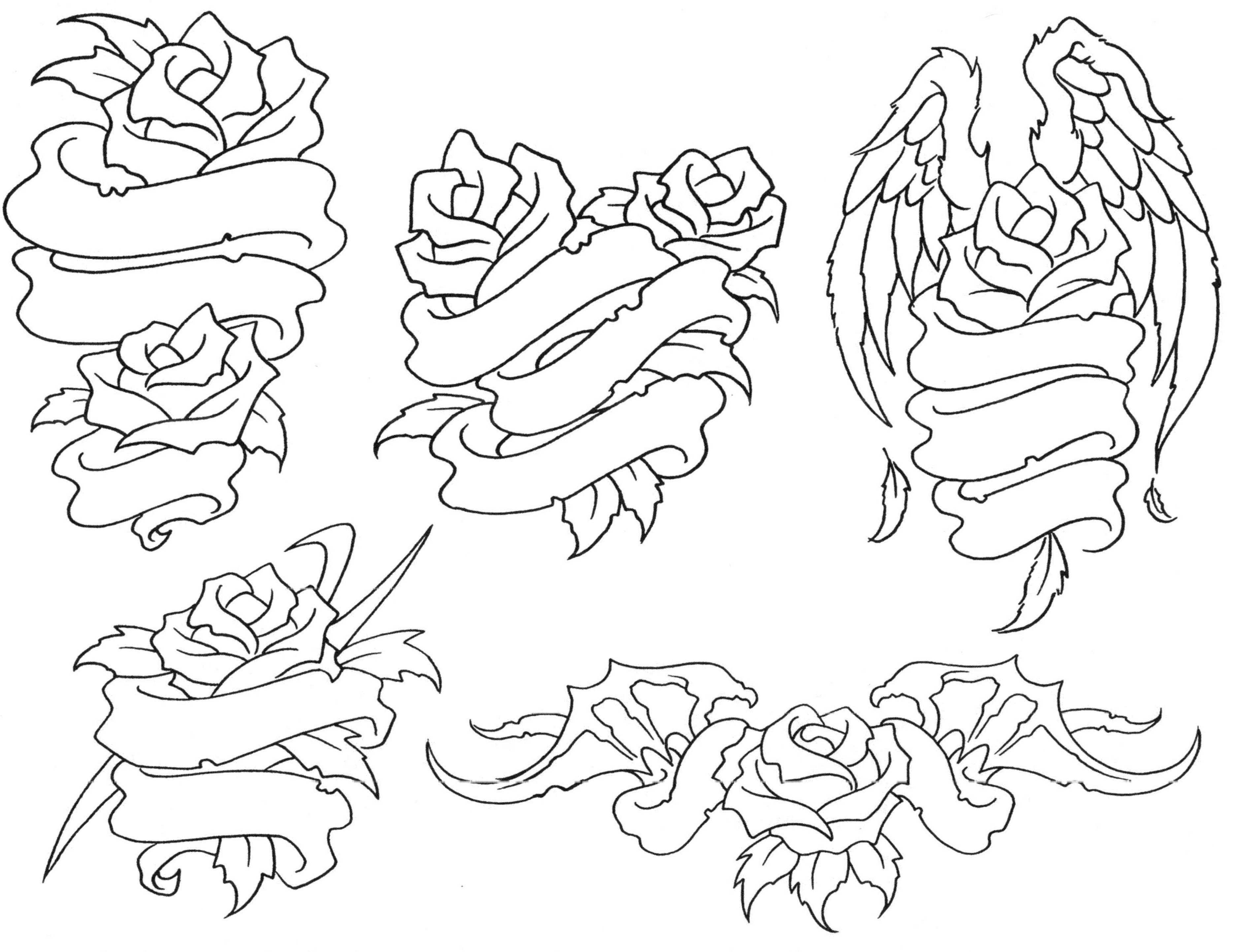

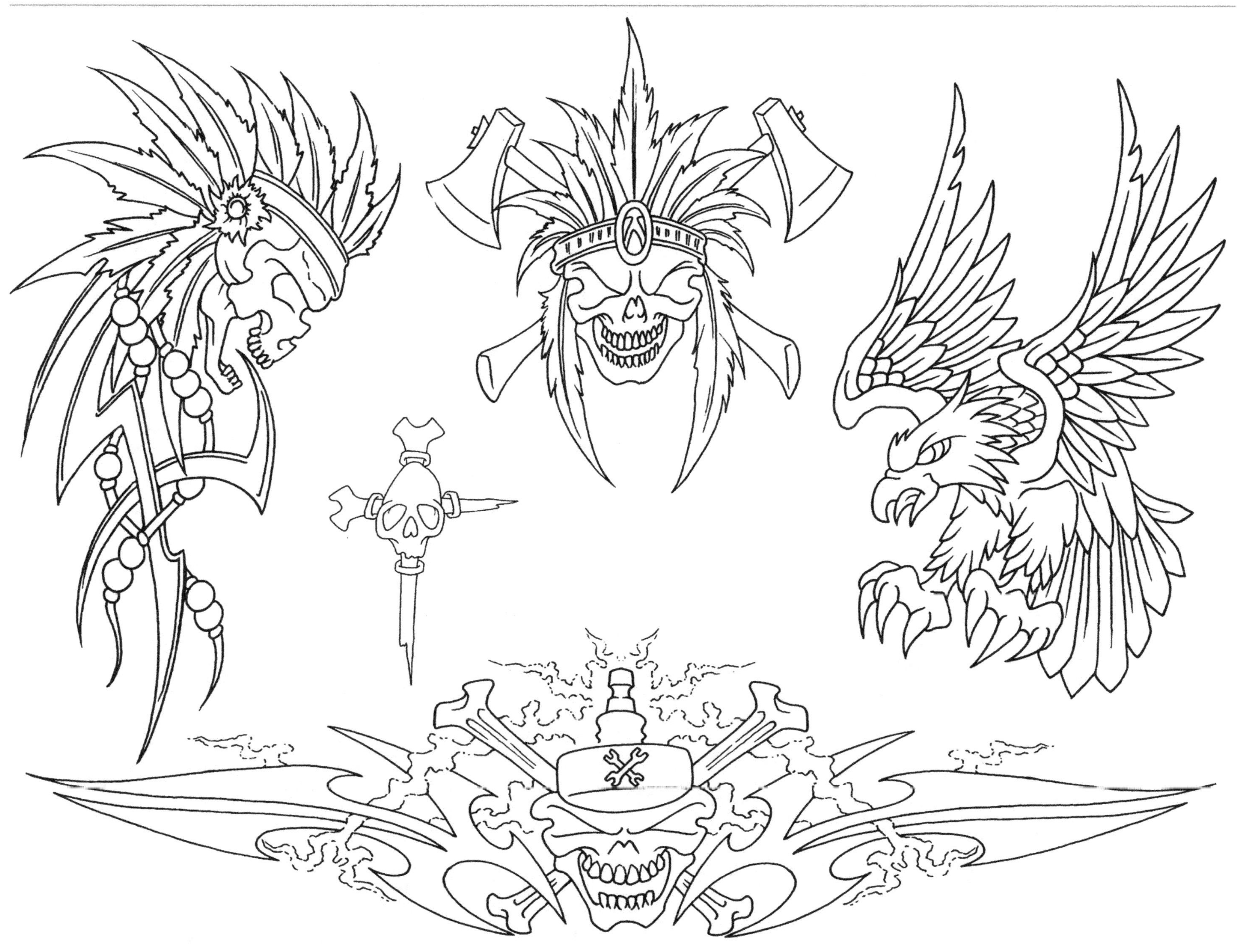

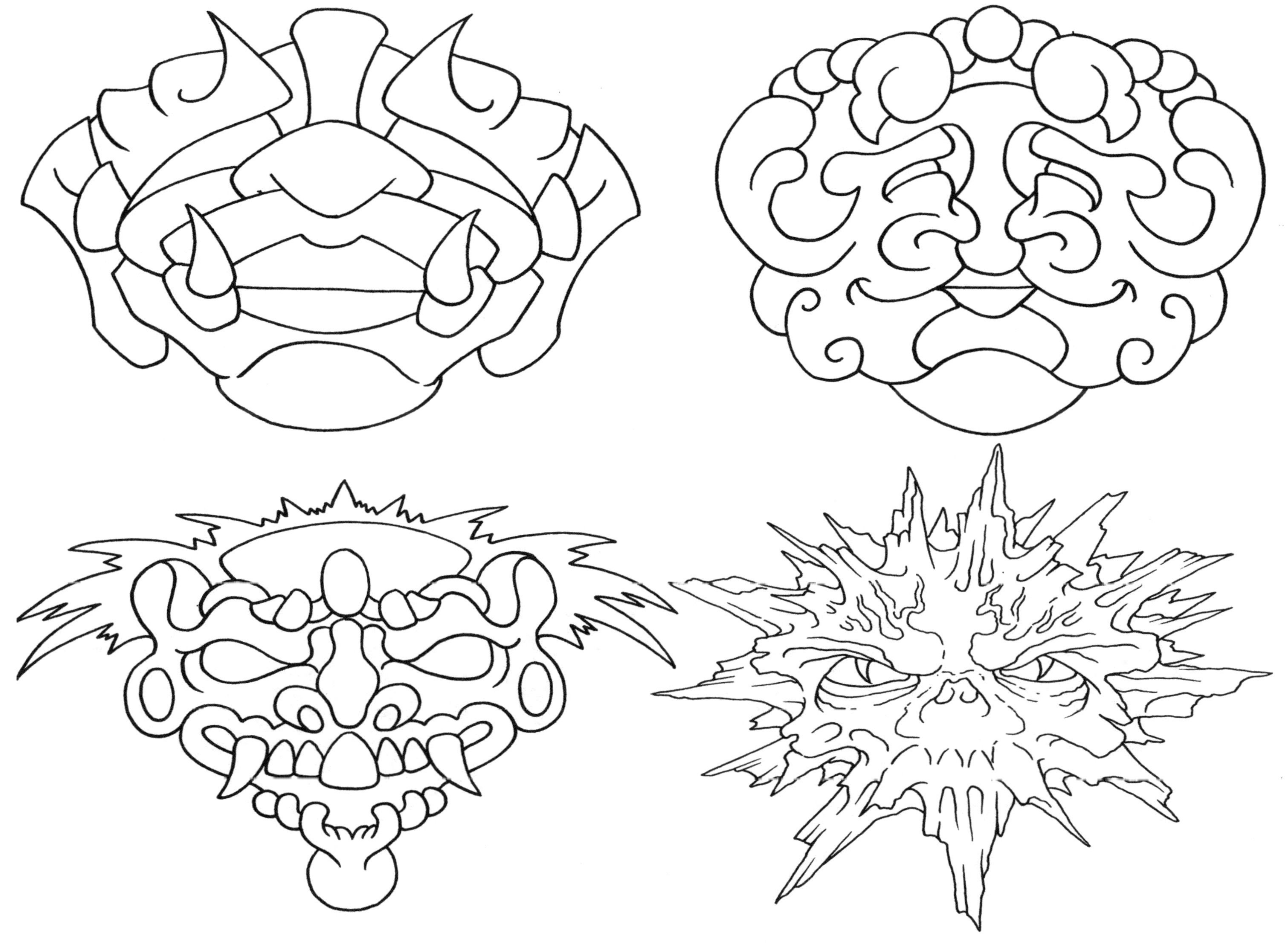

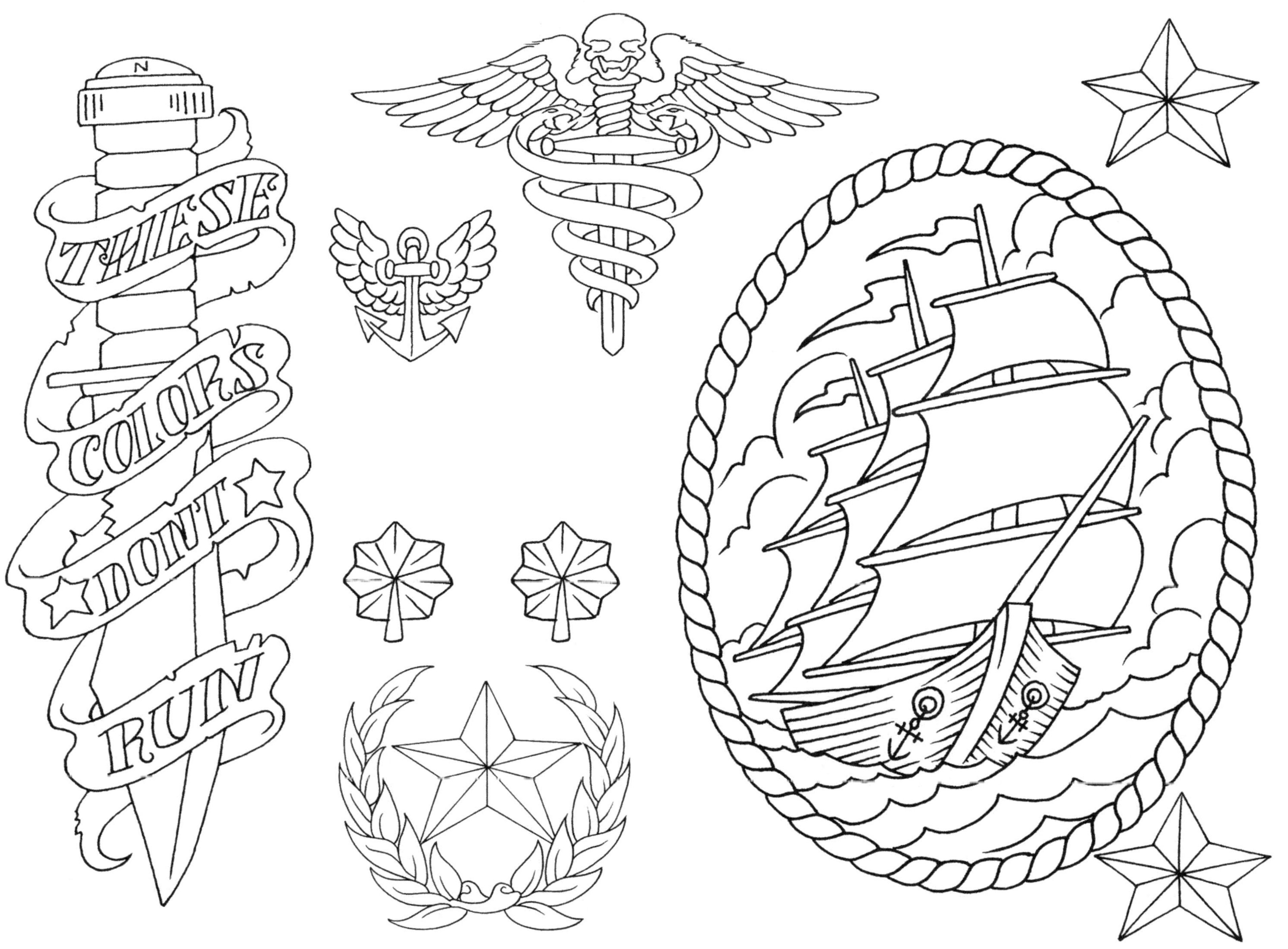

N
THESE
COLORS
DONT
RUN

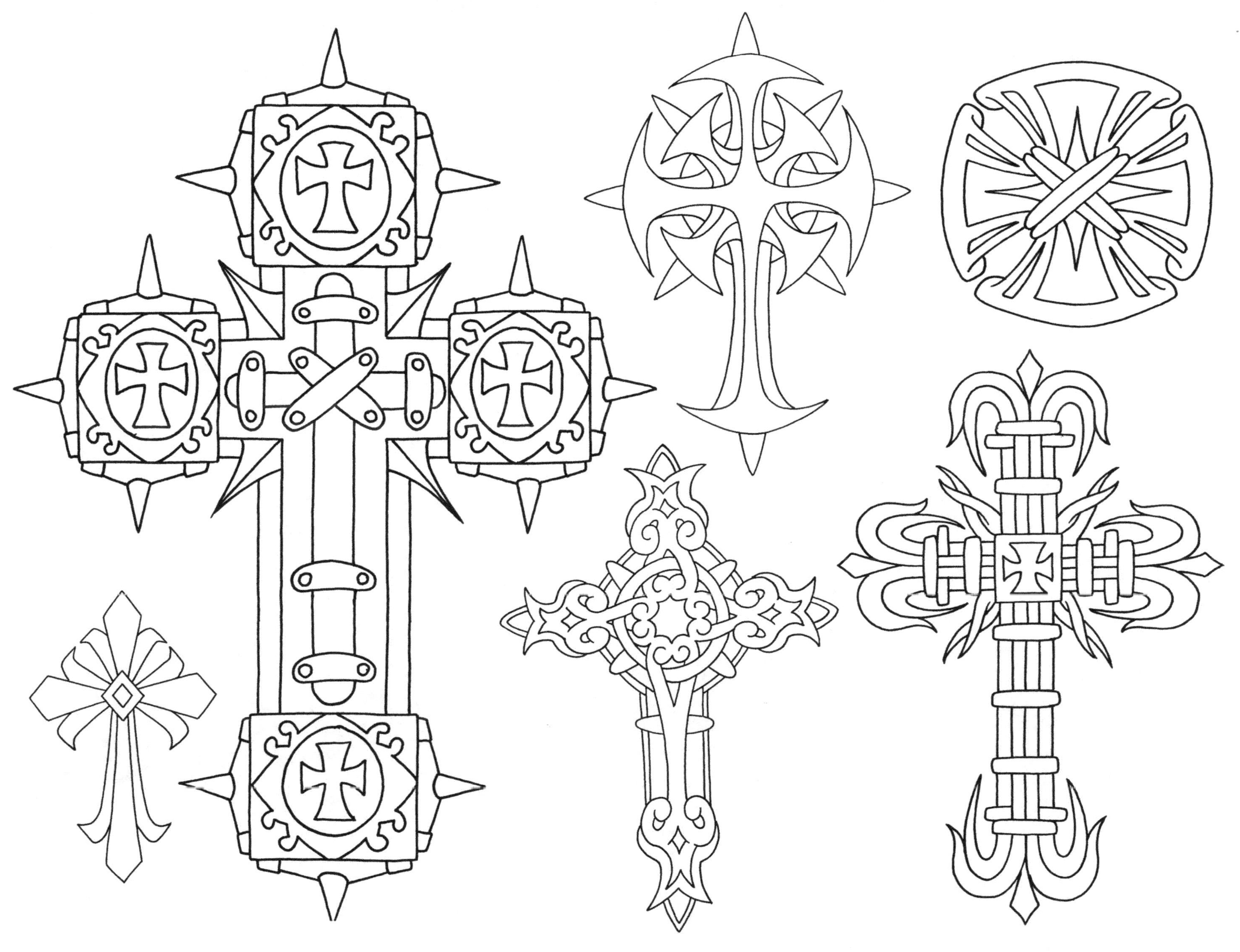

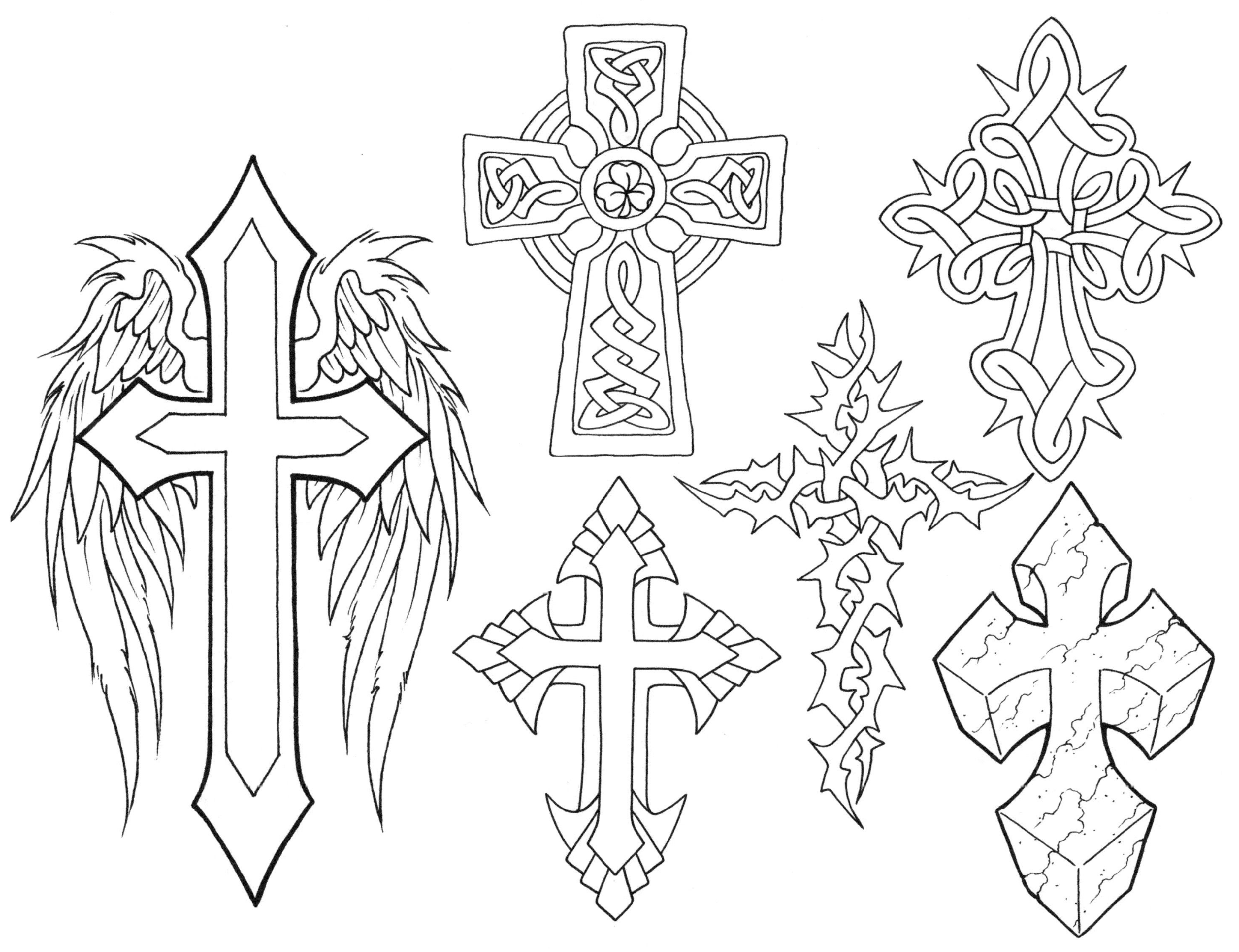

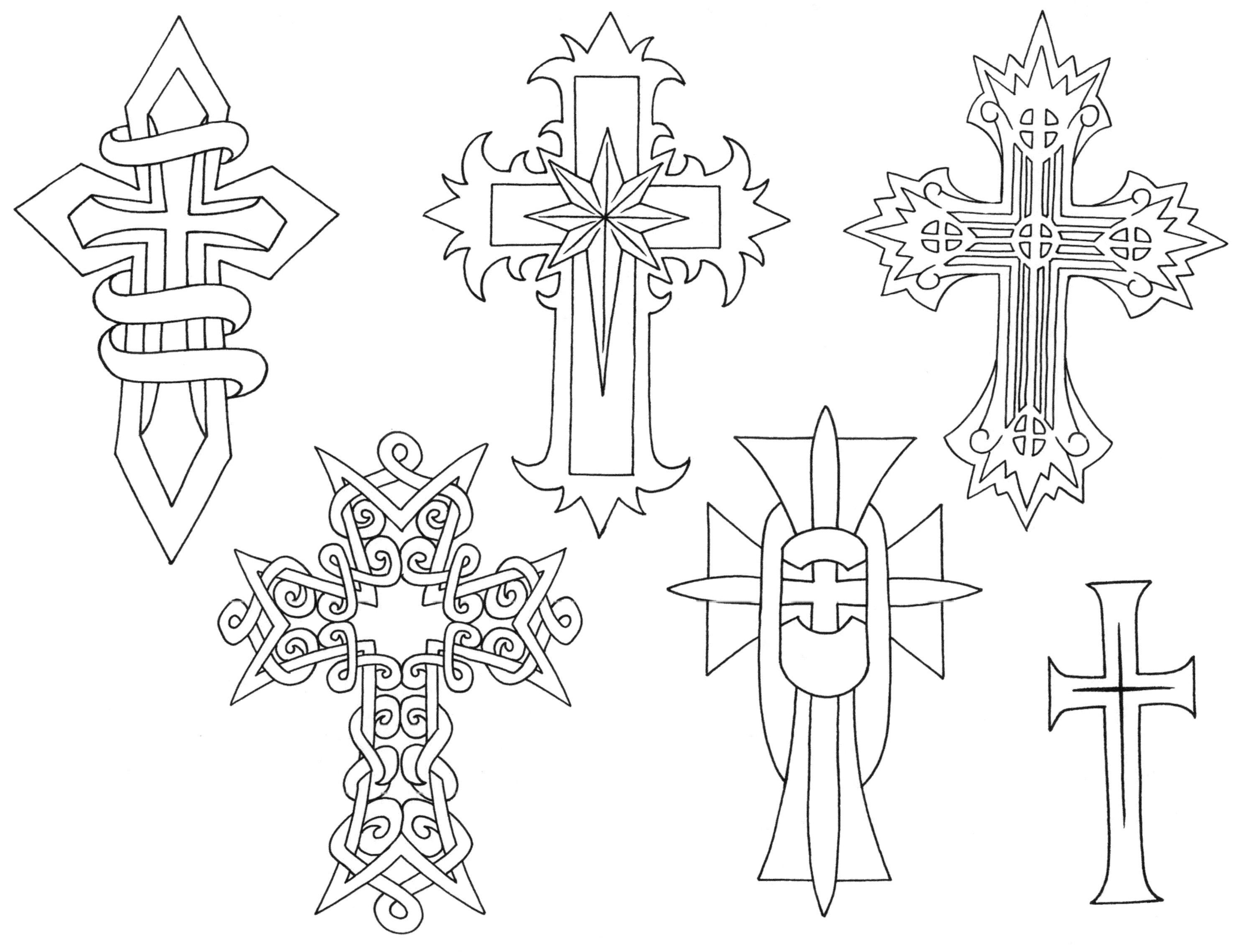

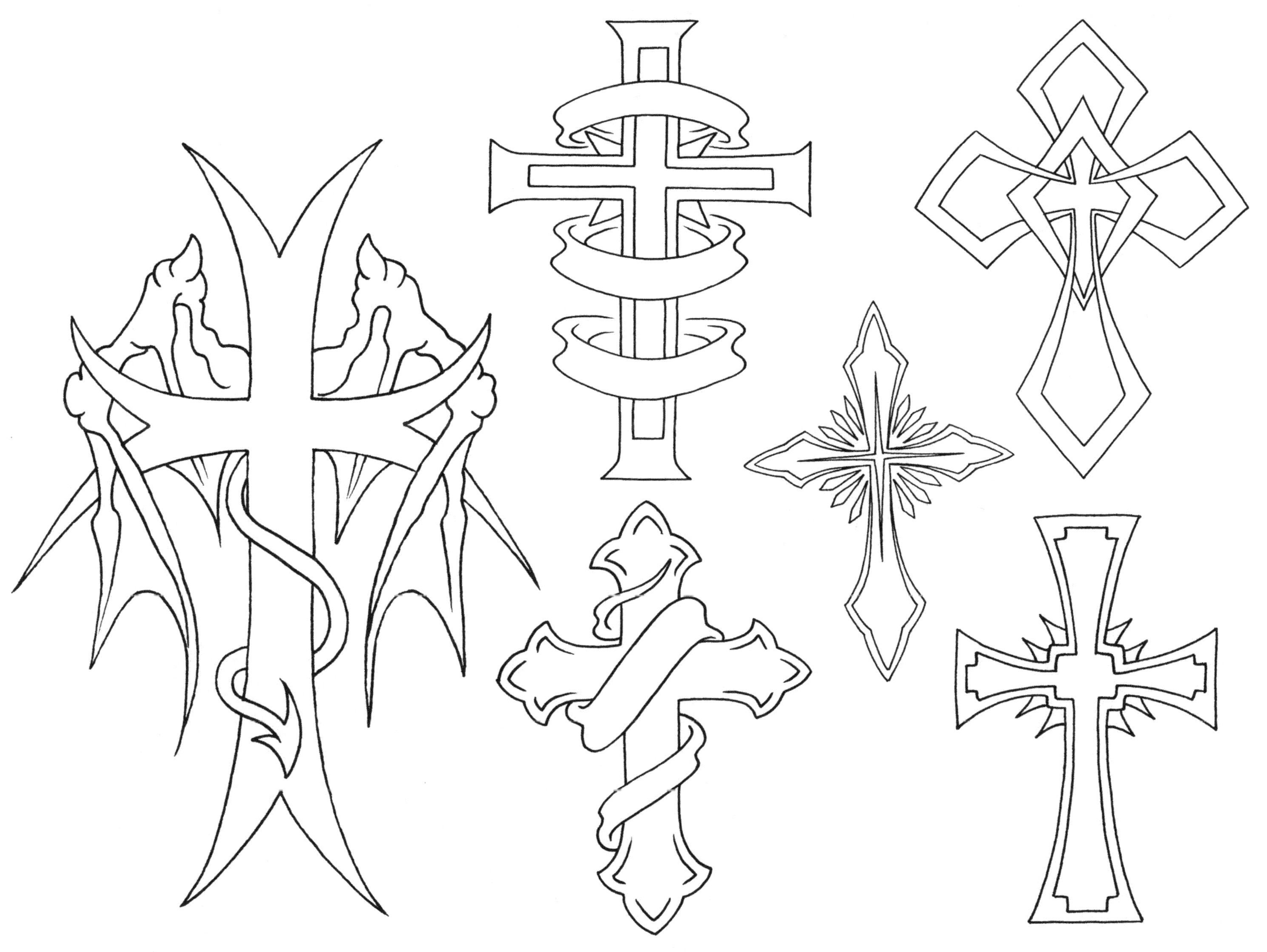

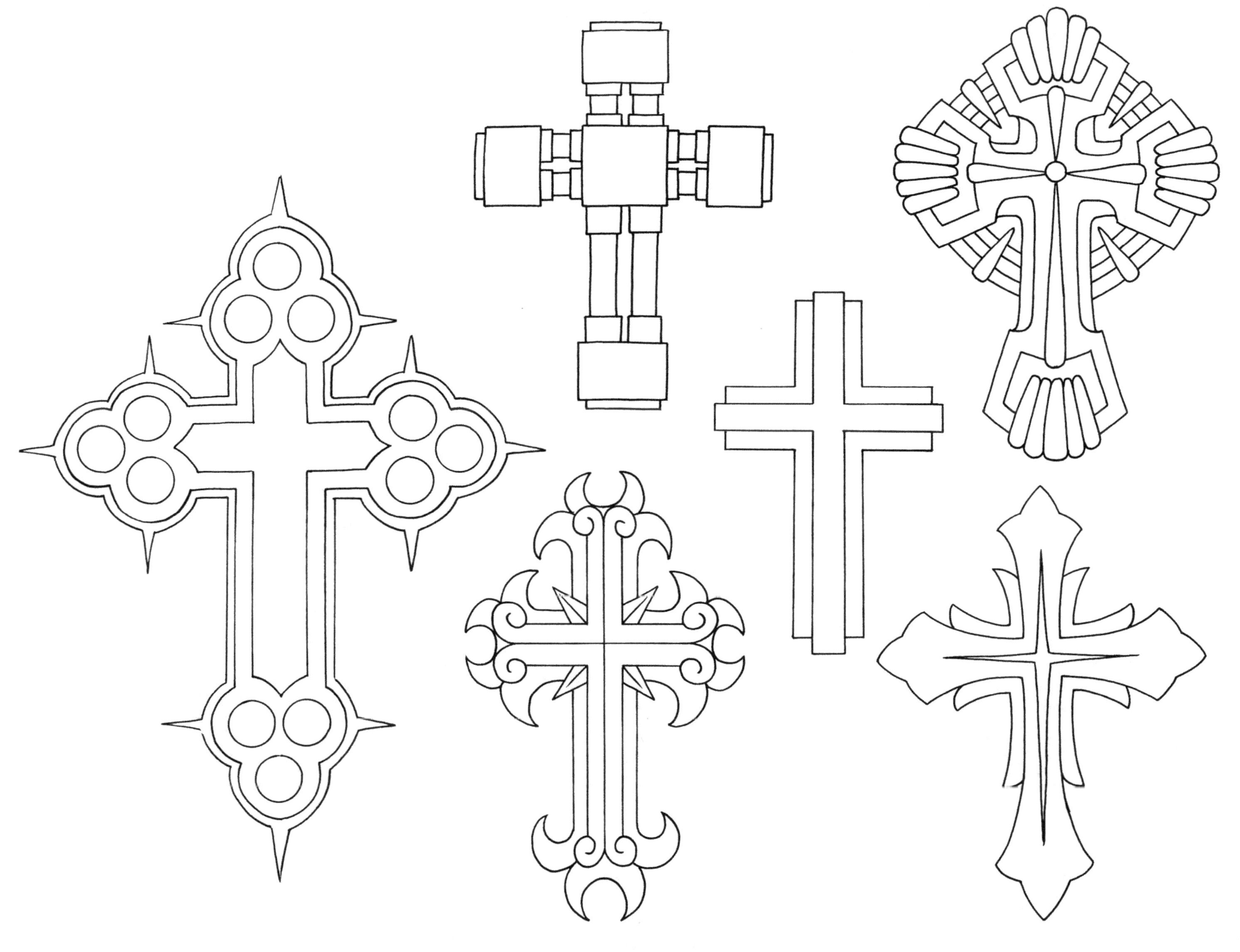

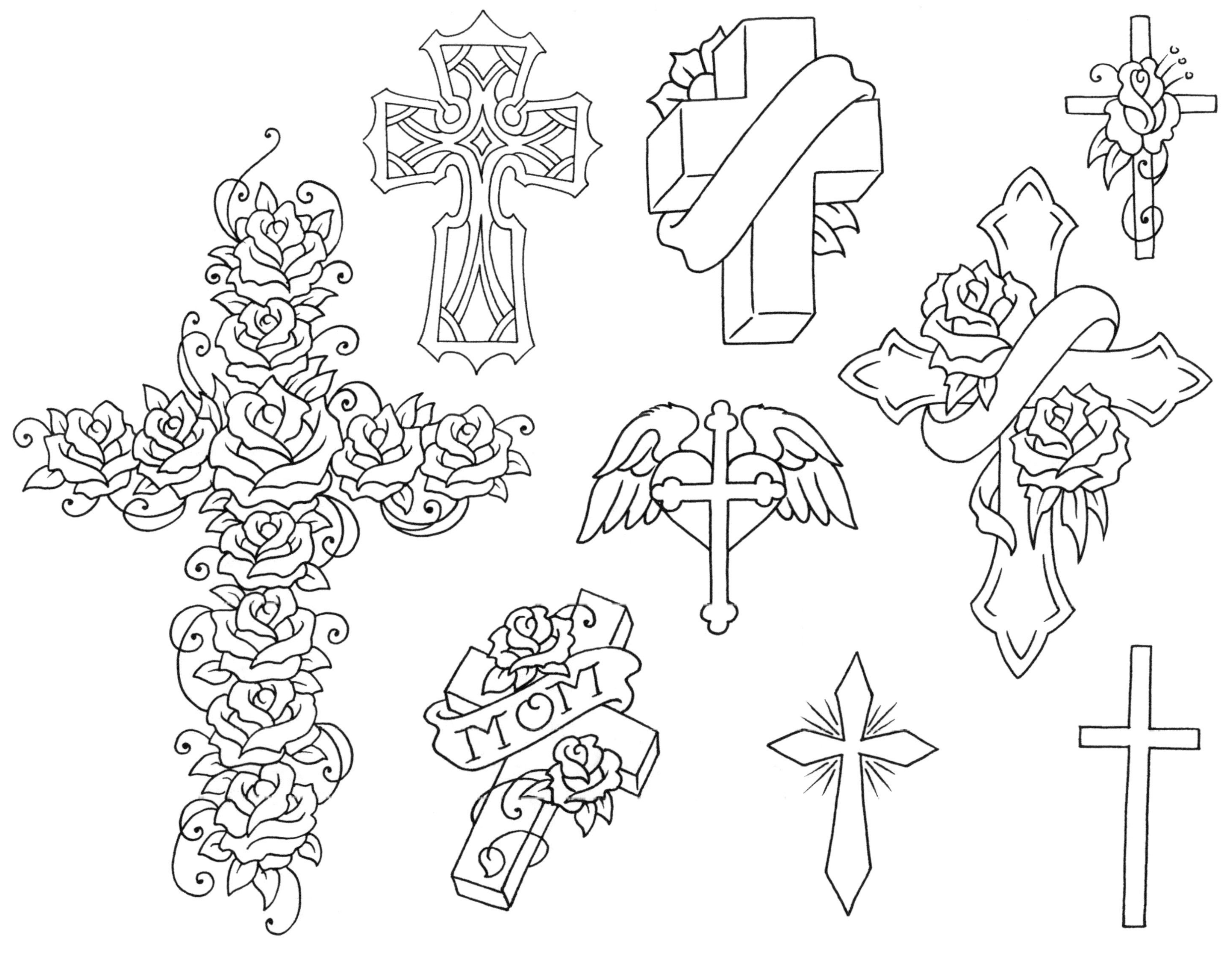
MOM

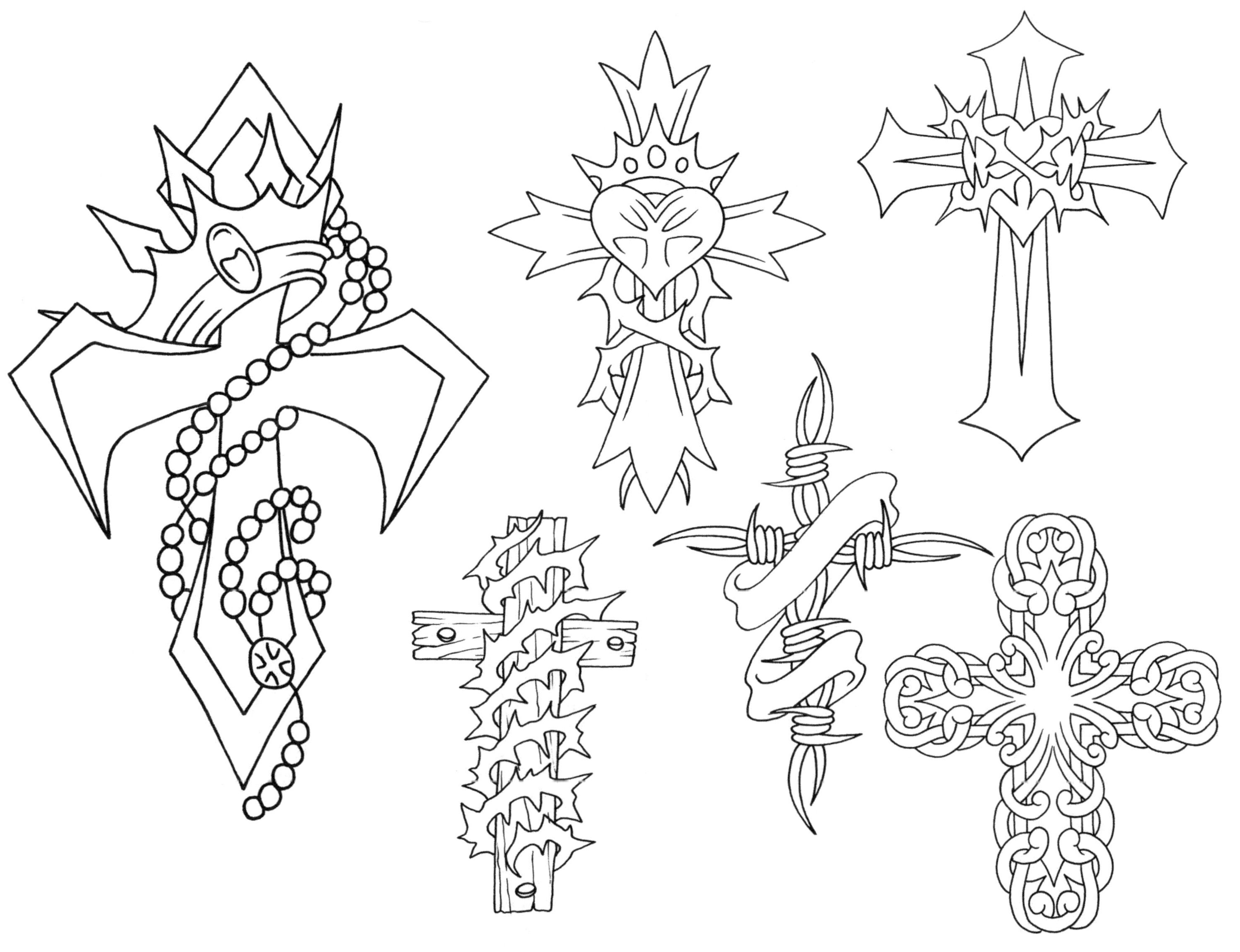

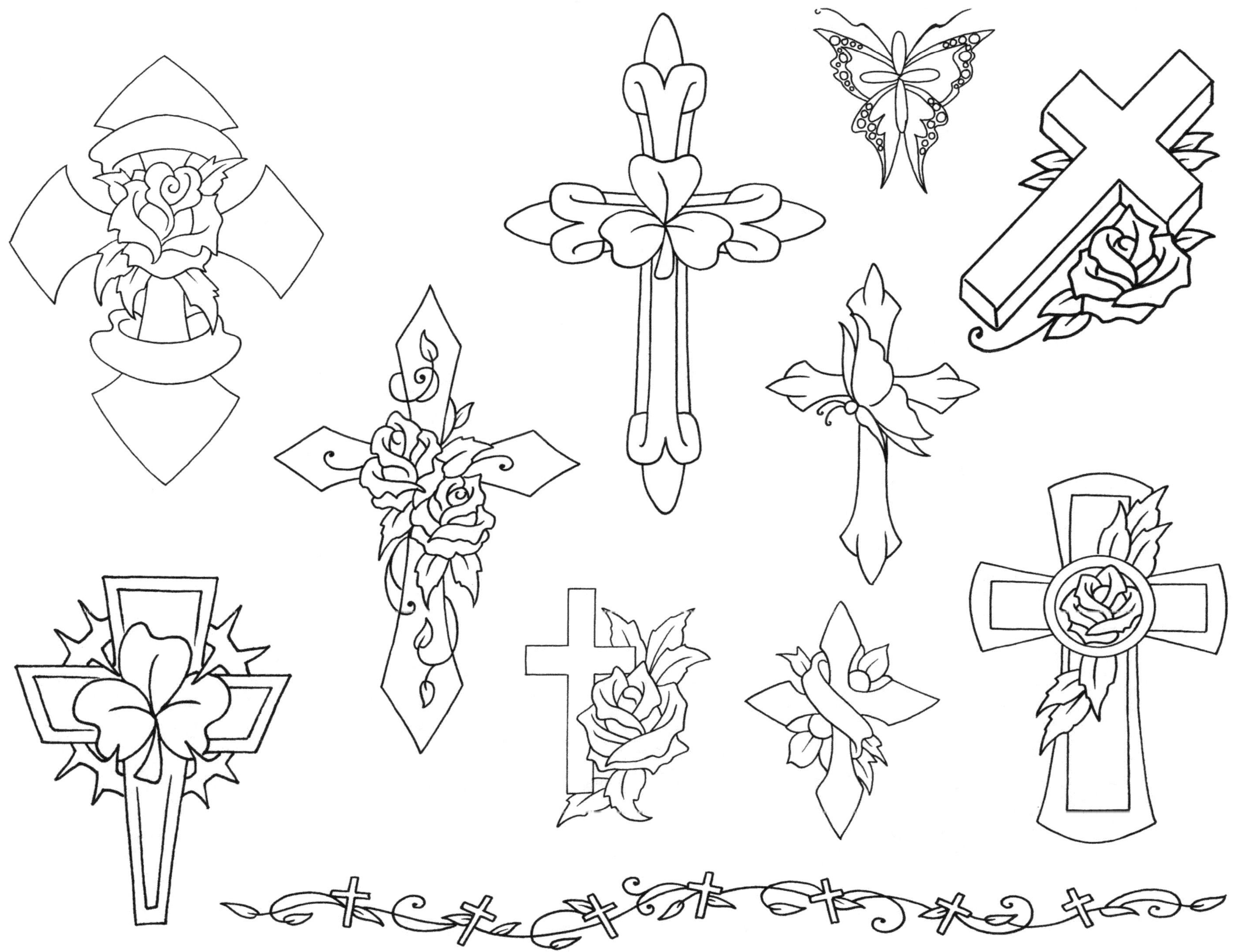

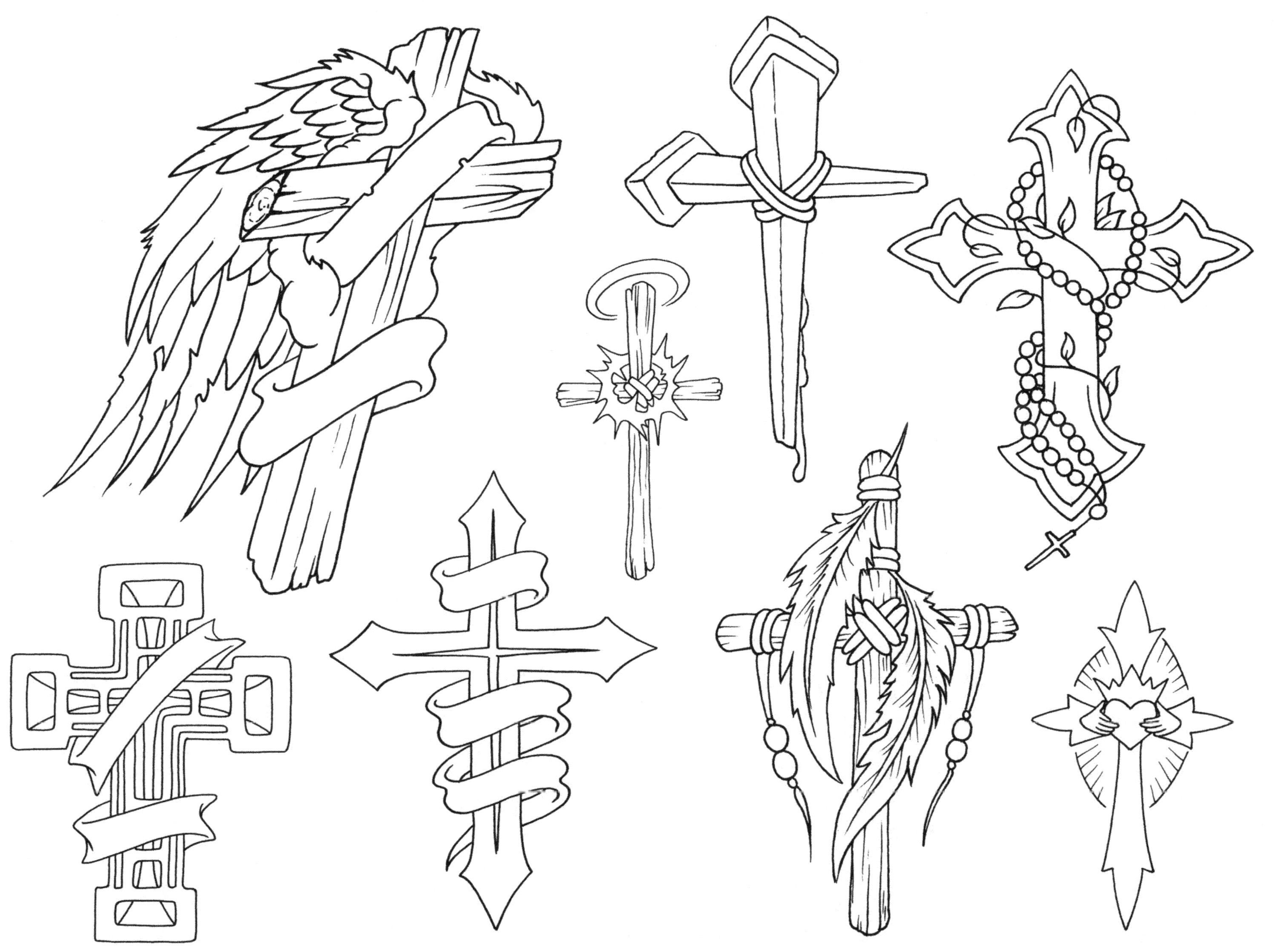

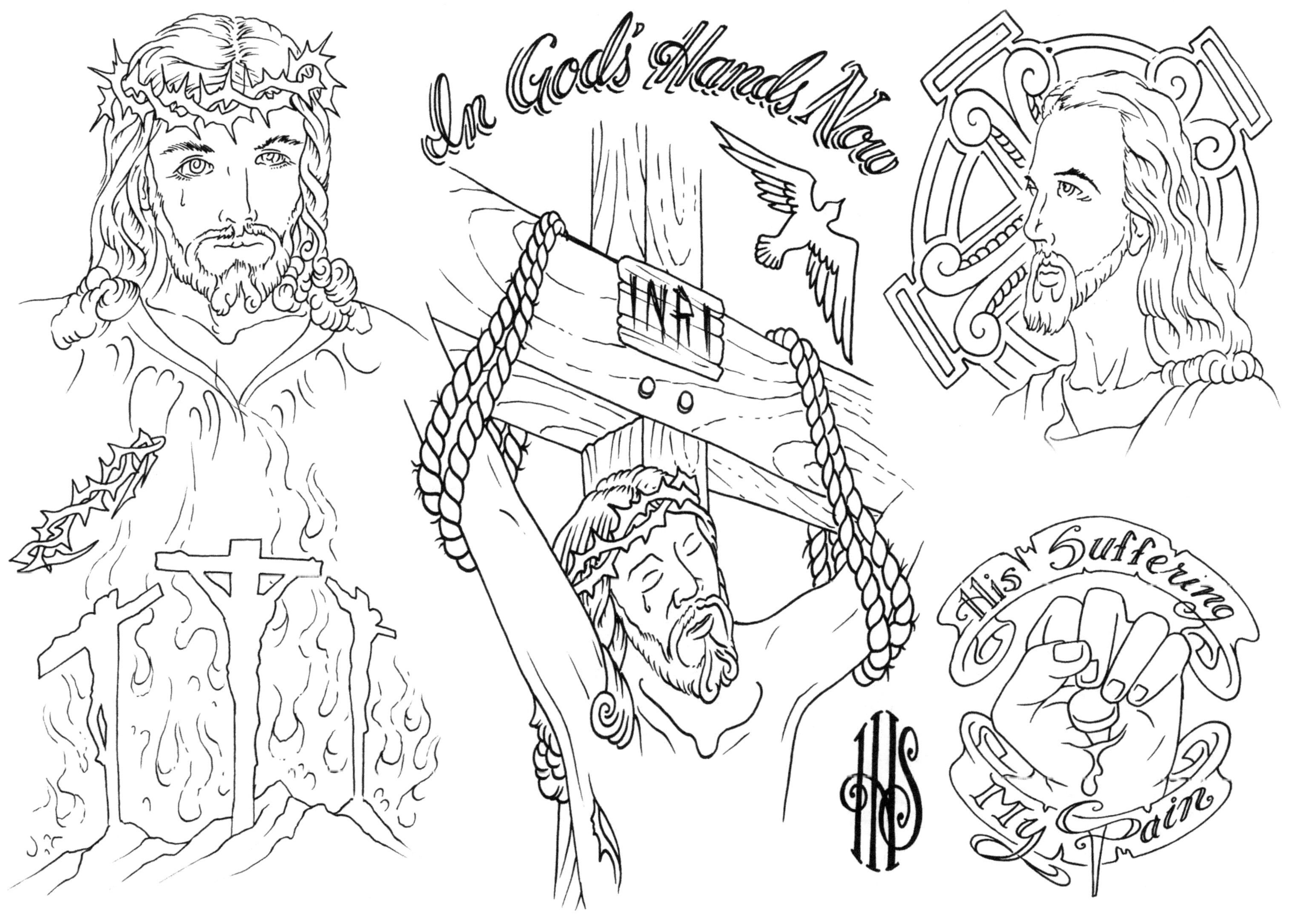
In God's Hands Now
INRI
His Suffering
My Pain
IHS

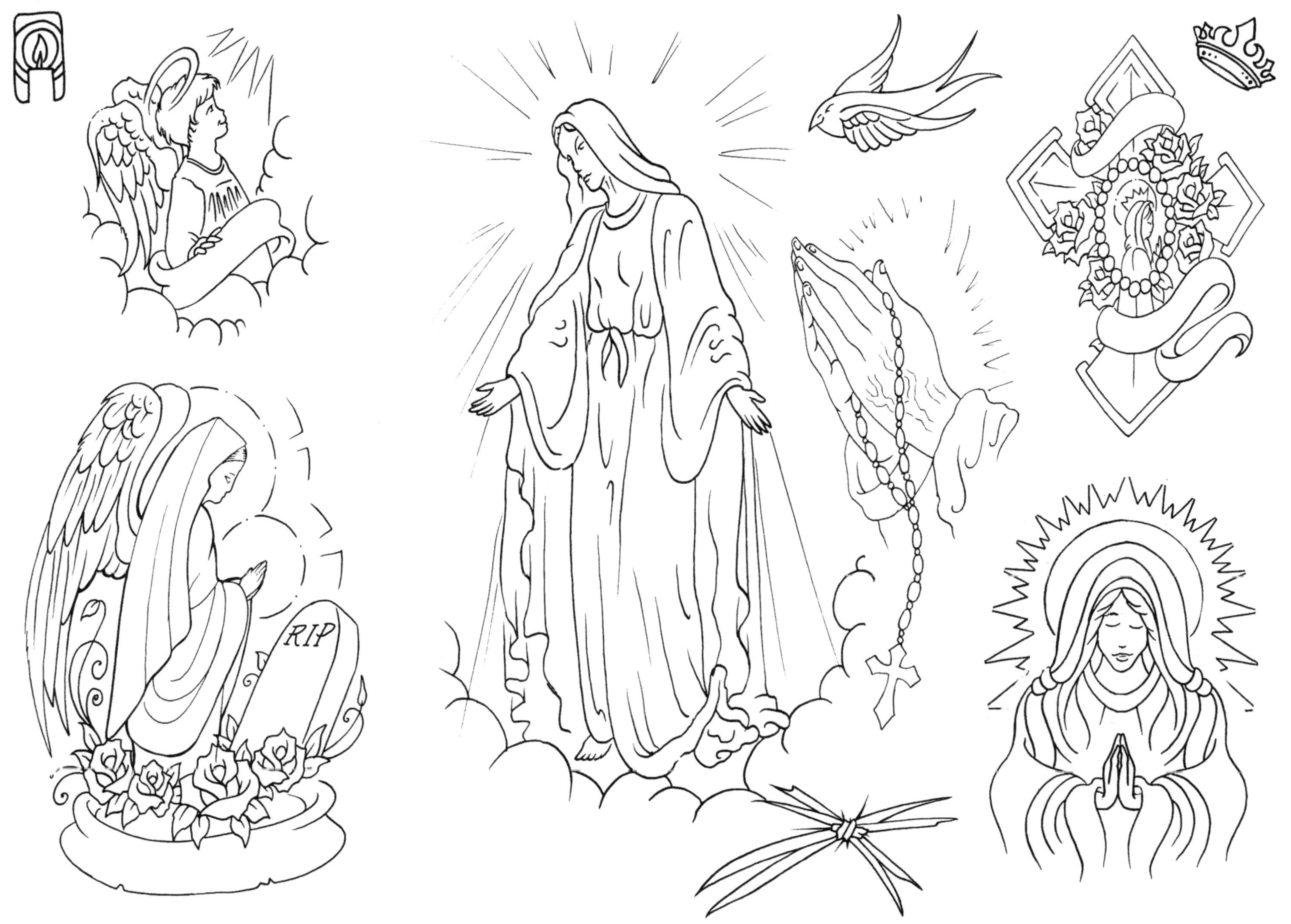
RIP

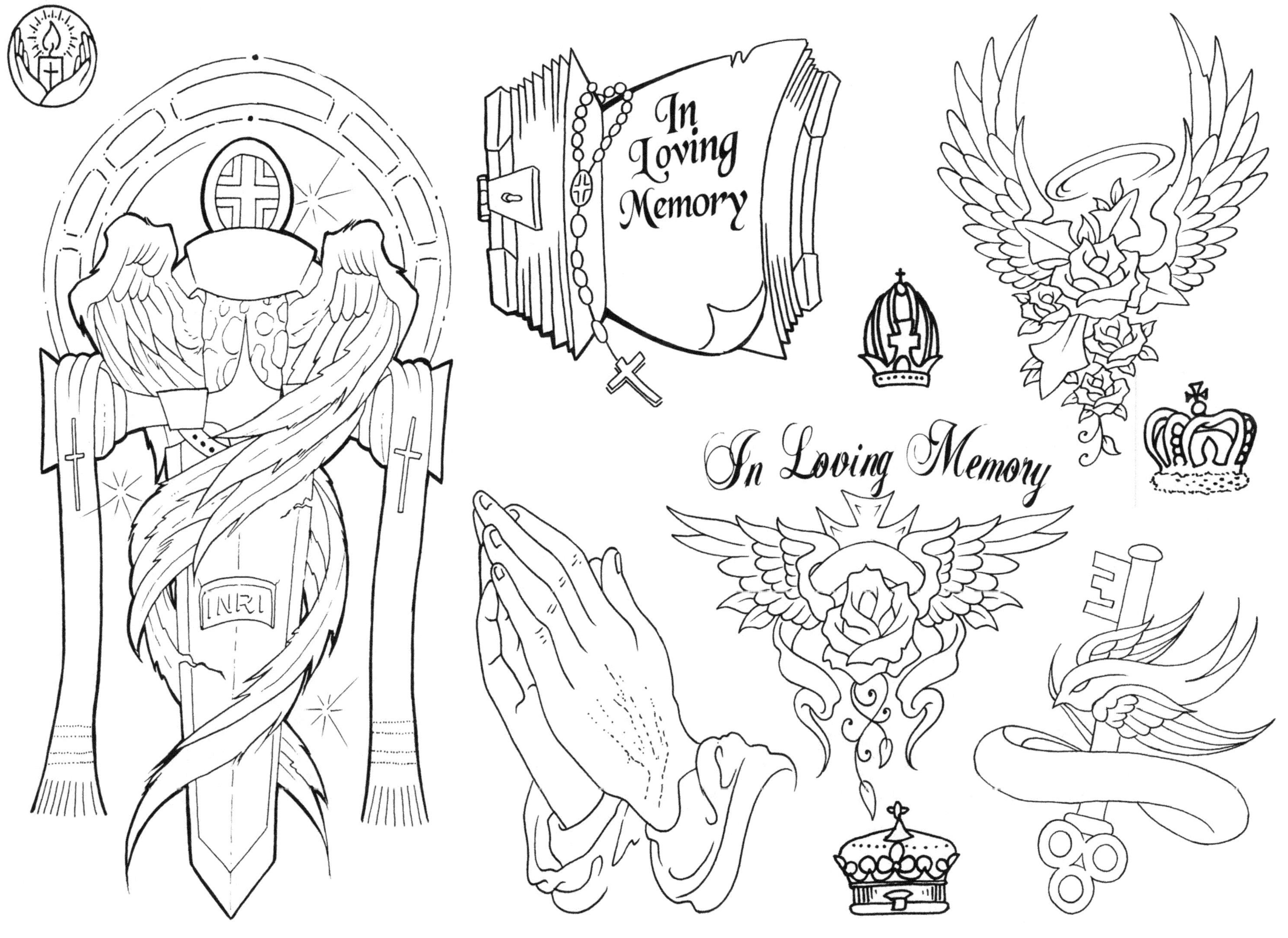

In Loving Memory
INRI
In Loving Memory

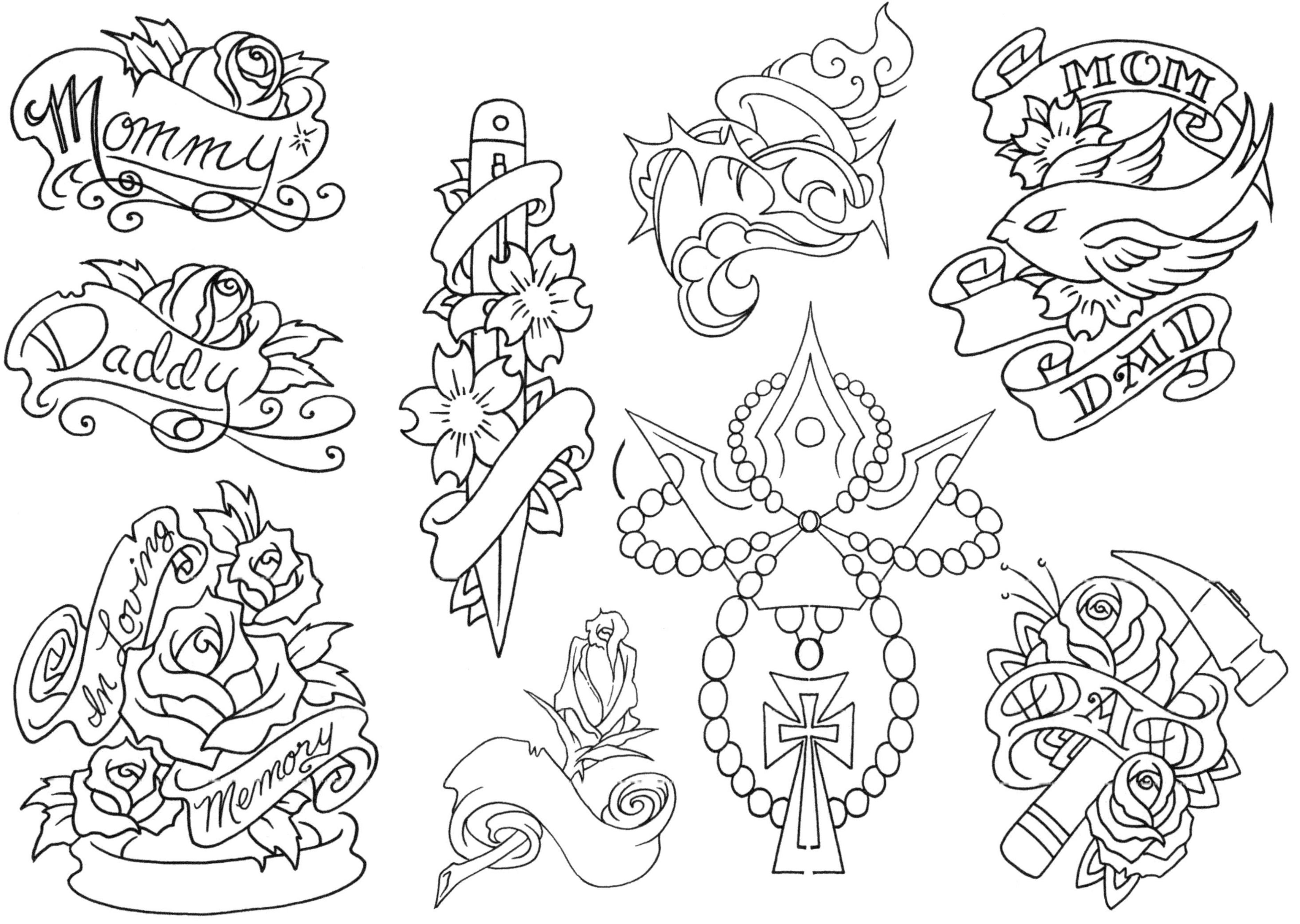
Mommy
Daddy
In loving
Memory
MOM
DAD
DAD

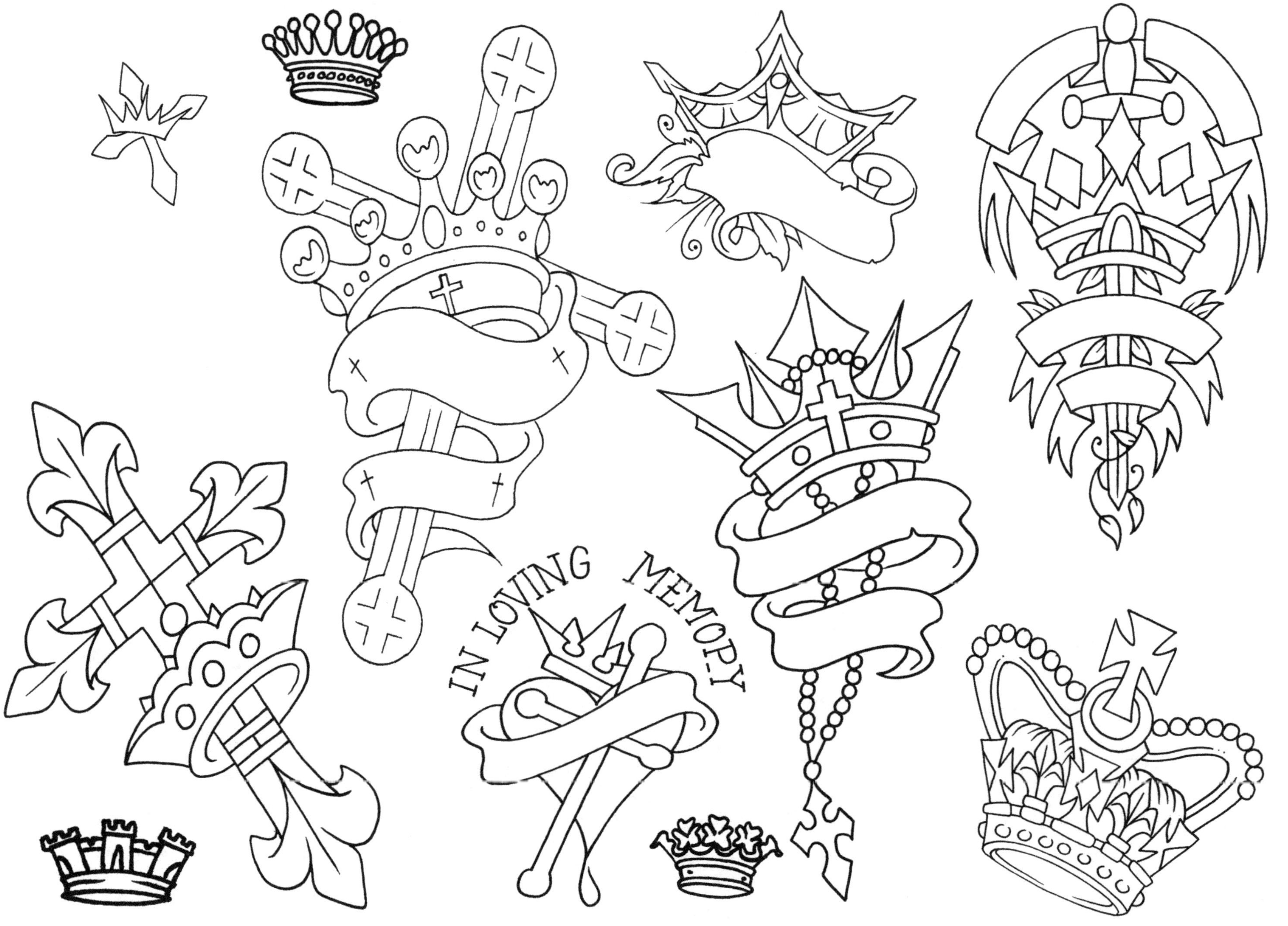
IN LOVING MEMORY

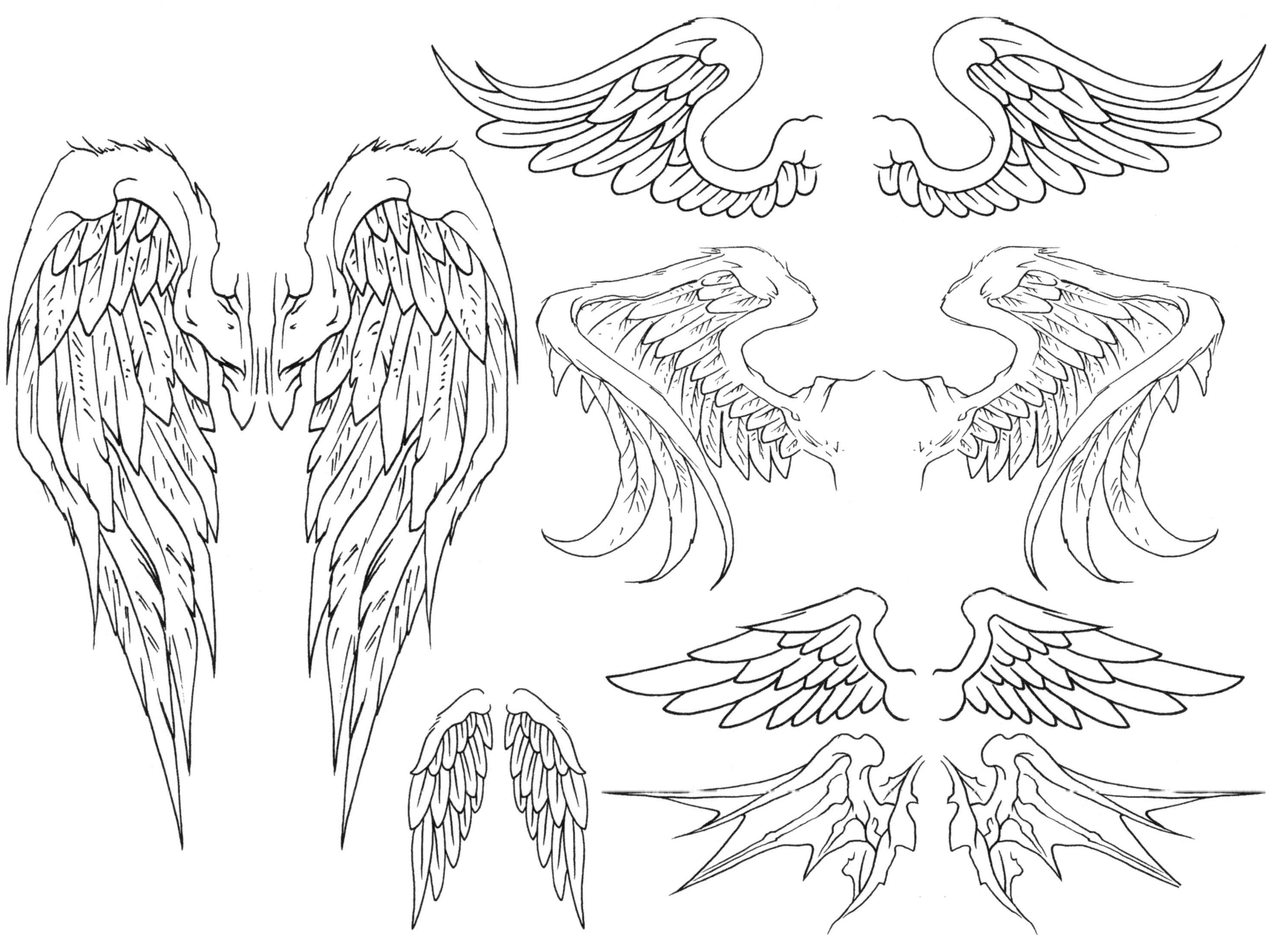

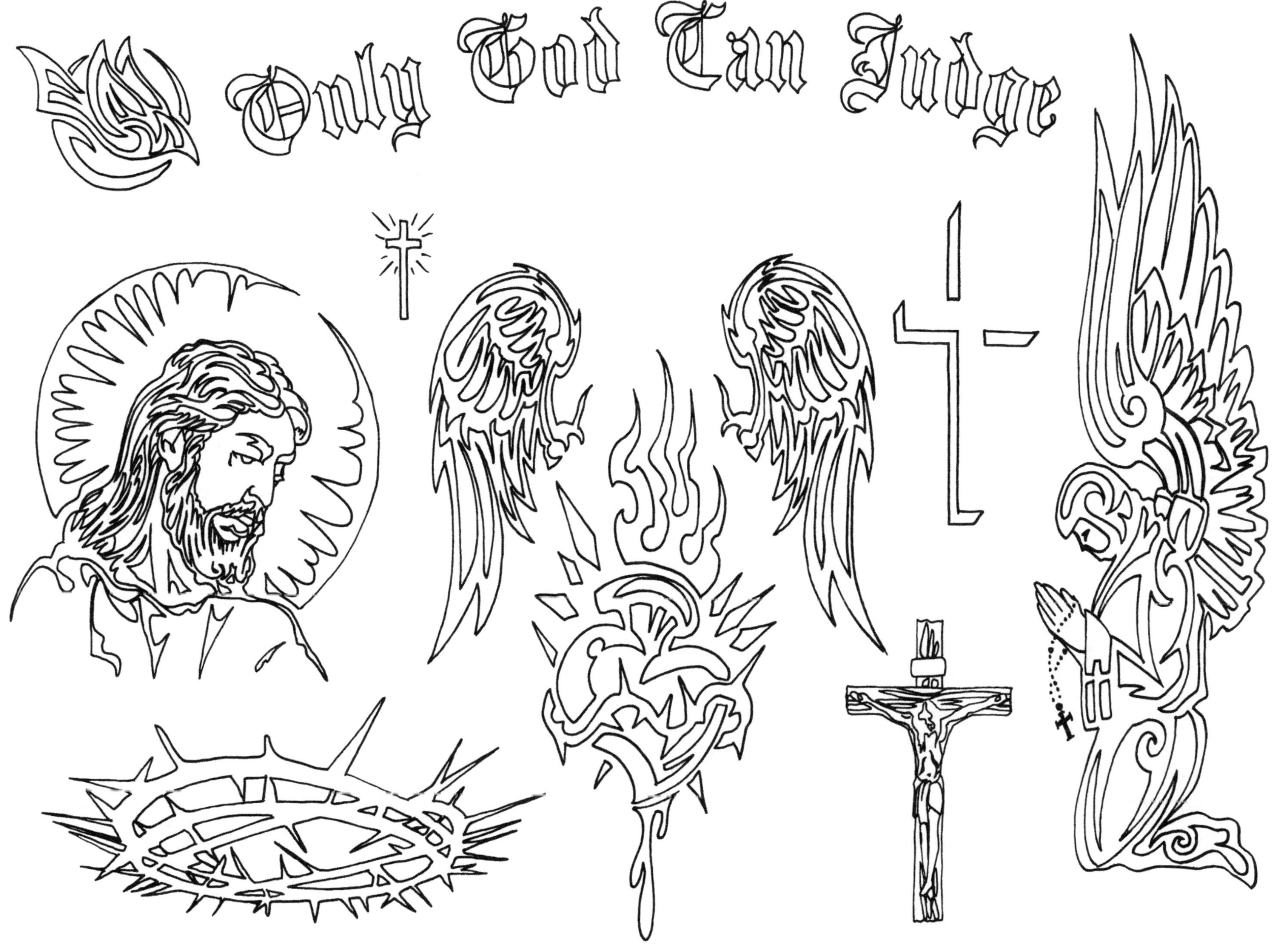
Only God Can Judge

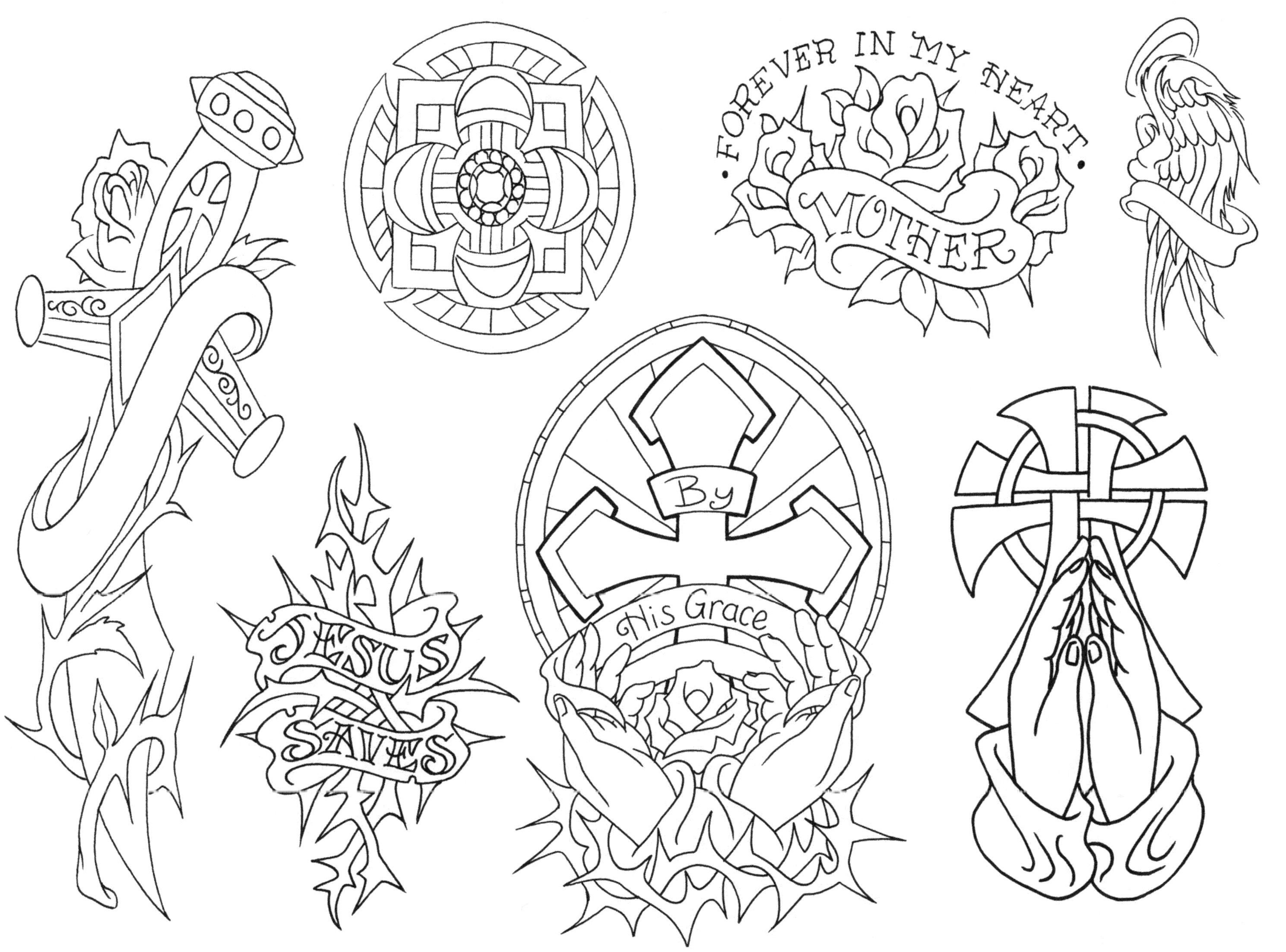

FOREVER IN MY HEART
MOTHER
By
His Grace
JESUS
SAVES

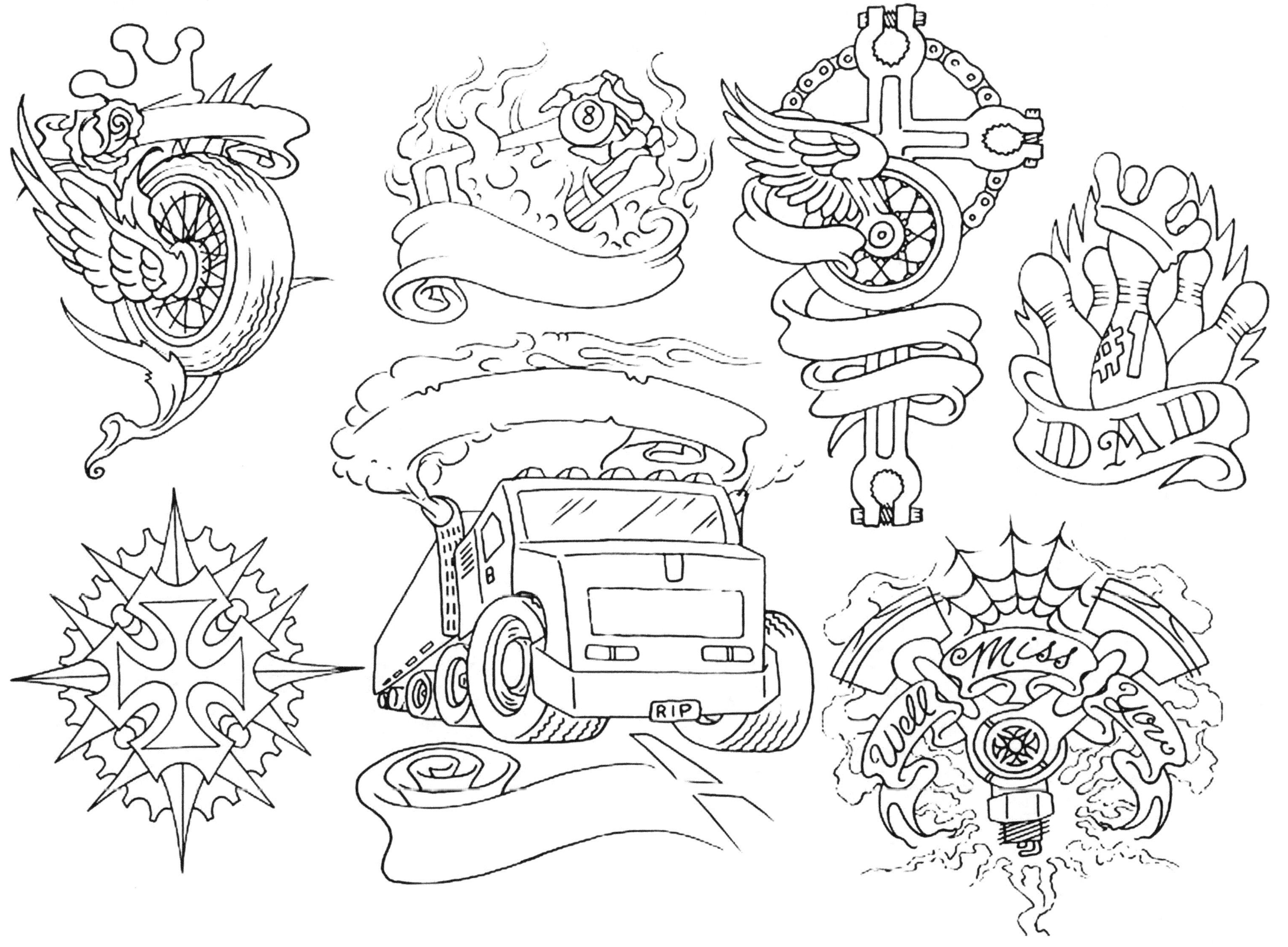

8
#1
DAD
B
RIP
Well
Miss
You

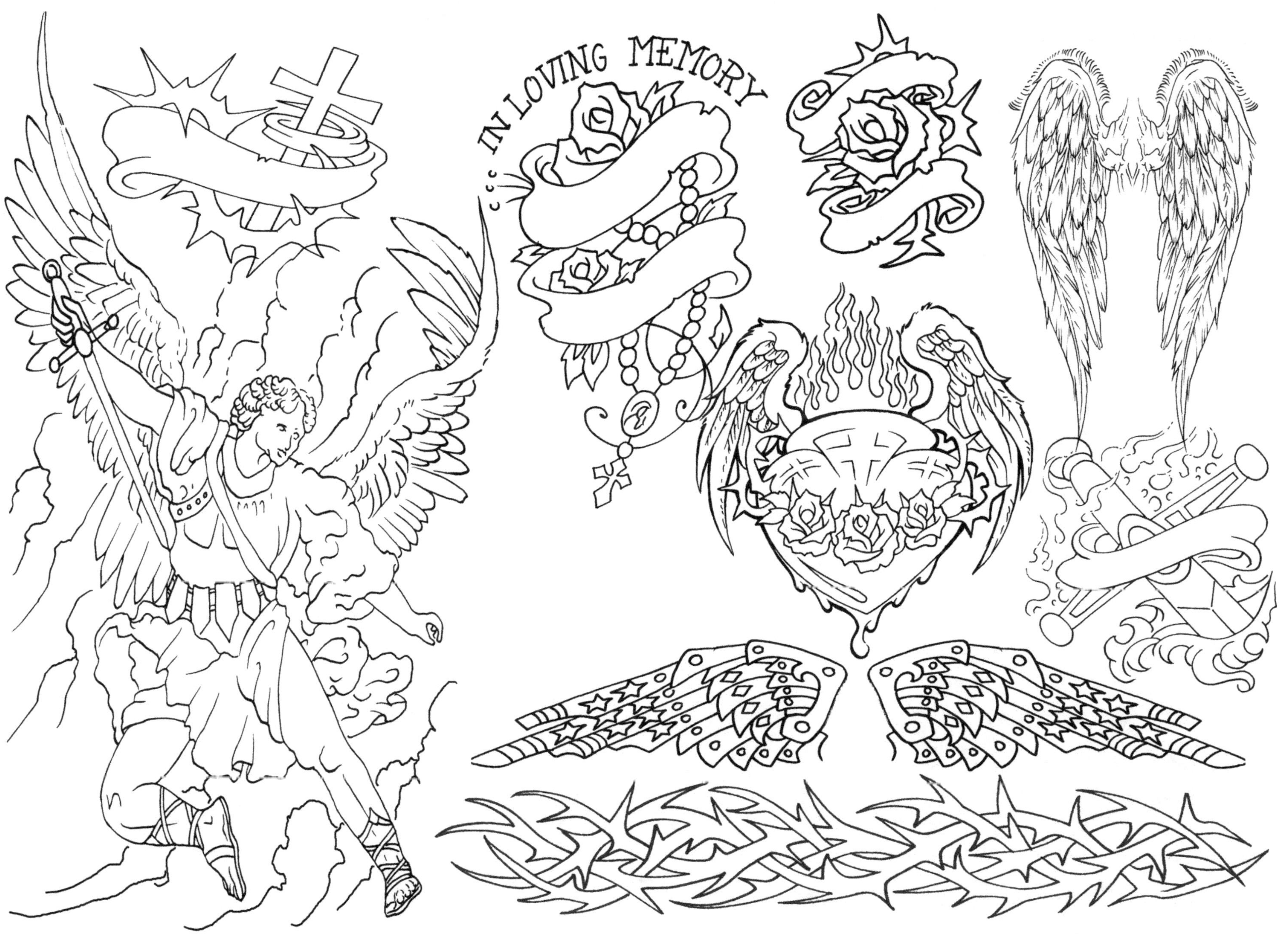
IN LOVING MEMORY

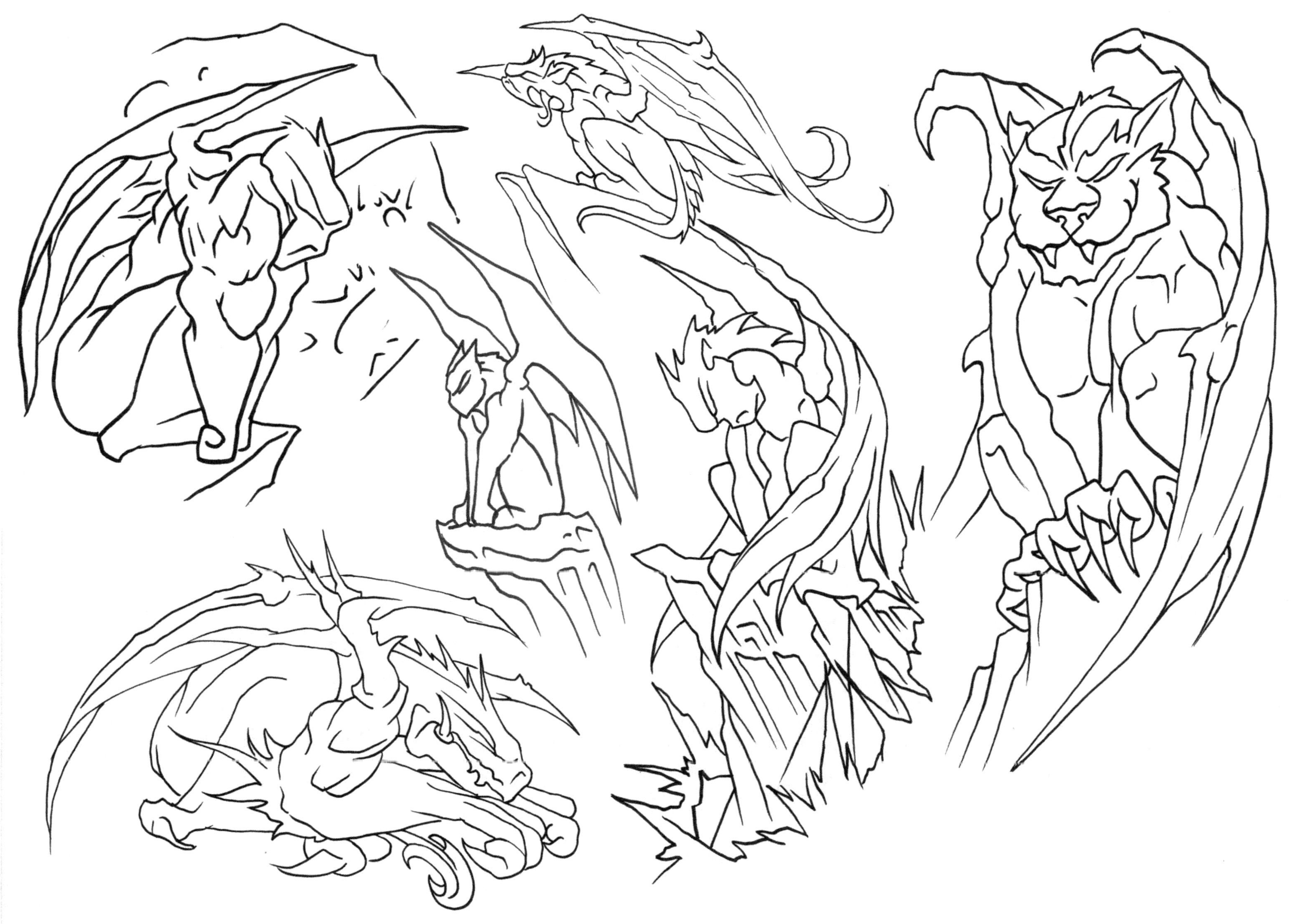

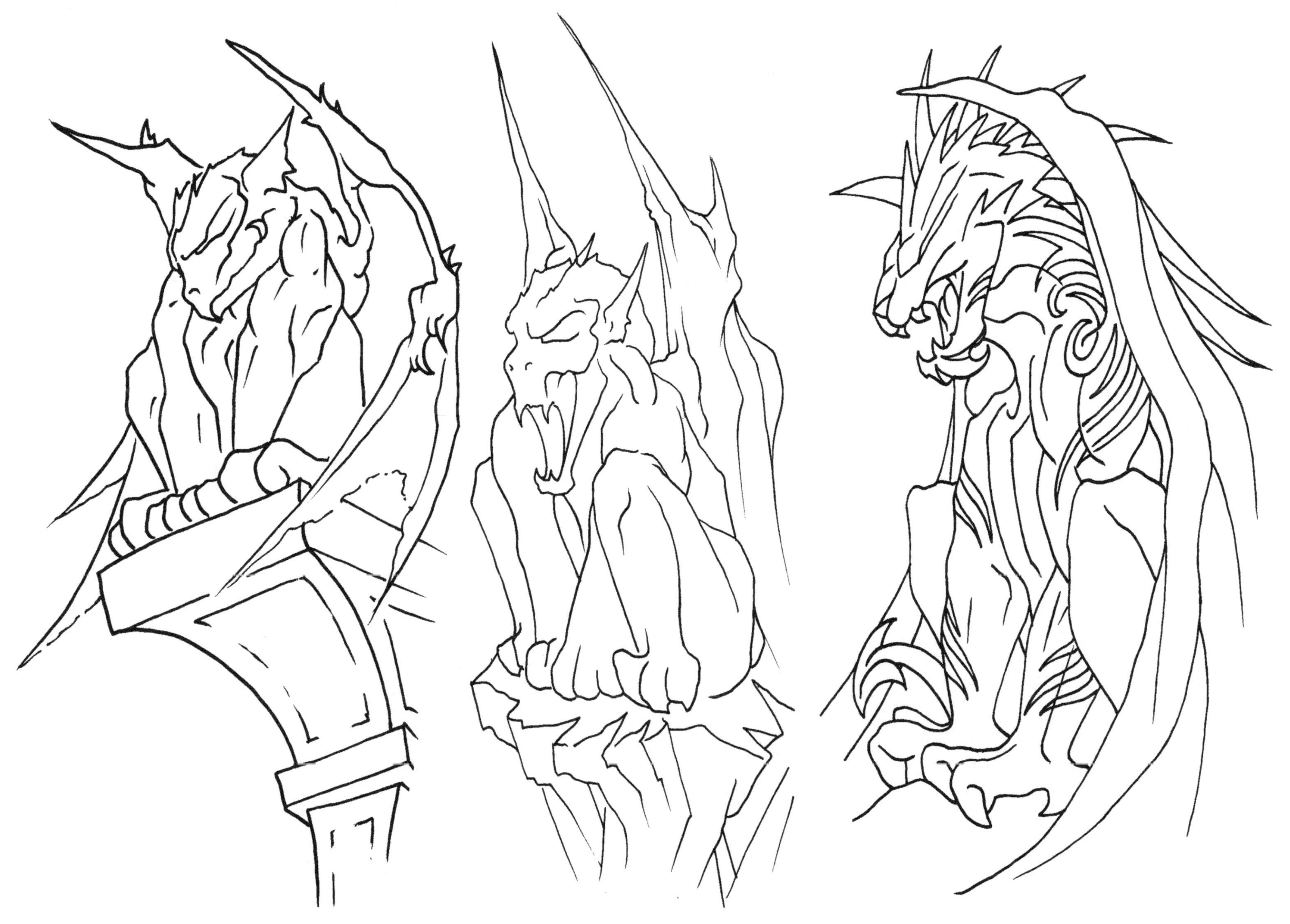

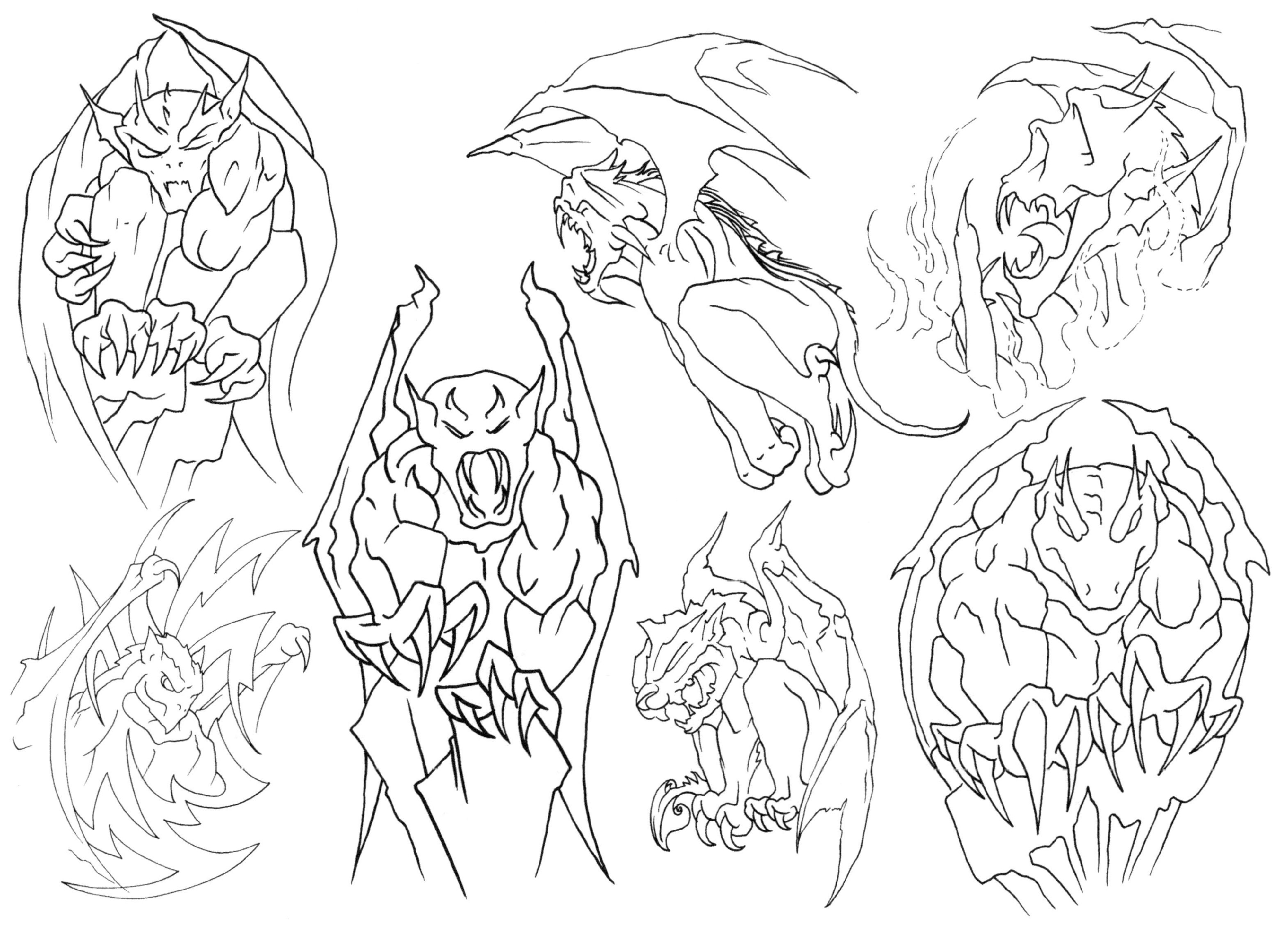

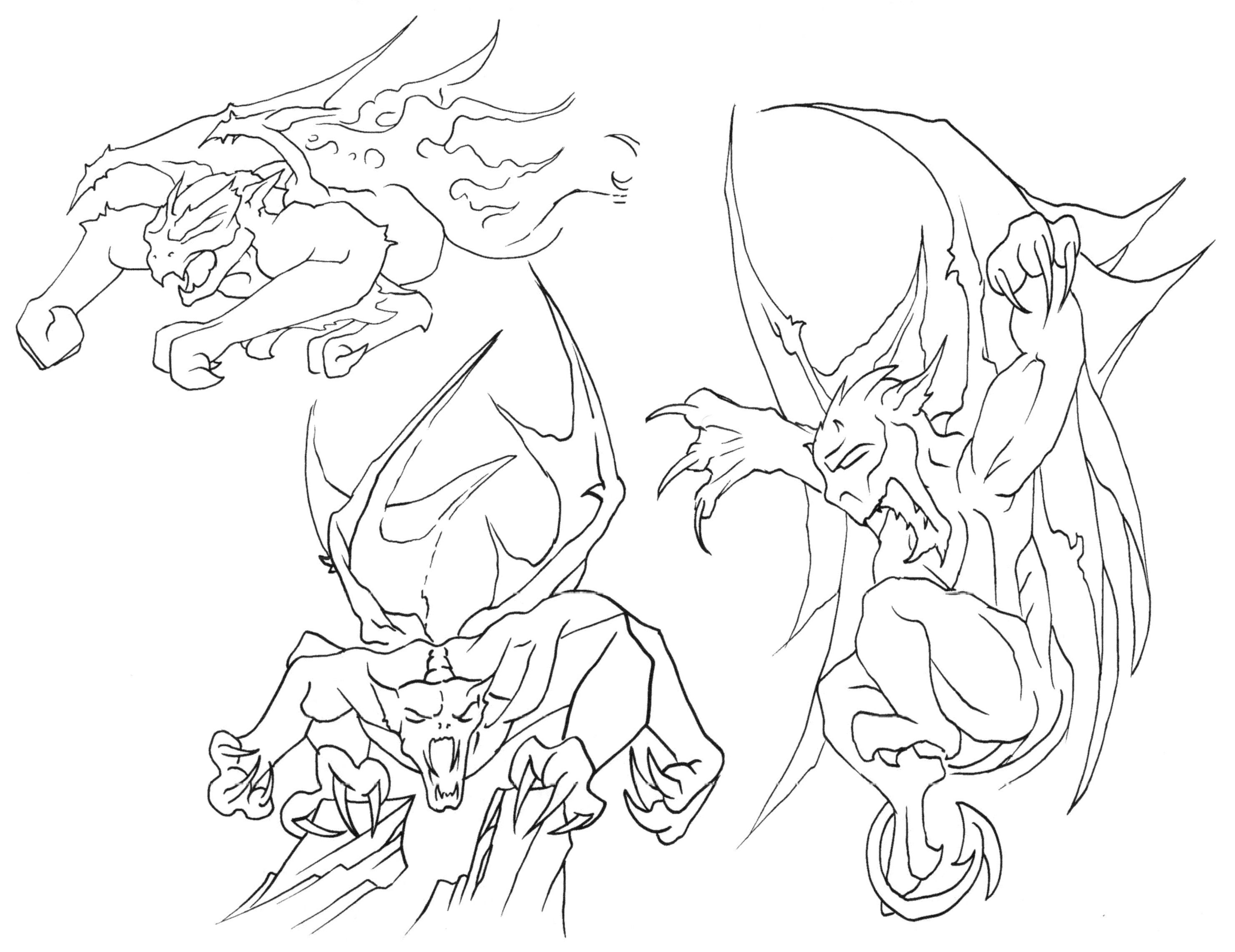

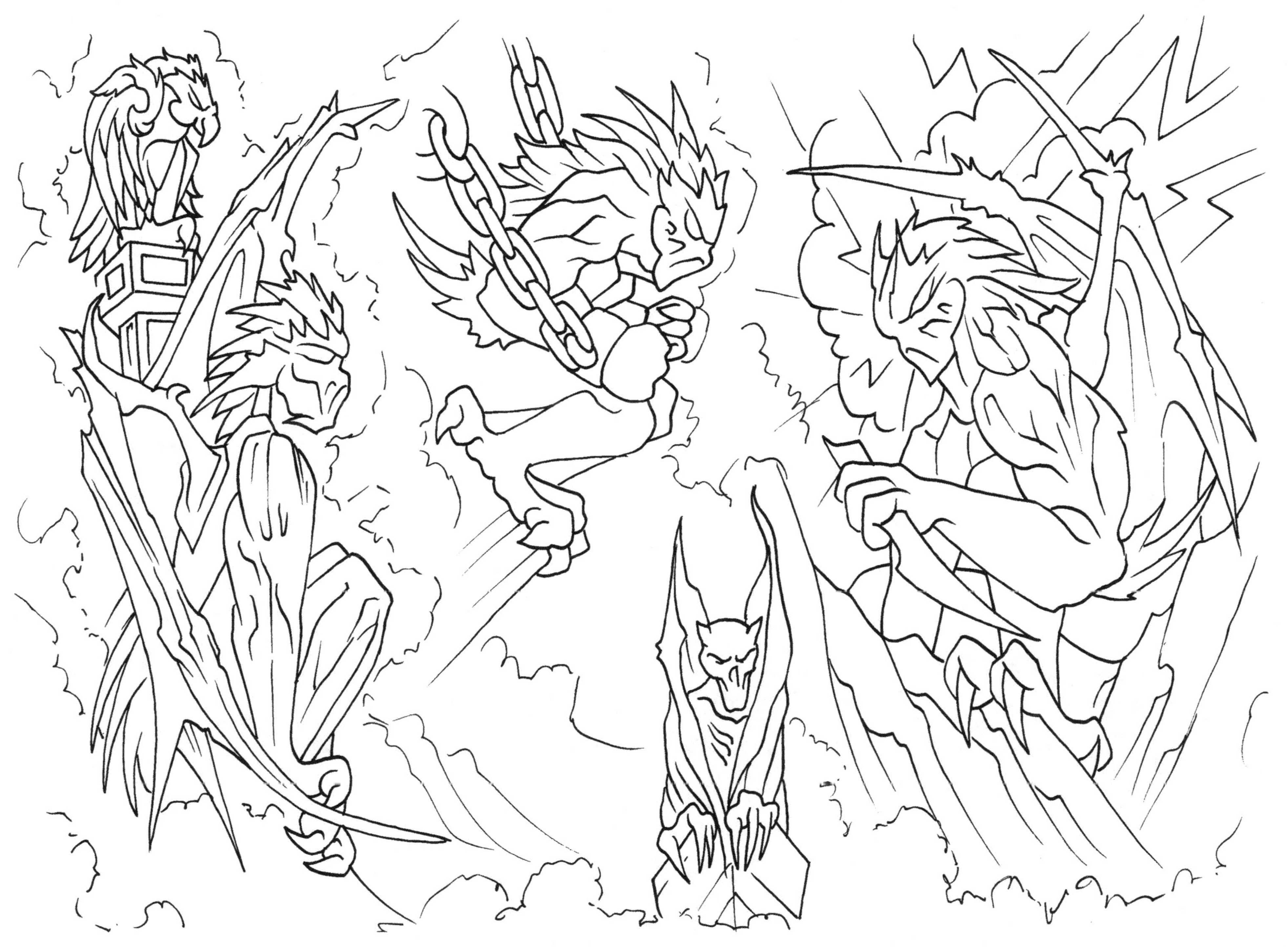

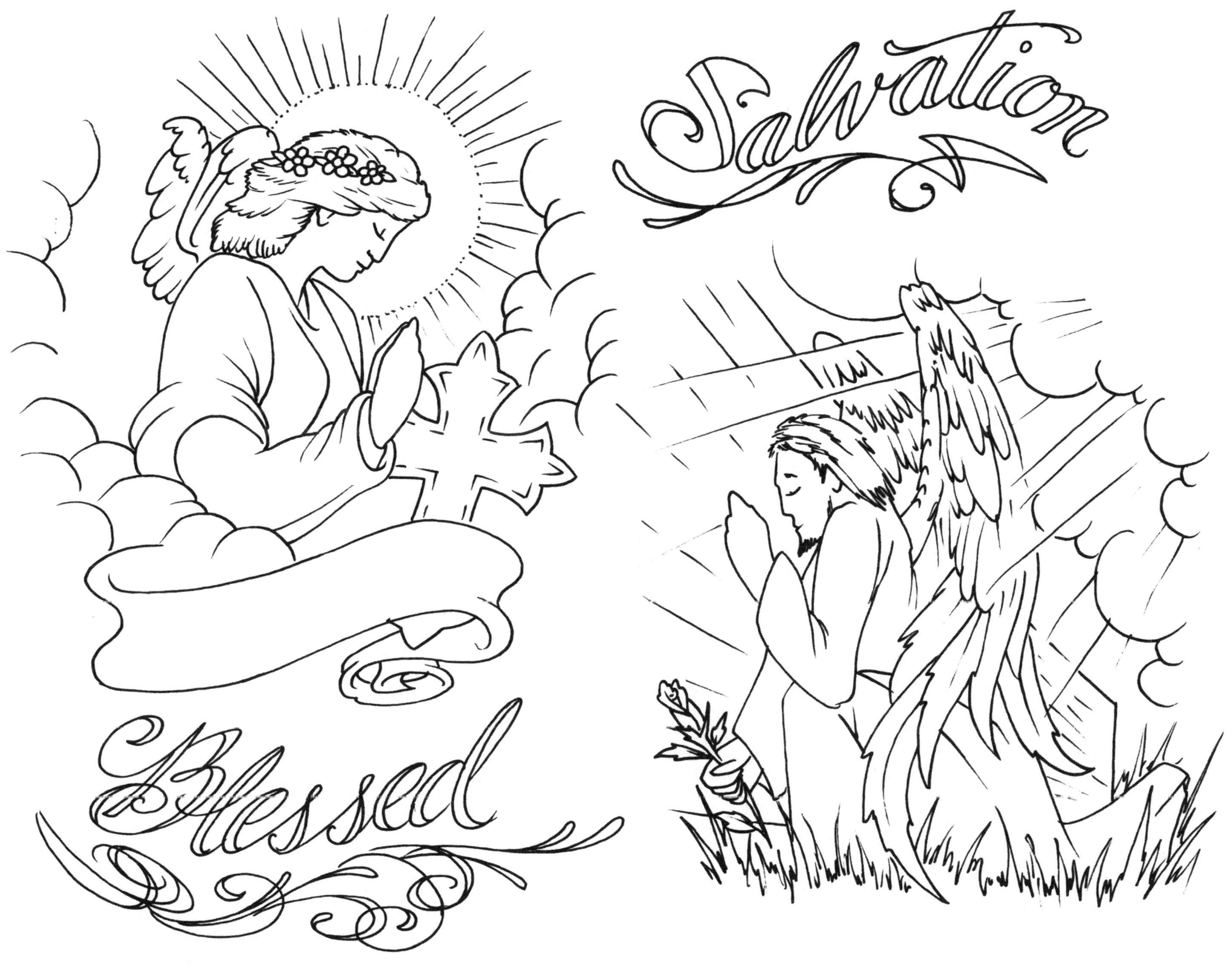
Salvation
Blessed

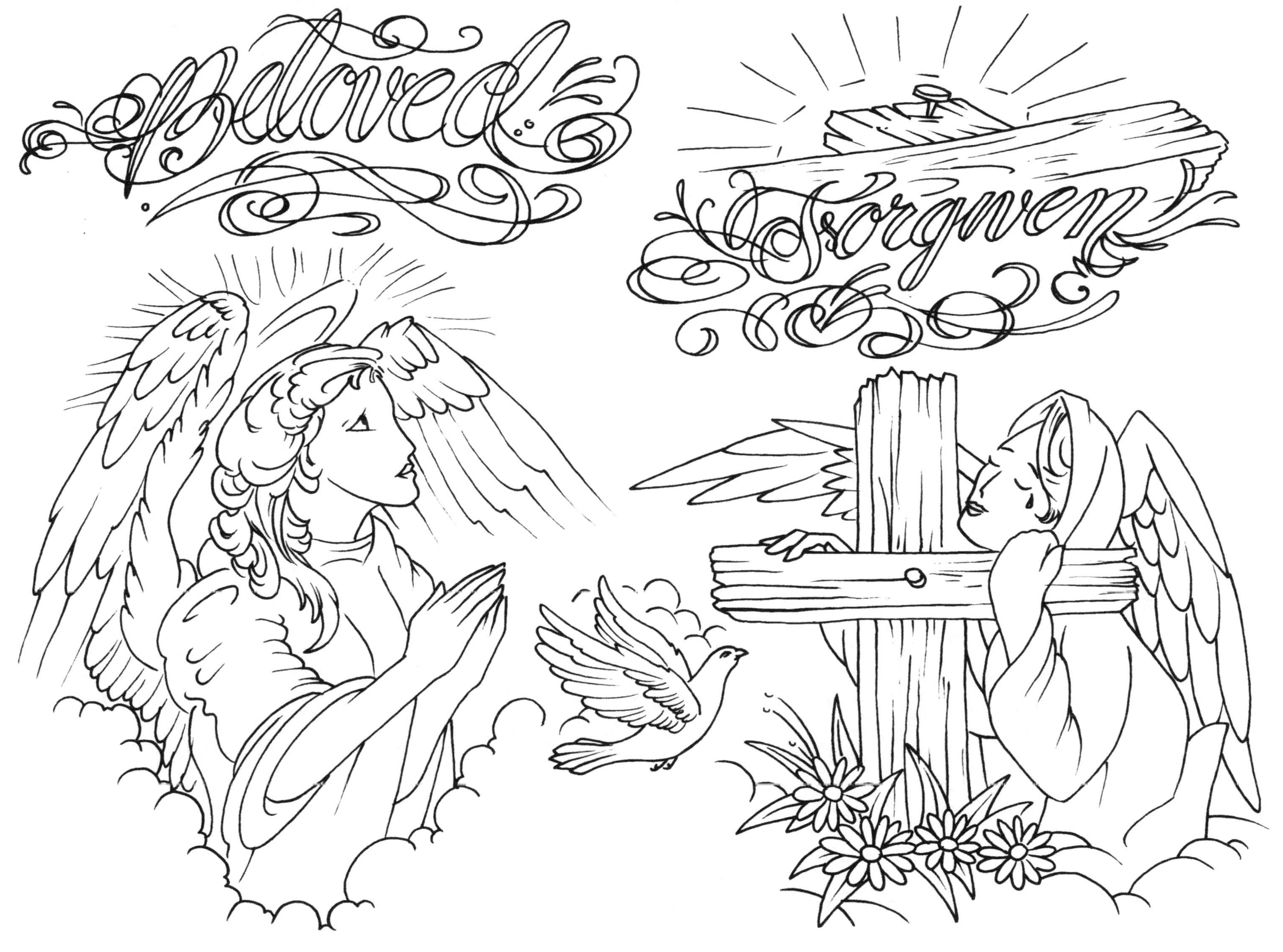
Beloved
Forgiven

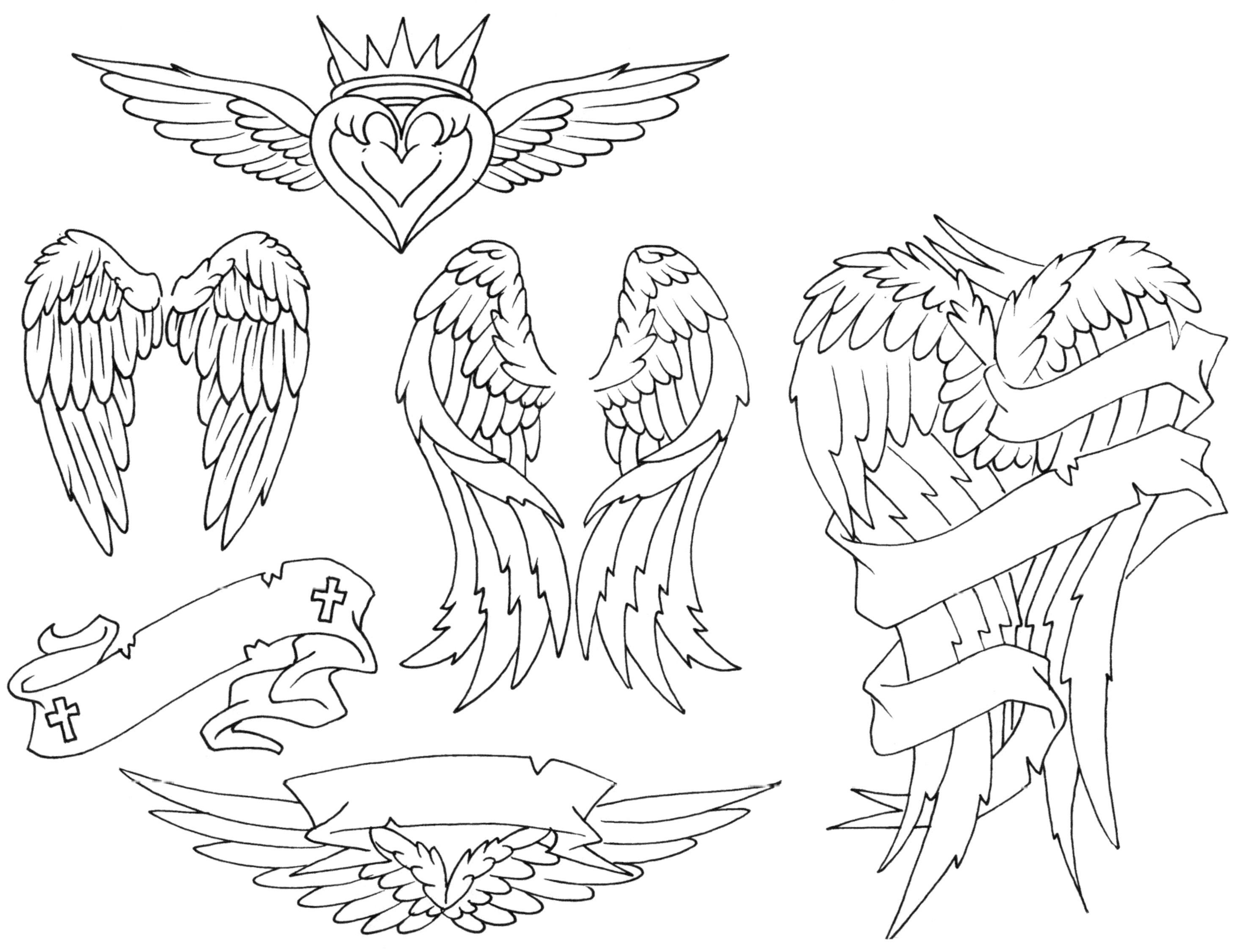

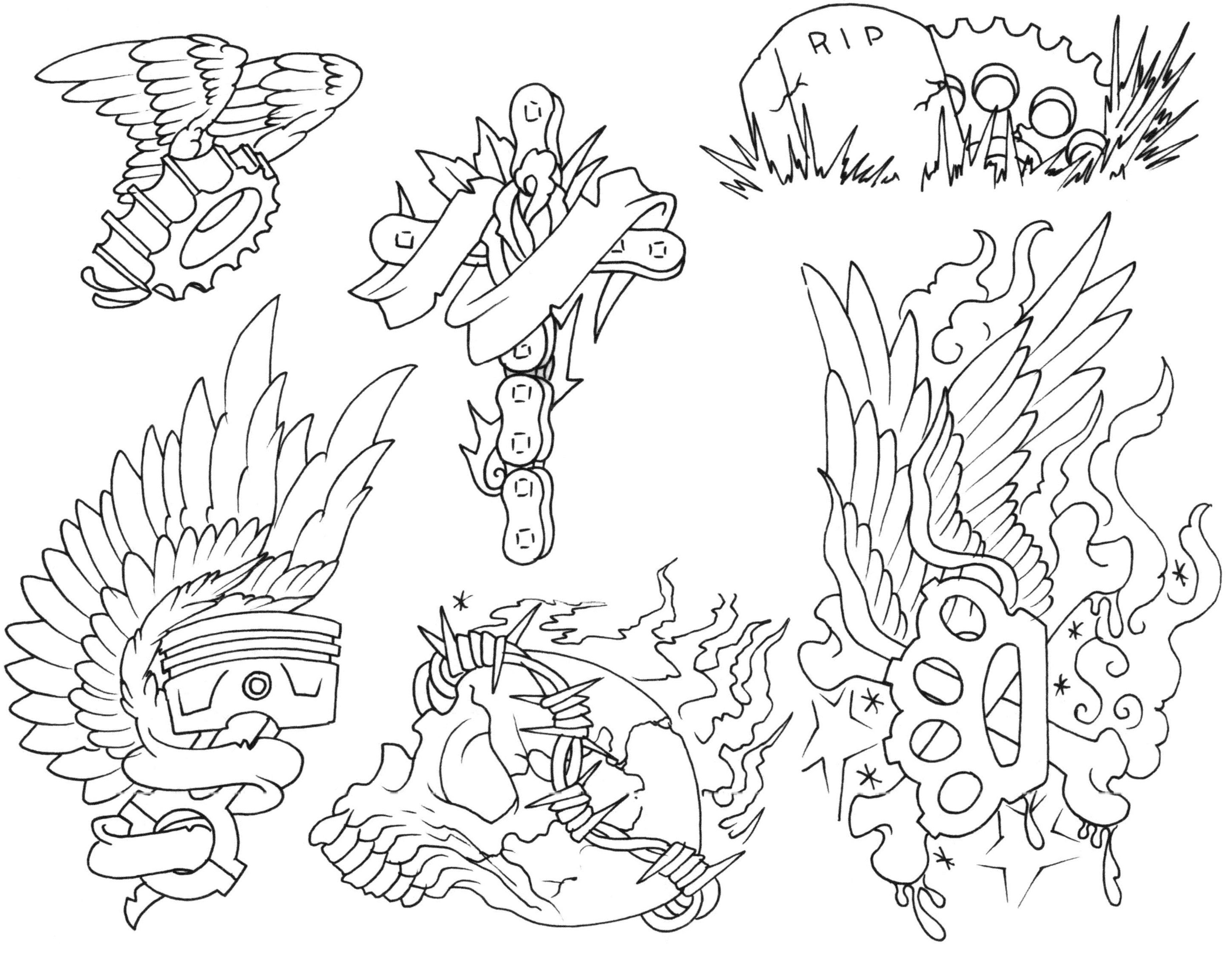
RIP

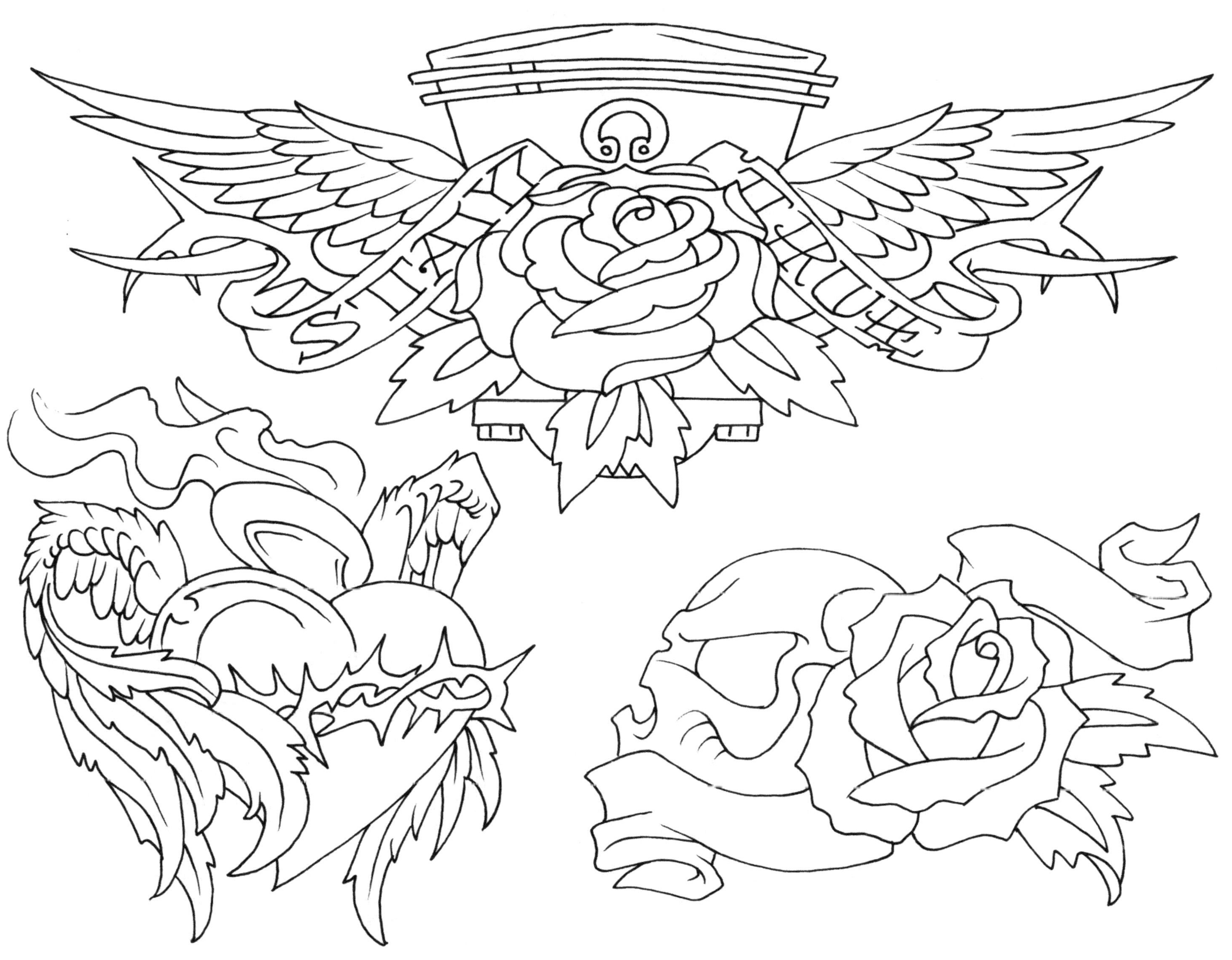

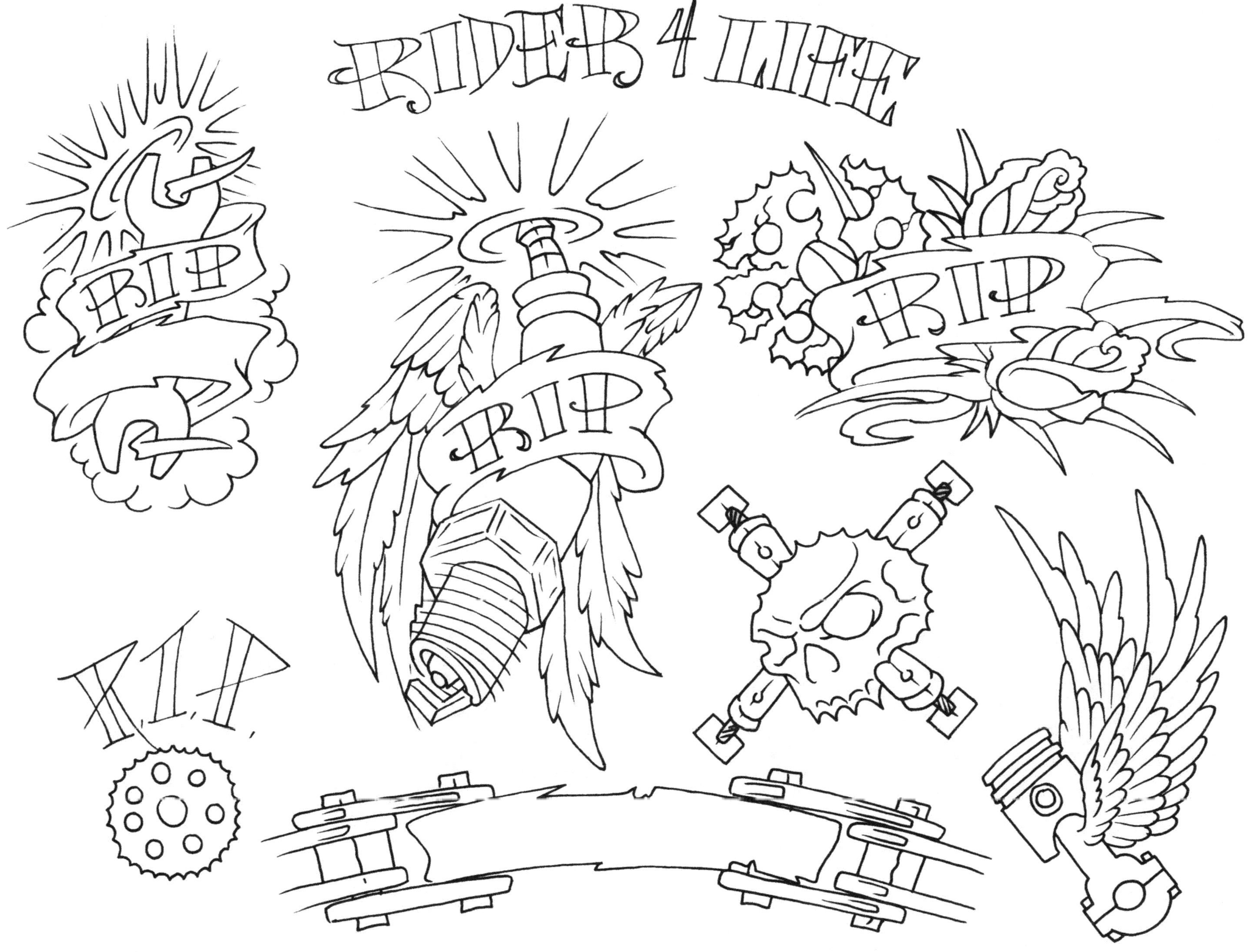
RIDER 4 LIFE
RIP
RIP
RIP
R.I.P.

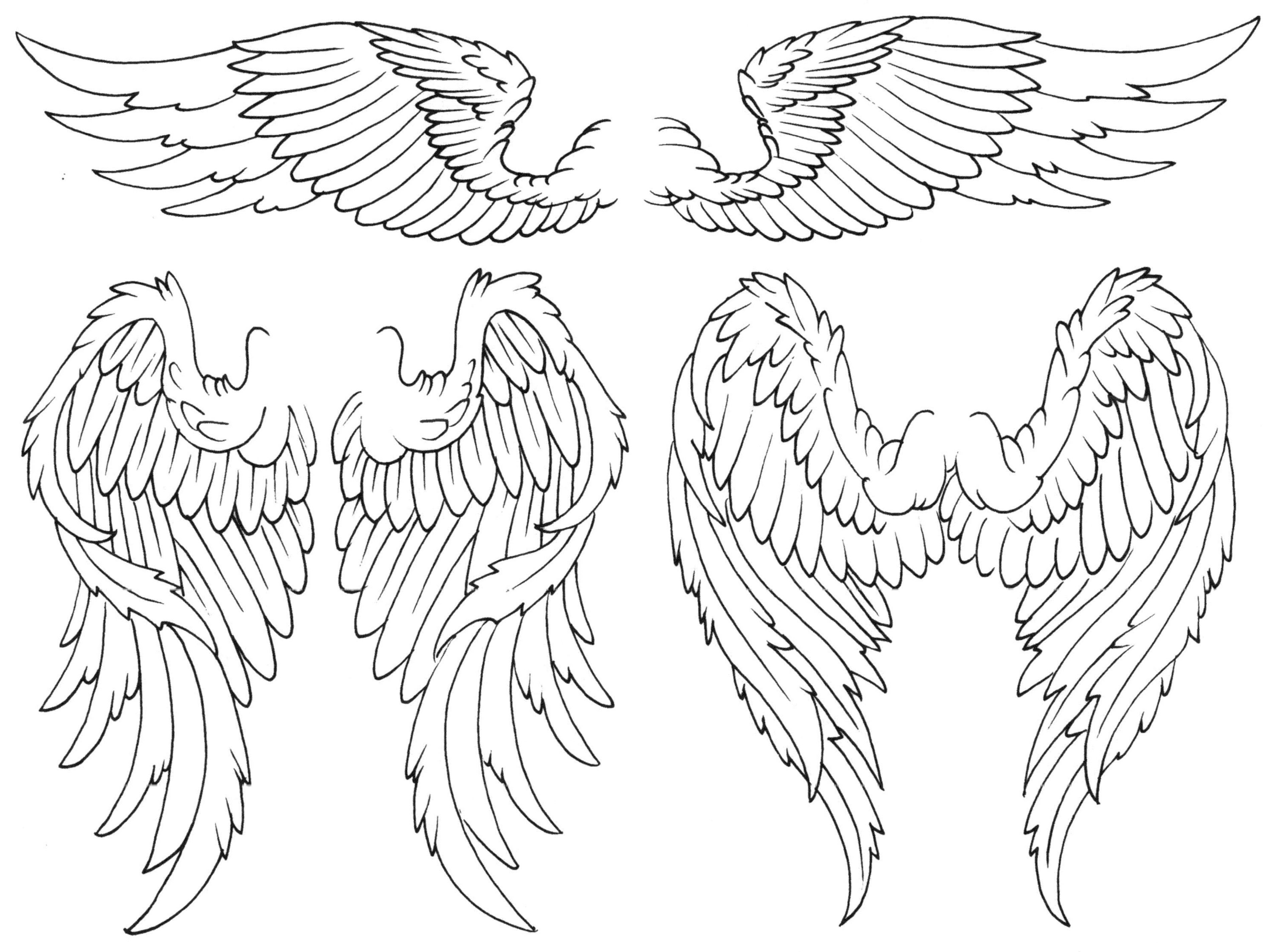

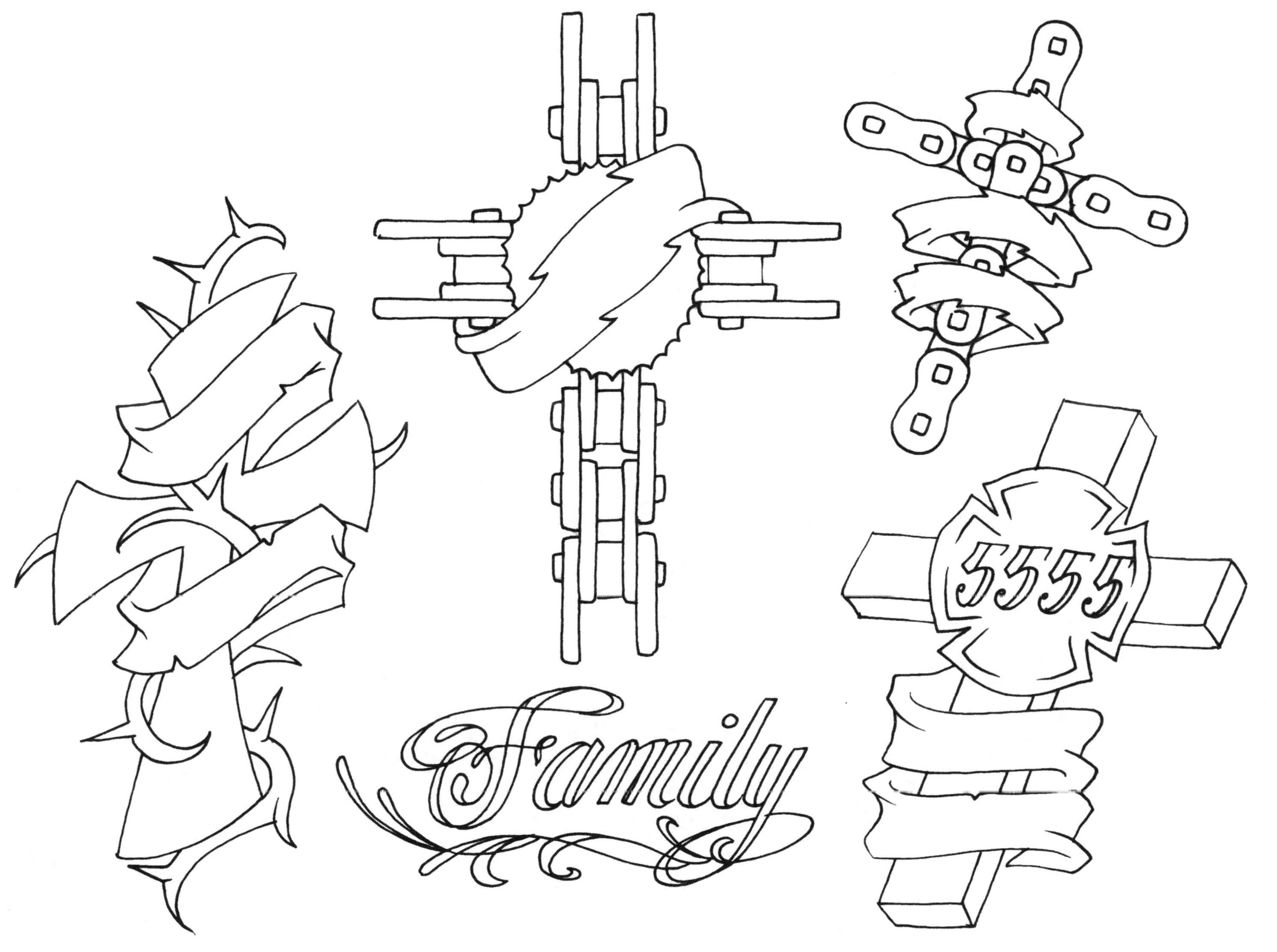

5555
Family

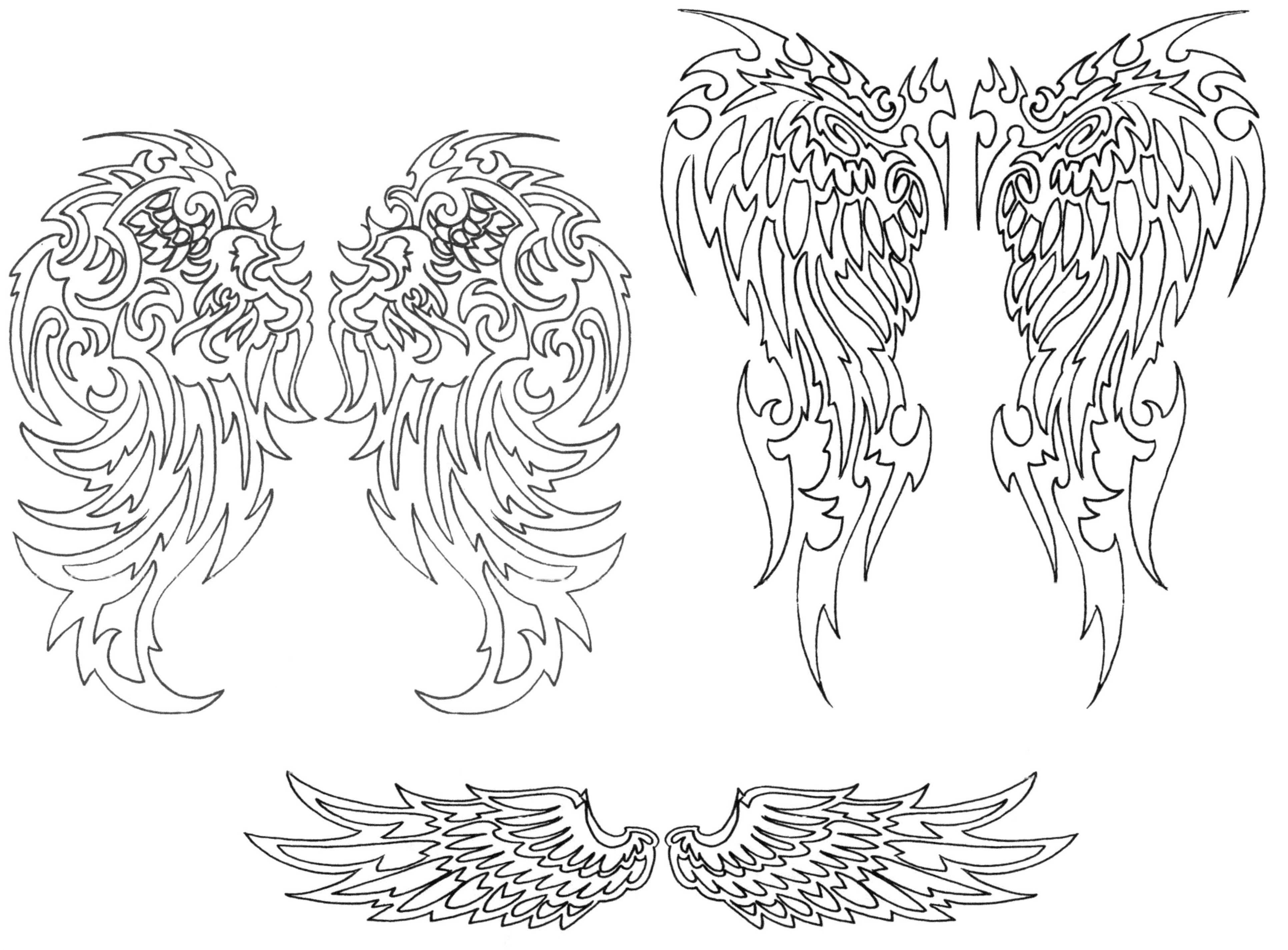

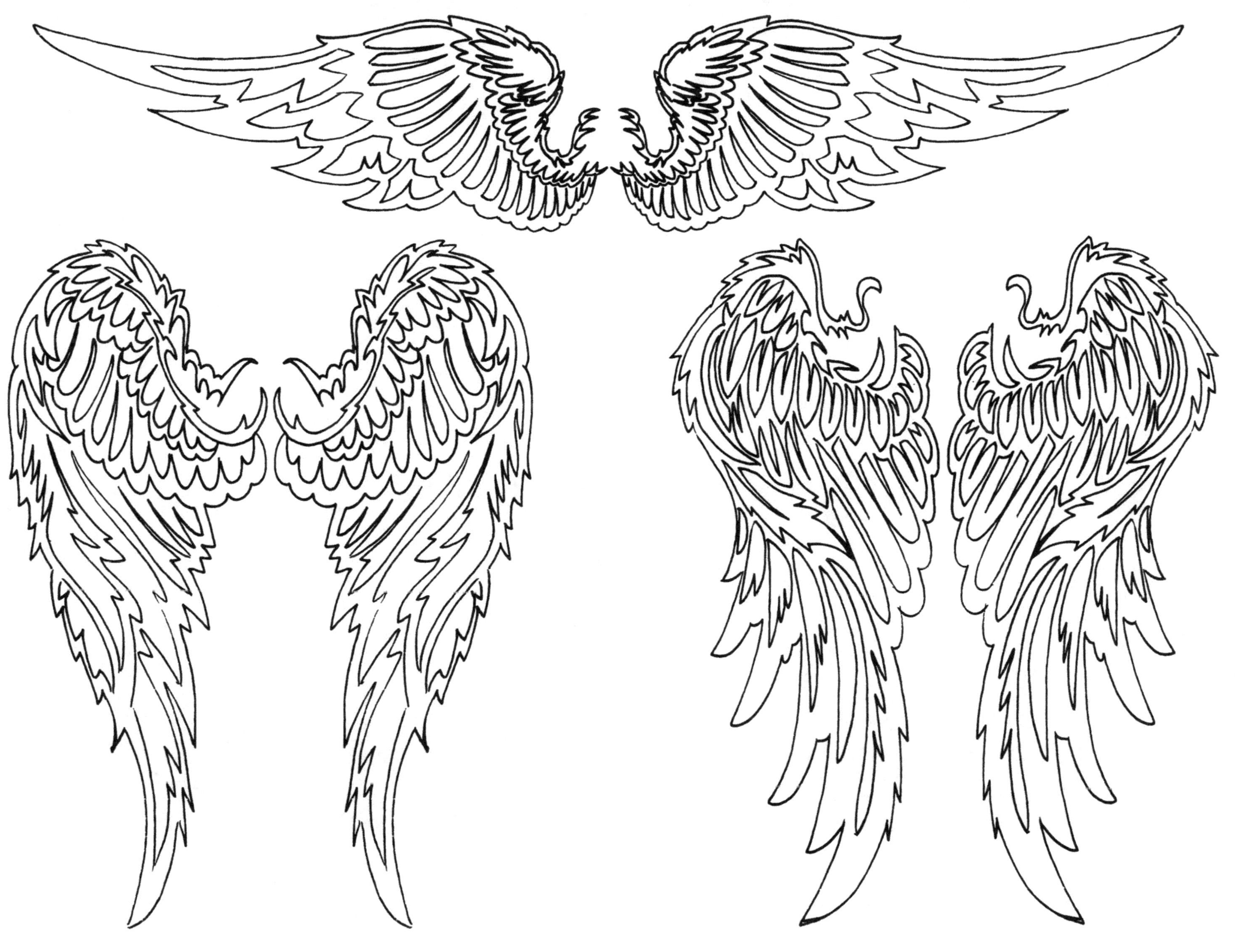

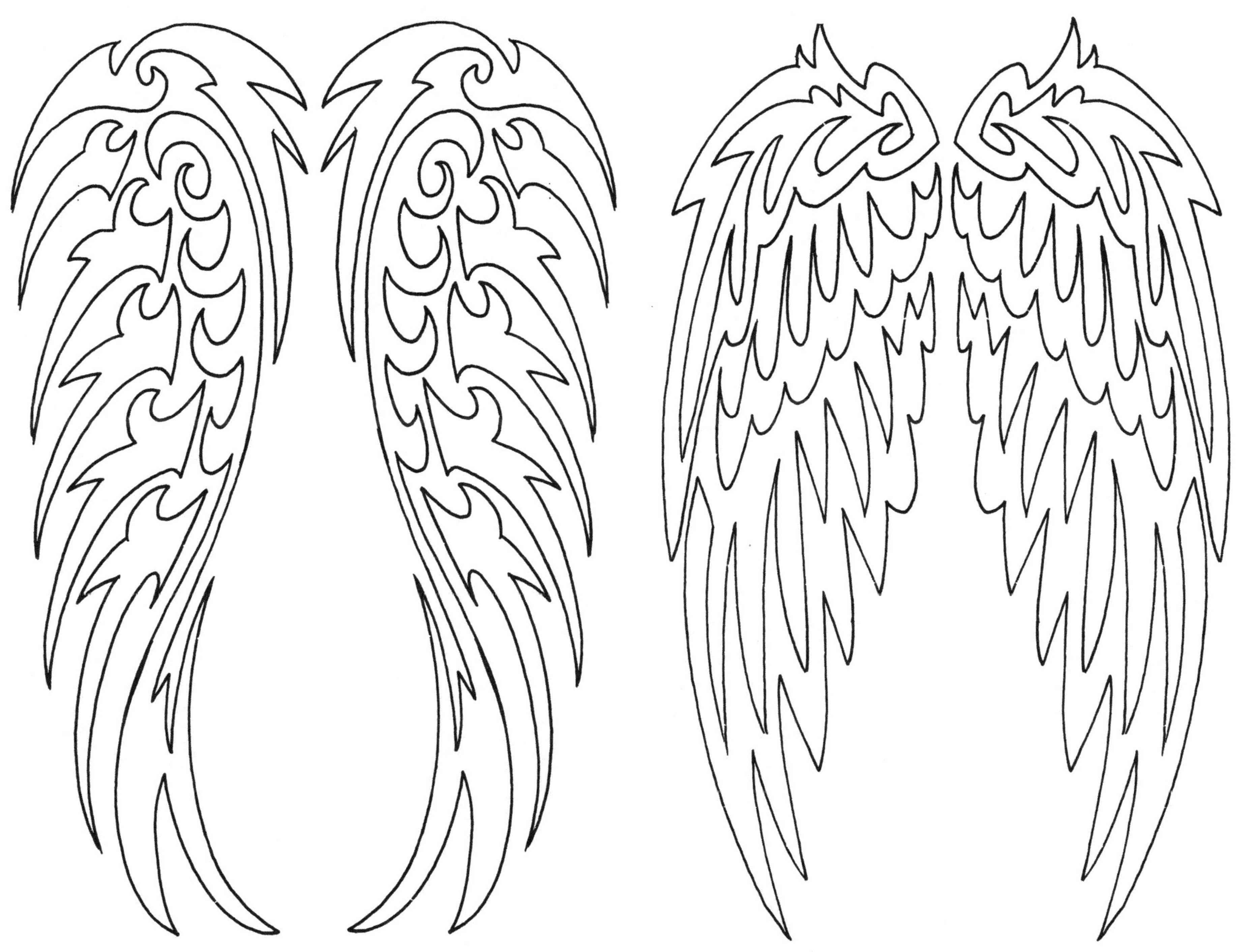

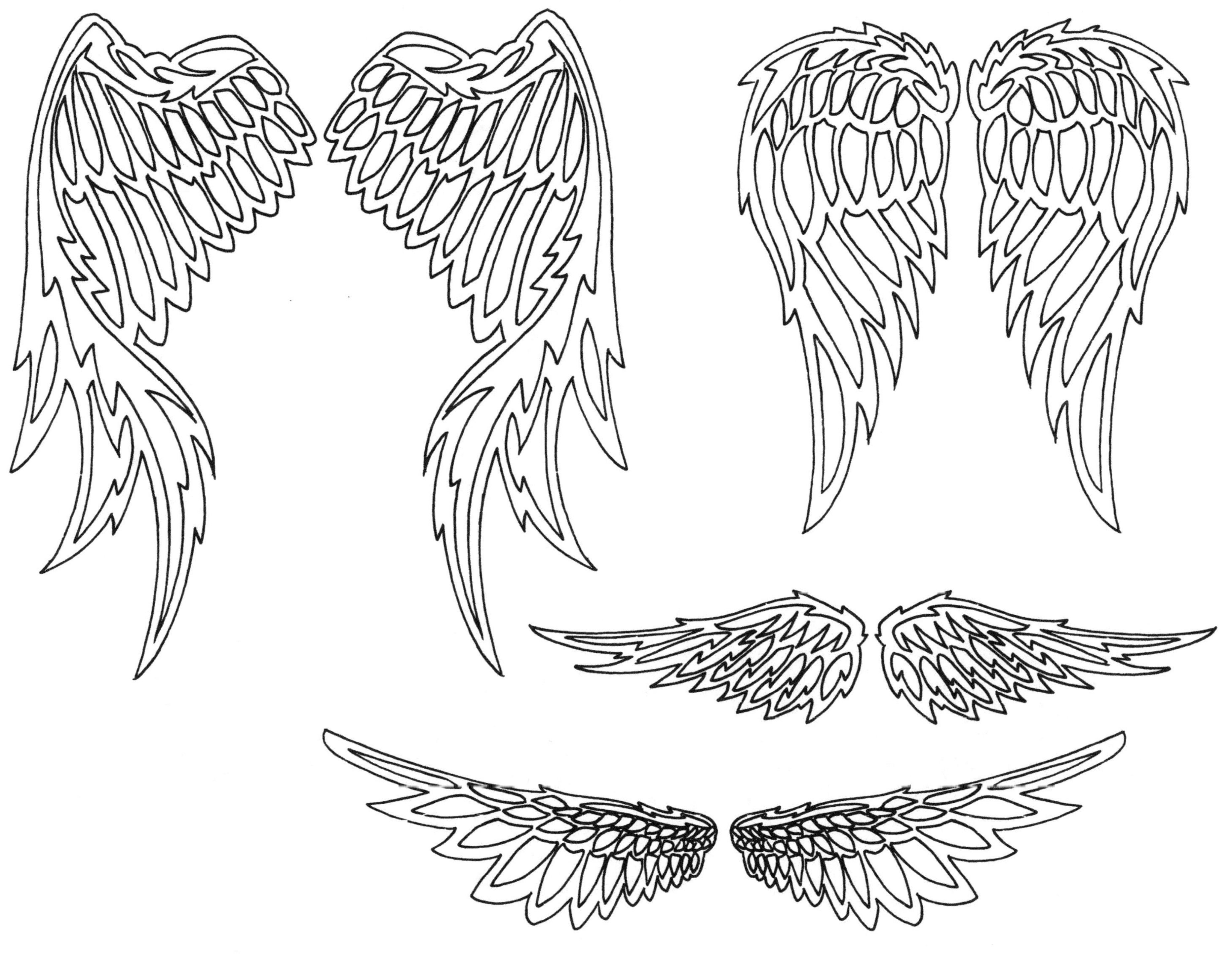

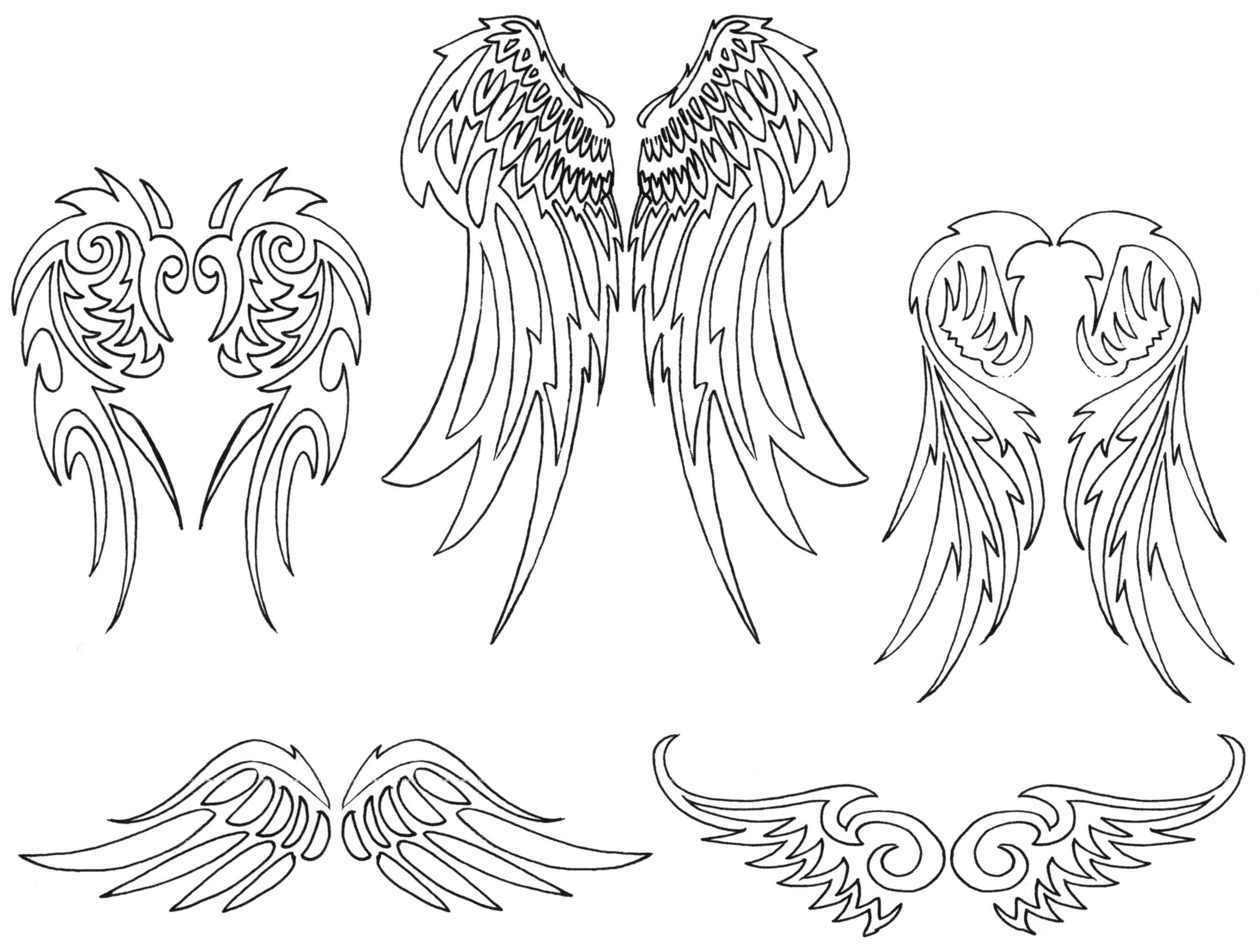

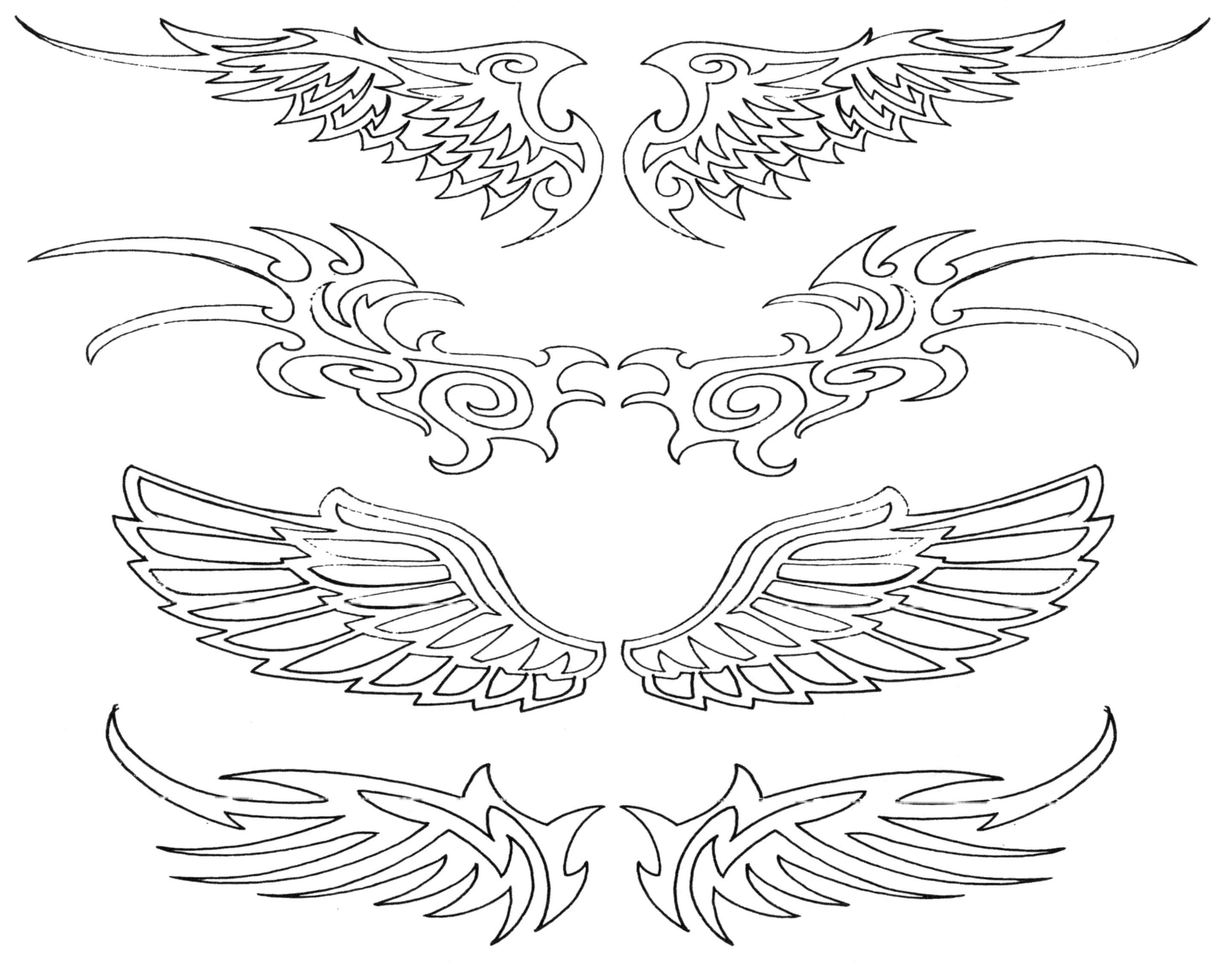

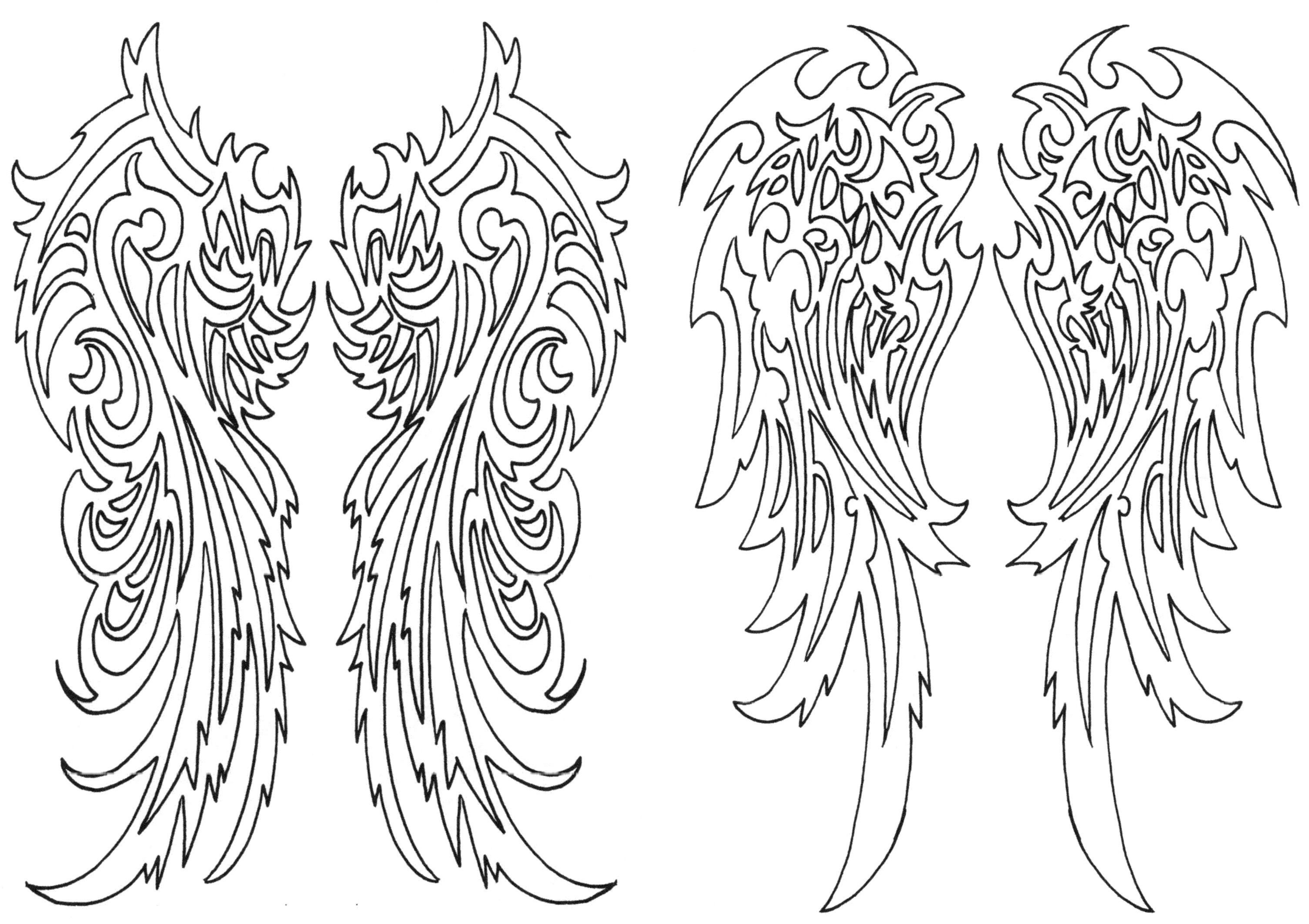

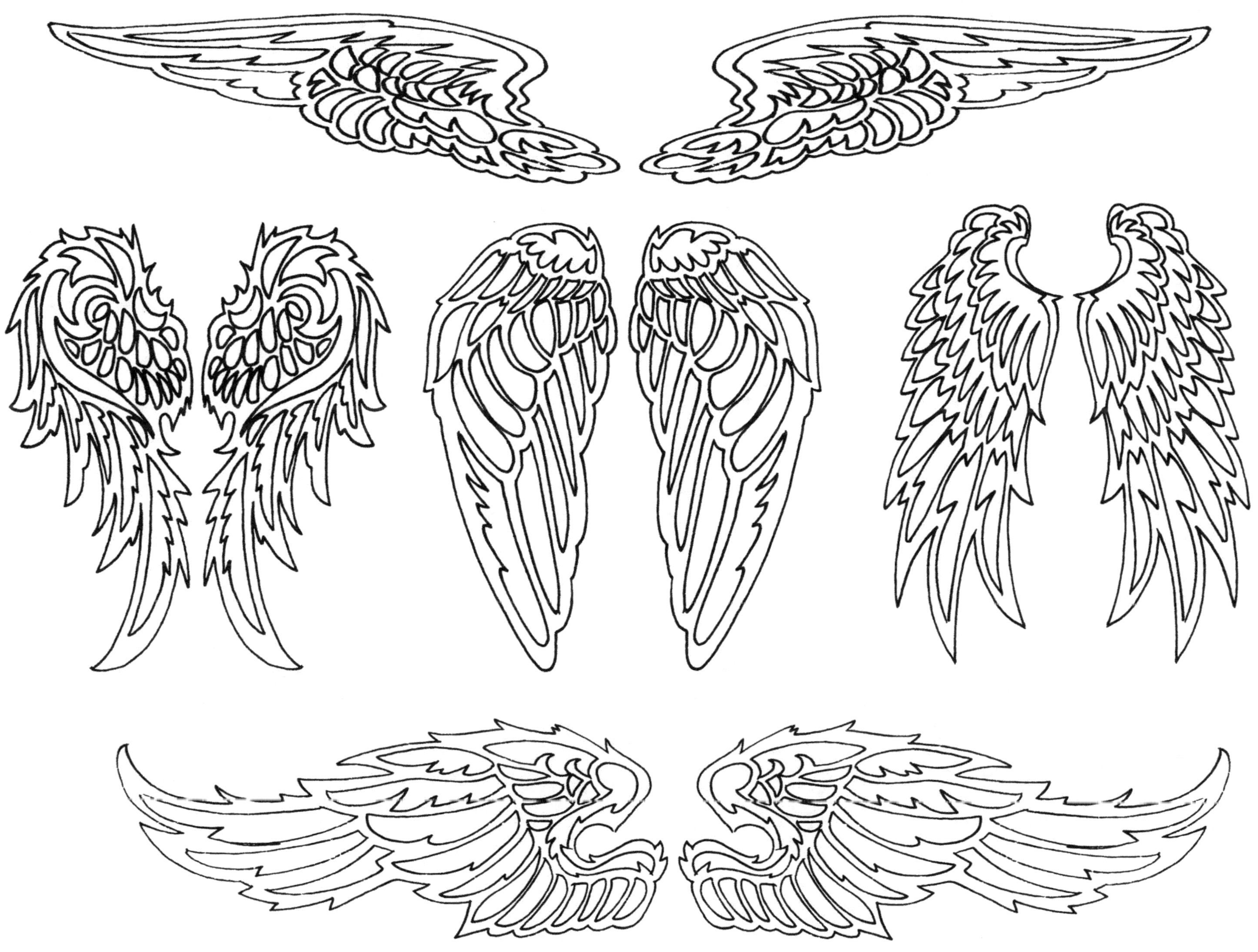

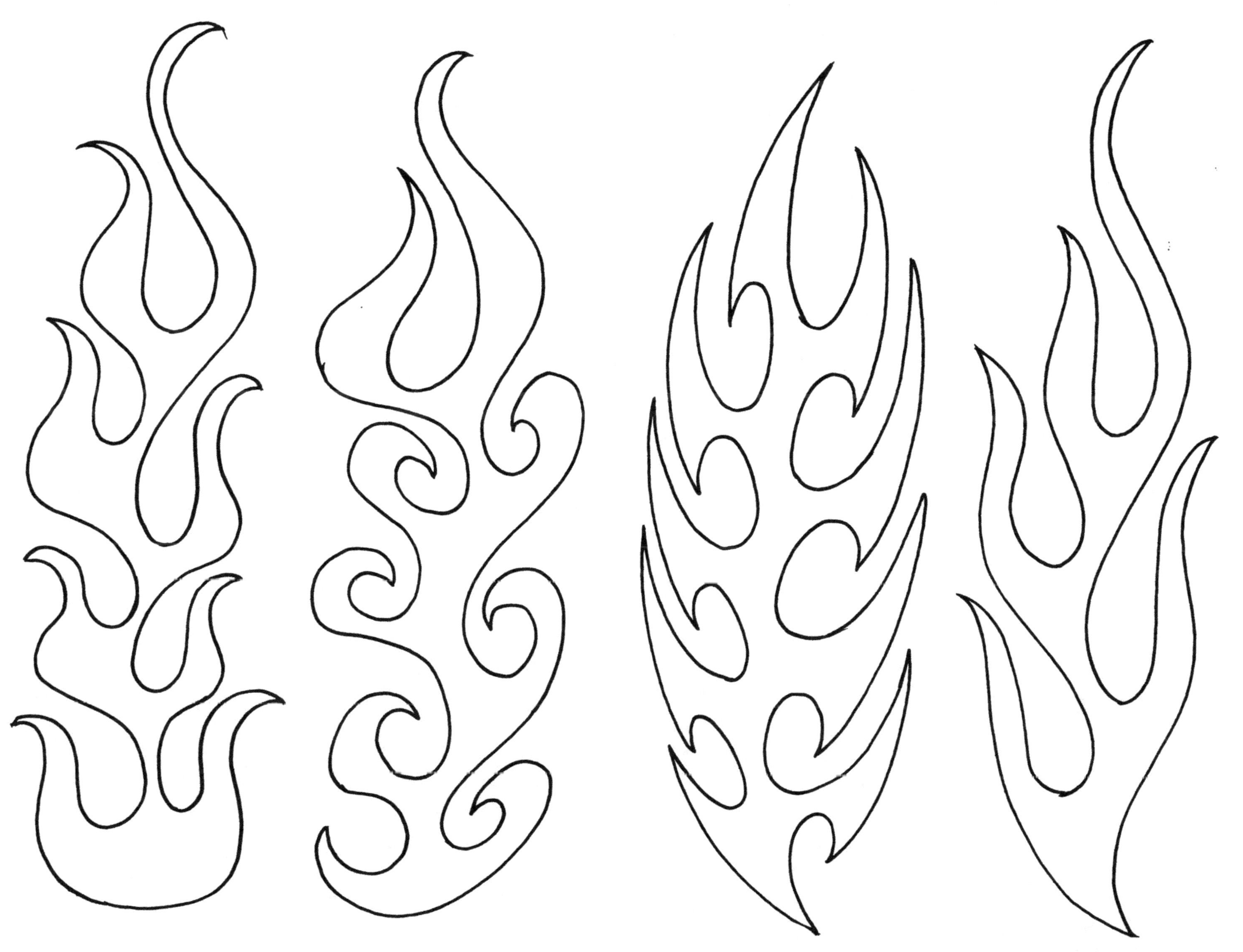

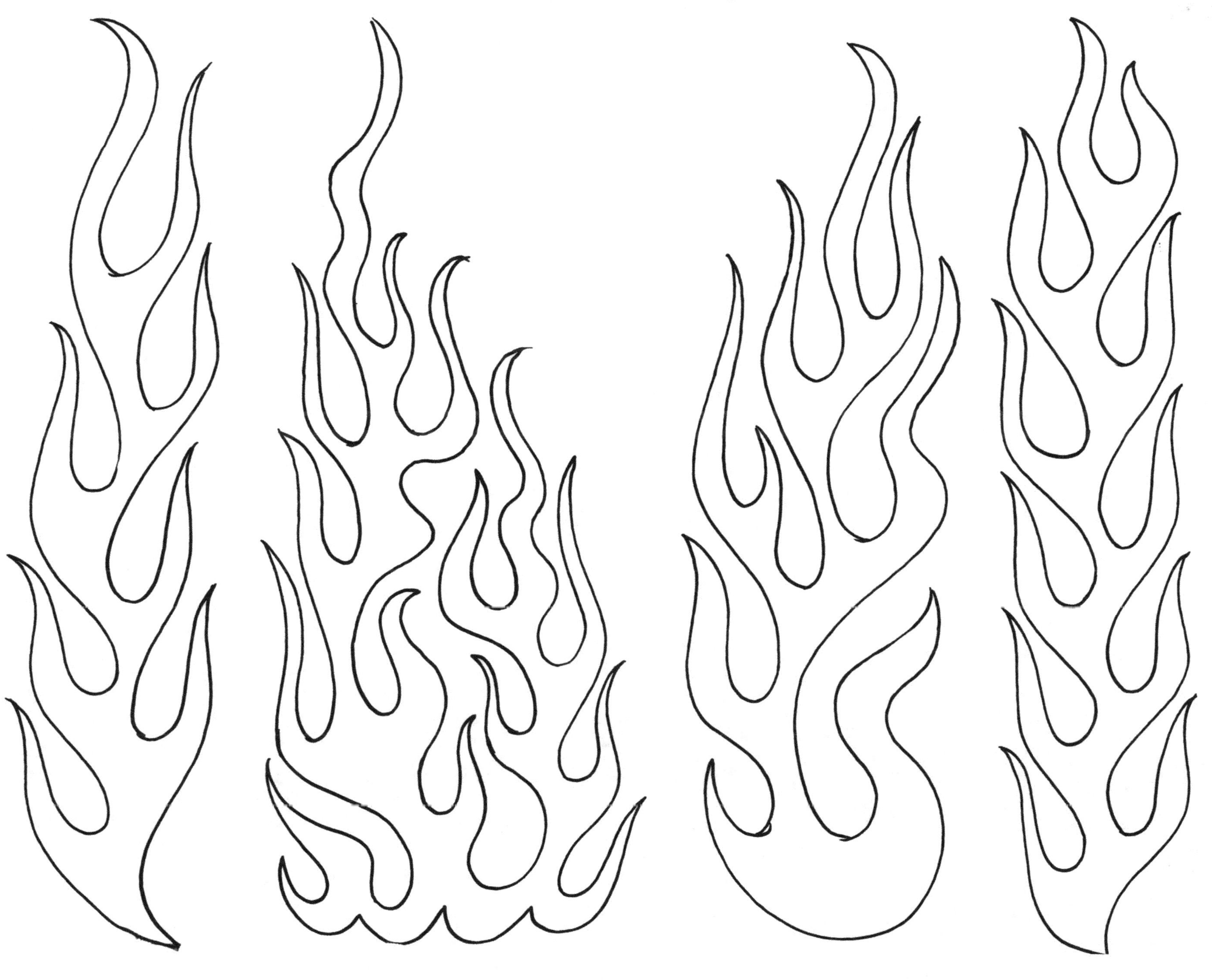

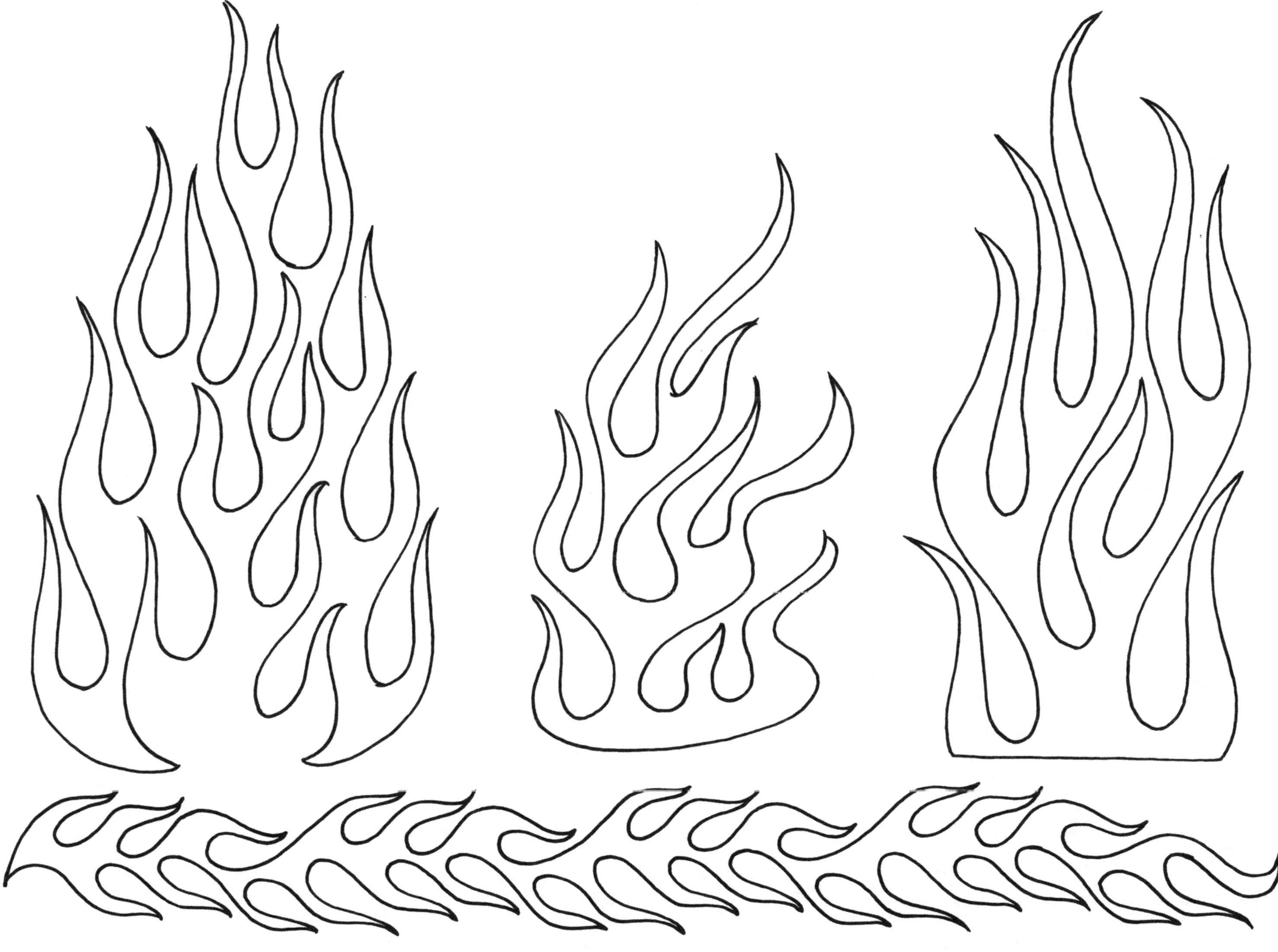

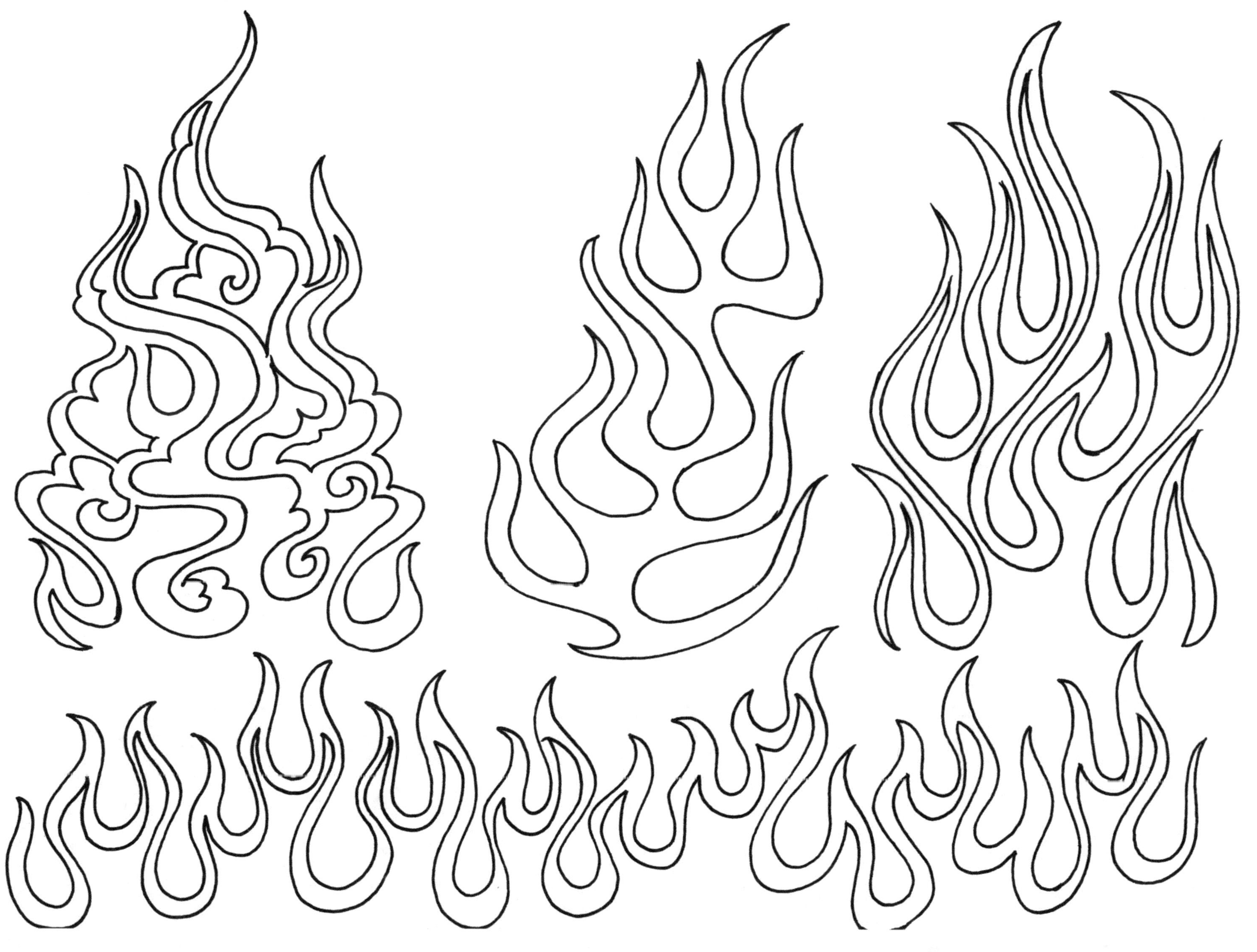

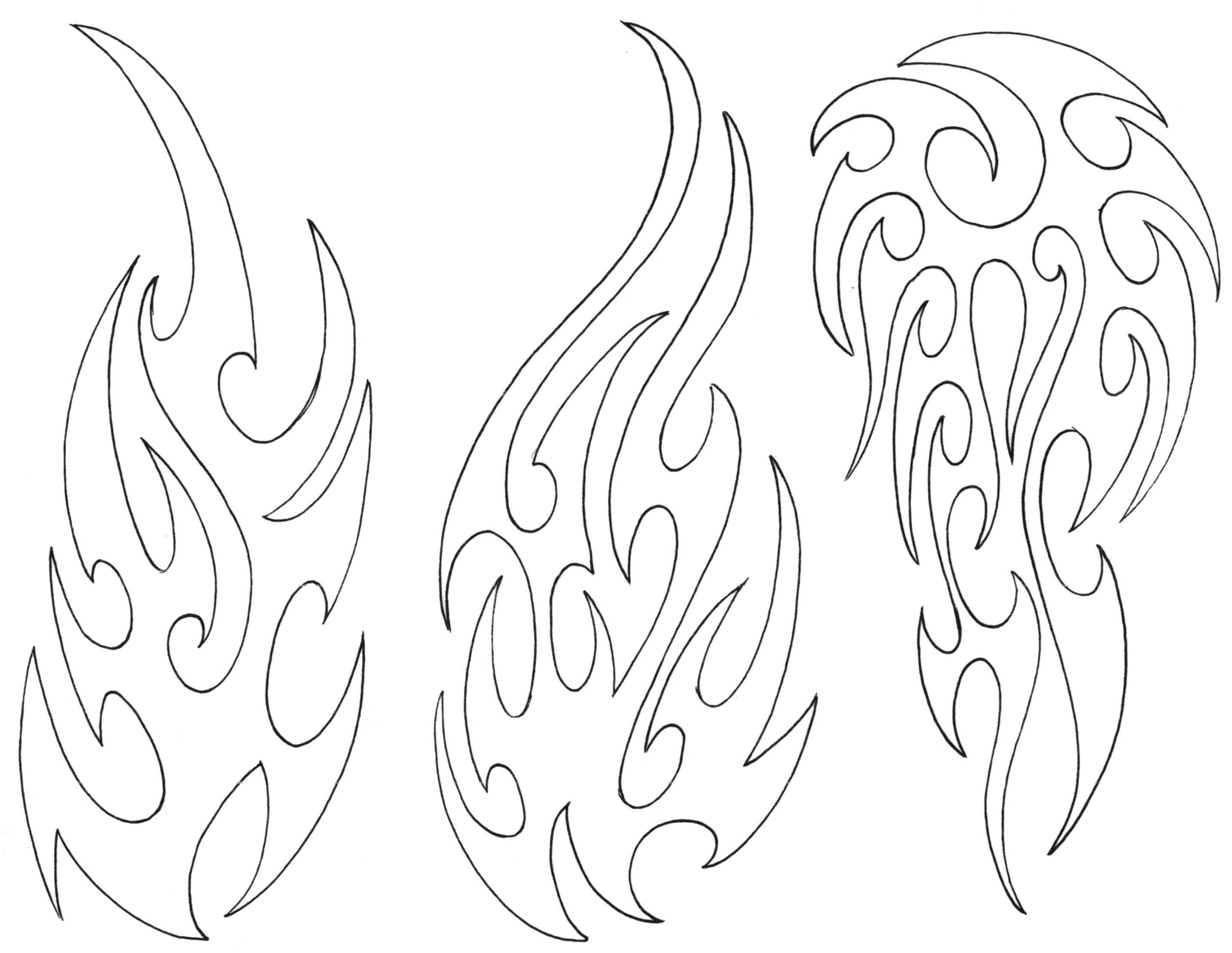

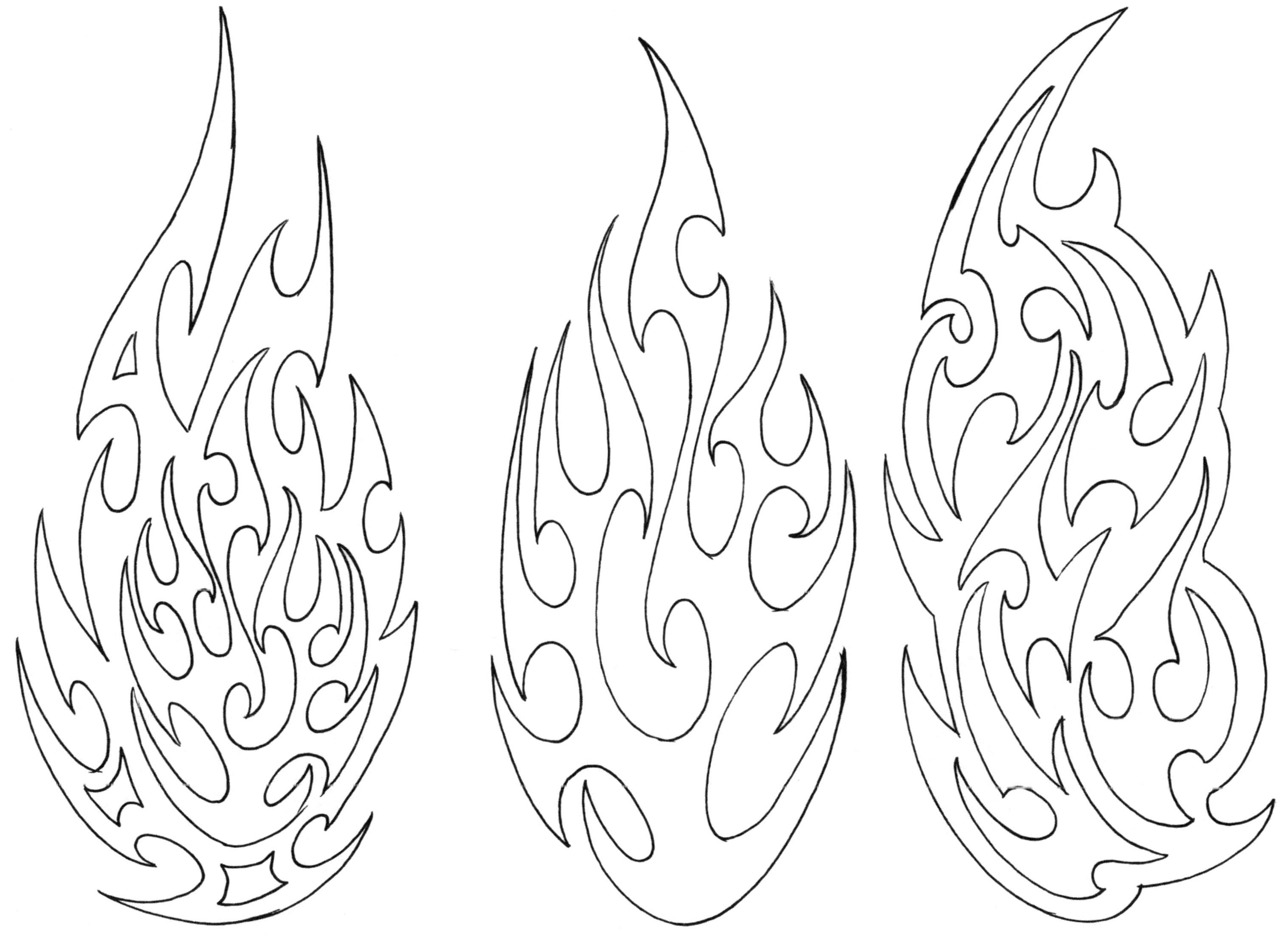

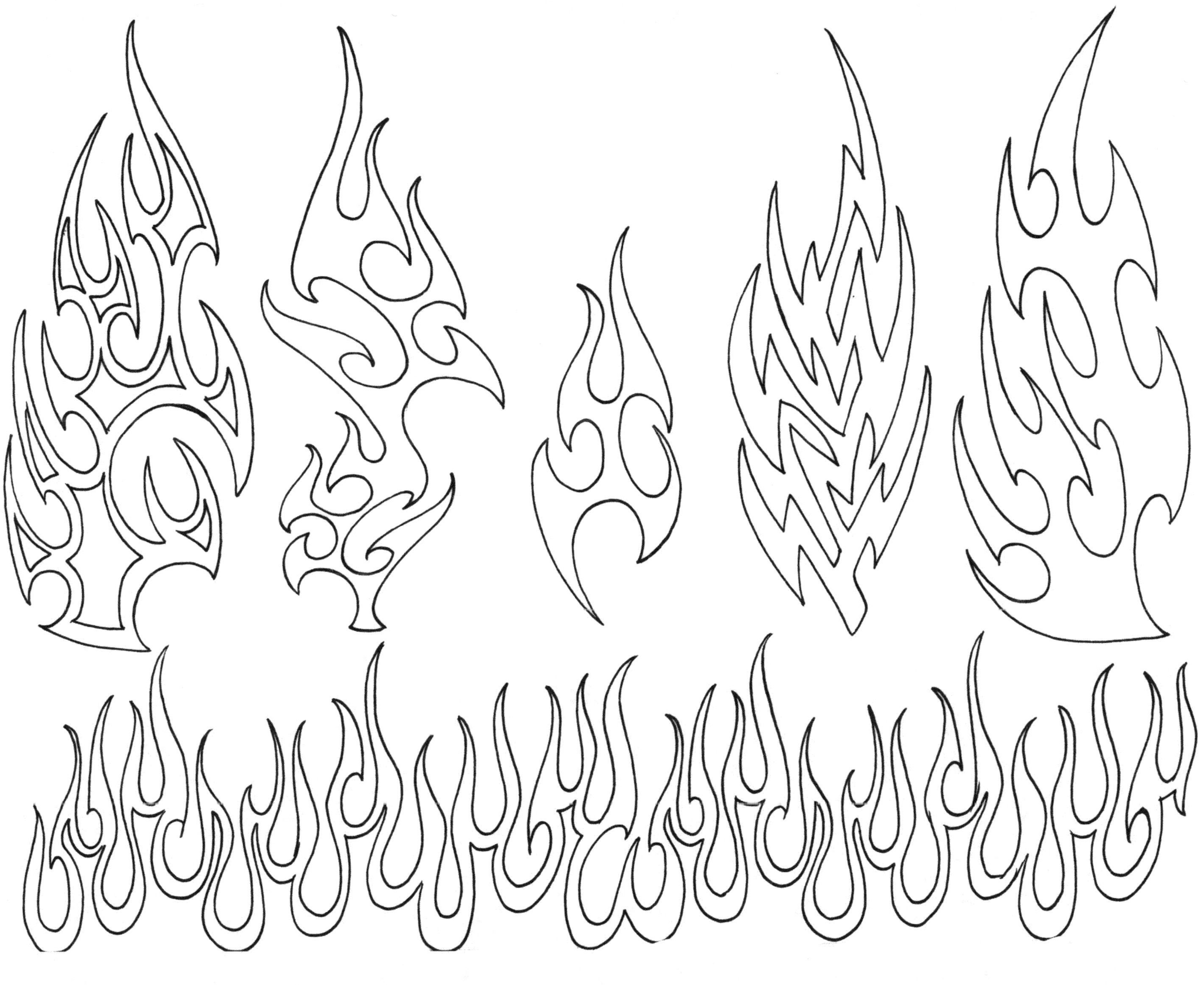

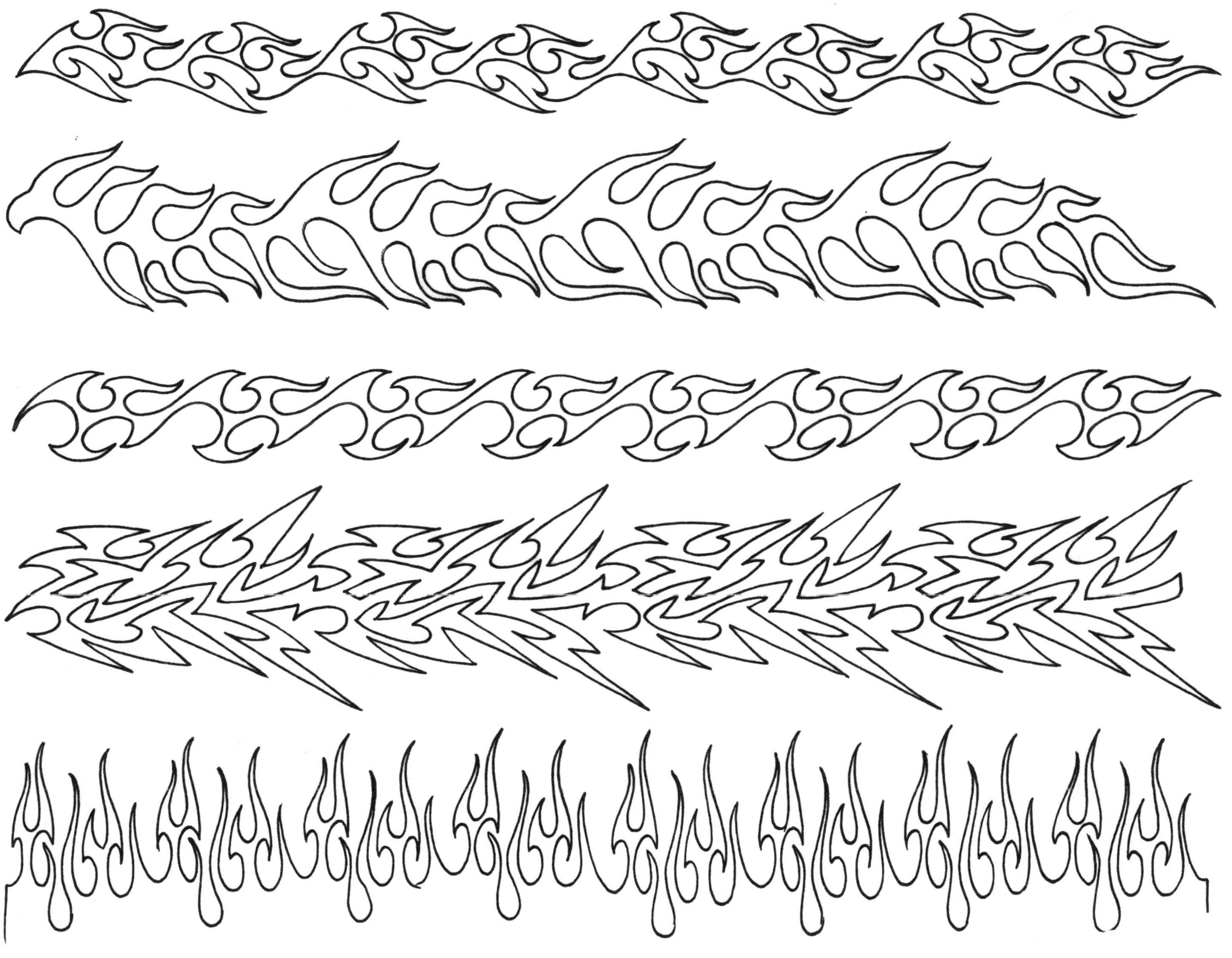

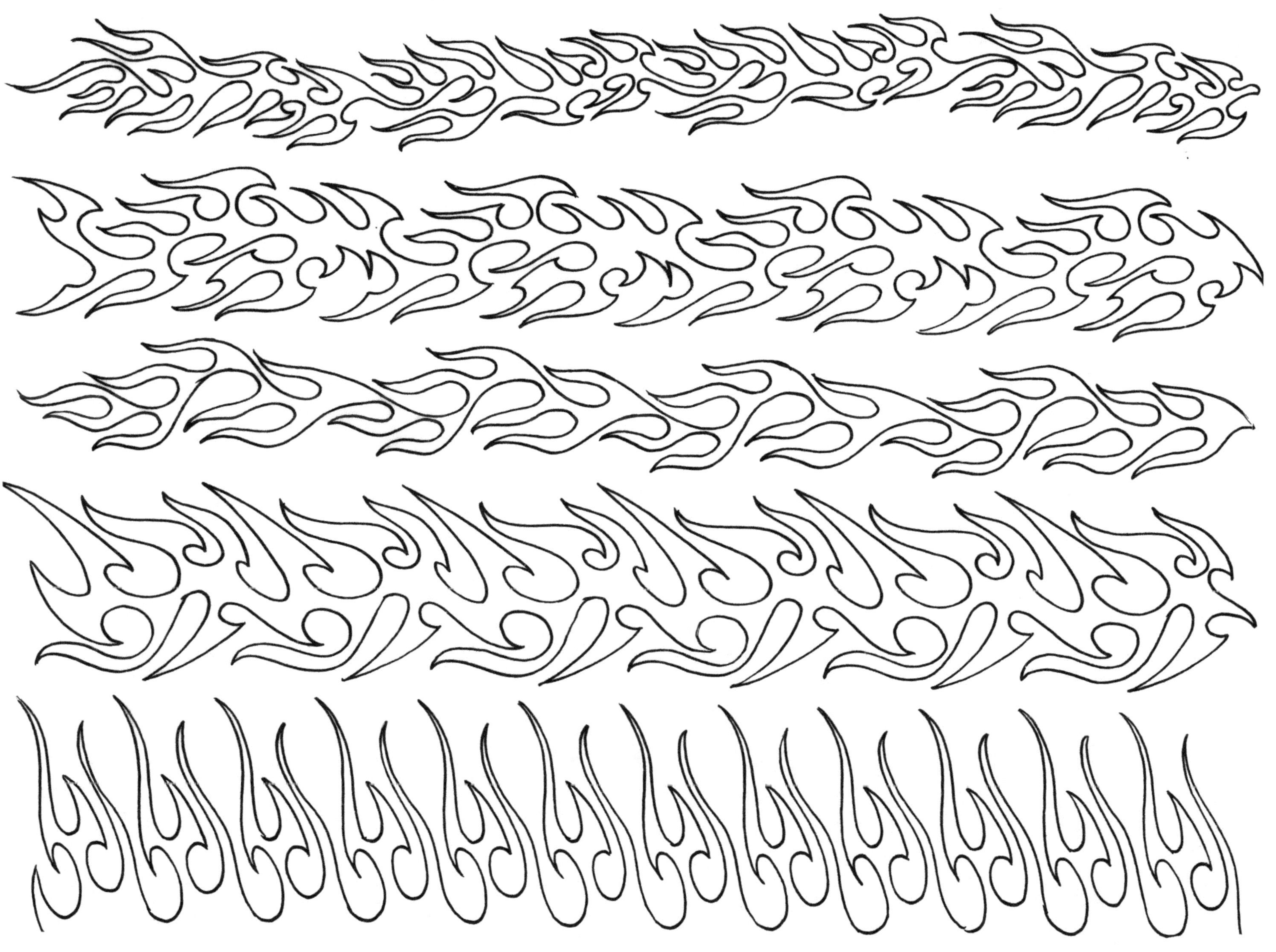

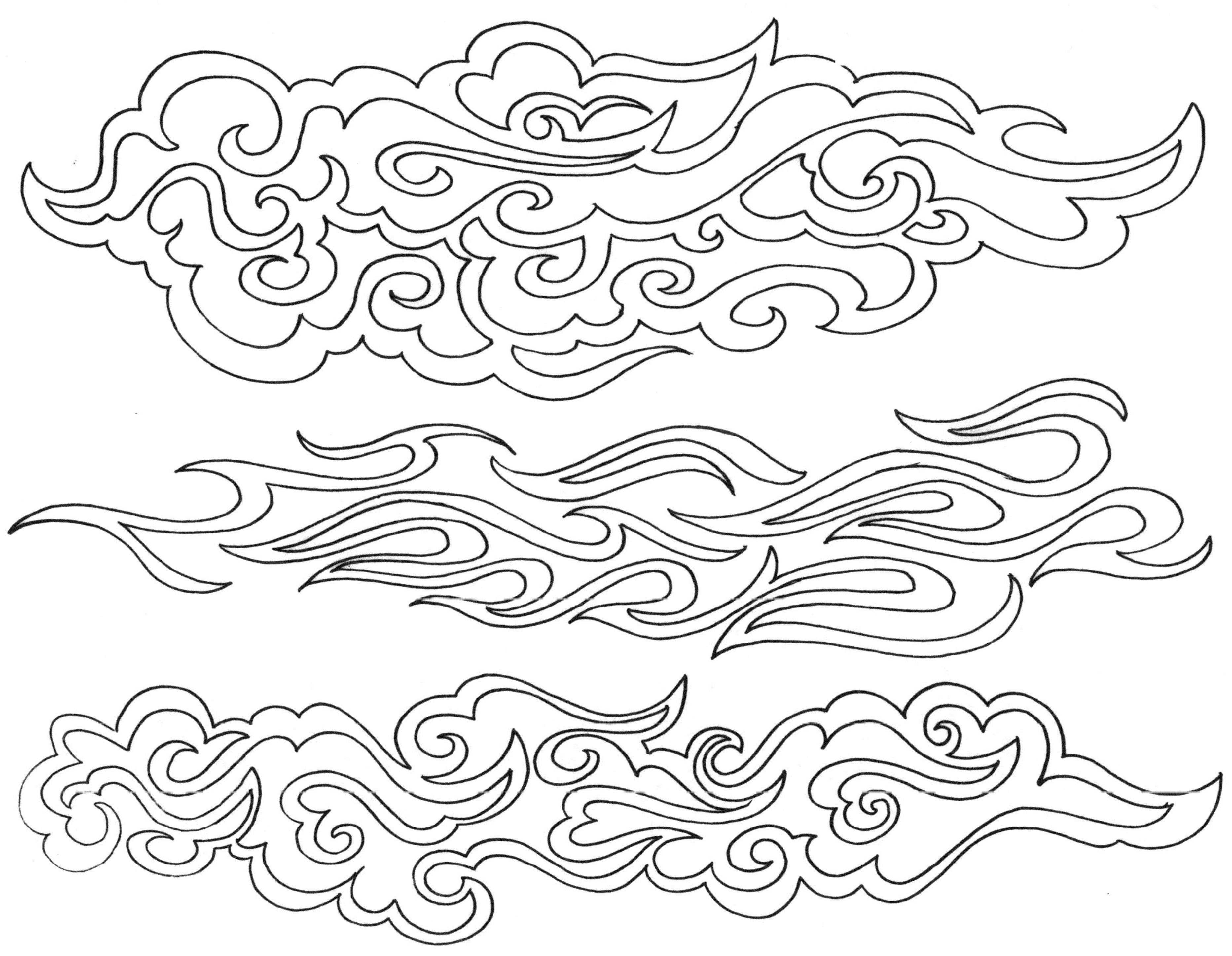

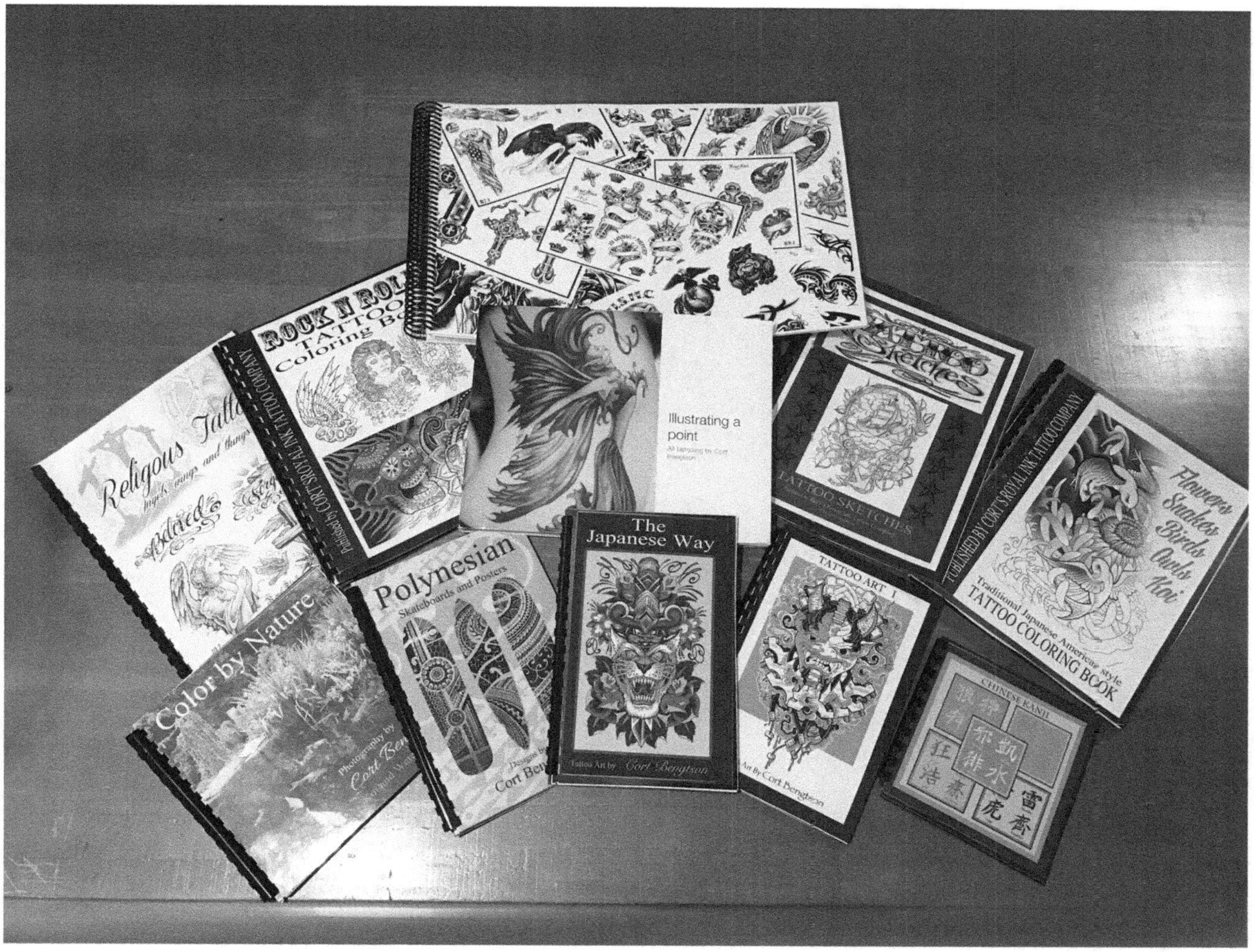

From Japanese style to surreal black and gray, to watercolors and computer art, we have something you will love. Prints ranging in size from 11" x 17" to 40" x 50" will adjust the visual appeal of any room.

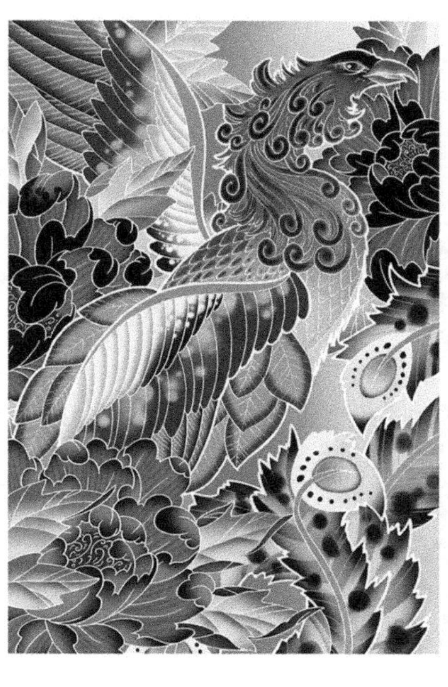
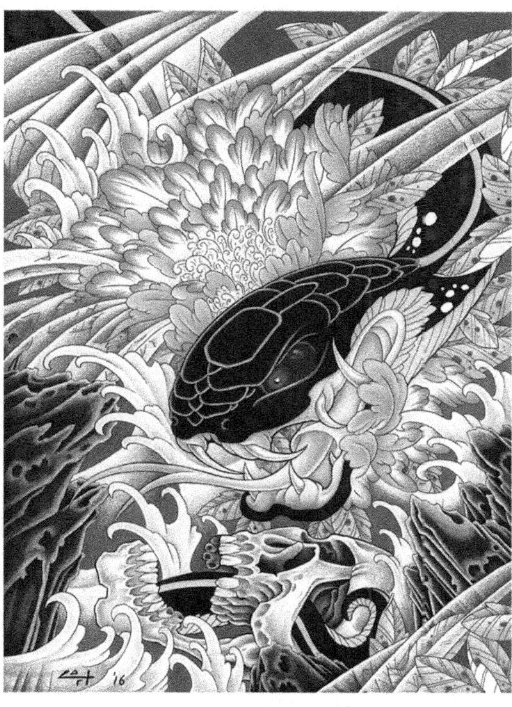
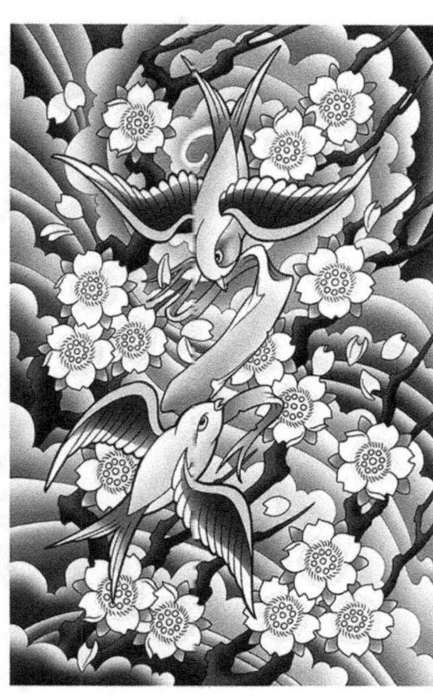
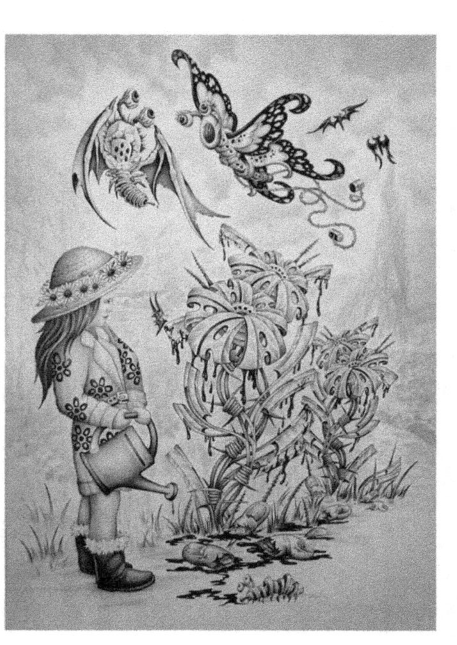
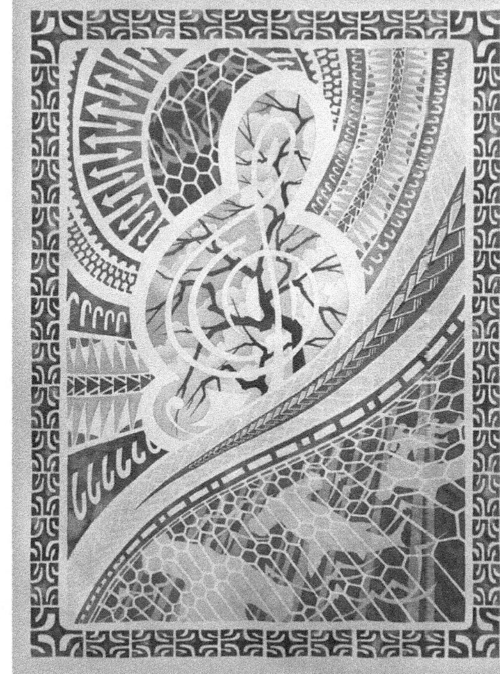
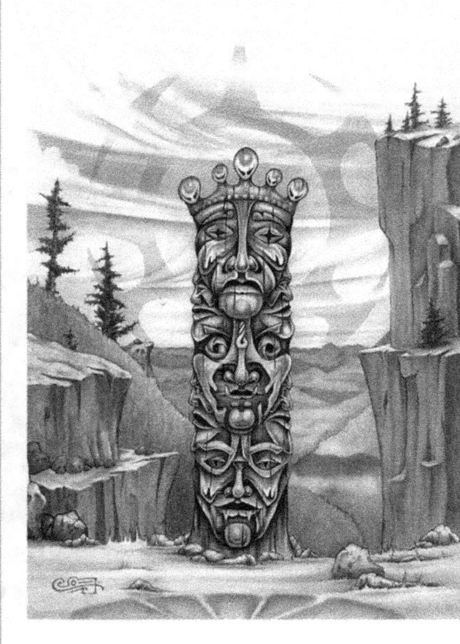

www.ingramcontent.com/pod-product-compliance
Lightning Source LLC
LaVergne TN
LVHW080319110826
845155LV00026B/160
* 9 7 8 1 9 4 8 1 8 7 1 3 8 *